400
and
Counting

Farley Dunn

THREE SKILLET

400 AND COUNTING, Dunn, Farley

First Edition

THE SE'YAN'T CHRONICLES, Book 3

 THREE SKILLET

www.ThreeSkilletPublishing.com

Cover design by Farley L Dunn

ISBN: 978-1-943189-30-4

400
and
Counting

—Chapter 1—

"Hitting the Enter key will reformat your hard drive. Are you sure you want to proceed?"

—*Early 21st Century old-Earth programming prompt*

"CHECK THE intercept alarm!"

Kratt Balanchine turned to the malfunctioning cryo-rejuv panel. Why did problems always have to come in layers? The eight colonists sleeping on the other side of the cargo bay would be mighty disappointed if they woke up back on Correigo Prime. He shook his head, hitting the unit with the flat of his hand. He had to get this cryo-rejuv back up or no credits would fill the till on this trip. He pulled the panel out, the flashing red light flickering off as he laid it aside.

Thudding in the corridor caused him to look up just as the door burst open.

"This'n's real! It's sending *us* a message this time."

The face disappeared just as fast as it had shown up.

Kratt leaped up, brushing his hands on his chest. He looked over at the eight cryo pods he was transporting and then at the door still standing open.

"Forget the colonists!" Catching the door and flinging himself through, he cursed under his breath. He couldn't get there fast enough, not with his pilot halfway across the ship already.

Then it hit him what she'd said, and he called out, "Contacting us?"

"Yes, Kratt." Jarring his attention, the ship's voice permeated the air. "The message is contacting this ship. However, it is a general message and not specifically aimed at this vessel. I could have already told you this if you would just let me into the rest of the ship. Installing my sensors and speakers only on the bridge, in the corridors, and at other limited locations severely limits my productivity."

"Crazy machine, I didn't want you on this ship in the first place. If the new space regs didn't require you here, I'd rip you out quick as I could get your service panel off." He glanced at the sensors in the ceiling, one after the other falling behind him as he ran. "At least I got by without the Vid sensors."

The corridor was quiet for a moment, with only the sound of his feet on the floor, before he heard the warning message-ding he'd insisted on before that cursed machine was insinuated into his private cargo vessel.

"I am only here to help if you need me. Many ships consider me an irreplaceable member of their crews."

"Not here, baby. Not here. Just keep your sensors off. I

can fly this tub just fine without your help." He rounded the corner and flung open the door to the bridge. His breath coming in gasps, he stopped, his hand on the wall. He looked over his navigator's shoulder.

"Synrnn." He touched her lightly. "What's it look like?" He stepped to the console, trying to interpret the readout even without the visor.

"Strange, Boss," whispered Synrnn Har-Zahav. "I don't even believe this." She reached one hand up, slowly slipping the visor over her head, her eyes still glued on the cryptic displays in front of her. Without looking, she held the info-reader out to him. "And I thought my kibbutz family was odd. You'll want to check this out. Look for yourself. You'll not believe me, even if I tell you the truth."

"Yeah, well, it seems you're the one being odd. What gives?"

"Boss," and she turned and thrust the reader up to him, "you'll see. MegaCorp."

"Grow up, girl. You know MegaCorp can't be way out here. They haven't had true interplanetary flight capabilities since shortly after that big incident hundreds of years ago. You do remember that one, or did you sleep through *all* your academy classes?"

"Yeah, Boss. I slept through them all. That's why they stuck me on this boat with you. You'd better be glad they did, too. I'm the one keeping this crate on course. Now, check the visor."

He grinned at her, well aware how many times he'd told her she was the best thing that had ever happened to him. He grabbed the info-reader from her and slapped it to his face.

She laughed as his chin dropped. She already had her hand over the info-comm when his hand blindly waved at the console.

"Patch me through to the Information Retrieval and Communication module. We'll see if she can at least start to pay her way. She cost enough for us to put in." He continued to look in the visor, his hand reaching out, touching nothing, his fingers meshing the information in the visor with the reality of his physical world. "Are we patched in, yet?"

"I am here, Kratt," IRaC inserted into the conversation. "Thank you for giving me the opportunity to help. I will certainly try to prove my indispensability to you. How can I help?" The voice modulating throughout the bridge was filled with warmth and helpfulness.

"Quit the niceties, module. Just scan this input. What is that thing out there? It's sending us a signal, and it looks like MegaCorp. Everyone knows MegaCorp's interplanetary capability is history lesson fodder. Run through the files and see what's compatible with this signal. Something out there's talking to us."

"Of course, Kratt. I will get it done as you have requested. Thank—"

"Can it. Just download the results to a reader." He turned to Synrnn. "What do you make of this? It sure looks real, I give you that." He paused, laying the visor on the console. She picked it up and held it to her face. Then he turned and walked to the door, pausing before exiting

10

the bridge. "That message says starstrike class battle cruiser. Isn't that the same class as that military ship that disappeared out by that binary star system? Can't remember the planet's name. We learned about it at the academy, though." His hand drummed the wall, his brow furrowed in thought for a moment. With a deep sigh of resignation, he stepped through the door, leaving Synrnn to the signal.

Turning to the empty doorway, she called out, "You're welcome, Boss. I enjoy working with you, too." With a laugh, she turned back to the console, the visor already covering her eyes, immersed in the unusual signal being sent her way.

—Chapter 2—

cryo·bi·ol·o·gy (krī-ō-bī-ä'-lə-jē) n. the
study of the effect of extremely low
temperatures on living things

—*NewWebster's Thirty-Seventh*
Secondary Dictionary

"IRAC, WHERE'S that info I requested about that Mega-Corp signal?" Kratt reached a hand to the readout panel, tripping a sensor, pulling in a secondary level of signals from the object. "Well?"

"I have downloaded the information you requested to the reader. However, if you prefer, I can put it on the visor, instead. Would you like me to do that for you?"

"Gods, IRaC, you are so conciliatory. Yes, you may put it on the visor, instead. Thank you. Would you please fade away, now?"

"As you please, Kratt. Feel free to use me again."

He'd throttle that module before they got back to Correigo Prime. He frowned as he watched the infor-

12

mation in the visor shift to IRaC's display. This couldn't be right. He reached across the board and slapped a comm relay. "Synrnn. Are you there?" He twisted his chair around, his visor-covered face looking at an image only he could see. He yelled out, "Hey, Synrnn!"

"Yeah!" The word unexpectedly barked out of the air just behind him, the humor in its sharpness clearly intentional, causing him to jump, nearly falling over in his chair. He threw the visor off his head.

"Gods, don't do that to me! How'd I know you were right here? I nearly peed myself."

Synrnn pushed him back into his seat. "You'd know if you'd turn the comm to send *and* receive. Are you sure you made that trip from Aregas 4 alone? Maybe you just didn't want to get some beautiful stowaway in a bucket of muck." She looked up at the ceiling. "IRaC, did you get that recorded?"

"Thank you, Synrnn. Yes, I did. Is there a particular part you wish me to pay close attention to?"

"The peed part, IRaC. Mark it as priority." She smirked at Kratt. "Got that, IRaC? Keep it on top of your priority recordings."

"Yes, Synrnn. I have posted it as you have requested. Will there be anything else?"

"We're good for now. Thanks."

"You are most welcome, Synrnn. I am glad to be of service."

"Glad to have you around, IRaC." She turned to Kratt. "See, Boss. Be nice to the help, and they'll be nice to you." She leaned over him, putting her elbows and

13

forearms across his chest. With her eyes looking directly into his, she intoned, "Important message for Synrnn. Important message for Synrnn." Standing, she cocked an eyebrow. "Well?"

"How long do you think a power charge could maintain a military emergency escape pod?" He picked up the visor, glancing inside it as he did.

"That depends. A slow-sleep pod or a full cryo model?"

"Either one. Listen. That message. I had IRaC pull some information together." He thrust the visor at her. "Check this out. The signature is definitely old military, so old it registers as an out-of-date pattern from the Mega-Corp military files."

"It seems I do remember that from those history classes. I didn't sleep through all my academy lessons. I actually woke up once or twice." She tapped the visor with her fingernail. "Old MegaCorp military. If we're talking about the end of the MegaCorp era, they were building pretty good stuff. Let's see. What were those really big ships called? Star something? I think they were the same class of ship the pod's message identified itself as hailing from."

"Starstrike class."

"Yeah, that's it. You are a smart one. You probably kept awake the whole seven standards. Starstrike. Yeah, those were some good ships. We still use some of that same technology currently. Of course, we've improved on a lot of it, too. Hm. An emergency escape pod. They weren't used often. No time, and very frowned on by the

14

higher-ups. Too many versions of events that didn't always support the official military one. I remember reports of a few used for prisonplanet containment. Slow-sleep used more power. Maybe eighty to a hundred standard years. Full cryo barely used any power at all. Easy three twenty-five or three-fifty. Why?"

"These records in the visor? I know that planet now."

"Quit beating the bush. What are you talking about?"

"There was a binary star system with a habitable planet way out the other side of the arm, name of Rejuvenant. It seems MegaCorp lost a starstrike cruiser there, one with the same signal we've been receiving. Guess how long ago."

"C'mon, Boss. Let me just pull the answer out of the air. Before the dawn of time. Just tell me, for the gods' sake."

"Three hundred seventy years. Synrnn, this could really be from that ship." He grinned. "A little piece of history."

"Junk history." She stared at him. "You're not thinking of pulling that piece of space trash in, are you, Kratt? Three hundred seventy standard years. Full cryo's not even assured for that long. You could pull in a stinking mess. Even the technology would be so far gone, you'd be lucky to sell it for scrap."

"Wait before you write me off. It's still powered. Think. Maybe even a person. Even if they are in cryo-decay, they might have valuables with them." His eyes pleaded with her skeptical glare. "Remember that pod found over in the Treset sector about seventy standards ago? That old guy was deader'n a powerless jumpship, but he must've been some important someone. That or a courier. Salvage on that one set up that crew with a brand new ship. What do you think?"

She snorted, trying to divert his attention back to more practical matters. "Your ship, Boss. Did you ever get the cryo-rejuv up? Those colonists won't pay if they can't be brought around and we have to take them back home again. Without their credits, you don't have much room for error on this run."

"IRaC's working on it. She thinks she can run down the problem." He leaned back and laughed. "Run down the problem. How ironic! She can't even run. She's an artificial personality, and she asked me if I'd like her to run down the problem."

"Boss, you work on that with IRaC." She turned to exit the bridge, glancing in the visor as if wanting to wish the information away. "Get the colonists up walking, and I'll check coordinates on that pod. If you want a toy to play with, we'll round it up for you. Who'd have thought I'd be plying the universe with a twelve-year-old boy?" She rolled her eyes as she walked down the corridor.

He yelled after her, "Fun, isn't it? It's the only way to travel. Wahoo!"

—Chapter 3—

Take one hardboiled egg.
Rap sharply against a hard surface.
Peel shell away.
Slice egg in half.
Scoop out yolk.
Mix yolk with mayo and onion.
Spoon back into egg.
Serve.

—Recipe from an old-Earth
cookbook

"HEY, PUDZ." Synrnn leaned against the door. "You and IRaC got that rejuver back up again?" She drummed her fingers against her arm. "Hm?" Walking over to stand over Kratt as he lay prone on the floor, his arms inside an access panel, she grinned. "Or would you like me to take a stab at it?"

"Well, well. It's the fire brigade to the rescue. Thanks, Synrnn." He puffed his mouth out, revealing a rising level of frustration. "Like IRaC is helping. What I could really use is a smaller pair of hands to be able to reach into this cursed thing. I can't get my hands inside and *twist* at the same time. IRaC's got me testing each one of these nodes. Twist it out, test it, and twist it back in." Pausing, he pulled his hands out, flexing his knuckles. "I'm beginning to think this is just busywork to keep me out of the way."

"You know we all love you, Boss. However," and she blew onto her fingers, rubbing her nails on her jacket, "I think I've come up with something for you. I've run some old mech preassembly programs on this cryo-rejuv. Did you know this thing was obsolete even before the Archa'Lades Conflict? In fact, parts have to be custom built anytime these units need repairs."

"Obsolete is exactly why colonists use them. They're cheaper to lease. These colonists usually spend the bulk of their credits paying the likes of you and me to get them there. If they were rich, they'd be called tourists."

"Ha! Good one!" She slapped him sharply on the leg. "Well, I've found a setup routine that's not in IRaC's data file. I think I'd like to try it and see if I'm as good as I think I am. Wanna move your butt over and let me at the board?"

He looked at her, continuing to twist on a node inside the invisible confines of the access bay. "Give me a chance to force this connection back in place. Then you can have this, and those crazy frozen colonists, too. It always creeps me out to be in here with 'em for this long. An hour or two, no sweat. After a while, though. You know. That creepy gel they're immersed in. With the

18

lights on, it glows that bilious green color, and my stomach can only take so much. I'd hate to travel in one of those. No air, no nothing." He shivered as he pulled his hands from the shadowy interior.

"Safer'n us. We get holed, and they go right on until they get picked up." She walked over and tapped the translucent shell of the cryo pod. "Right near impervious. These are some of the best things they ever came up with for travel across space."

"Creepy safe, if you ask me. Let's just get the rejuver up so we can get paid when we get there. Oh, and I want to know about that pod that's sending us that signal."

She stepped to the cryo-rejuv and ran her fingers up and down the lighted panel, the dancing of her fingers telling the machine to run through routines long forgotten. With a rapid flickering of status indicators, the machine suddenly went dark.

"Hey! Not even I managed to kill it dead." He squatted to peer inside the access panel. "Did you break it for good?"

"Patience, moron. I'm not exactly sure, but I think it's resetting its operating parameters. Hold your breath for a moment and let it play with itself." Stepping back and looking for signs of life, she let out a sigh of relief when a lone green light blinked on. "Whew! I was actually starting to worry there." She laughed, kicking Kratt's boot as ready light after ready light began turning green. "Ha! I am as smart as I thought I was. Get your tail up, and let's go get us a space toy. No need to babysit these colonists any longer. They're just credits in our account from here on out."

Kratt gave her an admiring look. "I'm actually going to admit this, even though I know you'll hold it over me." He grinned as he shook his head back and forth. "But you deserve it this time. You're good."

"You know it, Boss. I thought that's why you hired me on."

"Well, that and those long legs. Maybe mostly those long legs."

"Watch it. You'll steal a girl's heart with that sweet-talking. Can't be too careful, now." She leaned over and pinched his cheek. "Now, let's go get you that space toy." She walked out the door, leaving him sitting on the floor.

He looked around the room, reached over, and clicked the access door shut. A quick glance at the eight cryo pods was enough to give him a shudder and a reason to exit the room as quickly as possible. "Good night, and sleep tight," he muttered as he jumped to his feet, letting the light wink off as he headed out the door.

"CAN WE PULL it alongside without compromising our flight path?" Kratt stared into the visor, the virtual world inside as real to him as the one he could touch around him. "IRaC, put this up for Synrnn to see, also."

Synrnn murmured something she had learned about the old MegaCorp escape pods. "These pods were designed for easy retrieval, self-guidance systems and all. This is just so far out from everything that if this is truly what that signal says it is, the sensors may not have had enough reference points to triangulate. IRaC, what do you think?

Will it be safe enough to pull in?" She glanced at Kratt with a grin. "I wouldn't want the ship to blow a seal doing this." She was pleased to see Kratt's hand jerk the visor up, his eyes darting her direction. They both looked up at the two-dimensional display on the wall as IRaC replied.

"I foresee no real problems with retrieving the pod, Synrnn. I can recalibrate the magnetic grappling arm for tight-beam focus, and by matching velocities as we intersect its trajectory, we should be able to easily divert it. Keeping it in tow will add little drain to our power supplies, allowing us to operate well within acceptable margins. However, if Kratt wishes to bring the cryo pod aboard, I will need to recalculate the risk assessment. Would you like me to begin that now?"

Kratt interrupted the little tête-à-tête. "Later, girl. Synrnn, you *know* I want this on board. Wow, starstrike cruiser! This is the stuff of prehistory." He grinned and rubbed his hands in glee. "I do feel like a twelve-year-old with a new toy just waiting to be unwrapped. I can hardly wait." He jumped up. "Let's go get some grub. We have hours before that pod'll be in range. IRaC can keep track of our course corrections for a while, can't you, machine?"

"Thank you, Kratt. That is within my design parameters. I will monitor the location of the signal and adjust course accordingly. Thank you for requesting my help. Please enjoy your meal."

KRATT THREW one long leg over the back of the stool, expertly sliding the tray of food onto the table. He watched Synrnn take a few bites, and then he pushed his plate back.

"You know, I've been on this tub for years. Every time I'm hungry, I get so juiced up about a good meal, and then when I get it, I wish I hadn't." He grabbed the edge of her tray, jiggling it back and forth. "Hey, Synrnn. How about you? Do you think that personality module we took on board could help out in this area, like maybe actually prepare food instead of mush?"

She looked at him over a bite of her meal and just smiled as a voice replied.

"I am sorry, Kratt. I would like to be able to adjust your meals for taste and preference. However, please remember I am in minimum install mode, and while I will be glad to provide whatever services I am capable of, I am bound to the parameters you chose to purchase."

"Crikes! I'm being lectured by an artificial personality, a machine, by dog!" He grinned at Synrnn. "I guess I just have to take my lumps." One hand stirred the mixture on his tray. "Literally." A first bite bringing on a grimace, he cut his eyes to Synrnn's response.

"Dog, Boss? Been back reviewing your old-Earth files? Besides, you're just a big baby. You do it to yourself. I tried to tell you the full install was only marginally more when you purchased IRaC. You didn't want her, and now you're beating yourself up about what she can't do. It'll cost you, but you can always get the upgrade next time we're in port."

"Kratt," IRaC's modulated voice floated over them, "me being in minimum install mode will give you the chance to see what features you might like added to my personality. Waiting might not be such a bad idea. I will keep a list for you if you would like."

"Sure thing, IRaC. You keep a list, and we'll see what we can do. First on that list of yours, cooks great meals. Can you do that?"

"It is already there. Synrnn, I can make a list for you also, if you wish."

She laughed out loud. "Ha! That's fine, IRaC. Just keep Kratt's list. He'll come up with ideas for us both." Turning to him she whispered, "I think you've won her heart, Boss, you old womanizer, you." She laughed again as the personality module responded.

"Yes, Synrnn, Kratt has 'won my heart' as you say. That is within my working parameters. I always wish to please in whatever way I can."

Synrnn threw her head back and laughed as she tossed her tray into the recycle slot, watching Kratt sink farther and farther into his seat at the machine's words.

SYNRNN'S EYES flew open at the sound of Kratt beating several times on her door.

"Come on, Synrnn. It's Christmas time." The sound of his footsteps disappeared down the corridor without waiting on her response.

Leaping to her feet, she flung open the door, yelling, "I thought you didn't believe in religious holidays."

She listened to the sound of his words as they echoed back. "For this cryo pod, I'll believe in anything. Even IRaC as a beautiful woman!"

"Thank you, Kratt," the machine's melodious voice floated through the corridor.

Synrnn smiled as she pulled a top over her head and walked down the passageway. This was going to be a good waking cycle, and even IRaC was at the top of her form. At the bridge, she leaned her head in and poked Kratt's shoulder.

"You need me more here or at cargo?"

His hand waved to her. "Meet me at Cargo 4. I'm getting IRaC set up with drive sequences, then I'll be there to suit up. You can go ahead and suit up if you want."

"Gotcha, Boss." She swung herself out and down the corridor, the lighting blinking on and off as she triggered the sensors. She shivered under her clothing, although the ship wasn't really cold, as she came up to Cargo 4. Pressing her hand to the sensor, then rotating her palm, she triggered the door to cycle open, stepping inside. Gods, I love this, she thought, as she floated off into the vastness of the bay. The one big space on the ship, and hardly ever a reason to come here between ports.

She drew herself into a ball and launched into the space, a much practiced double backflip unwinding just as her hand encircled the grab bar by her exosuit. Touching the clasp at the throat, she let the suit peel itself back before lying back onto the exposed interior. Sensing she was completely inside, the suit wrapped back around her, the powerpack disengaging from the bay wall, releasing her to freefall. This was the way to travel. She was going to be glad Kratt had sprung for these suits. The latest thing, and expensive, too. All she had to do was act like she wanted to go a certain direction, and the suit jets fired up, the internal algorithms calculating how fast and how far.

"IRaC, displays up." When there was no change, she realized she'd forgotten this one detail. Her exosuit needed to be calibrated to the new personality module. Seeing the corridor door open, she nudged her suit mike. "Boss, have IRaC reroute the displays and vocals to the suit screens. Also, have her connect with my exosuit. She should be able to find my frequency easily enough."

He gave a thumbs-up sign, hitting the comm switch on the wall. "Should be pulling up as we speak."

She smiled as she saw the edges of her faceplate begin to mist with scrolling displays. Not quite the virtual world of the visor, at full res she would see the bay as a ghost world within her displays. Toned down at present, the virtual displays kept themselves to the edges of her world, easy enough to tune out.

She saw Kratt's suit enclose itself around him as he launched from the wall. She knew he was in business mode as his voice rang out, "Magnetic grappler on." Her stomach twisted, and the displays in her faceplate doubled. They slowly resolved back to their original rendition as the power surge hurtled through the cargo bay.

"Gods, Boss. I always forget."

"You haven't forgotten, Synrnn. It's the recalibration. When IRaC tightened that magnetic beam, she routed it all right through there. We were already on a potent spike, and this is exponentially more powerful. Nothing else'll pull that pod in. Get ready to open the bay doors. Strapped in?"

"As we speak, Boss." She backed up to one of the

mechanical grapplers, allowing a tether to latch to her suit. When the tether light in her suit display turned a friendly green, she moved forward.

"Extract air, IRaC." Kratt's voice rang in her suit. "Bay doors open."

She moved forward, this unimpeded view one she'd trade her mother for: the blackness of the heavens counter-balanced by the pinpoint brilliance of the stars. No matter what they told 'em back at the academy, space was a jeweled velvet cape with all the colors of the rainbow. Those groundies just needed to get out here and see the real world as she saw it now. This never transposed onto Vidpics, but she knew she wasn't the only one who saw it. Spacers spoke of it, although only in quiet whispers to each other.

"Synrnn. Psst, Synrnn. Come back to the bay. It's tough. I feel the same way every time. Just pull back. Focus on your faceplate displays. IRaC, pull Synrnn's displays up to sixty percent."

"I am bringing it up now, Kratt."

"Thanks, IRaC. Better, Synrnn?"

She shook her head, not wanting to let go of the sensuousness of the moment. "I'm good, Boss. I just need to bleed a little adrenalin. Let me haul a deep breath or two."

"That's a good girl. It hits me hard every time, too. I always think I'm over it, and I have to come out with my faceplate on full res just to be able to think. I'd wonder about you if you didn't do this every time, wonder if you're a real spacer or not. Ready to proceed?" He waved a suited arm at her.

"Let's go, Boss. IRaC, drop the res to twenty. I want the center of my faceplate clear. I want to see the boss's toy when it comes into view." She laughed to herself. The boss's toy. How many boys got to play ball in the vast reaches of space? Just Kratt. What a lucky girl she was to have snagged this berth on this ship! Gods, she was having fun!

"Kratt, Synrnn, the object is within grappler range. Be prepared for contact. There will be a jolt to this ship. Five. Four. Three. Two. One. Contact."

The entire bay lurched as the magnetic grappler made contact with the cryo pod flinging itself along its track through space; and it wrenched the pod out of its trajectory, forcing it to dutifully trot in the wake of its new master.

"Kratt, Synrnn, are you okay?"

"Didn't feel a thing. Thank the universe for zero gee. Life is good, IRaC." The enthusiasm belonged to Kratt.

"Fine, IRaC. Thanks." Synrnn made sure to be polite, even if it was to a fault.

"I am glad to hear that. I would hate to have initiated a procedure that resulted in your harm. How close would you like me to bring the pod?"

Excitement bubbling in his voice, Kratt blasted, "I want to see it, IRaC. Get it at least that close."

"The power is ramping up. I am pulling near-maximum without drawing down the reserves. I would like to proceed cautiously, Kratt. Is that acceptable with you?"

"Yeah, sure. How long 'til we see it?"

"Perhaps . . . about now. Can you locate it, Kratt?"

"Flaming stars, there it is! Synrnn, catch a sight of that. It's real. That's the real thing." They watched as it grew larger. "Gods, it's been out here a long time. Look at that. It's burnt black on one side. There! There, Synrnn! Right on the side. It says it! MegaCorp. Wow! External mechanical grapplers ready, IRaC. Synrnn, man those on the far side of the door. I'll get these."

Synrnn did her jetted spacewalk as fast as her suit would take her in the relative confines of Cargo 4 bay. "Pushy, pushy. It'll still be there in five. I'll tell you what, Boss." She turned to face him.

"What?"

"I'll *wo*-man them for you. How 'bout that, Boss?"

He laughed. "Fine. You *wo*-man them for me, and we'll call it even. I just want that pod in this hold."

"Trigger the mechanical grapplers now." IRaC's voice rang insistently in their suits. "There is no time to delay. The pod will pass us by if we do not hold on to it. It is coming in too fast and will slip from the grasp of the magnetic grappler within a few moments. Pulling it in this closely this quickly is more than the magnetic grappler tolerances will allow. We do not want to lose it."

"Ready, Boss." Synrnn slapped the panel to ready, the lights tripping to green.

"Go on my mark, Synrnn. Ready. Set. Mark." The grapplers flung themselves from the ship, the distant thunk of attaching to the pod felt rather than heard. "Pull her in, IRaC."

"My pleasure, Kratt. I am glad I have been able to help

you pull in your toy."

"You're welcome. You know, I may even fall in love with you after all, old girl." He grinned and winked at Synrnn through his faceplate, as she shot him a thumbs-up hand signal.

"Nothing would please me more," IRaC crooned back.

"GODS, BOSS. This pod's a mess." Synrnn ran her hand over the pitted and scarred surface. "Are you sure you want to take up space with this?"

"We've got the space. Besides, check this out." He floated over to a blackened panel and brushed it with a cloth. "Here's something." He spat on the cloth, rubbing vigorously to reveal what was underneath.

"Boss, let's get this back into the gravity well. This zero gee is great for playtime, but it's hard to work in." She swam back to her suit dock, hitting the seal sensor, nodding satisfactorily as the high-tech suit sealed itself for recharge and the light flipped from orange to green. "I'm cycling out. Play with your toy awhile, then come back inside. Wipe your feet when you do. Wouldn't want to get any dirt tracked into the house."

She nodded to him as he waved her off, his efforts at polishing the panel sending his legs comically parallel to the floor. Machines and boys. That's a mix that'd never change. She whistled to herself as the ship's gravity pulled her feet back to a direction they recognized as down.

"IRAC, CAN you access any of the data from this pod?" Synrnn circled the salvaged pod, occasionally stopping to touch it on the surface.

"I am trying, Synrnn. The transponder signal is all that is coming through at this time. There is a three-century lag in technology. I will keep trying."

"Thank you, IRaC." She rubbed a series of pits in the curve of the pod, tracing them with a finger. Centuries of microscopic collisions. Could anyone be in there? She glanced at the pods protecting the colonists, noting their perfect unscarred and translucent surfaces. This one they'd dragged in was of a totally different design. Opaque. Military, beyond question. The scarring didn't help, either.

"Ah, Synrnn. Enjoying the company of the dead, huh?" Kratt's head appeared in the doorway.

"Don't know, Boss. Just thinking."

"Trust me. No matter what we find in that cryo pod, you are in the company of dead people. Anyone who travels in green goop, well, that seems to me as good as dead. Ugh!"

"Boss, you are afflicted with morosity. It seeps from you all over this ship. Just give me time to work on this. IRaC?"

"Yes, Synrnn."

"Can you access that file I asked you to find?"

"I have it up now."

"Good. It's an old military file, right?"

"Yes, Synrnn. The encryption code has long since been broken. It is fully accessible."

"Excellent. I seem to recall seeing a section in there about maintenance on these pods. Feed those algorithms to this pod, and let's see if we can get a response." She turned to a noise from the door. "No! Absolutely not, Kratt!"

He held a metal bar, flattened on one end. An outsized mallet was also in his hand.

"It's ours, Synrnn. This'll get us inside."

"Boss, you've got to let me work this. I'm good at this. Give me some time, and then have a go with your mallet and pry bar. I'll get this opened. I wish I could see inside, though. They always opaqued these old military pods." She crossed her arms and leaned against the pod, blocking his access to the old relic. "I was on a prisonplanet once. Rant, I think. Well, on the station that orbits above it, anyway. They wouldn't let me downsides to the surface, not that I minded about that. There'd been a breakout attempt. It seems like a couple of the inmates had escaped, stolen a transport or something. They finally captured them, but that's the time I saw these pods being used as containment for incorrigibles. All of those were like this except they had triple security voice locks on them. This one seems to just have an environment lock on it, at least as far as I can tell. Boss, what could have blasted the side of this pod like this? Under all this black, the surface is melted."

"Who cares? You as good as said anyone inside would already be in cryo-decay, and the technology would be worthless. Let me break the bank, Synrnn. You can play with the onboard systems just as well with the thing cracked wide." He walked the circumference of the pod, his eyes glancing back to the glowing pods the colonists were in. "Four hundred years." He nodded at Synrnn,

31

tapping the pod's surface with his mallet.

"Three seventy, Boss. That battleship disappeared three hundred seventy standard years ago." She moved to stand in his way, separating him from the scarred orb.

"The person inside would be four hundred, if he's a cycle."

"Yeah, but not really. Besides, you want to break in. Four hundred and very dead if you use that mallet to bypass the seal." She leaned against the pod's side, looking him in the face. "Cryo is a full stop, Boss. They'd still be twenty-five or thirty, or however old they were when they went inside."

"Synrnn, Kratt."

They both looked up as if to find IRaC on the ceiling. Kratt started, his eyes opening wide, as if just realizing the artificial personality was speaking with them in an area outside her installed parameters. "Dang it, IRaC! How're you doing that? You don't have any sensors in here." He turned his head to Synrnn to see her split a grin. "Wha—"

"Kratt, Synrnn patched me into the secondary comm system. I now have full access to all areas of the ship. Of course, I am auditory only, but Synrnn and I are working on a patch into the ship's optical sensors. Would you rather we did not?"

"It's like I'm being conspired against. No, IRaC, this is fine. I actually like having you in here. I just didn't expect it, that's all." He dropped his proposed break-in tools on the floor, the items clattering noisily, then paused, running a hand across his head.

"I apologize, Kratt. You should have been told. Would

you like to be informed of such activities in the future?"

"Yes. No. Um, I'm not sure, IRaC. It's just . . . let me think about it, okay?"

"I understand. I will monitor your daily input and attempt to determine an optimal time to revisit the question. Will that be acceptable to you?"

"Sure. That'll work. Thanks for being so understanding." He glanced around at the empty walls, just Synrnn watching him, an amused look on her face. "What am I saying, thanking a personality module for being understanding? I'm turning into a loony."

"Already there," Synrnn said under her breath.

"I agree with you, Synrnn," softly washed IRaC's melodious voice.

Kratt turned at the words. "What was that, Synrnn?"

"That's between me and IRaC. Never you mind."

Suddenly a sharp snap and hiss yanked the attention of both Kratt and Synrnn to the mysterious pod.

"IRaC, did you do that?"

"I am sorry, Kratt. I had nothing to do with that. I am monitoring the situation as closely as I can."

They turned to look at each other, then back to the pod. Together they began to search its space-scarred surface for evidence of the noise.

"Do you smell anything strange, Boss? Anything that smells suspicious, or," and Synrnn made a face, "perhaps rotten?" *Dead* was what she meant.

"Not that I can tell. Come over here. I want you to see this."

As she walked around, she saw Kratt running his

hands down the heat-slagged surface of the pod.

"This looks like it might have been a seam. This dark streak, right here. Look at that panel I was cleaning earlier. Has it changed?"

"Like what?"

"It seemed to be glowing a faint orange before. On the modern pods, that indicates atmospheric instability detected. The colonists' pods won't open under an orange code. See what it looks like now."

"Green? I think maybe green. It's pretty faint."

"Get me that pry bar, Synrnn."

"Boss!"

"He is right, Synrnn. The signal from the pod has changed. It needs to be opened now. If anyone is alive inside, they will not be much longer unless access and retrieval is achieved."

Leaping to the pry bar and mallet, Synrnn kicked them over to Kratt. "Quick, Boss. You were right. Crack 'er like an egg. Let's whip up an omelet." She laughed. "I'll get the cryo-rejuv online just in case the little chicken isn't already spoiled."

Grabbing the pry bar and placing it along the slagged seam, Kratt began whacking it with the mallet. Over and over the sound rang through the room. His clothing growing damp with sweat, he gasped and wiped his face on his sleeve. Handing the tool to Synrnn, he put his hands on his knees and stood panting.

"Let a real man do it, Boss. A *wo*-man." She worked around the opening, driving the slagged seam apart. "I think I've just about got it. Help me rock the far side to see if we can jar it loose. Ready?"

"Let me get over there." Placing his hands on the blackened face of the pod, he counted, "One. Two. *Three!*" With a shove they began to rock the panel until it shifted, giving them room get the pry bar underneath. As they did, cold fog began to seep from around the crack.

"Quick, Boss. That's a sign of cryo-breach. We'll only have a few moments to start resuscitation. Work it with the bar."

"I am, Synrnn. You try it!"

"Kratt, Synrnn, the pod is sending a system failure message. It is critical to evacuate the contents now."

"Thank you," Synrnn yelled at no one in particular. "Boss, I'm getting the ripper." She yanked open a stor'lok, grabbed a large tool, and slammed the end into a socket on the wall. "Move aside. This can opener will do some damage."

Backing up, Kratt watched her do one of the things he most appreciated about her. With the tip of the tool in the exposed seam, she hit the power, and he watched the metal fly. Throwing the panel off, exposing a glassine panel in the darkened interior, he put his face close and took a deep breath. "Smells fine, Synrnn. Open the rejuv socket."

"No rotted meat, huh?" She let the ripper fall deafeningly to the floor.

He danced over and yanked the connector from the cryo-rejuv. Dragging it over and plugging it in, he leaned back on the pod, panting. "Got it! IRaC, can we take time to check the reading, now?"

"I currently have full access to the pod. Thank you,

Kratt. Well done, Synrnn. I will run diagnostics and see what you have found. Give me a moment." A steady hum started from the direction of the rejuver, and as they watched, the interior of the pod began to glow.

"Yellow? Whoever heard of yellow cryo gel?"

"Chill, Boss. We've only had green for the last hundred and fifty standard years, one seventy tops. This is old military." She ran her hand along the inside of the opening until she felt a notch. "There," she said with satisfaction. "I knew it should be here." She stepped back as a row of indicators blinked on, only the final one gleaming an ominous red. She peered at it, a frown on her face. "Not good, Boss. This is certainly not good. Check the rejuver. See if it gives us any suggestions." She tapped the red light. "Green, please. I need green."

"One indicator here also showing red. It says life-force regeneration isn't powering up. Life-force regeneration means there *is* someone inside. We may have to pull whoever it is from the pod. Can we do that? Safely?"

"Never did that, Boss. Maybe we'll find out. Maybe we can drop 'em into a medbath. IRaC? Have you been listening?"

"Of course, Synrnn. How can I help?"

"Run the stats on a medbath. See if the parameters are sufficient to bring someone out of full cryo. Stat. We've gotta transfer *now*. Boss, I'm taking the assumption we can do this. It's going to be the only way. I'm heading out to pick up a medbath and get it back here." She was gone before he could answer.

"IRaC, will it work?"

36

"There may be a chance, Kratt. I am running the simulation now. Current projections for success hover at slightly under sixty percent."

"Keep at it, IRaC. It looks like that's the only way we might keep this person alive."

"MEDBATH. Let me see."

Synrnn counted down the wall and popped the correct stor'lok door aside, reaching inside for the portable trauma device. It was designed to handle the most devastating physical injury imaginable. Anything short of decapitation was theoretically within the repair ability of a medbath. Grabbing coldpaks, gloves, and a medkit, she threw them into the medbath unit.

"IRaC, is there any way I can start this to get it ready faster?"

"Get it to the bay, Synrnn. I will guide you from there. This was good thinking. I am running simulations using the bath right now. I am currently projecting a seventy-eight percent probability of success."

"Thank you, IRaC. I'm on my way." She strapped the bath on a portable gurney, her time back to the bay disappearing as fast as its wheels would turn. Clipping the door, she flew the gurney inside. "Boss?"

Following a muffled, "Bring it over here," she saw his head deep in the pod. "We've got to get him out, and I do mean him, and into that medbath. The gel's already softened, and none of his systems are up and functional yet." He pulled out of the pod, his arms covered with the yellow gel. "It's making my arms numb, even inert like this. It

37

still creeps me out thinking of getting in one of these intentionally." He shivered, looking over what Synrnn had brought with her. "Good. Coldpaks. He'll need that. Clear the bed and help me move him. Use gloves if you brought 'em. We'll need someone who can still work her fingers."

Snapping the gloves on, she reached in to help pull the body out. "How'd you know it's a man?"

"He's in uniform. MegaCorp. Not high up, but still a man's. You'll see."

As they began to lift him, she cursed her sloppiness out loud as her arm brushed some of the gel away from the body.

IRaC's voice rang out, "Keep the gel on him, Synrnn. There is still life left in it. In my simulations, success falls to less than thirty-two percent without it."

"I'll be more careful, IRaC." Aside, she turned to Kratt. "You hear that? Now my mother's aboard with us."

"You do want to keep him alive, Synrnn. Am I correct?"

"Yes, IRaC. I stand chastised. I'll be more careful."

"Thank you, Synrnn. As soon as you have him loaded, fill the medbath with as much gel as you can. Close it and apply the coldpaks. Then roll him to the medcenter. After only a short time with no cryo support, projected success for resuscitation will start to drop exponentially."

"Got it, IRaC. Boss, let's move him." Four arms reached deep into the cryo gel, pulling the fetally-curled body from deep within, shifting him to the medbath. Quickly dumping in as much of the gel as they could reach, the man was sealed inside.

"Hit the road, Synrnn. Let's get this buggy parked and the horses unhitched. It's time to kiss the bride."

"Ha! Boss, you can still make me laugh, even under circumstances like these. Where you come up with this stuff, I'll never figure out. Now, let's get to the medbay and kiss the bride, whatever that means." She ran behind him, guiding the rear of the gurney, keeping the trip as concise as possible.

"Synrnn, Kratt, probability of success now stands at seventy-three percent and falling. Please hurry." IRaC's voice followed them down the corridor.

"Go, Boss." As the gurney rounded the door into the medbay, Kratt slapped the access panel to the medical table. As the glassine door raised and the table slid out, he guided the gurney up to it. They slid the medbath onto the table, plugging the bath into each end. Hitting the access panel once again, they both stood back and watched the table slide back into the wall, the glassine slipping down, the chamber sealing itself.

"How'd we do, IRaC?"

"I now estimate successful resuscitation at eighty-one percent and rising, allowing for eighteen to twenty-three shipboard cycles within the medbath. I have recalibrated the medbath specifically for attempted cryo-rejuv. From the readings I am already getting from the medbath, apparent cryo-decay had set in even before pod retrieval. Damage seems to be consistent with gradual power loss in cryo maintenance systems in the pod. I should be able to adjust settings in the medbath to compensate. I am readjusting my estimate for success to eighty-seven percent. Would you like to receive regular updates on the subject's progress?"

Kratt looked at Synrnn with a grin. "I guess that means we did all right." Louder, "Thanks, IRaC, and yes."

"I am glad I could be of help to you, Kratt."

He motioned to Synrnn. "C'mon. Lunch is on me."

"You do know how to woo a girl, Boss. I'll take you up on that. Give me just a moment, though. I'll meet you there." She stepped to the glassine panel, the medbath inside infused with a glow of photonic healing compounds. Planet-side weeks. It would be several sevendays before they would know how well they did. She pressed her palm against the window, watching. Waiting. Maybe even hoping. She wasn't even sure. She turned to go as she heard Kratt yell out for her to join him. "That's my Kratt," she said to the silent walls, only IRaC to hear her, and IRaC didn't seem inclined to reply.

"I'M TELLING you, Synrnn." Kratt tossed the portable glass he'd been searching through onto the shelf above his bunk. "If we find anything old military in that pod, people'll pay big time." He scratched absently at the side of his nose. "At least, I hope they will."

Reaching to pick up the glass, she flipped through the images of MegaCorp history archives. "Boss, why do you keep these old relics?"

"What? The glass?"

"Yeah." She turned. "They're nothing more than old-fashioned toys. I haven't owned one of these since I was a kid."

"They're sturdy, and they're dependable. I've also never had one fail. Tell me that about those dermal readers kids use now. I like tried and true. That's me."

She handed him the glass. "You've certainly got that, Boss. It's true you try everyone's patience. But we'll keep you around a while."

"What do you think happened to cause this pod to wind up all the way out here?"

"I don't know, Boss. I really don't." She tapped her fingernail against the doorframe. "I bet I know someone who does, though."

"Yeah, but he's not talking. You think he'll come out of it? That's a long time to be in cryo, even full cryo. I once traveled in slow-sleep, you know." He grinned as she cut her eyes to him. "Surprised you, didn't I?"

"I thought you hated all that cryo stuff, and slow-sleep is just a step under full cryo."

"Yeah, well, that's why I hate it so." He traced a circle with his finger on his bunk. "I was stone broke. My family couldn't even send me to the academy. I had to pay myself, working three standard years. I was cheap—"

"Even then?" She laughed.

"Even then." He laughed with her. "I had worked hard for those credits. It was three times the cost to ship on top, so I opted for a sealed bunk. Waking up was death boiled by two. I swore never again, and I never have, either." He put both feet up on his bunk, leaning back against the pillow. "I'll pay whatever. It's not worth the savings, no matter what they say."

"This guy's gonna have a tough time, even if he does

41

come out. IRaC says eighty-seven percent chance. What's your guess?"

"My guess? He'll walk and talk, but he'll be a scrubber, that's what. Food-sucking menial labor. Might've been better to've spaced him."

"Just what I was thinking, Boss. Too late now. He's on ship's records, and that carries a lot of weight in any port we enter. 'Cepting Rutger's World. And, just so you know, I have no desire to ever go to Rutger's World. Even the stories give me the heebie-jeebies." She picked at one rough nail. "How long do you think before the medbath'll drop, and we can see what he looks like?"

"IRaC, did you get that? Got an estimate, yet? Synrnn wants to check him out."

"It is a bit early for a firm estimate, Kratt. However, I feel I can say with a high degree of confidence that two sevendays in the medbath should be sufficient for the initial phase. He is still fully clothed, though. When the medbath is removed for the final recalibrated immersion treatment, he will need to have the clothing removed."

"Gods, IRaC! Did you have to share that now? I haven't had my meal, yet."

"I am sorry, Kratt. I will try to be more sensitive on future occasions. However, I am just stating a medical necessity. The clothing will interfere with the rejuvenation of the skin. As you may recall, cryo-decay had set in, and the skin does indicate damage. A full epidermal rebuild may be necessary."

"Sure, IRaC. I'll be there in full scrub gear. Synrnn might have too much fun on her own."

She laughed and kicked his bunk, and he grinned mischievously as he tossed his pillow at her.

Turning, she stepped outside the door. "Let's go see what else is inside your new toy, Boss." She hit the wall with the flat of her hand, the noise resonating in his quarters. "Stat!"

The lights clicked off, and the door slid shut as he bounded after her.

"DO YOU THINK this gel is good for anything?" Kratt stared inside the cryo pod, the yellow cryo gel in a semiliquid state, the mallet in his hand. He reached out with the mallet and knocked down several of the rough edges left by the ripper. "Do you think it'd still work if we charged it up?"

"Jump in, Boss. I'll power you up."

"No thanks. Just wondering if I should dump it or keep it. On Carney's World, there's a demand for old cryo gel." He grinned. "Old-school technology winning once again, modified to save the day, or at least their limited food supplies. Think we might make it there someday? Might be some credits in it, if it still holds a charge. Course, we might find someone closer who'll put it to a similar use. How about it, Synrnn?"

"No opinions, there. Sorry, Boss. I'm heading over to drop off these access node connectors. Might be able to give IRaC some visual interface capabilities."

"Ouch, and all I wanted was a good cook. Now I'm getting a peeping Tom. Er, maybe a peeping Tom-ette. IRaC, any opinions about this gel?"

"Thank you for asking, Kratt. However, I really cannot answer that question without additional information. The gel is old military and was the highest grade available at the time. It was still holding a charge when we retrieved the pod even though the occupant was entering cryo-decay. The decay may have been due to a power loss and not to a decline in the actual composition of the gel, itself. I would suggest storage for the short term with an analysis to determine viability for resale. Does that satisfy your request, Kratt?"

"That's good enough for me. Thanks."

"Do not mention it, Kratt. I am always glad to be of service."

He dropped the mallet and pulled a retractable hose from a wall stor'lok, attaching it to an arm suspended from the ceiling. Keying in storage retrieval mode, he initiated the suction in the hose. Working it over the inside of the cryo pod, he evacuated the remaining gel.

"Tight quarters," he muttered to himself. "How do people manage to fit in these?" Eyeing the pod, he pulled himself up and squirmed inside, settling into the built-in seat, his knees to his chest and his arms at his side. He placed his hands into the recesses designed for them and shivered. "Gads!"

"Taking a nap, there? Want me to power it up?" Synrnn strolled up, her arms resting on the lip of the pod. "Do I get to pilot the ship while you're out for a century or two?"

"Help me out." He offered a hand. "This is tight."

"That's why it's called an *emergency* pod, Boss. It's

just for *emergencies,* not for daytime naps. Here, grab my hand." Grasping his, she popped him back to full size. "No sweet dreams, huh, Boss? What about high-tech military secrets?" When he shook his head, she continued, "Maybe the high tech is in that man's head back in the medcenter. You never know." She felt of the opening where the panel had been cut off. "Slagged on one side and still like new inside. Well-built. I'd love to know the story about what must have happened to degrade this metal like this."

"You may never find out. That's what makes it so much fun." He glanced at her and winked. "Here's what I think. He was probably guarding a prison construction crew. The crew went renegade and started blowing the place up. Our guy was the last guard being held hostage, and the prison crew was promised clemency if they let him go. When the crew was setting our guard free in this cryo pod, the military blasted the smithereens out of the bunch of them, nearly taking out this pod in the process."

"Except, Boss, what little I could see of it, that was no guard suit."

"Fair enough." He rubbed his chin, the stubble darkening its surface producing a scratching sound. "There was a mutiny aboard a military vessel. Once all the shooting was done, the ship was busted up pretty well. Our guy was on the wrong side, and there wasn't enough ship left to support everyone. The losing side was given just one option. Join the usurpers or jump ship. Our guy was true blue, and rather than join in, he decided to take his chances in an escape pod."

"Yeah, Boss. One problem with that scenario. How'd

45

the pod get blasted?"

"Minor detail I left out. Sorry. Our guy wasn't so dumb. He set the main engines to overload just as his pod exited the ship. Bye, bye, ship. Almost bye, bye, our guy."

"I like that one. Can you give me one that doesn't involve blowing thousands of other men up?"

"Sure. There was this guy who had found his true love. Only, she didn't love him. See, she never had, and he just couldn't figure it out. Then, on one assignment, she was bored and let him have his way with her. However, once he started to proclaim his love out loud, she kicked him out. He was so distraught he threw himself into an escape pod and aimed it right into a nearby sun. He happened to be a little off in his calculations, and he bounced off the sun, frying the outer shell of the pod rather than sucking down into the solar gravity well. Now, here he is aboard our good ship."

"The best rendition for sure. I really like that one, Boss. Unrequited love." Synrnn smirked as her next barb came at him. "I wonder where in that head of yours you came up with that. Perhaps personal experience? Hm?"

"Yeah, my mother. Or better yet," sidling up to her, "sweet love of my heart. You never do seem to warm up to me. What goes on in that cold, cold heart of yours?"

"Only my pounding love for you, Boss. I just keep it under lock and key." She put her hand flat on his chest and pushed him away. Walking over to the pod, she reached in, running her hand over the interior. "I've never played with one of these. Really tight inside, was it?"

"Pretty much." He leaned in beside her. "No one

46

travels in these without the cryo on. Just fall in, and it self-initiates an emergency cryo cycle. Before it's even away from the ship, the gel has pumped in, and photonic cryo compounds are flooding the occupant's system. From what I understand, you're out so quick, you never even feel the high-speed jettison from the mothership." He chuckled. "How's that for travel accommodations? Now picture yourself on an exploding ship. When these cycle up to ready status, the lid pops up, and you back in. The pod senses you're inside and clear. Pop! You're sealed in. You barely even have time to know it's dark before the gel shoots in from eighty-five injectors all over the inside of the pod." He pointed inside at barely visible indentations on the interior surface. "Eighty-five. I know. I looked it up. Isn't that right, IRaC?"

"Yes, Kratt. You are correct. Eighty-five became an industry standard on full cryo models well before our pod was manufactured. Several versions of multiple occupant pods have substantially more, though."

"Thanks, IRaC. See, Synrnn, when this pod ejected from that cruiser, it was moving at five gees, and it ramped up to twenty gees almost immediately. That gel had to already be in place to cushion our poor, fragile human from being crushed to death. Imagine. Within two seconds, our guy had gone from awake to encased in fully energized cryo gel, his pod under nearly twenty gees of acceleration."

"A speedaholic's dream, Boss."

"See? That's what I'd like." Kratt leaned over, both arms resting on the opening, taking care around the areas cut by the ripper. His eyes were filled with possibilities, and they sparkled.

"To be spaced in a cryo pod?"

"Nah. A fighter pod. Military grade. Twenty gees or more. Instant acceleration, my suit encased in energized suspension gel. Wow! Wouldn't that be a trip!"

"Until the first laser strike. Maybe a sonic disrupter. Boss, you could look forward to hitting a piece of space debris at twenty gees. Do you have any idea how much of you'd be left? Bye, bye, little bits."

"Spoil sport." He pursed his lips. "That's my dream, though. Low, sleek, and it has to be red. With manual thruster controls. Yeah, manual." He grinned playfully. "If I ever strike it really big, if enough of a paycycle ever comes my way, I might just do it. You know, by George, I just might!"

"Good gods, Boss! And why's the color important?"

"So I can stand back and admire it in the docking bay."

"Crikes, Boss. You're the only one who'll ever see yourself flying it."

"It's more than that. I guess it's a guy thing." He looked at Synrnn, the longing bringing a mournful look to his features.

"I think you mean it, Boss. I think you'd really do it. Well, I hope you do strike it big on one of these runs. I hope you open one of these pods one cycle and find it filled with diamonds and gold."

"Thanks. Except that since they found that diamond reserve on Shirlson 3, even natural diamonds have become almost worthless. That'd be my luck."

Synrnn laughed out loud. "Yeah, mine, too."

"KRATT."

He jerked his head up and looked around. He was alone in his quarters, and the room was dark. He frowned and groaned, knowing it couldn't have been a full night, yet.

"Yes?"

"Kratt, please wake up. We have an emergency. Your attention is needed."

"Ahh." He groaned, letting his head sink back onto his pillow. "What sort of emergency?"

"The medbath has reached critical overload. The occupant needs to be removed as quickly as possible."

"Crikes, IRaC. I thought you had recalibrated the operating parameters for the medbath." He threw his face into his pillow, his arms pulling it around his head.

"You are correct, Kratt. However, to achieve maximum cryo-rejuv from the non-cryo medbath, I have had to push the bath past its designed operating parameters. I have known the medbath was under strain for some time, but I had hoped it would continue to complete the rejuv procedure. It has now failed. With failure of the medbath, successful completion of the rejuv process has now dropped to an estimated sixty-one percent and falling. Synrnn is already on her way to the medbay."

"Shike! Shike! Shike!" He vented into his pillow. Rolling over, he said under his breath, "Why always at night? Can't these things ever happen when I'm *up?*"

"Would you like me to answer that question, Kratt, or

49

is it rhetorical?"

"Let it go. Tell Synrnn I'm on my way."

"I will let her know. Thank you, Kratt. Your help will be appreciated."

"Anytime. Just remember, daytime is better."

"I will keep that in mind. I appreciate your suggestion."

With a slapping sound, Kratt's feet hit the floor. Grabbing a shirt, he headed out the door, the medbay foremost in his mind.

"You owe me for this, Synrnn. I would've been happy to've busted in, curse the occupant inside. No one would have faulted me for it, either."

However, even his reservations did not slow him as he hustled down the corridor and into the medbay.

"BOSS, THANK the stars you're here. The whole medbath's gone down. IRaC tells me the initial rejuv process is essentially complete, but with the bath down, this gel's got to come off quick."

"Also, the uniform must be removed, Synrnn."

Kratt guffawed. "Duh, IRaC." He bounded to Synrnn's side, helping her pull on long gloves and an emergency smock, turning to allow her to do the same for him. "Ready, Synrnn."

"Ready, Boss. IRaC?"

"Ready could not come soon enough, Synrnn. Proceed, and I will offer suggestions."

"Thank you, IRaC. Boss, hit the release."

As the glassine enclosing the front of the medbath

50

audibly released its seal and slipped upward into the wall, they stood back, allowing the medical table to extend itself between them. The medbath looked like a long satchel with a spring-loaded top. It now appeared dull and lifeless.

"Medbath releasing. Kratt, Synrnn, please press it into the surface of the table. It will be absorbed."

"Thanks, IRaC. Synrnn, ready?"

"Got it, Boss. Ready. Set. Push." Together, both sets of hands on the opening medbath, the stiff seal dropped closer and closer to the table as the flexible sides began to liquefy.

"The medbath liquefaction is complete. Remove the seal from the bed. Subject is now fully exposed."

"Not fully, IRaC. We've got a goo-covered man here." Kratt raised his eyebrows, looking up at the ceiling from where IRaC's voice emanated.

"Begin to remove the gel, Kratt. Removing the uniform will take care of much of it. Inventory logs show a slicing tool underneath the table. Please work carefully so as not to damage the skin underneath. When you are finished, use the overhead sprayer to wash him down."

They began slicing the man's clothes, peeling the cloth away. Synrnn stepped back.

"IRaC, he's moving."

"He is alive. Cryo-rejuv outside of a pod takes much longer, but he is definitely alive. Please use the sprayer now. Wash the gel from his face. He will need to evacuate gel from his lungs, also."

She grabbed the sprayer from the overhead rack and set the temperature for warm. Spraying gently, the man's likeness began to show through the gel for the first time, revealing pale hair and skin, and emphasizing slender, almost pretty features. She watched as he coughed, sending yellow gel oozing from his mouth.

IRaC's strident instructions interrupted her observations.

"Turn him on his side, Synrnn. Kratt, help her remove the rest of his clothes. He must be returned to the medchamber as soon as his lungs are clear. My revised estimate for survival is down to fifty-five percent."

Synrnn worked to keep the man's mouth clear as Kratt stripped the rest of the uniform off, dropping it on the floor at their feet for further study later. Using the sprayer, he rinsed the man's limbs clean, surprised at the lack of injury.

"He seems to be in perfect condition." Synrnn looked at Kratt, puzzled.

"Surprising, huh? I agree it's odd. In battlefield conditions, people who made it away in these pods were often injured when they entered. Ready to roll him on his back?" He placed his hands on the man's hip and ankle. "Grab his shoulder and head."

"Almost. Let me move around the table. Ready. Set. Roll." As the man rolled onto his back, they heard a groan. Looking at each other, she was the first to call out, "IRaC? Is he conscious, already?"

"He is not awake, Synrnn. The medchamber will continue to keep him unconscious. Please place his arms at his side and prepare to close the chamber. Survival probability has now fallen to fifty-one percent and will continue to drop until he is returned to the chamber."

Straightening the man's arms, Kratt slipped off a glove and palmed the switch. The prone figure glided inside the medchamber, with the glassine panel sealing him in.

"Full immersion in photonic compounds has been initiated," IRaC intoned. "Kratt, Synrnn, do not open the medchamber for any reason."

"Thank you, IRaC." She leaned against the glass. "I'm so tired, Boss. Look at all this stuff on the floor. IRaC, will it be all right here until morning?"

"It will need to be cleaned as soon as possible. The gel will start to destabilize in continued exposure to air and will begin to infiltrate the ventilation system. I am sorry, Synrnn. I know it is very late."

"That's all right. Boss, hand me the hose and key it for storage retrieval. Is the setting entered for the same destination as before?"

"It will be." He tapped a few times on the panel. "Done. You get that, and I'll get the uniform. I want to keep his clothing just in case I find something interesting about it." He gathered the gel-covered fabric, stacking it in a tray from under the medical bed, and slipped a self-sealing lid on it. "I'll drop this in a cleaner tomorrow. I'll want to go through it, first." He stood, setting the tray on a shelf. "Thanks, Synrnn. I know this has been more work than we both bargained for." He stepped to the glassine separating the blond-haired man from them. "Just look at that, though. A man. Nearly four hundred years old, if a single cycle."

"Not really, remember. That body has only what,

twenty-five, thirty standard years at most on it, if that. When the skin rebuilds, he'll probably look even younger. Twenty, at most."

"You know what I mean. Stuff that happened nearly four hundred years ago is just like last cycle in that brain. Look at him in there. A little slice of history is in those legs and arms. That face. The last time it showed an expression or spoke a word was to one of my grandparents. With ten greats added on!" Kratt looked at Synrnn with a grin as she walked up to the window. "Just because that pod gelled him one cycle."

"I just hope his brain isn't gelled, too. He's kinda cute."

Kratt finally laughed at the situation. "Leave it to you, girl." He rubbed the glassine as he watched the figure lying still, finally noticing the chest moving up and down. "Get this. For the first time, I think we might have a chance with him. He's actually breathing. That body is actually working on its own. IRaC, has our probability improved?"

"Kratt, the transfer from the medbath went very well, indeed. The subject's breathing and heart rate are both stabilizing. Within another cycle I should be able to verify brain wave restoration levels. The latest estimated probability of complete physical rejuv is now at seventy-six percent and climbing. It is still too early to estimate with confidence the probability of complete cognitive rejuv. I will continue to monitor the situation."

"That's good news. Thanks."

"You are welcome, Kratt."

As Kratt and Synrnn watched the living, breathing relic in the chamber, they saw the man shift his position. "Looks like we may have pulled in a live one after all, Synrnn. I can't wait to talk with him. He hasn't even lost his muscle tone."

This time she laughed. "Yeah, he might have you beat, there. Boss, did I hear you say something about the exercise gyro? Or do I need to introduce the two of you again?" By the time she reached the door, she was laughing so hard she had to hold her hand on her side.

—Chapter 4—

"I had a really bad nightmare."

"What happened?"

"A beautiful girl was kissing me. Man! She just couldn't keep her hands off me. Then she forced me into bed with her."

"How is that a nightmare?"

"The nightmare happened after I woke up. I looked next to me, and lying there was my wife."

—Joke sent via Interlink

KRATT FLICKED his eyes upward and watched the display in the lens shift. With a double blink, he drew the information closer. Keeping his gaze on a pinpoint of light for a moment brought up a label showing the information he'd preset the ship to display about various types of celestial objects. A jerk of his head, and the entire scene rotated a half circle. A bright river at the bottom of his view was the ion stream from the propulsion drive. He studied it for a moment as the ship read his intentions, enlarging his view, each particle in the stream slowing for him to scrutinize. Twelve, fifteen, nineteen, twenty-six. He read the numbers to himself as he saw them pop up. Not bad, he thought. Might need to tweak the propulsion thrusters in the next few cycles. Another jerk of his head, and the scene rotated again. He subvocalized, "Backup. Backup. Backup, backup, backup. Stop. Forward. Stop. Enlarge." He felt his heart start to race all over again. Gods, he wished he'd been in here when that signal first came in. What an adrenalin spike! He watched the overlay appear over the small pinprick with the signal information they'd received those couple sevendays ago. *MegaCorp. Emergency escape cryo pod. Starstrike 143Z.45. Please intercept.* Seeing something flick around the edges of his vision, he brushed his hand in front of his face, the motion useless.

"Current view." As the scene shifted to one of normal space, he reached up and pulled the visor off his head with one hand.

"Kratt, I did not want to interrupt." It was IRaC. "I am sorry. I did let you know that I would keep you informed."

"What do you need?" He laid the visor down on the console and rubbed his eyes, the hours of replaying that first contact telling on him.

"I have REM waves."

"What?"

"Our visitor, Kratt. Brain waves have been detected.

He is dreaming."

Kratt jerked himself to his feet. "That's good, isn't it? That means we've got brain power?"

"That is a reasonable assumption."

"Assessment, IRaC?"

"I now feel confident in assigning an assessment of a seventy-one percent chance of unimpeded cognitive function."

"That means he'll be able to talk, huh, IRaC?"

"There is a good chance. Long-term memory retention is a more real concern."

"Speak human, machine."

"He may have no memories of his previous life. He may need to be retrained with a number of basic skills."

"No! I refuse to potty-train another adult human."

"You may have no choice, Kratt."

"Talk to Synrnn. Tell her she'll need to be responsible for this little jewel."

"I already have. She was my first choice. She claimed right of first refusal should this be a necessity. She sent me to you. I am sorry, Kratt. I know this will not be a pleasant job. However, things are looking up. My prediction for unimpeded mental recovery has risen to seventy-three percent just in the time we have been talking."

"You work on that, IRaC. I want that mental thing up to a hundred ten percent. There'll be no potty-training on my watch. And IRaC?"

"Yes, Kratt."

"The next time you need to give away a grubbin' duty like this, you give me right of first refusal."

"Synrnn said you would say that, Kratt."

"Star-sucking females. I should've taken the male program."

"She said you would say that, too."

"Voice off, program." At least he'd have another male on board, even if he did have to rear him from a baby.

IN THE DARKENED medbay, a light glowed from behind the misted glassine panel. Photonic compounds clung to and sparkled all over the young man inside, their inherent healing properties infusing his cryo-damaged body with the warmth of proffered continuation.

The rise and fall of his chest and the twitches of dreams in his muscles betrayed the man living inside.

Dreams.

His eyes twitched underneath closed lids. Small movements along his slender body—a quivering leg as if taking a step, the small movement of a finger grasping for an unseen object—revealed the reliving of a lifetime of experiences.

The man, brought back from his nearly four-hundred-year sleep, not yet aware that life was not the same and would never be the same, was in fact living in a world from long ago, the flashing synapses in his brain renewing his thinking processes as they reenacted his memories. He was becoming once again what he had been so many years before. Much of it was very good. Some of it he would wish he had been able to let go. All of it was him.

He dreamed.

"JO'N!"

The man remembered a time when he was only a boy, and his older brother was home for a visit.

"Jo'n!" he called again, his excitement overwhelming him. Crashing into his brother, he flung his arms and legs around him, the familiar feel making his world right again.

"Little Rom'n!" Jo'n Rezalton mussed the hair on his head. "I guess this means you missed me."

He set his duffel on a grassy patch and knelt by the small boy. Grabbing his brother's head between his hands, he looked into his face. "What do I see here? Tears? Now I know you missed me." He wrapped both his arms around the boy, drawing him as close as he could.

Muffled, Rom'n Rezalton snuffled, "Smells like you."

"What?" Jo'n leaned back, looking at the top of his brother's head, giving him a smile.

"Your shirt. Always smells like you." Rom'n rubbed his face against his brother's shirt.

"Little bro, of course it does. This *is* me. I guess I always smell like me." He laughed at the thought.

"I miss this smell. When you're gone, I need you here to smell." The small boy pulled in even tighter.

"Space, Rom'n. Give me a little space. I've got to at least breathe." He took a deep breath and laughed again. "I've never had anyone tell me they wanted me for my *smell*."

"Not your smell, Jo'n. I miss you. Your smell is you. I love you, Jo'n."

"Me, too, Rom'n. I love you, too, little bro."

"I COULD watch him for hours, Boss." Synrnn pushed her tray away, propping her feet up on the bench. "He looks so beautiful there. This morning, I could have sworn I saw him smile. IRaC tells me his cognitive projection is up to seventy-eight percent."

"Don't get too attached. This is a prehistoric guy. He may have great-greats out there older than you."

"No, it's not like that at all. It's more the idea behind what's happened to him." She handed him her tray to slide into the recycle slot. "Have you ever wished for a fresh start in life? One where your past could just go away, and the world would be fresh and new?"

He grinned. "Yeah. One time on Goltine's Treasure, you know, out there in the Southern Arm, I met this beautiful girl at this drinking establishment." He grinned broader when he saw her roll her eyes. "Yeah, she was some looker, too, with a chest out to the kazoo." He held his hands out in front of him, laughing out loud when she covered her eyes.

"That wasn't necessary. I know what motivates your gonads, Boss."

"She was all that and more, you know. We had this wild planetside week, see. Her father, or so she told me, had this place out on a river. We were in the middle of nowhere. No one to see, and no one to see us. We spent that whole week with nothing on except our skin."

"Boss! Remember that there's a woman present."

"No, really. We had the best time. We swam in the river, lounged on the grass, and ate picnics every one of those planetside days."

She interjected, "And probably did a few other things, too."

He smiled. "Well, we weren't exactly innocent play-mates, I will admit that."

"I bet you weren't."

"I wanted it to go on and on. Then, on one of those idyllic days, this transport landed. Well, to get to the point of the story, it wasn't her father. It was her bonded partner, and there we were, jaybirds, naked on the lawn. I could have used a fresh start right about then. Have you ever spent three sevendays hiding in the forest with naught on except what your momma gave you? There are more places on a body for nasty bugs and plants to get you than you ever dreamed of in your wildest nightmares."

She smiled. "As in?"

"Let's not go there. Let's just say, it wasn't fun. I could'a used a fresh start after that three sevendays, though."

"I bet you could, Boss. I certainly bet you could."

"Yeah, you should have seen the faces of the family I finally found downriver. I think they were still laughing when they dropped me off at the spaceport wearing a borrowed pair of gran's trousers."

"Still, Boss. You wouldn't trade a thing. Your life. You. You're a one-of-a-kind guy."

"That what that girl said, right up to the time her part-ner came home. Then all she said was to run!"

At that, Synrnn let out a hoot over Kratt's rendition of his misfortune.

"Synrnn, Kratt." IRaC's melodious voice whispered

into the conversation.

"Yes, IRaC. Is there a problem?"

"No, Kratt. I have a new cognitive projection to report. REM waves are surging, and my current prediction is at eighty-two percent for a full recovery. Would you like me to continue to keep you updated?"

"That would be nice, IRaC. Thank you."

"Cross your fingers, Synrnn."

"And my toes. That I will, Boss."

"ROM'N."

The small boy in Rom'n's dream turned, snuggling deeper into too thin covers in the cold night, unable to wake.

"Rom'n, wake up."

"Hm? What?" He rolled over, the air in the cramped, unheated room freezing.

"Rom'n, move over! I'm cold, and I'm coming up." The bed shifted as his brother jumped up in one quick leap, pulling the covers off the small boy to slip underneath next to him.

"You're cold, Jo'n." Rom'n grabbed for the thin blanket as his brother slipped his long legs beside his shorter ones, sliding next to him.

"This feels good. You're warm." Jo'n rubbed his hair, still wet from his bath, over Rom'n's face.

"That's cold." Now awake, Rom'n giggled, and he squeezed under his big brother's arm. He barely fit, anymore. Jo'n had told him so. Jo'n had told him he was getting big, just like him. "You're warm, now, Jo'n."

Jo'n laughed softly. "Well, I wasn't a moment ago. All those years away at the academy, I've never had as good a place to sleep as this. Here, let me have your hand." He took it, laying his own arm over it. "You'll always be my best little brother, you know that, Rom'n. I'll always love you. Now, go back to sleep."

After a time Jo'n's breathing slowed, as sleep finally overtook him. Rom'n moved his fingers underneath his brother's arm, feeling the strength of the grown-up military man lying next to him. He wanted to be strong like Jo'n. He whispered to his brother's soft snore, "I love you, too, Jo'n. I want to be just like you."

"BOSS." When there was no response, Synrnn became insistent. "Kratt, quit playing in the virtual world and talk to me."

"Sure, Synrnn. What?" He pulled the visor off his head.

"I was wondering about the stuff you found in that guy's uniform. What did you do with it?"

"Oh, yeah. I emptied the pockets and dropped it all into a rinser. There wasn't much. I set everything up to dry and forgot all about it. There was only a packet of cards and a couple of old style information crystals, the kind you might find in a secondhand shop. I'm through here. Want me to go with you to check it all out?"

"If you don't mind. I've been trying to download info from that pod." She backed out of the bridge, talking to Kratt as they walked. "Remember getting that second layer of info when that signal was coming in?"

"Sure. What of it?"

"I think the first layer was a public broadcast for civvies, but that second. We never could get it to break down. I've been guessing military. It's the same with the pod. IRaC can access the pod, and she says she has full right-to-use. Yet, I keep pulling that secondary layer, one she can't even register."

"You think this might be something? Valuable, even?"

"I don't know, yet. But I was wondering if there was something in that man's things, anything that might help me out. I just don't know what."

"None of it makes sense to me. Communications are your field. You play, girl." He reached up to a drying shelf. "These are the cards and crystals. They might trigger something in that pod. Who knows? But, I don't really think this was anyone especially important. He'd have been picked up if they knew about him."

"Maybe, Boss. If they knew." She took the tray from the past and rifled through it with her finger. "Where's the actual uniform? The buttons and other trim were sometimes old-MegaCorp triggers for access, a log-in shortcut that served as a security firewall."

"You are the wellspring of information. I never knew that." He handed her a stack of folded material. "Not in very good condition anymore."

"No, it wouldn't be. We put our security tricks in the skin, now. Like those dermal readers you dislike so. All the military have them. Every one."

Kratt grinned. "Just one more reason to be glad I never joined up."

She paused and raised one eyebrow at him. "They wouldn't take a pudzo, anyway. I love you, Boss, but I'm sorry. They just wouldn't." She flicked a finger teasingly against his collar.

He called after her as she strode down the corridor, "I wouldn't take them, either." Then, to himself, "Not even if they asked me."

SYNRNN LOOKED at her palm, studying the bare skin under the overhead light. Her eyes slipped to the eight pods, with eight people inside. She'd never met them, and she wouldn't until they reached their destination world several sevendays away. She placed her palm on the translucent, glowing surface of one of the cryo pods and watched her hand become translucent with color.

People did this. They just backed in and let the pod gel them in. She laughed to herself, remembering seeing Kratt in that empty pod. She had never seen someone actually inside one. It was very tight.

She walked around one of the colonists' pods. Not much bigger than the one they'd retrieved, these weren't designed for deep space survival. They didn't have navigation triangulation capabilities or beacon projectors. They were vacuum proof, though, life sustaining at little or no power for many centuries if an emergency occurred.

"IRaC, can you find some information for me?"

"I will be glad to try, Synrnn. What would you like me to look for?"

"Just for curiosity, there was a world a number of years ago that suffered a cataclysmic asteroid impact. I don't remember anything much except that at one of the spaceports, decades later, several powered-up cryo pods were found. It seems there were people in them. Also, check to see if there were any slow-sleep chambers."

"Occupied or unoccupied, Synrnn?"

"Either."

"Of course, Synrnn. I will get right on it."

"Thank you, IRaC." She patted the luminous pod, the photonic glow making her imagine she could sense the outline of the person inside. She might meet this person, she knew. Maybe not. Rejuv inside a pod was relatively quick, unlike the man in the medcenter. She patted the pod one last time and strode through the door to check on how her refugee was doing.

"Hey!" Kratt rounded a corner.

"Hey, Boss." She motioned for him to join her.

"You'll want to hear this." He held out one of their visitor's memory crystals. "This. I ran an autosearch on the cargo manifest for the colonists' supplies, and guess what I found."

She stopped and took the crystal from him. "Hm." She turned to look him in the face, waving the crystal in front of him. "Well, this certainly isn't the new girlfriend." She handed it back to him. "Even more old memory crystals?"

He grinned. "You wish. I found a reader for this memory crystal."

"Why would these colonists have a reader for something like this?"

"Old technology is dependable and, even more importantly, cheap."

"What good does that do us? Do we just wait until the colonists are defrosted and then ask in a friendly way for the use of their reader?"

"Better, Synrnn. Much better. Spacing transport rules state the captain of the vessel has the right to open and inspect any and all items during shipping whether or not the owner is present to give permission. All we have to do is find the reader. My manifest says it's in Crate 17d. Want to go with me to look? It's in zero gee, and I know how much you love that."

"I'm game, Boss. Better yet, I'll bring a ball of my own to play. I'll meet you there." She stopped at the medbay door, and she shot him a thumbs-up. "Give me a moment to check on our passenger. You'll be toast when I'm done."

"Toaster strudel, Synrnn. Hot and sweet. That's me."

She made her way inside the door, murmuring to herself, "That's not exactly what I meant, Boss. Not quite."

As she stepped up to the glassine, she used her hand to wipe aside a film of condensation. Looking inside was like seeing another world. Inside that world, the man she hoped to find more about was turning, his fingers twitching. She could see he was dreaming, another memory bringing his mental abilities back to life.

"IRaC, how's the REM going?"

"Hello, Synrnn. Our subject is experiencing very strong REM waves as much as fifty percent of the time. This is a very good sign."

"Your current prediction?"

"I feel very confident in making a prediction in the

ninety to ninety-two percent range. I can be more precise if you wish me to access his current dream state."

"That's close enough. Are the hand movements normal during REM?"

"Very much so, Synrnn. As his brain reestablishes the pathways for his memories, his body responds. His internal temperature is currently elevated, and his pulse rate is high. He would seem to be reliving a very powerful memory."

"That will help him out, you say?"

"It is the best of the indicators I have measured so far. The stronger the reaction to the dream, the better the chance he will wake up with no damage."

"It's been several sevendays. Is he almost done?"

"See the photonic energy and the way it has pooled about the hands and feet?"

"Yeah, I noticed that. What makes it do that?"

"The most damaged areas of skin take the longest to repair."

"I hope he has sweet dreams."

"Instead, you should hope he has powerful dreams. Those are his best bet."

"Thank you, IRaC. You've been very informative."

"I am pleased to have been able to help. Kratt would like to know if you are still interested in joining him in zero gee."

"Scab blisters! Tell him he couldn't beat me off if he tried. I'm on my way." She kissed her hand and placed it against the glassine. "Sweet dreams, anyway." Then she was off, her expression making it clear she would brook no nonsense from the opponent she was headed to meet.

As she turned away, the man's face tightened, his dream living itself out through him.

ROM'N, STILL A small boy, backed into the corner as his mother pushed the box away, her eyes filled with pain. He watched her face, the tears already staining her clothing.

"No! I don't want it." Her words were ragged, bleeding her desperation into the air. "Just leave me alone. Jo'n's not dead."

His heart caught, shoving itself into his throat. He watched his father put his arm around his mother's grief, hugging her close to him.

"We'll just set it up on the shelf. You don't have to think about it."

The pale-haired boy sank to the floor, knowing what the box was, and crushed inside. His eyes burning, he forced his slender frame into the crevice that was the darkness behind the big chair. Jo'n! Flashes of his brother crashed through his head, too many for his heart to bear. As whimpers of *knowing* seeped from his throat, his memories faded to just one, more special than all the rest.

In the darkness he ran. He had missed the smell of Jo'n, needed to see him, to hold him close. He ran faster.

"Oomph!" Arms clasped tightly around him. "I've got you, little bro. Oh, you feel good to me." A hand ran fingers through his hair. "I've missed you more than you can know, little one."

"Jo'n!" He pressed his face into his brother's shirt, drawing in his smell. "Are we really going to the city?"

70

Looking up at his face, dark in the darkness of the evening, he knew it as well as his own without even seeing it.

"Can you walk, bro?" His brother rubbed his back, his fingernails tracing up and down his backbone. "It's a long way for me to carry a big boy like you."

"Sure, Jo'n. I can walk. Just let me go."

"Bro, I'll never let you go." Jo'n quietly laughed. "But, I will let you walk. Can I hold your hand?"

"Sure, Jo'n. I'll hold *your* hand, okay?"

"That'll be fine with me. That'll be extra fine with me."

As they walked, he held Jo'n's arm with both hands, all the way to town.

He awoke, still behind the big chair, and his little sister was crying. He was used to her crying. She was hungry a lot. His side hurt. The corner was no longer soft and dark.

He looked around the room, the light shining in where his mother had stood, where his father had tried to help her be strong. He remembered the box, the box his mother hadn't wanted. He wanted to look. He wanted Jo'n, to smell Jo'n's smell.

He could feel the burning start again in his eyes, and he blinked the tears away.

BEHIND HIS WALL of glassine, shrouded in his chamber of light aboard Kratt's ship, the slender, pale man in the medchamber shifted on the table. His bare skin, pink in its newness, seemed to glimmer with the photonic compounds surrounding him as they worked their magic. Moisture pooled at the corner of his eyes.

ROM'N, OLDER, now a cadet at the military academy, shoved his legs into his emergency survival suit. The section of the academy ship Ma'jene and he were in had collapsed around them, and it was their fault.

His heart was in his throat. He leaned in to her, barely choking out her name, "Ma'jene! What if they find us?"

"Shut up. Just get your suit on. Remember, we're here by accident." Fellow cadet Ma'jene Holcum turned away from him, shoving her arms into her ESS, the motions quick, practiced, and smooth.

As he snapped his headpiece on, he heard the helmet speaker come to life.

"Set to my private channel, Rom'n. Stat."

"Got it up. What?"

"We've still got to get in there. It's two corridors over. I've got the emergency codes for the loc-seals. That's the only way we can get in there with all this damage." She nodded her head inside the suit, indicating the direction they'd find the most severely damaged section of the ship.

"Ma'jene, we did this!" He started to shake, the horror and sense of responsibility wreaking a new layer of indescribable havoc on his body.

She turned and glared at him through her faceplate. "I told you, shut up! Timons did this. Not us. He should've let me come up. No! He shut me out. All this is his fault, and don't you forget it!" She turned, her anger and determination filling her survival suit. "Let's go, and keep up. Don't wimp out now." She strode off, her righteousness her strength, even if Timons was dead at her own

72

hands.

He looked down at his suited hands. At *his* own hands. His own hands. He felt himself retch and swallowed it quickly. His head throbbing and his mind going into shock, he saw Ma'jene's receding form. He felt his legs start to move, following her vindictiveness, and he had no choice but to tag along.

IRAC'S UPCOMING message dinged in the corridor, the sound alerting the humans to pay attention.

Kratt stepped into the bridge and nudged Synrnn. "Hey," he whispered. She slipped the visor off her head and looked at him quizzically. "It's IRaC. This must be the update you've been expecting." He disappeared back into the passage.

"Thank you, Kratt. I can speak with you both in the bridge. I did not want to disrupt Synrnn while she was under the visor."

Synrnn moved to the door, pausing before following her employer. "That was sweet of you, IRaC. Wasn't it, Boss?" She blew a kiss toward the ceiling.

"She can't see that, you know." Kratt leaned back inside.

"I know, but you can. That, and I know I did it. That makes a difference to me. It makes a big difference to me." She rubbed one hand on her shoulder, absent-mindedly massaging a sore spot from their zero gee game.

Kratt touched her chin. "You are the sweetheart of this ship, Synrnn. You know that? Without you, this'd be a sad, dry place." He looked around the corridor, and he softly rapped the wall with the knuckles of one hand. "I love all this, but you've made it a home."

She chuckled. "Yeah, even a boy's very big toy gets boring without a woman to liven it up."

"That's right." His eyes sparkled. "IRaC?"

"Yes, Kratt."

"Hit it!" Loud, throbbing music resounded throughout the corridor. Kratt yelled over it to Synrnn, "How do ya' like it?" He put a hand to one ear. "Loud, huh?"

She waved her hand and yelled, "IRaC!" The music settled to a dull throb. "Kratt, where did you get that?" She put her fingers in her ears as if to clean out the sounds. "Colonists' music?"

He grinned, nodding.

"When they climb out of those pods, I hope they don't tweak their contract with you over this piracy."

"It'll all be back in place by then. Anyway, IRaC's already pulled this off their system. It's mine, now."

"Leave it to you, Boss. Free music downloads, even in deepest space. What's next?"

"I don't know, Synrnn. I just hope it's as interesting as my life has been so far."

"CHECK THIS manifest, Synrnn." Kratt held out one of his old-fashioned glass readers. As he did, he used a thumb to flick the information up for her to see. "The auto program said 17d. It wasn't there when we unloaded it the other night, though. Now look, the crates themselves show the crystal reader to be in 17e. Let's try that one." He held a palmcrypter over the crate's lock. Centering his open hand over it, he pressed his palm flat and rotated it a quarter turn, hearing the mechanism inside the crate's door shift and click, now unlocked. "You didn't know I carried this, huh? All my contracts write this into the small print. I don't usually have a need to open stuff, but this is one time it's coming in handy."

"I'm hoping, Boss. Moving all this stuff is hard work. It's crazy what people think they need when they head off across the galaxy. How much of that stuff in that last crate do you think they will really use?"

"It's all credits to me. The more they move, the more we make."

"If the cryo-rejuv works!"

"Yeah. I get ya' there. If. But, it's their stuff."

"I just like to travel light. The less the better."

"These people never know if they'll ever make it home again. Who knows what they might miss in a lifetime on a distant world? That's why they'll opt to leave the water-synther behind and carry Grandma's old thingy. Memories count to them."

"I know you're right, Boss. I just don't *feel* it inside. This *stuff.*"

"Stuff to me and you. Indispensable treasures to them. If we find this reader, at least one piece of all this will be an indispensable treasure to us." He grinned and looked at her as he tugged at the door to Crate 17e.

ROM'N WRESTLED with the gyros in the small craft. Three local days unassisted on an unfamiliar world hung ominously before him, the final exercise before graduation

75

from the academy. He couldn't tell if he was having trouble because of the ship or his nerves.

"Ma'jene, the gyros won't stabilize." He knew the trainers were designed to be primitive, to test the potential graduates' skills, but going through this maelstrom without an interactive ship interface could prove to be deadly.

"Don't complain to me. Just fix it," she barked. "I wanna make it down alive, even if it does mean three of this world's grubbing days on this rock they call a planet."

He glanced at her, beautiful to him even in her anger. He grabbed the manual velocity regulators, damning himself for being the sucker she knew he was. All she had to do was batt her eyes, and there'd be that familiar feeling in his legs, his knees going weak, and he would respond, yes, yes, yes.

Gods, he was stupid.

He also knew she coupled with anybody who could give her a leg up. She's had a leg up or two, just never by him.

Yeah, and she was still beautiful.

"Look at where you're going, kiddo," his partner snarled.

Despite seeing Ma'jene for what she was, that familiar sensation in his knees ensured that no matter what she said to him, he did as he was told. After all, whatever it took to be with her. Whatever it took.

"BORED, YET?" Ma'jene flicked a wet thumb at Rom'n, the water catching him in the face. "Want to kill a few hours?"

76

It was the third night of their survival exercise, three hot days of nothing to do except find food and water. It had been excruciating.

"Of course, I'm bored. What else can we do except wait out the rest of the night?" He looked at her, the light of their glowwands casting strange shadows. He was certain she winked at him, and he felt his anticipation. "Damn you," he whispered, looking away.

"Come on. Have some backbone for a change. Let's do something fun."

"Like what?" He glanced up to see her pulling her overjacket off. His heart began to pound.

"I am beautiful, aren't I?" Her top slipped completely off, thrown to the side, and she had on nothing underneath.

"What if they do an inspection, just drop in on us to check our progress? It's in the book. They do that sometimes." His voice shook. He knew what she offered was completely against the rules, even as he felt he would explode with the desire that ripped through him.

"Yeah. And did you look this one up, Rom'n? The last inspection was forty-six quarters ago. Kill yourself with boredom, if you want." She walked away, her slender shape in her unders tantalizing his eyes.

"Gods, come back, Ma'jene. Don't you know what you do to me?"

She turned. "I know. I'm yours if you want me."

"I didn't think you'd ever noticed." With a silly grin, he grabbed at his pants, releasing the fasteners, and dropping them where he stood.

As she watched him fumble his clothing off, she muttered, "And with you and me alone on this hellish rock, nobody'll have to know."

By then, however, Rom'n was too immersed in removing the final bits of his uniform to care.

ROM'N JERKED awake. He squinted his eyes, the sun hot on his face. The night had been a blur of senses, and he hadn't wanted it to end. Apparently it had, because morning was here.

He glanced down at himself, the sun bright on his bare skin. He laid his head back and smiled as he reached to his side for Ma'jene, where she had been all night long, anyway, and where she wasn't any more.

Leaping up, he stood, his desire for her fading in the brilliance of the sun as his eyes searched for her, then their things, their clothes, *his clothes!* His heart thumping with the uncertainty of what he didn't want to contemplate, he ran from the clearing, topping the rise nearby. The equipment. The trainer. Gone. All gone. She had abandoned him, left him here. To miss his rendezvous with his ship was tantamount to career suicide.

"No! Ma'jene! You didn't." He knew she had, though. She hadn't changed, just used him once again as she had all along. He called, "I loved you. I've loved you always. How could you do this to me?"

He turned to where they'd lain during the night, wondering how to make a simple sheet of cloth into presentable clothing. Nothing came to mind, and anger boiled up inside.

"Just wait," he muttered, a new firmness coalescing in

his chest. "You've made a fool of me. But I'll come out of this. You'll see. I'll be a better man alone than I've been around you."

Even the laughter of the rescue crew didn't shake his resolve. He stood there, his emerging sunburn turning bright in places no shipboard soldier should ever have sunburn, and he became the man inside he had never before been.

He was very grateful to see they carried a spare pair of trousers and a shirt. Expecting a scathing condescension from his rescuers, once back on the modern, automated rescue ship, he began to laugh at the good-natured gibes of the crew, their appreciation of a man wronged by a woman providing a calming salve to his wounded pride.

"IRAC, HE LOOKS like his repair is complete. We're getting impatient. How much longer?" Synrnn sat on a low bench she and Kratt had brought in for their more and more frequent vigils.

"Be patient, Synrnn. He will come around when he is ready. The photonic healing compounds are completely dissipated. The medchamber has done all it can. Now, he is being provided nutrients only. His REM state is exceptionally high but well within tolerable limits. I am estimating his successful cognitive rejuv at ninety-eight percent."

"Does that mean no potty duty, IRaC?" Kratt teased.

"I cannot assure you that some retraining will not be necessary. However, in all probability, successful retention of basic skills is anticipated."

He gave a mock sigh of relief. "Thank you for that, old girl."

"Kratt, I believe I am beginning to learn humor. Ha. Ha."

"Very good, IRaC. We'll raise you to be a real person after all."

"I will certainly do my best to exceed your expectations. Thank you, Kratt."

Synrnn turned from the medchamber and winked at Kratt. "Then we'll each have someone to chum up with. I'll have our blond guy in here, and you'll have the girl in the ceiling. How charming!"

"That's all right, Synrnn," he chided. "If we tire of them, we can always harass each other."

"We already do that," and she laughed.

"YEAH, DON'T tell anyone I said this, but I knew Holcum before she was a loser." Rom'n lay on his bunk, his hands behind his head. The planetside incident that had cost him his rank as an officer was long past, his demotion a footnote in an otherwise lackluster military career.

"How could she have ever been anything else?" Redzik Ajadijon glanced across the space between the two shipboard bunks, laughing at the story his good friend had shared. His red hair and freckles were in sharp contrast to Rom'n's pale skin and white hair.

Rom'n leaped down, and in one smooth jump he was sitting on his friend's bunk. He looked around the dorm as if not wanting anyone else to hear. Putting one finger to his lips, he confided, "Shush. This is for your ears only.

We were on a routine T404 planetside training exercise, and you'll never guess." He winked at Redzik.

"What?" Redzik snorted with a smile, propping himself up on his elbows.

Rom'n crossed his first and second fingers. "Just like that, Holcum and me." He winked again suggestively.

"No! Not Holcum! Tell me no way! She's vicious." Redzik flopped back on his pillow. "That must be a lie."

"We were bunkmates at the academy. Rose in the ranks together. It wasn't until later that she turned." Rom'n looked away for a moment, thinking of Timons.

"Yeah, and hey, if you came up in the ranks with her, how come you're down here with us now? You should be an offic'r." Redzik punched him on the shoulder, laughing.

"Yeah. Apparently, she wasn't as thrilled with me as I was with her. I woke up that last morning, and she'd stranded me buck naked."

"Nah! Stranded?" Redzik sat up. Everyone knew about T404 exercises. You graduated or flamed on the results of your T404 score. Then, picturing Rom'n as he must have looked, he laughed. "Naked?"

"When I woke, I was there in the sun, and everything was gone. And, well, now here I am. All trained and no place to go, except here with you. It's been a good trade so far. Good friends are hard to find, and you've been the best." He rolled off Redzik's bunk, putting his hands on his own and leaping up in one thrust.

"Thanks, Rom'n," Redzik called, shooting his friend a mock salute.

"You're very welcome, good friend." Rom'n reached

to his side and triggered his bunk light.

"Night," Redzik replied. He reached up and doused his own bunk light, one more cycle over and done.

"HEY, REDZIK! I've been looking for you." Rom'n stopped him in the corridor. "Scuttlebutt is we're leaving out next cycle. Planet's been cleared of insurrectionists."

"You ever get downside?"

"Nah! Only the crack troops went. I've been up in interrogation a few times. Messy stuff." The interrogees hadn't often survived. It wasn't his responsibility, though. UnderGen'l Holcum had been one of the major instigators in the interrogation room, along with CaptGen'l Bofsky, of course. They had the rank, and that meant they accepted the ramifications of what went on under their watch.

He followed Redzik into the dorm, pulling a fresh shirt from his stor'lok. "I need to run to stores and pick up a few things before we get underway. Go with me? I'd like the company."

"Let me see." Redzik glanced at a portable glass he had with him. He patted a package at his side. "I've got to drop this at the medbay. Tell you what, I'll cut through the comm control section and meet you on D. How's that sound?"

Rom'n smiled with pleasure. "That'd be great." He buttoned the last of his uniform, and reaching on the stor'lok shelf, in a sweep of his hands, he slipped all his personal ID and credit information into his pocket. He looked at his friend and nodded his head. "Might be forced to stop by for a drink afterwards."

"Yeah," Redzik responded. "I'd like that. I'll hustle and see you on D."

Rom'n laughed, shooting his friend a mock salute as he exited the door. He took a moment to smooth his bunk. Closing his stor'lok, he stepped back to survey his small area of the ship, satisfied with the way his life had turned out. Exiting the dorm with a smooth, easy gait, he waved at those he saw, spoke to ones close by, and made others glad they could count him as a friend.

Rounding the corner into D Corridor, his eyes fell on that red hair that was so easy to find. Stepping up behind him, he swung his arm over Redzik's shoulder and spoke into his friend's ear.

"Looking for someone?"

"Gods!" Redzik jumped. "You do that, and I almost pee my pants every time."

"There's a solution to that. Just carry an extra pair." He laughed at his own joke.

Both men froze at the unexpected braying of the ship's emergency klaxons. Looking at Redzik, Rom'n asked, "Were you aware of a drill?"

"Not me." He turned and looked both ways in the corridor. They jumped when a mechanical voice droned around them.

"Evacuate ship. This is not a drill. Emergency escape pods now cycling online."

As the voice continued to sequence through the same message over and over, Redzik looked at Rom'n with surprise on his face. "That's definitely not part of any drill I've ever participated in." He turned. "Follow me."

Jogging down the corridor, they saw the emergency pod panels retracting at carefully spaced intervals far into the distance. The ship jerked under their feet. The two men looked at each other as the lights dimmed and then brightened, with many of the opening panels groaning before freezing halfway up. As the two men began to run once more, they had to dodge others who were racing in opposing directions around them. The great vessel creaked ominously, and sparks showered from fracturing seams. They came to a corridor junction and stopped. Glancing at each other, they noticed one panel completely retracted with an open escape pod inside. The interior glowed with blue light, the form-fitting seat welcoming them in. The inside surface was covered with recessed nozzles, ready to flood its life-preserving cryo gel around its occupant. Down one side, flanking the opening, a panel blinked with green indicator lights. One was bright yellow, proclaiming the pod's readiness to seal and thrust its cargo far from the savagery certain to tear the big starstrike cruiser apart. A colorful display blinked numbers, revealing a full charge and the timespan it could ensure the safety of its occupant. It offered more than enough years to be rescued in even the most extreme cases. Yet another announcement to evacuate reverberated throughout the ship, interrupting the ever-present klaxons blaring their warning cries.

"Not me," yelled Rom'n, barely able to hear himself speak. "I'm not sure I could even fit. I'll save it for a real battle, maybe for a little guy."

"I think this is for real." Redzik turned his head to search for the source of a repeated thumping noise coming at them. "Back."

As a squad of armed troops jogged past, they crowded far into the escape pod's recess to give the passing fighters room. Without additional warning, the ship's lights went dark, with only emergency lighting left to brighten the dimness. With a violent shudder, loud explosions began rocking the ship. The emergency lights dimmed for a moment, leaving them in total blackness, then came up again.

Rom'n yelled, "Take it, Redzik. The pod. It's yours."

"No!" Redzik suddenly and unexpectedly slammed into him, the force of his body careening him off his feet and into the pod. When he grasped at the opening to drag himself back out, Redzik grabbed his hand in his and held it for a moment, then forced it inside the pod.

As the door to the escape pod drew closed, shutting off his shipboard world for the last time, the final words Rom'n heard were, "Farewell, my friend!"

Two seconds later, he knew nothing at all and was traveling at twenty gees, a missile rocketing through space.

—Chapter 5—

Wake little child;
Your time has flown.
The world is new.
You won't be alone.

Morning is here,
And your dreams are done.
Wash your sleep away.
It's time for fun.

—*From* Grandma's Songs for
Bedtime

"RUN THAT by me again, IRaC. None survived?"

"That is correct, Synrnn. The asteroid impact was unexpected as the world was a relatively new settlement, and the satellite warning net was incomplete. Full cryo takes several cycles of intensive preparation before full immersion."

"Wait, IRaC. I know my information about cryo pods

is spotty, but I do understand some things. Emergency escape pods are just that. An emergency doesn't give you cycles. You get maybe two or three breaths of desperate indecision, and that's if you're lucky."

"You are correct. However, your reference applies specifically to emergency pods designed for military craft. Civilian transport pods are configured for optimal cryo immersion only after having a gradual build-up of photonic compounds introduced into the bloodstream. The gel compound for civilian transports uses a completely different substrate than the military version."

"Hm. That might be why that pod we pulled in contained that yellow gel."

"Yes, Synrnn. That is a reasonable assumption."

"What happened to those pods? Were they just down or what? Does your information tell that much?"

"Yes, it does, Synrnn. When news was received of the asteroid impact, some years had already passed. My sources are unclear as to exactly how many."

"That doesn't matter. Go on."

"It was not known that any cryo pods were on the planet's surface. A survey mission team located them many years later. When the pods were retrieved, the systems were fully functional. A number of important planetary dignitaries had taken the opportunity to avail themselves of civilian pods that were waiting for pickup and return to their place of origin. The dignitaries were apparently unaware of the proper process for civilian pod immersion."

"So they were dead?"

"No, Synrnn. They were alive, and although not cognitively responsive, it seemed they might have suffered only minor cryo-decay due to the inadequate preparation for immersion. However, after some planetside weeks of medical care, it soon became obvious the damage was more invasive than previously thought. Body systems began failing, and within six local lunar months, all had died."

"And any slow-sleepers?"

"By the time of the survey team's arrival, all were past their functioning time limit. No survivors were found."

"What about our guy? Is he going the way of those people that tried to avoid that asteroid strike? Are we going to lose him after all this?"

"Do not overlay the two situations too closely, Synrnn. There are similarities, but the core facts are vastly different. Our subject meets all the medical criteria for full cryo recovery."

"Even without the rejuver? I just don't want to lose him after all this. He lays there, his eyes twitching, and his body shifting like he's dreaming, but he doesn't wake up."

"His REM waves are indicating full cognitive function. All physiological functions are at or above optimal levels. Please give him time. I will continue to monitor the situation. If there are any changes, I will let you know immediately."

"I know. I'm just getting jittery. I want this to be real. I want him to be real, to have his second chance at life."

"I understand. If you do not mind, I have a message for you from Kratt. He would like you to know he has been able to decode the information crystal from the pod. He would like you to see what he has before he returns the reader to the cargo bay."

"Got it. Thanks, IRaC. Just keep an eye on our man, here."

"You are most welcome, Synrnn, and I will keep an eye on him. I hope for the best along with you."

"SYNRNN, GET in here." The excitement could be seen all over Kratt even under the visor.

"What? Another cryo pod?" She stepped in the bridge, her arms crossed on her chest. "Well?"

"I've got it all here. You've got to see this."

"Obtuse." She snickered, but she didn't elaborate.

"Obtuse?" he murmured, his hands shifting position as he responded to the unseen information in the visor.

"You heard me. Obtuse. You know that's a math term, Boss." She glared as best she could as he pulled up the visor, looking at her. "It's also you, Boss. How about that?"

He leaned his elbow on the console. "What the devil are you talking about? Obtuse?"

"It means stupid, Boss." She smirked at him. "Got what? You can't expect me to know what you're seeing in that visor."

"You're right. Sorry. The information on that crystal, well, IRaC was able to pull it up on the visor. She's good."

"I told you, Boss. You learn quick, though, I'll have to give you that. What'd you find?"

"Career military. Hey, and I've even got a name. What do you think about that? Guess."

"Come on." She hiked one leg up on the console. "How do you expect me to do that? I have no clue."

"Try a name from the ancient past. And we were right on the money. Four hundred years. Well, at least almost that many. C'mon. At least one try."

"Tell me, Kratt. Better, give me the visor. I'll find it."

He yanked the visor away with a laugh. "No. Guess."

"IRaC?"

"Yes, Synrnn. What can I do for you?"

"Kratt's being a jerk. Can you give me the name of our friend?" She looked up at the ceiling, her call for help sent to the sensors.

"Yes, I can, Synrnn. Kratt has asked me not to. He wants to use this information to tease you. I believe this falls under the definition of humor."

"Boss! You didn't!" She leaned over him, reaching out, her hand on his chest, pushing him into the chair. With her other hand, she grabbed the visor from his out-stretched fist. "Let me see in there. IRaC, I want to see." She slipped the visor over her face.

"Have fun, Synrnn." He leaned back, his feet dangling, laughter on his face.

Without looking, she barked at him, "Quit laughing, pudzo. Let's see. There. Rezalton. Underpriv't." She raised the visor. "That's bound to be a disappointment for you, Boss. Only an underpriv't. I don't even think that's a classification any longer. Three hundred seventy years. Wow! Things have changed. I wonder what he'll think when he wakes up." She slipped the visor back down. "Rom'n. It's funny how they used to shorten names using all those apostrophes back then. Archaic, even. Looks like he had a brother in the military at one time. Hm. Killed in action. Hey," and she pulled the visor off. "This guy attended the MegaCorp academy. Back then I think that was a big deal. I wonder what got him demoted back to priv't." She handed the visor back to Kratt.

"Underpriv't, Synrnn. Not priv't. But, you didn't see the good stuff. That was just some of the information I was able to dig out of all those cards. Out of those information crystals, I got the good stuff. One's his military pay account."

"Pay?"

"Yeah. He has an account. I just wonder. Nearly four hundred years. If it were still valid, think how much it would have in it."

She slapped him upside the head, her laugh making it gentle. "Greedy. Hoping he'll share? He might, you know. Just for the joy of being alive."

"It's intriguing to think about. An account sitting for that many years. Interest? It could have been building interest. Maybe even accumulating back pay for all that time. He'd be so rich that he couldn't even spend it all."

"Yeah, Boss. I think if that's the case, he's paid for it with everything he's ever known. Have fun dreaming, but what's his is his. Give him that."

"Yeah. It's just a dream, Synrnn. I know that. But it's fun to dream. A new ship, or at least this one refurbished. Maybe a small two-man for outside work. But that's neither here nor there."

Both turned at the sound of a chime.

"Kratt, Synrnn, please move to the medbay. Our subject is waking. Please move quickly."

With a crash, two sets of feet tore up the floor in their dash to be there when their unexpected passenger, Rom'n Rezalton, first learned the truth. The life he led ended three hundred seventy years ago. He was now living in his future.

—Chapter 6—

*"It's called relativity, Sergei. Because of
the time-space principle, the two people
involved sense time moving at different
speeds. Theoretically, three hundred years
could pass in my perception, and yet to you,
it might seem as if no time had passed at
all."*

—*Discussion overheard after
Einstein's presentation
of his Theory of Special Relativity*

KRATT AND SYNRNN ran, the lights barely able to keep up, flicking on then off again in their wake as the pair ran down the corridor and turned into the medbay, the excitement flushing their faces scarlet.

"Gods, Boss!" Synrnn gasped with exertion. "Look!" She could see the man as he moved, groggily still, but obviously no longer fully sedated.

IRaC instructed, "Open the medtable, Synrnn. He is

awake."

She leaped to the access plate and slapped her hand to it, the glassine sliding into the wall. The cold air spilling from the recess puddled in a cloud of fog on the floor.

"Rom'n." Synrnn called his name, reaching out to steady him as the table slid out into the room. "Rom'n Rezalton, you're going to be fine. I'm Synrnn Har-Zahav, and with me is ship's captain, Kratt Balanchine."

The man moaned as he turned his head, arching his back and twisting in his disoriented dream, trying to wake, yet obviously unable to accept the reality of waking. Synrnn watched as Kratt put his hands on the man's shoulders, pressing them to the table, keeping him in a prone position.

"Easy, guy. Take it easy." The man twisted under Kratt's hands as he fought against waking. "Synrnn, get something to cover him. He's going to be awfully embarrassed to see two people standing over him and him wearing nothing at all. I'd feel better, too."

"Kratt, Synrnn. He needs a nutrient pack. He will be hungry." IRaC's voice prodded them.

Kratt looked at his partner. "Do you know where they're stored? Check the stor'lok above the bed, right up there." He lifted one hand to point out the correct locker. "Four hundred years. He hasn't eaten in nearly four hundred years, Synrnn. I guess I'd be pretty hungry, too."

"A few sevendays, Boss. That's all, really. You know that."

"Yeah, but four hundred sounds better. Suddenly, our man, no, *Rom'n* stands and makes an announcement.

94

Folks, I haven't eaten in nearly four hundred years, and I'm very hungry, if you don't mind. I think I might take a snack." He looked at the face of the man under his hands, grinning.

Synrnn laid the nutrient pack on his chest. "Here," she said, turning to slip a large sheet of heavy cloth out of yet another stor'lok. Shaking it out, she laid it over him.

"Um." A moaning sound came from the man on the med bed.

Synrnn's eyes flew to his face. "His lips." She looked at Kratt. "They moved. He made a sound." She laughed. "He made a sound."

He grinned at her. "That's what men do."

"Synrnn, feed him the nutrient pack. He will need the nourishment and stimulants from the mixture. Please feed him now."

As she tore it open, the man moaned again. "Hungry. So hungry. Thirsty."

Synrnn leaned toward him. "Here, take this." She slipped the flap of the pack in his mouth and squeezed. "Swallow, Rom'n. Swallow." She watched the man suck on the mixture as his eyes opened, looking at her.

"Look at that!" Kratt chuckled with excitement.

"He'll be all right, Boss. He's lying still. You can let go." Synrnn squeezed the pack gently, a pleased grin on her face.

Kratt stepped back. "IRaC? How about it? Is he going to be okay?"

"He is no longer in the med bed, Kratt. I no longer have direct input from him. My last information shows a fully functional normalcy. Please be reassured. He seems to be holding true to my prediction of a ninety-eight percent probability of cognitive recovery."

"Hey, IRaC?"

"Yes, Synrnn."

"Now that we know his name and he's awake, can you *use* his name?"

"I am sorry. I did not intend to be insensitive. I will certainly use his name in the future. Please sit Rom'n Rezalton up. He needs to stand as quickly as possible, Synrnn."

Synrnn slapped Kratt on the arm. "Boss, I could use a little help with this. Rom'n, swallow the last of it. Now we need to help you sit." Together they placed hands under his shoulders, lifting him until he was in a sitting position. "Boss, get his legs, please."

Kratt lifted Rom'n's legs with one arm, swinging him around to sit on the edge of the table, as he huddled in his blanket, pulling it close around him, his eyes moving from unfamiliar item to unfamiliar item in the room.

"How do you know me, my name?" he croaked, looking into Kratt and Synrnn's faces. "I don't know how . . . how I got here." His body started to shiver, his skin quivering with the cold.

"Boss, he's freezing!" Synrnn reached to pull the cloth around his shoulders, tucking it in tightly. "Let's get him into some clothes. Here, Rom'n." She pulled him to his feet, as he stepped down unsteadily from the table. "You can walk? This way. We'll get you dressed. You'll feel better."

96

"Food first, Synrnn." Kratt grabbed one of his arms. "Come on, guy. We'll get you some food. Then we can talk. We've got a lot to talk about, you and me." He glanced behind Rom'n's head at Synrnn. "Help him with this blanket, Synrnn. Keep him wrapped tight."

"Aye, aye, Boss."

Between the two of them, the barefoot man was walked, pulled, and carried down the corridor to find something to eat.

CROWDING THE SMALL table in the mess, three people sat where there was only room for two. Wrapped in loose sheeting, his pale hair tousled, his skin pink from its newness, and blond bristles spattering his jaw, Rom'n's eyes glistened.

"Redzik." He glanced from Kratt to Synrnn. "Gone." He dropped his eyes to the floor. "Everything, gone." He took a deep breath, adjusting the fabric around his shoulders.

"I'm sorry, Rom'n. I really am."

"He was just here. I touched him. I told him a joke. He laughed with me. And he's been dead how long?"

"Over three centuries. We don't know the story except what we've been able to surmise from the pod and from the things you had in your pockets."

"He just pushed me in. The alarms were going off, and I was telling Redzik to get in the pod, that I wasn't going to, and he just rammed me, knocking me in. He did that for me." His eyes teared up, the moisture rolling down his cheeks. With a ragged breath, he whispered, "Redzik,

97

why?"

Kratt reached out and squeezed his shoulder. "He must have really cared about you. You must have been a good friend to him." He stood. "Now that you've eaten, let's get you some clothes and get you started on a place to sleep. Cabins are scarce on this baby, but we'll set you up with something. Need the personal facilities?"

"Um, yes. Could you point me the way?" Standing, one hand holding his wrap, the other on the table to steady himself, he paused. "Thanks for the help earlier. I'm sure I can make it on my own. Which way?" Following the finger pointing out directions, he hunched his temporary clothing higher around his neck and headed out the door.

"Enjoy going alone," Kratt called. He jerked, an oomph jumping from his throat. "Hey!"

"You deserved that, Boss." Synrnn stood. "That's been on your mind ever since he climbed off that table. You admit it. It's true." Moving to the door, she looked at their guest as he carefully made his way down the corridor. "He's all there. He's gonna be okay." Pausing for a moment, a decision made, she announced, "I think we're gonna like him, too. That'd be nice."

"Since we brought him on board, and he's staying with us, I sure hope so."

"You won't regret it. I have a feeling. Trust me, Boss."

"No problem there, Synrnn. I trust you with my life every waking cycle. This shouldn't be any different. No different at all."

ROM'N STUDIED himself in the mirror. Was it really

true? Could he trust his own eyes? Three hundred seventy years since falling into that escape pod? Who else escaped?

He thought of the people he'd left behind, gone. Whoever else that had been able to get to an escape pod would have been picked up long ago, living out lives and dying already, their remains dust on distant worlds. However, that line of thinking wasn't a safe well to fall into. He might never climb out.

These spacers he'd fallen in with seemed good enough. They'd scanned his IDs and read his information crystals, but they hadn't tried to hide it. He rubbed his face. He realized he would need a shave soon.

Rom'n palmed the hand sensor by the door, the shipboard control not too different from those he remembered, and called to those who had rescued him.

"Synrnn? Kratt? What about clothes?" A bundle was thrust into his hand.

"Try these, guy." Kratt's hand released the folded items as Rom'n pulled them from his grasp. "See what you think."

"Thanks!" Leaving the door cracked a bit, he called into the corridor, "Don't leave just yet. I'm really in your debt, you know. Without you, I guess I'd be dead, just a smear on the annals of MegaCorp. Now I think I might have a life to look forward to."

"No problem. We didn't even know you were aboard that pod. Had no idea what it was until it came right up to us. Still, it'd have been a shame to leave you out there."

"Tell me about MegaCorp again, Kratt. It's been my

life. You say it's gone?"

"Not exactly. Just its military presence. You can find MegaCorp's commercial establishments galaxy wide. Military is left up to the military now, those controlled by planetary governments and the like."

Rom'n stepped through the door adjusting his new clothing. "How's it fit?"

"Better'n me, guy. Better'n me. As many years as I've worn this stuff, I never thought it was intended to look good, but it's like it was made for you. Synrnn'll be impressed, that's for sure." He motioned for Rom'n to follow. "I have something to show you. This might be to your advantage."

"Kratt, does the ship's, um, interactive personality only have sensors in certain parts of the ship?"

He looked sheepish. "That's a sore spot. These shipboard personalities are a new requirement on all deep spacers. I fought until the last possible moment, only giving in when they wouldn't let me leave port. Synrnn tried to talk me into a full upgrade model, but I wouldn't go there. Minimum install, I demanded of the port authorities. She was right, and I've had to eat crow. It'll be everywhere on ship once we hit port."

"I just wondered. Do you know if it will respond to my voice?"

"Anything I can help you with?"

"No. Well, yes. Maybe. If MegaCorp is gone, the military arm, anyway, I guess I don't have a job anymore, do I?" He ran his hand through his hair, the unconscious action reassuring to him.

100

Excitement flooding his face, Kratt turned to him, stepping backwards down the corridor. "That's what I want to show you." He opened his cabin door. "Come on in. My cabin. Look at this." He picked up a glass from his bunk and thumbed his hand across the surface, scrolling through information, finally pulling up just one item. "Here." He handed the glass to Rom'n.

Rom'n smiled at the familiar shape and texture of the instrument, so similar to ones he'd held a hundred times. "Finally, something I recognize. Not exactly the same, probably a newer model, but this I can operate."

"Yeah, I collect these out-of-date toys, so Synrnn calls 'em. I like them, though."

"Thanks, Kratt. 'Out-of-date toys.' You know how to hit close to home." He let a half-grin ghost his face.

"I didn't think. You have my apologies. Synrnn always says I'm a pudzo, whatever that is. I guess she's right." He put his hand on the younger man's shoulder. "I didn't intend to hit a sore spot. It's just that everyone makes fun of me for keeping this old technology around."

"No offense taken. If I get sore at every unintended slight, I'll never learn to get along." He looked at the glass. "Hey, this is my military record." He looked up at Kratt. "How'd you get this?"

"Off your ID cards. Your crystals, too. You had all that stuff in your pocket, and we found an old reader in the colonists' cargo."

"I only had it because the ship was readying to move out, and Redzik and I planned to be a little rowdy for the evening, to live it up. We never made it, though. Lucky

101

me, I guess. Unlucky Redzik. Well, it probably wouldn't have made a difference no matter where Redzik was. The ship was under some sort of attack." He shook his head as if to clear the memory away. "You know, you're throwing me again. Colonists?"

"You'll see later. Look at the glass." He reached and thumbed sideways. "Your military pay account. When I tagged it in, guess what?" At Rom'n's puzzled frown, he pointed, "It's still green. Look at it!"

"I never had cause to spend much. My account was never in the red."

"You're still living in your now, and this is your future, kiddo. What if those funds have been accumulating all these years? What if, my boy?"

Trying to shift his thinking, the possibility of what Kratt was getting at just skimming his awareness, Rom'n shook his head. "Probably not. I was dead, remember. At least as far as they were concerned. Anyway, MegaCorp doesn't have a military arm anymore."

"I looked into that. IRaC?"

"Yes, Kratt?"

"Summarize that ruling you found for me about Mega-Corp and its military dissolution. The part about missing-in-action and duty pay."

"Yes, Kratt. I remember." IRaC continued as if quoting, "Section 534.34c. Active duty status may not be removed from a member of the MegaCorp Military Arm unless verifiable DNA has been established as proof of physical death. Full active duty pay must be set aside, compounded in perpetuity, disbursable upon the member's legally pursuant claim upon such account. At no time shall MegaCorp or its assigns be relieved of this obligation under full penalty of intersolar law." IRaC paused. "That is what you wanted, Kratt. Am I correct?"

"Always, IRaC. Thank you." He was almost dancing with his discovery. "You are really you, aren't you, Rom'n?" He looked at him as if daring him to answer otherwise.

"The last time I looked I was." He paused and took a deep breath, looking away then back at Kratt. "It's still three-hundred-seventy years ago for me. To me, the pay I got was just another entry into my accounts, one that I'd never spend aboard my ship. I never wanted to have a lot of credits."

"Tsk. Tsk. I've had multiple sevendays to think. You're the man with the golden hand. Of course, here my files only tell me your accounts are green. But when we make landfall, a good medscan and a good DNA sample, and you might just be richer than God, boy. Richer'n God. What do you think about that?"

"Give me some time. In the military, I never had to worry about funds or balances. Remember, I never spent everything I received, ever. I never needed to check my accounts or think about it at all."

"Well, old man. Here in the real world, we have to think about it a lot. A whole lot." He grinned at Rom'n. "You may be the luckiest S.O.B. in MegaCorp history."

—Chapter 7—

"Danged spiders. A billion miles from old-Earth, and they still got here."

—*Bird, in* Exiled on Rant,
*talking to Renhant, Jer'son,
and Barn't*

ROM'N LIFTED the visor in his hand. "I just slip this on over my head?" He glanced at Synrnn. She smiled at him, pushing the visor toward his face. When he hesitated, she pushed at it again.

"Just do it."

"How will it know what I want? Do I talk to it?" He set it on top of his head, one hand still holding the visor, hesitating before slipping it over his face.

"It's adaptive. You can talk to it if you want. It will also learn your eye movements." She reached up and pulled it down over his eyes. "We could go through everything step by step, but you'll pick it up. Just sit and play. You can't mess anything up." She reached to his shoulders, her hands pressing him into the seat. "I'll leave you alone to play. Have fun."

"Synrnn?"

"Yes, Rom'n?"

"How much longer until we're in a port?"

"IRaC?" She looked up.

"I have been listening, Synrnn. I hope you do not mind. Rom'n, we will arrive at the colonists' destination in about four shipboard cycles. I can be more precise if you wish."

Rom'n waved from under the visor. "That's close enough. I just want time to learn about them." Louder he called, "Thanks, IRaC."

"You are most welcome," she returned.

Without further conversation, the visor took Rom'n's attention as Synrnn exited the bridge. His hands and arms moved in conjunction with the unseen pictures on the visor. It would have made for an amusing scene had any-one been watching.

Inside the visor, he watched as stars flickered past. He observed one becoming brighter, his eyes stopping on it. He saw a label pop up. Hm, he reasoned to himself. That's interesting how it did that. He turned his eyes to another star, and watching it, saw the original label fade, a new one popping up where he was watching. This is easy, he thought. Flicking his eyes back to the first star, he saw the label reappear. Watching it, trying to read it, suddenly it enlarged, then again.

"Stop!" he said involuntarily. When it stopped enlarg-ing, he knew he had two types of commands down, vocal and iris tracking algorithms. It was good design, because it made sense. He realized the label was giving him information about what the object was, and after a moment, he knew it was him. Rather, his pod. This was the recorded sequence where his pod had been detected.

"This is all civilian output from that pod. There should be a military overlay in all this information," he said absently to himself. He was surprised to hear the visor softly reply to him.

"Military clearance sequence not received by pod. Please input clearance sequence now."

What the blazing stars? he thought. He pondered for a moment. It couldn't hurt to try. "Alpha. Delta. Delta. Niner. Niner. Tango. Tango. Delta." The visor blazed into a red-tinted overlay of charts, graphs, and rolling columns of information, all obviously military. "I know this stuff," he murmured. "I spent time on this during the ship's last assignment near that binary star system just before all hell broke loose. I had several cycles of duty inputting some of this. Star charts, system coordinates, and military exercise information. Ship? IRaC?"

"IRaC overriding visor feed. Yes, Rom'n. What can I do for you?"

"Are you recording all this?"

"This is itself a recording."

"What about this military input? I think I gave a clearance code and unlocked a second layer of information."

"I am checking as we speak. Yes, I see it now. It was present in the recording all along. It is strange that I should just now be recognizing it."

106

"No, IRaC." His heart raced with excitement. "It's not strange at all. This new information is a coded military channel designed to be invisible unless the proper clearance sequence is given. You couldn't see it because the program was designed to hide itself, disguising my pod as civilian. Preventative protection. This information is for military eyes only. Is this new stuff being recorded?"

"The information is part of the original broadcast received from your pod. There is no reason to rerecord it. I can do so if you wish, however."

"Please. This might be the answer to what happened to my ship. As it was cycling up, this pod should have been downloading all pertinent shipboard information about the confrontation we were currently involved in. If the ship survived even a few moments after my pod ejected, additional information about other pods and the occupants they carried would have continued to be broadcast to the pod. Find Kratt for me. I need to get to that pod." He pulled the visor off, already standing, too excited to probe its uses any longer.

"Shall I have Kratt meet you in the ship's bay, Rom'n?"

"That's where I'm heading. Tell him stat."

"Yes, I already have."

He panted all the way, his endurance still under par, the effort unnoticed in his anticipation.

He did forget to thank IRaC.

With barely a whisper, she responded, "I understand, Rom'n. You are welcome, anyway."

"CAN YOU believe this, Rom'n? I would have never thought all this was here." Kratt reached into the cryo pod, waving the tattered military uniform inside. "That woman keeps getting smarter and smarter all the time." He leaned closer to him. "Mind you don't need to tell her that. Her head barely fits in her cap as it is."

"Tell me what? That I'm the best you've ever seen? I know that, Kratt, my boy." Synrnn strode in and rested her elbows on the cryo pod, her hands under her chin. "What's with the uniform?"

Excitement bubbling all over him, Rom'n leaped in. "The second layer. I've unlocked it. I didn't even think about it until I was under the visor. I gave a code I remembered, and there it was."

She straightened up, impressed. "You remembered a four-hundred-year-old code? Wow!"

"Not four hundred years, Synrnn. Now. I remembered a code from now. My now, anyway. For me, that code was only two sevendays ago. It was just there in my head when the ship prompted me, and out it came! I had it all." He smiled, energized. "That was only the bones, though. The meat of it is stored here in the pod."

"I'm glad I couldn't convince Kratt to space it." She laughed. "I tried. What's with the jacket?"

Kratt put his finger to his lips and winked. "Classified. Very classified. You were right about the buttons. Rom'n says he thinks one of the metal pieces, probably inlaid with an ionic-pulse key, is the second part of the code for opening up the bulk of the military information. I mean, it doesn't actually decode anything, but it permits the information to be downloaded and read by IRaC."

"I tried what you're doing, Boss. You watched me. IRaC couldn't see anything even with that."

"Well, she can now." He grinned and pointed at Rom'n. "That's our magic key, right there. Our boy knew the rest of the magic words."

Rom'n smiled at Kratt's interplay with Synrnn.

She rolled her eyes. "It took magic words?"

Kratt knocked on the pod as he let his thoughts flood from his head. "Yeah, magic words, that military code from three hundred seventy years ago. Three hundred seventy years, Synrnn, and Rom'n remembered them from just a few sevendays ago. I have to keep the suit in the proximity of the pod, though. This is *so* fantastic. You have got to see all this stuff. Go look at the rejuver. It's opening up there, and IRaC's pulling a recording of it directly from there."

She shook her head as she turned her attention to the displays telling the pod's story.

Rom'n grinned at her as she stepped to the console, running her eyes across the information pouring through it. He explained, "It's everything that happened to my ship. The internal ship's communications, the orders, the star charts, everything. Even the escape pods that managed to get away, maybe even the people aboard. Well, at least up until the broadcast unit was destroyed."

"Kratt," IRaC intoned. "The download is complete. You may put away the uniform. I am assimilating the information as we speak. I should soon be able to present a realistic picture of events as they occurred. Would you like me to prepare that scenario for you at this time?"

Rom'n jumped in without waiting, "I really want to see the cryo pod list, IRaC. Can you get me that first?"

"Of course, Rom'n. Will you be using the visor, or would you rather use one of Kratt's glass units?"

He looked at Kratt, who gave an affirmative nod.

"The glass, please."

"I will have it ready when you wish to download. Please notify me of your intentions."

"I appreciate it, IRaC." He turned to Kratt. "May I?"

"Sure, go on, kid. Use the one above my bunk. I'll know where it is when you're finished. Just put it near the terminal so IRaC can do an info dump."

"Thanks, Kratt. Synrnn, IRaC, thanks so much!" He ran, the door no hindrance to his speed.

"I guess I never thought about how important this'd be to him." Kratt folded the remains of the uniform, placing it back on the shelf. "He's all over himself with this information from the past. I expected excitement about being in the future, but not this."

"Give him time. All that information he just unlocked is still the now he's been living. He'll make the transition. Finding this is like finding home for him. I'm just glad I'm not dealing with this like he is." Synrnn leaned over the pod, running her hand around the inside. "Poor guy."

ROM'N STEPPED inside Kratt's cabin. One of only two on the ship, it wasn't large, more an overgrown closet as much as anything. Still, it was larger than the space given to him. Stepping to Kratt's bunk, he reached up to the glass on the shelf. He laid it on the console and stepped into the corridor. "IRaC?"

"Yes, Rom'n."

"You can download, now."

"One moment." A slight pause, then she continued, "You may remove the glass. The download is complete."

"Thanks. This is exciting to have this."

"Good luck in your search. Do well."

"I will, IRaC." Reaching into Kratt's quarters, he grabbed the glass and all the information the pod had carried through nearly four centuries of travel. With it, he hoped he could piece parts of his past back together again. It wouldn't bring it back, but he hoped it might help him put it behind him. It was a long hope, but any was better than none at all.

Reaching his "room," he sat on his "bunk." Actually just a bend in a little used section of a corridor, the bunk a low bench with bedding across it, he sat, propping his feet up, the glass in his lap.

"IRaC?" He looked around, knowing she was only a sensor and couldn't see him, but feeling the need to treat her as real.

"Yes, Rom'n." Her response was immediate.

"All this from the pod. Do you still have it?" He looked at the glass, stroking through the layers of military information.

"Of course. I do not clear any information from my memory unless I am specifically instructed to do so. How may I help you?"

"You are much faster at searching through files than I

am. Can you search this for me?"

"I will be pleased to help. However, at my current level of installation aboard this ship, I can only search directly on the portable glass you have in your hand while it is in close proximity to a terminal. I will be glad to search my databanks and direct you to it on your glass. Will that be sufficient?"

"Yes. Look for any information about emergency cryo pods, their occupants, and the direction of their transit paths when evacuated from the main ship. Can you do all that?" He continued to manipulate the glass's information, pulling, pushing, and thumbing it around almost blindly in his desire to see evacuated personnel.

"Yes, I can. Throw away your current information, and bring the glass up to its default display. Swipe three times left, pull out the image of the cryo pod on the left, and spin it twice. You will see several choices. Choose any one of these except the first. You will find the information you seek. If you wish more details, feel free to request my help at any time."

He laughed. "I'm there, IRaC. How you do that so fast, I don't know. You had the information before I even finished the question. I'd have been all night. This is just what I wanted. You're good. Too bad we didn't have you around back in my time."

"I am here in your time, Rom'n. I was just not there in your past."

"Right, right. Literal to the end."

"I am trying to respond in a more human fashion. Please be patient. I will improve."

112

"No offense, IRaC. I'm going to work on this now. Thanks."

"You are welcome, Rom'n."

Time melted away for him as he relived the last few moments of the ship's life. He realized most of the crew did not escape. Of course, of those that did, he had no record of who might have been rescued or after how long. He searched for name after name. None were there. Not even Redzik. He hadn't really expected to find his friend, but he had hoped.

The biggest ship MegaCorp had ever built, the crew numbered in the thousands. From the records he had, only a few hundred had managed to escape. He pulled their names as a group, instructing the glass to plot possible interception points based on known trajectories upon expulsion from the ship. All were approximate, of course. A difference of only one-tenth degree over a great distance made for a very wide arc of possible destinations.

There. He had it. Many had blown out into the blackness away from the inhabited systems that had been colonized at the time. He had known that the binary star his ship was stationed near was far from the densely starred regions traveled by most of mankind. Only twelve of those systems had been heavily populated. He searched for the location of the binary star on the glass, and identifying it, tapped on the image. The world's name popped into view. Rejuvenant. He'd never known that. Pushing it away, the name unimportant to him, he tapped at the lines pointing toward the area of space when his host ship was most likely to travel in the near future. Of all those evacuees recorded in the pod's records, only seventeen showed possible intersection points in his near space. His eyes moistened. Seventeen out of the thousands that had been aboard.

He grabbed the group of names and tumbled them to the surface of the glass, their letters unraveling themselves into names and ranks. Glancing down the list, one made his heart stop, his memories of only a few sevendays ago, although nearly four hundred years old in real time, still fresh to him. He paused, his eyes looking up at the ceiling as the events flooded his head. They had been bunkmates at the academy, rising in the ranks together. She had been beautiful to him then.

He glanced back down at her name on the glass.

Holcum. UnderGen'l Ma'jene Holcum.

He set the glass down, memories crowding in, ones of more than just the last few years on board when the dorms of the underpriv'ts was his home. There were memories of the years he had spent at the academy, his longing for her. She had been everything to him at that time. Jo'n had been gone, his parents and sisters never seen again. His first friend at the academy, dead.

Grief surged through him, and he mourned his old friend for a time. Dead, and he couldn't remember his name.

He had needed someone. He had thought it was Ma'jene. She had always seemed so beautiful. Even at the end when she was cruel to everyone, her beauty becoming hard, he could still see her prettiness as his youthful self once had.

He had grown past her, though, her final cruelty to him opening his eyes to her as she really was. But now, with no rock to ground himself on, his memories of *before* were hitting him strong.

He glanced at the glass, drawn to those old memories, taking one small look just to see. Where would she have wound up if no one were to have picked up her cryo pod? He traced out her path.

"IRaC, I need to overlay our current position on this display. Can you help?"

With IRaC assisting, there it was. Only a few systems away, give or take a tenth-degree error in calculations, if her pod had traveled this far. Why her? In his thoughts, he pleaded with the gods, Why not Redzik?

Fighting through his melancholy, he marked the possible systems, then moved on, indicating those for each pod that had come his way. Just finding out the stories would make it easier to turn loose.

Soon, realizing just how much time he had allowed to slip away, the ship's corridors now darkened in their energy-saving semblance of night, he laid the glass aside and headed off to the facilities. Once finished, he padded barefoot back to his sleeping niche, slipping his newly refreshed skin underneath bedding only one-hundredth the age of the body it covered. As he drifted off to sleep, he mused at the idea of being so very old.

His thoughts were murky as he drifted into the world of dreams. Ma'jene's hard-earned reputation for cruelty was forgotten for a span, and he drifted in a world filled with her earlier beauty and charm, hardly aware that she'd lived out her life on an unknown world, now shriveled and dead, while he remained barely more than a youth.

For that one evening as he slept, he held her in his arms once again.

—Chapter 8—

snowbush (Breynia nivosa) – in colder
climates, a greenhouse plant grown for its
gracefully slender branches and delicate
green and white leaves: from old-Earth
Polynesia

"WATCH YOUR step, Rom'n." Kratt hit the release
panel, twisting his hand, and he watched the doors to the
bay swing open. "Zero gee." He flung himself inside,
hooting as he floated across. "Fun!"

"Our military ships, even the training areas and cargo
bays, were always under a full gee. I don't think I've ever
been in zero gee. I'll try, though." He jumped, flying right
to the ceiling. "Hey!"

"Small movements. Small movements are safe. Swim
to me. You'll get it with practice."

"No gravity to save credits, Kratt?" Rom'n moved his
arms and feet, eventually ending up at least close to the
captain of the ship. "With no gravity to hold things down
in here, you just strap them in?"

117

"Pretty much. Margins are close on small ships like this. This saves me a lot." Kratt knocked on one of the crates. "All for the colonists."

"This zero gee, and all the colonists' things. That I can understand. But the pods, for the colonists to get in one voluntarily. I couldn't do it even on the battleship. I would have rather died, although I'm glad I didn't."

"It all comes back to credits. Let's head to the corridor, and I'll tell you about it." Kratt pushed expertly off while Rom'n fought for balance and grace, finding neither. "If colonists were rich, we'd no longer call them colonists. We'd call them tourists. And they'd ride up top in a really nice ship. Colonists go full cryo on these slow barge runs to save credits. The credits for slow runs like this are a fraction of the ones on the big boys' ships. However, I take my time because I like it."

Stepping outside, gravity finally took its hold on them, pulling their feet in a downward direction. Rom'n pointed back through the door. "What about all these crates?"

"That's part of the slowboat thing. Full cryo costs almost nothing, just the lease on the pod. The crates are the colonists' biggest expense. They bring everything with them. Stuff they pay for. That's where my real funds are." He closed the doors. "Let's look in on the colonists. We've only got another cycle with them."

"Do you have bios on each one?"

"Nah. Nothing. I don't know what we've got until we cycle 'em up. Sometimes not even then. We hook the rejuver up, then let the miracle of technology take its course. Sometimes, Synrnn or I am here when they step

118

out, but mostly, the destination planet sends in help. You came out a mess, cryo gel all over you. You had to be kept in the pod's gel for several sevendays while the medbath attempted to pull you back from nothing. The pods can do it in half a day or less. The colonists spring forth all fresh and air-dried. Hungry, perhaps, but that's because many of them are too nervous to eat when they go in."

"Um, yeah. I've been wondering about that. My uniform was all cut up. Um—"

Kratt chuckled. "Yeah. You wonder right. I know your birthday suit better than you know it yourself. You can say thank you any time, because when we were doing the suit thing—" He shuddered. "I wasn't about to say anything, but since you asked."

Rom'n looked sheepish. "And Synrnn?"

"We work together. We weren't even sure you were alive, and then we weren't sure you would stay alive. Once you were out of the medbath and on the med table, we kept a pretty close eye on you."

Rom'n snorted with a grin, muttering, "That med table with the glass front."

"For two sevendays. Dreams, nightmares, and all. IRaC monitored, but we were in it, too. We had a stake in keeping your best interest forefront. Like, and I haven't mentioned this either, IRaC thought you might not remember everything, see. She thought there was a chance you might need some basic retraining, if you get my drift. Synrnn copped out of that, so that was to be my duty. I was sure glad when you managed to be all there, going to the facilities on your own. I'm telling you, I had my own

119

special interest in seeing you come out one hundred per-cent whole. I kept a *close* eye on you the whole time." Kratt turned and gave Rom'n a giant, overplayed wink, together with a big grin.

"I guess I thought it was an open and shut case. Plug me in and wake me up. One thing, though, I don't guess I could have been *covered.* I've seen the med beds. Glass fronts, Kratt?"

"I know, and I apologize. Your skin was heavily dam-aged, and nothing could be touching you while the final repairs were in process. Thank IRaC for that. I think Synrnn was as embarrassed as I was. She knew you'd be mortified. You don't have to mention you know, if you don't want."

Rom'n paused, his face scarlet. "No, I don't think I will mention it. Thanks for the heads up. IRaC, did you hear that? Synrnn doesn't need to know I know."

"Of course, Rom'n. My lips are sealed. I am the pic-ture of propriety."

And she was, as always.

"POWER UP, Synrnn." Kratt started pulling hoses from the rejuver to the colonists' pods as she slapped the power pads, the console lighting up like a swarm of fireflies. "Tell me when we're ready to plug 'em in."

She turned to Rom'n. "Here. When these bars turn green, give Kratt a thumbs-up. I'm heading to the bridge to navigate us in. Got it?"

He threw her a mock salute as she exited the room, bringing a smile to her face, before turning to the cryo-rejuv console to monitor the readouts.

"Almost there, Rom'n?"

"Almost." He held up a balled fist, and then he threw a thumb in the air. "Go!"

"Come plug a few. You'll get it." Kratt waved him over.

"Thanks." He watched Kratt, and following his lead he began plugging in the pods. "At last I feel I'm doing something to make myself useful to pay you and Synrnn back."

Kratt stopped, a look of exasperation on his face. Rom'n took a deep breath, imagining that he'd done something wrong on the pods. Kratt's words told him otherwise.

"Kid, you owe me nothing. You've been my toy for this trip. You've kept me interested, told me things about the past I'd never known or understood, and listened to me go on and on about this ship I love. You've paid me back just by being here. Trust me, Synrnn feels the same way."

A chime sounded, causing them to both look up.

"Rom'n, I want to join in Kratt's sentiments. You have made my first trip as Kratt and Synrnn's onboard personality very pleasurable. I hope to have you travel with us again."

"She's right, kiddo. My ship is your ship, anytime, anywhere. You just contact me, and you've got a bunk. Well, er, maybe an unused corridor, but you're always welcome aboard." Kratt walked through the maze of pods, brushing his hand over the readouts, occasionally pushing a power cord out of the way with his foot. At one point, he jostled one of the connections to see that it was solid. Finally, he stopped and pointed a finger Rom'n's way. "However, if you like this world here and would rather not leave, I'm sure you'll be welcome to stay. Understand, you won't hear me encouraging you to do so, because I'm not tired of you." He balled his hand into a fist and gently bumped Rom'n's shoulder.

"Thank you. I appreciate that." He was watching the readout on the console by then, holding a cord that still had to be attached.

Kratt waited until he looked up, and then he gave him an old-fashioned thumbs-up hand sign. "Three local weeks we'll be here. Plenty of time for you to decide. I'll be glad to have you along if you want to throw in your duffel, so to speak." He slapped the younger man on the shoulder.

Rom'n's eyes teared up as he took several deep breaths. "That's the best thing I think anyone has ever told me. You've become a good friend to me. Thanks."

"You're welcome. Now, let's get the rest of these guys plugged in. They're our paycheck, and I like to eat when I'm en route." When all eight were done, he brushed his hand over the lights on the console. "All green. Rom'n, check the pods. Each one should have a green panel lit just by the hatch."

Rom'n walked by and touched each one. "All green, Boss." He smiled. "I like that."

"What? The green lights?"

"No. Boss. I like you being my boss."

"Then get your butt to the bridge. Keep Synrnn company. It gets boring navigating the ship in, and I need to go to the facilities."

"Sure thing, Boss."

"GET READY, Rom'n. I've been here before. Snowbush World is one that's hot and damp. You'll want those goggles on." Synrnn faced the outside bay door and slapped her palm on the lock. With a twist of her hand, the doors unsealed with a thunk and slid aside. Immediately, she squinted. Noise from outside poured in with the sun. "Told you," she yelled over the sounds of industrial machines, rumbling transports, and voices chattering in several languages, while slipping a pair of gold-tinted goggles over her eyes. "Follow me." She stepped into the sun.

Rom'n moved after her, the sun, the moisture, and the smell of the planet assaulting him. Buried in the smells of the spaceport, the odor of trees and earth jarred his thoughts. A sudden rush of long-ago memories flooded his senses, and he froze in his tracks.

Ma'jene stepped away, her slender shape in her unders tantalizing his eyes.

"Gods, come back, Ma'jene. Don't you know what you do to me?"

She turned. "I know. I'm yours if you want me."

His muscles released their lockdown on his body, and he caught himself as a wave of dizziness flashed over him. He shook his head at the memory. That was all, just a memory. The real world was this place, with its noises filled with life and vibrancy, wrapped in the heat and sun that had nearly overwhelmed him. He took a deep breath, attempting to gather his thoughts.

"Rom'n?" Synrnn turned at the bottom of the ramp.

"I'm coming. I was disoriented for a moment."

"Happens to us all. Join the club. Wait'll Kratt comes out. He'll probably fall down the ramp."

They both laughed at that one.

"I'm thinking food, Synrnn. You say you know this place?"

"Been here once. It's grown a bit since then. However, I think I recognize that house over there. They have a little room just in back with three tables. The finest fried meat pies this side of The Three Sisters. Are you game?" She turned, taking several steps backwards as she waited for his answer.

"I trust you, Synrnn. If you like it, then I'll like it."

"Good answer. That's a man I can enjoy being around." She turned and led the way to the best fried pies on the planet.

—Chapter 9—

"I think love is big to a lonely heart."

—*Kreeian*

"BOSS, GET in here!" Synrnn yelled through the open door. The heavily goggled man walking by did a quick turnaround and poked his head in the doorway of the small eatery.

"Synrnn? Have you got Rom'n in there?" Kratt leaned farther in, his gold-tinted goggles making him appear bug-eyed. "I don't want to lose that guy." He stepped inside and pulled the goggles from his face, blinking his eyes as he waited for them to adjust.

She smiled. "You may not have much choice with that, Boss." She turned to wink at the blond, pale-skinned man next to her, reaching out and putting a hand on his arm. "I've gotten used to living with the face of a god, but the serving girl here hasn't." She laughed at the rising blush from under Rom'n's collar.

"Oh?" Kratt rubbed around his eyes where the goggles

had rested.

"Enough, Synrnn." Rom'n fought to keep a mortified grin off his face. "Leave it be." Cutting his eyes to the door he had last seen his supposed *amour* walk through, he smiled at her next comment.

"She's completely sotted."

Kratt took in the inside of the eating establishment, and he chuckled. "I'd forgotten how small this place is." Glancing at the table where the only two diners sat, he pulled up a chair and flipped it around backwards. He sat, resting his arms on the back. Catching Rom'n's eye, he questioned him with a grin. "How's she look, kiddo?" He reached over, giving Rom'n a mock punch to the chin.

Relaxing in the familiar camaraderie of his shipmates and rescuers, Rom'n smiled and leaned back in his chair, running his hands back and forth along the edge of the table in front of him. His eyes darting around the room, making sure no other ears would hear, he replied, "Pretty good, Kratt."

"Ha!" Synrnn laughed. "Pretty good? You should see her, Boss. Better yet, you should have seen the attention she was giving to our boy, here." She tapped the table in front of Rom'n, grinning in her enjoyment at his discomfiture, as he grabbed her hand to stop the noise.

"Shush, Synrnn." He put his other hand out to quiet her. "She'll hear."

Quieter, she continued, "She really is quite a looker, Boss. Once she began to speak, I remembered her from my last time onworld. She waited on me then. Just a kid with promise, but she was charming everyone who came through that door. Wow, now. Not all chest, either. Seems that charm I remember from then has continued to improve. Or, maybe it's just our Rom'n, here. He could pull the charmer out of a wallflower. Quiet. Here she comes." She put one finger to her lips.

"Oh, I see your friend has joined you." The girl, a young woman, in reality, placed plates of steaming pies before Synrnn and Rom'n, turning a smile to her new customer. "I thought you might show up. Most people do, us here just off the landing. We don't get a lot of visitors onworld, but those that do make the landing often manage to get this direction, and, well, we make 'em welcome. I brought you a pie, too." She placed a third in front of Kratt. "I thought you might like the house drink along with your friends," she continued, placing a mug before him. She wiped her hands on a towel she carried over her shoulder.

"Kratt." He held his hand out, palm up, in greeting. "Kratt Balanchine."

"My name is Kreeian Potgieter." She squatted at the tableside as the three sank their teeth into the pies. "I love your friend's name. So old-fashioned and elegant, like someone from an old 3Vid. I've never known anyone with a name like that. I had him spell it for me three times just to hear it." She smiled at Rom'n, touching him on the arm for a quick moment, and then she looked around at the other two empty tables, extending one hand, and placing it on the table before her. "I hope you don't mind my company. We've no other customers, and I do enjoy visiting with the offworlders who come in for a bite to eat."

"I know our 3Vid friend here doesn't mind." Synrnn smiled, watching Kreeian drop her eyes in embarrassment. "Kreeian, I seem to remember you as a girl from last time I was insystem."

"I have been serving here for," and she looked at the ceiling as if counting, "eight of our years." She stood, hearing a noise from the direction of the kitchen. "The last five full time. I was in my schooling forms before." She backed up, taking her towel from her shoulder. "I must go. Ring the bell if you need assistance." With a smile and a wave, she disappeared into the back of the eatery.

Kratt turned to Rom'n, wiping a bit of his meat pie's juice from his chin. "Well, it doesn't get any easier than that. We land, and in the space of an hour, you've found a local girl who's besotted with you." He laughed and shook his head. "You aren't lucky, my boy. You are charmed. Charmed. In every way."

Rom'n laughed. "I don't know about charmed. My life hasn't been exactly that. Remember those three hundred seventy years? Plus, there's a lot more I can't even bring myself to talk about." He set his pie down and licked one finger, before lifting a cloth to wipe his hands. "But I do know that I've been lucky to fall in with you guys. So, if that counts for charmed, then I'll take it." He looked around the room, his eyes finally resting on the door that had swallowed Kreeian. "I'll take her, too, if she wants." He laughed again at the sparkle in Kratt's eye. "Not like that, Kratt. Gods! Give me *some* credit for good sense. I don't even know the girl."

"Kiddo," Kratt tapped a fingernail on the table for

emphasis, "I'm a spacer, and trust me. Not knowing the girls is better. Then it's not a big deal to leave 'em." He looked over at his navigator. "Right, Synrnn?"

Shrugging and putting both palms in the air, she replied, "Don't look at me. I don't go that direction." Turning to Rom'n, she rolled her eyes. "Ignore Bozo, here. Trust your heart." She reached out and tapped him on his breastbone. "This will not lead you wrong. Kratt just doesn't have one."

Kratt raised his palms this time, mock surprise on his face, as he mouthed the question, *Me?* Synrnn wadded a napkin and tossed it his direction.

"I've watched you the past few sevendays, Rom'n. There's a heart of gold in that chest. Give it away carefully. Take your time, and some girl'll appreciate you for it." She stood, dropping a pile of coins on the table. "I'm out of here. Boss, are the packages delivered?"

"Colonists are away, off to their colonizing duties. Loaders are taking the crates as we sit here."

"Good. I'm headed to find some local lodgings. It'll be good to have my feet on the dirt for a while. I love spacing, but I love the breaks in between, too. Rom'n, Kratt'll take care of you. You know that. Just watch him with women. Well, don't watch him too closely. You might get more of an eyeful than you bargained for. The boss'll know how to find me when you need me or just want something to do. This is a great world, better than most. Just be careful with that heart." She kissed her hand and tapped his forehead, and then she turned and walked out the door.

"I couldn't ask for better than that one." Kratt let his eyes follow her. Then he grinned. "Except when I'm onworld. Then I like to have a really good time. Let's go, Rom'n. Your girl'll still be here tomorrow. Let's get you set up for life on a rock. Maybe for three of these local weeks. Maybe for a lifetime. If that girl, Kreeian, steals that golden heart of yours, that is." He laughed, leading Rom'n out into the brilliant sunshine, his hands fumbling for his goggles to block the glare.

ROM'N STEPPED onto the second-floor balcony. The plants, the varied ivies growing all around, shaded him from the brightness of the sun as he stood watching the street below. This city was busy. His remembered world, lived in just a couple sevendays ago in a past that could only be his, in reality many centuries gone to those around him, was one of shipboard order. His world consisted of stock clothing, any differences indicating rank or duty assignment. Here, all was a riot.

He glanced down at himself, at what Kratt had insisted on at the shopkeeper's establishment. The brilliance of the colors had made him feel garish in the shop, but once outside, no one had looked or stared. He was just one of many, those wearing the plain patterns and simple designs the sore thumbs.

He caressed the fabric absently between two fingers, recalling those he'd worn all his life. Compared to the fabrics he remembered aboard ship, this was exceedingly soft. He glanced down at the bright colors between his fingers, and then looked back up to watch for his friend.

Would he even recognize the Kratt who had come out of the shop, the colors and patterns exceeding even his? He wasn't sure, so he stepped back into the coolness of the room to wait.

A sharp rap on the door pulled him from his reverie. A voice pushed its welcome intrusion into the room, calling, "Rom'n?"

"Yes! Let me open." He fumbled with the catch, the shipboard palm sensor expected and not found, the old-fashioned latch strange for a moment. Apologizing through the door for his slowness, he finally mastered the primitive mechanism, and the door swung wide.

"Thought I wasn't getting invited in for a moment, my boy." Kratt brought in a stack of boxes and dropped them on the bed. He turned to grin triumphantly at Rom'n.

"Kratt! All this stuff! For just three local weeks?" He caught one box as it tumbled from the pile.

"Life onworld is brief. We live it to the fullest." Kratt slapped him on the shoulder, pulling out tall boots. "These are made for the damp forests of this world." He threw them aside and chortled. From another box he pulled sandals that were more sole than strap.

"These?" Rom'n reached a finger and picked one up.

"For the heat." Kratt scooped them up and dropped them back into a box.

"What about when you leave? You take all this stuff?" Rom'n pushed through the stack of boxes. Finding one in a very bright blue, he pulled open a corner just to explore, not recognizing what sort of garment the scrap of fabric represented, and then put it back on the stack.

"Gods, no!" Kratt pushed several of the boxes aside and pulled out one, this time in a vivid red, handing it to Rom'n. "Open it. All this is yours."

"Mine? I have no funds, Kratt. I don't even have a job."

"What? I'm Kratt, now? What happened to *Boss*?" He put his hands on his hips, a mock look of consternation on his face. "You're still crew by your own admission, and crew gets paid. Besides, once we get to the money house, we'll see who has the real funds. If you insist, consider it a loan." He slapped Rom'n on the back. "Besides, I like you and want you to have the best. Enjoy, my boy."

As he opened the box Kratt had handed him, Kratt laughed.

"You'll like that. Local sleeping attire. Like gauze. It's too hot to wear anything else at night. Just don't walk out onto the balcony without putting on a robe first." He let out peals of laughter as he strode down the hallway. "I've got more stuff below. Help if you want."

Rom'n tossed the box and its contents to the bed and ran after him. "Coming, Boss. I'm on the way."

"SYNRNN, YOU should see what Kratt bought me, and all just for three of this world's weeks." Rom'n followed her lead as she walked through the outdoor shopping stalls. She had been here before, and while she had explained to him there was a much better shopping area on the other side of the city, this was more convenient to where they were staying.

"Or for a lifetime, Rom'n. Like it here? You might

even want to stay." She held her hands up, her fingers forming a heart shape.

"It's only been a few hours. I have no idea what I want. I've only known shipboard life, ever since I was thirteen." He paused at a vendor's stall. Taking a container of a red liquid for himself, he also handed one to Synrnn, leaving a paper credit on the counter. "Is Kratt really that wild when he's downside? Can I trust him not to steer me wrong, or do I need to watch myself?"

"He doesn't really have many vices, not aboard ship. He's the best I've ever crewed with," she mused. "He just lets it all out on each planet when we lay over. For all that, trouble from his misdeeds never seems to follow us off-world." She paused as if caught in a misrepresentation, a smile growing on her face. "Except for that time on Regglet Colony. They have a station there, a refueling station, and you have to ferry downplanet. The boss didn't like not having access to his ship. He didn't exactly get fined for borrowing that shuttle, but he hasn't been invited back, either." She looked at Rom'n with a chuckle. "Other than that, he's been pretty mild."

"I gather I don't have to worry overmuch. At least he won't lead me to ruin."

"Not quite." She turned to a stall. "Hey! These are my favorites!" She stepped over, pulling a huge flower from a basket.

"Very pretty." He pushed his nose into its center. "The smell. It's like a thousand worlds all rolled into one."

She reached into her pocket and handed a paper credit to the smiling flower vendor. "I always get flowers when

I'm downside. They don't last on board, and the fragrance gets cloying after a while, anyway. Here, onworld, it's just wonderful."

"You deserve it, something so beautiful. It suits you."

She jerked her head around, grabbing his forearm. "Rom'n, shush! Behind you. There's your girl, three stalls over."

He started to turn.

"No! Don't turn around. Here. Take this flower."

He raised his free palm to refuse. To his dismay, she pressed the stem of the flower into his hand, using her other hand to wrap his fingers around it.

"Take it. Walk over to her and smile. *Now*, Rom'n. She's walking this way." She turned her back to him as if he were a stranger, leaving him to greet the girl, her nose buried in whatever she could find to look at deep in the stall.

He turned, his eyes searching. Everything was bright outside of the stall awnings. Underneath their shade, he and Synrnn had removed their goggles. Now, when he looked up and caught the light, the glare made everything else look black. He glanced back and forth under the shadows cast by the awnings, and then he found her in the dimness, not yet seeing him. He stepped her direction, and he cleared his throat.

"Excuse me."

"I'm sorry," Kreeian said without looking up, moving to the side, reaching to touch an item that interested her.

"Humph," he tried again, stepping in front of her, and then again as she moved. "Excuse me."

134

She looked up, perplexity twisting her eyes, a mystified smile playing across her lips. Her expression cleared as recognition set in.

"From the eatery. I know you. These clothes make such a difference. Um, um." She snapped her fingers. "Rom'n, with an apostrophe. Am I right? I am, aren't I?" She smiled, resting one hand on his arm. "What a beautiful flower!" She leaned over to place her nose next to it, inhaling deeply. "These are the most beautiful on our world."

As she looked at it, he glanced sideways, his eyes catching Synrnn's. She made a motion with her hand for him to get on with it. He glanced back at Kreeian. He took a deep breath and cleared his throat. "For a beautiful girl. You."

She looked up at him, surprise on her face. She whispered, "Me?" reaching a hand to take it.

"Of course, for you, Kreeian. Where are you headed today, or are you just out looking?"

"Business is slow sometimes, so I have the rest of the day off. I'm passing the time."

"I don't know this city, or this world, in fact." He looked around at the stalls, this time keeping his eyes from the intensity of the sunlit ways beyond. "I could use a guide for the afternoon." He began walking down the aisle between the stalls, using his hand to motion to all the unfamiliar things. "I know none of this."

She chuckled and offered, "I know a man who is very good at taking offworlders through the city." Reaching to touch an especially beautiful piece of fabric, she paused. "I do have the afternoon, though. I would be cheaper." Her voice brightened. "Faster, too. I'm already here." She smiled broadly.

"Sold!" He offered her a hand, and they shook. "Where to first?"

Their voices melted into the hubbub of the market as Kreeian started off, offering a narrative, "The real flower market is over here . . ."

ROM'N STOOD, his back to the water, his elbow perched on the rail. His shirt was open, the breeze ruffling the fabric against his waist. In the waning of the day, the heat had become welcome, and he wasn't uncomfortable at all.

He looked at Kreeian, the candlelight at the table glistening on the sweep of her hair, the glow just catching the curve of one breast above her shirt. She turned her head to move a wisp of hair from where it had blown onto her face, and he watched her as she reached out, taking a sip of amber liquid from a clear container. Her eyes caught the light of the candle as she looked at him.

"See? It's so much cooler once the sun goes down. The oppressive heat of the day becomes the welcome warmth of the night." She stood, moving beside him, her elbows also on the rail, her face looking out over the water. "I do so love the river. It runs everywhere through the city."

"Will you tell me of it?" He turned to face the glassy expanse that stretched in front of him, dark in the night. His shoulder touched hers, and in the wind, his shirt billowed behind him, while the heat of the daytime left their skins shimmering. He glanced at her, shadowed against the reflections of the city lights on the surface of the river. The wind rifled her hair, pushing it from her face. He had found he enjoyed her sense of pleasure in just being near the water. He had never spent the day with someone like this, a woman who seemed to enjoy him as much as he enjoyed her. He would have listened just to watch her speak, no matter what topic she broached.

"The river comes directly from the mountains. It rains more there than even here. It's in one big torrent for a great, long distance, and then it reaches the plain. There, many fingers branch out, each deep and cold. On flood days, the shopkeepers all pack up their goods and move them to the upper floors. That's why all the ground floors are constructed of stone." She laughed, turning to glance at him as she made her next statement. "Most shopkeepers are glad the floods don't come every year. Me, I'm glad when they do. The waters rush through the city, and when all the rushing quiets down, everything is flooded for days. We use small gondolas to get around. Everyone has one." She reached to touch him on the arm. "Am I boring you, Rom'n?"

He laughed out loud at the absurdity of the question. "Never. Go on. I enjoy just listening to you."

He looked out over the river, not remembering such a day as this one. The heat had been incredible, but Kratt had been wise in his choice of clothes for him. The lightweight pants, the shirt that could be opened to the waist, and the footwear, just soles that strapped to his ankles. He had run and laughed with Kreeian, enjoying the open spaces, stopping to enjoy cool drinks. Then the darkness had become a welcome relief to the brilliance of the day. Now, light rain occasionally spattered the surroundings, and Kreeian assured him a torrent of showers would sweep the city before morning, leaving it pristine.

Looking down, he noticed a hand still resting on his arm. A ripple of sensation ran fingers down his spine, his knees suddenly unsure, the memories of long ago, the breathing in the smell of Ma'jene's hair suddenly strong. He closed his eyes, his senses raw with those remembered things, the joy vanishing from the day. He took a ragged breath and stepped away from the rail.

"Kreeian," he spoke quietly.

She was already telling her tale, though, moving ahead with her story. "After the waters are gone, the city is so beautiful. I hear other worlds have floods that leave behind a terrible mess, but our fast-running river follows a bed that's built of rock ledges, so the water comes to us pure and clean. The pureness of the water sweeps the tiredness of life from everything, and all is renewed and fresh."

He touched her shoulder, glad now for the darkness to shadow him. "Perhaps it's time to go. Will you show me the way back?"

"Are you sure? This is truly the best part of our day."

"Tomorrow, please." Damn you, Ma'jene, he silently cursed.

"I work until the afternoon. Can you come by the eatery then? I'll wait for you."

He felt crushed by Ma'jene's presence as Kreeian led him down dark paths, their voices now silent, the warmth and the damp smells of the plants lining the streets bringing back unwanted memories of long ago. The light rain had turned into a steady companion by then, darkening the footpaths and their shoulders, turning his mood even grayer. He thought he was over his years of longing. How quickly it had come back to him!

Damn you, Ma'jene, he railed again. And you, three hundred or more years dead!

ROM'N TOSSED his shirt aside. He stepped out to the balcony in the quiet evening air, the rain abated, and the street now clear. Store awnings and cobblestones shimmered under the misty glow of evenly spaced streetlamps. Clouds still covered the sky, and it smelled of yet more impending rain. He knew it would again be hot tomorrow, but in comparison, this was a time of coolness. He stood in the breeze, the lightweight fabric of his pants stroking his legs with its embrace, its energies taken from the gentle wind and wrapping him with motion.

He tried to remember the many cruelties he had seen Ma'jene inflict on him, and others, as well. He wanted to remember the hurt he had felt from her betrayal. All he could recall was his face in her hair and her touch on his skin as the clouds finally erupted, and rain lashed the street before him, this time in blinding curtains of moisture.

He remained on the balcony, his eyes moist at the loss, the cruelties forgotten, as that one night was real to him once again. With the emptiness of the city as his friend, the breeze as his caressing lover, and the street as his muse, finally, the sun brought him another day.

THE DOOR slammed open, breaking Rom'n's peace asunder. Laughing, Synrnn pushed Kratt through, ignoring his protests that they should have knocked first.

"Hey, you two." Rom'n lay uncovered on his bed, still in his pants from the night before, and he rolled to his back. "Kratt's right. Knock next time. Oh, I feel terrible."

"Are you sick?" Synrnn stepped over, touching his forehead. "A new world can sometimes do that to a man. We can call someone, a medic, perhaps."

"I don't think I slept at all last night." He sat up on the edge of the bed, leaning over with his hands at the back of his neck. "Oh, my head."

Kratt reached out to slap him on the bare skin of his back. "Well, if you're not sick," he grinned, "let's get you ready to go. We've got appointments to keep. Synrnn, flip the water on. Boy, a bath'll do you wonders." He grabbed Rom'n's arm, pulling him from the bed. "Synrnn, help me with the pants." He pulled one long cord, untying the waist strap of Rom'n's pants in a quick tug.

"I can do it." Rom'n pushed him away. "Show me the tub."

"Shippies have to be more like brothers and sisters, and I'd certainly have let my brother undress himself, if I'd ever had one." Synrnn glared at Kratt, aiming her comment his direction.

"Oh?" Rom'n yawned, calling from the next room as he removed his clothing. "Didn't you?"

"Have a brother? Don't know. I was brought up in a kibbutz on Lacy's Veil Prime. A couple of the boys looked kinda like me, but we weren't allowed to ask, and if we

140

stayed, we had to mate outside of our kibbutz. I didn't stay." Louder, she called through the door, "I'll tell you why Kratt's so hot to get you out today."

"Hm?" Rom'n's response faded away as he sank under the water filling the tub, only coming up when his breath was gone.

"Money house. Kratt's set one up to check on your funds. He's been itching at the belt to find out from the time he found out your pay account was still active."

"Funds? My MegaCorp pay?"

"Yeah," Kratt's voice filtered through, "I want to know just how rich you are."

"Or just how rich I'm not."

"Well, maybe," Kratt said, "but I'm counting otherwise."

Standing from the tub, Rom'n picked up a thick towel and rubbed his skin, wrapping it around his waist when he didn't see a disposal or recycle slot. Looking for clean clothes, he stepped back into the room.

"Here." Kratt handed him fresh pants as Synrnn shifted through the boxes from the day before. "That one," Kratt called out.

She reached for the box he'd indicated and unfolded the contents, handing it to Rom'n, revealing a shirt with brightly colored flowers and birds, the fabric so thin as to almost not be there at all.

"What will I need with me for the money house?" Then Rom'n paused, the absurdity of the question striking him. "Silly question. I have nothing, so I'll just take myself, I guess."

"Good idea," Kratt replied. He pushed Rom'n back to sit on the bed, placing lightweight footwear on his feet and tying the straps around his ankles. He cut his eyes to his face with a grin. "Gotta get out the door, son."

"Ha, Boss. Who'd ever think to see you dressing another man? Rom'n, can you tell he's anxious?" Synrnn leaned her shoulder on the doorframe, her arms and legs crossed as she laughed.

"He's so slow, woman. Can't get him to get a move on." Kratt yanked Rom'n to his feet, and with his hands on his shoulders, guided him to the door. "Got it all, son?"

Rom'n turned around, looking for a moment, before clapping Kratt on the shoulder and saying, "One more thing, Kratt." He walked into the room and paused as if in thought. Then he turned back around and laughed. "Just kidding!" and he dodged the flat of Kratt's hand as he ran through the doorway past him.

"OH, MY, SER." The man behind the desk looked at the information in front of him. He had searched the money house's archives and pulled up Rom'n's military account to find it was still active. "This is a very old account. You say you are this person?" The clerk look at Rom'n as if unsure whether to call him a liar or not. "You do have your DNA verification?"

"Um, I don't think so. What is that, and can I get it here?" He looked across the room at Kratt and Synrnn, who waved at him.

"I'm sorry, ser. You'll have to come back when you've taken care of that. There's nothing I can do to help you out until then." The clerk had a relieved expression on his face. "Next."

"Wait. Where do I get a DNA verification? You haven't told me exactly what you need."

The clerk looked at him, clearly annoyed that he hadn't already moved on. He raised one hand and pointed to the building's exit. "Down the street in a clinic. Please move along, now."

Rom'n stepped away. As another customer took his place, he walked back through the room until he reached his friends and protested to Kratt and Synrnn, "He wasn't very friendly. He just kept trying to shoo me out the door."

"Probably thought you were a kook, what with you claiming to be a four-hundred-year-old dead man. That's what I'd have thought, for sure." Synrnn grinned at the prospect.

"Well, we need to go down the street. He said I have to find a clinic. Something about a DNA verification. However, I have a better idea. It's well into the morning, and who knows how long that will take." Rom'n slipped his hands in his pockets, a bright smile playing on his face. "Midmeal first, anyone?"

Kratt playfully slammed a fist into Rom'n's shoulder, his other hand grabbing the younger man's neck. "Midmeal? No way, kiddo. To the clinic. Let's go."

Rom'n grinned, throwing an arm around Kratt's shoulder. "Yeah, Boss. I was just teasing, you know." He stepped into the bright sunshine, no ivy shading these heavily traveled streets, and slipped his goggles onto his face. "We'll let them scan me and see if I'm still who I think I am. Ho, ho! Maybe not!"

"Lead on," Synrnn called out. "Did that nasty man in there point you in any particular direction?"

"Just outside." Rom'n squinted and then lifted an arm, indicating a building just down the roadway. "There, I think, a medical facility." He led them to a storefront with a giant red cross painted on the building.

Stepping inside the door, they approached a man at a table. "Ser, can you do DNA verification here?"

"Absolutely. We have the latest databanks in our files. We can verify the identity of any living person in the forty-two occupied systems." The medic seemed especially pleased to spout his information.

Synrnn chided, "That goes for dead people, too?" She looked at Kratt and Rom'n with a smirk.

"Pardon, me?" The man looked at her as if she might be serious.

"Ignore her," Kratt interjected. "She's making a very poor attempt at a joke." He turned to frown at her. Looking back, he questioned, "You are a qualified medic, right? You can verify the ID for us?"

"A very good medic," the man responded with an air of assurance. Looking from person to person, he questioned, "Which one of you?"

"The pretty one." Synrnn laughed, stepping aside to look out the door. She squinted against the glare, her goggles hanging from her neck. With one hand, she pushed them up on her face.

"Ah, miss. You needn't step away. In fact, if you'll just come this way." The medic stepped over to take her arm.

Kratt grabbed the medic's other arm. He said conspiratorially, "She's tied on one too many. I want the boy over there done."

The medic smiled knowingly. "I see, ser. Young man?" Taking Rom'n's arm, he led him back to a cubicle, seating him on a stationary med table in the middle of the floor, the table raised to an upright seating position. "Wait right here. I'll be back in a moment."

"How long will this take?"

"Not long at all." The medic touched the side of the table, and it started to lower itself. "Be right back, ser."

After a few moments, he returned and asked him to remove his shirt. When Rom'n asked if he needed to take his pants and shorts off, too, the medic laughed. "Absolutely not. We're here to scan you, not inspect you. Now, please remove your shirt and lie face down on the table." When he saw he had complied, the medic squirted a cream down Rom'n's back and massaged it in with very strong circular motions. Then he attached a wired strip along his backbone, pressing it very tightly in place, and he plugged it into a socket in the table. "Ready for a little sting?"

"Sure," he said, jerking, the sting up and down his backbone happening as he was replying.

"I find it much easier that way, as it's unexpected. Sorry," said the medic, not sounding sorry at all. "Let me take that off." With a ripping sound, he yanked the strip from Rom'n's back.

"Ow! Now that hurt!" He pushed himself into a sitting position to glare at the medic.

"Again, I'm very sorry. The unexpected hurts less, so I find it best to let the little things come without warning." The medic unplugged the strip, dropping it in a cleaning tank.

"Any more things I shouldn't expect to hurt?" He frowned at the man. He reached his hand over his shoulder to rub the back of his neck.

"No. We're finished. You may put your clothing back on."

"Why'd that last one hurt so much?" He slipped his shirt on and started fastening it up.

"The wires. To do this procedure in a manner that will allow the response for DNA verification to be instantaneous, the DNA must be pulled directly from the spinal fluid. Once in place, it sent a series of very fine wires directly into your spinal cord. That last painful jerk was me pulling the wires out."

"With no pain blockers?" He took a deep breath. It still stung, and he grimaced as he tucked his shirt in.

"Oh, we certainly use pain blockers when requested. I offered that to your friend, but he said to get the results the quickest way possible. That was it. I'm sorry," he said with a smile. He led Rom'n back to the front room of the clinic and touched his arm lightly to get his attention as he spoke. "I certainly hope you come again if you can ever use our services."

Rom'n walked up to Kratt. "Do you know the pain you just put me through? Fastest way possible. That hurt!"

He waved a hand at him along with a *tsk, tsk*. "Pain is for a moment. Credits are forever. How long until we know, medic?"

"One moment, ser. Usually results come back immediately." He paused, then turned with an apologetic look on his face. "There seems to be no result."

A voice just outside the clinic door called out a suggestion a second time. "Try dead people."

The medic looked at the two men in front of him. "Do you . . . want me . . . to do that? It will be an extra charge, as I must access a pay-for-information database."

"Yeah," said Kratt, looking off out the door.

"Do you have a specific time frame, ser? If I narrow the parameters, it will reduce the cost."

"Try about three hundred seventy standards ago."

"Oh, my, ser. The DNA records were not comprehensive that long ago. I may find a match, and I may not."

"Can you narrow the search more?"

"To a particular planet or system?" The medic looked unsure just what Kratt meant.

"Military."

Relief spread across the medic's face. "If our patient's a military man, there'll be no trouble pulling up an ID."

Rom'n leaned in to the medic, "That was our first order of business when I joined the military academy, getting a DNA scan. Didn't hurt like this one, though." He turned to Kratt. "Is my back bleeding onto my shirt?"

The medic interrupted, "Oh, ser. The scans never bleed. The wires that are injected into the backbone are microscopic."

Rom'n snorted. "They didn't feel microscopic when you yanked them out," glaring at Kratt, "without pain blockers."

The medic smiled, repeating, "I am so very sorry, ser. I only do that by special request." He glanced over at Kratt, who just grinned.

The medic looked at his machine, and an incredulous look came over his face. "Ah, here. No, this can't be correct. Why, you would be nearly four hundred years old. This is for a Rom'n Rezalton from the MegaCorp cruiser, hm, let me see." He looked up. "I don't see a name for the cruiser. It just says starstrike class battleship."

"It never was named officially. It was highly classified. Not even MegaCorp knew they had built it. We called it DeathMaker. However, that was never official." Rom'n felt more comfortable sharing information about his past than he had before, now that his identity was finally confirmed.

"But ser, you can't be . . ." The medic flicked through the display as if he might find that his results were in error after all.

Kratt interrupted, "Ever heard of cryo pods?"

"Of course. They've been in use for centuries. However, who would choose to stay in one that long? To do so would surely be unsurvivable. Cryo pods are used primarily for long-distance travel or transporting emergency medical cases."

Kratt grabbed one of Rom'n's shoulders with one hand. Leaning in to the medic for emphasis, he patted Rom'n's chest, saying, "Look and weep. Three hundred seventy years and a few odd cycles. That's exactly how long this man was in his little egg." He grinned.

Synrnn's voice bled in from the street, her goggle-covered face peering around the corner of the doorway. "Barely alive, though, when we pulled him out."

"This is our miracle boy." Kratt glanced back at the door, and then to Rom'n, who was grinning broadly at the exchange between the two.

The medic's eyes grew large as he put his facts together. "MegaCorp, you. Son, you've got a payout coming. There's a whopper waiting on you. I heard of this happening once before, years ago."

"Oh?" He looked at Kratt, surprised.

"Go on," Kratt instructed, leaning in toward the medic.

"My great-gran did a medscan on an ex-military officer. She was MegaCorp, too, although over in a neighboring system. She was old, even then. She raked in so many credits her six-times great-grans are surely still living high today."

Kratt yelled, "Hear that, Synrnn?"

"Got it, Boss! Happy, now?"

Kratt wrapped his arm around Rom'n's neck, his hand still on his chest. "Let's go open you an account, my boy. Let's see if they have enough credits." He laughed like he was drunk as he hugged Rom'n's neck on his way down the street.

Synrnn stepped inside just as the medic started out from behind the counter. "I'll take that." She pulled the DNA verification from the man's hand. "This is for you," and she placed a wad of credits in the man's hand, following Kratt and his golden boy back to the money house, yelling down the street, "Kratt, I hope you enjoy giving that clerk a for-what-it's-worth of our time."

She grinned. It was clear from the look on her face that she would enjoy it, too.

SYNRNN LAY BACK on the bed, laughter at the memory of the clerk in the money house keeping her in stitches. "Boss, you were so right. I'm so glad I went with the two of you today." She rolled onto her stomach. "The look on that clerk's face was priceless. All those credits going into one account. You'll never best that, Boss, not even if we both live longer than our friend, here." Rolling back over, her laughter exhausted, she let her breathing slow. After a moment, she glanced at Rom'n sitting next to her. "Of all the people alive today, you deserve this. I'm glad for you." She placed her hand on his shoulder, holding it for a moment, and finally letting her fingers brush his arm to fall onto the bed.

"You know I'll share with you and Kratt, Synrnn." He held up his credit crystal, offering it to her.

"You've paid dearly for those credits." She pulled herself up on her elbows. "Don't be so quick to give them away."

"I'll never be able to spend all this. Never. Not if I bought a dozen ships like Kratt's. I'm happy with you guys. The credits mean nothing."

Next to Synrnn, Kratt grinned, his new ship already his, only to have his face crash at Synrnn's reply.

"Just keep it. Rainy day funds." She paused, looking intently at the innocently generous man standing before her. She knew what would happen if he were not stopped.

"Never give it away, Rom'n. Never. You start that, and you'll have hangers on you'll never get rid of." She looked hard at Kratt. "Isn't that right, Boss? You do agree, don't you?"

He jerked his eyebrows up and let them slide back down as he chewed his lips. Finally, at a stern look from her, he grumbled, "She's right. I might be one of 'em, too, one of the hangers on. Keep the credits."

"Here," Rom'n smiled, handing the crystal toward Kratt in spite of Synrnn's exhortations. "This isn't all of it, but it's enough you'll never run out."

She jumped up, grabbing the credit crystal. "Let's put this away. I like who and what we are, and I don't want to lose that. This can be an emergency fund, how about that? Boss?"

With all three of them in agreement, that's what it became.

ROM'N WALKED up to the eatery door, removing his goggles against the dimness of the interior. As his eyes adjusted, he looked for Kreeian. Stepping to the door she had disappeared through the night before, he called out, an elderly man in a white smock arriving at his call.

"May I help you?" Then, as he looked up, the man squinted at the pale stranger facing him. "Ah, you must be Rom'n. Kreeian said you might be coming in. She was very afraid you were disappointed in her and wouldn't show today. She went early. Very sad. You must go to her. She needs a good boy. She needs to be reassured. Here." He wrote something on a piece of paper and placed it in

Rom'n's hand. "She's here. Go. I must return to my work. The midday is soon to be upon us."

With that, the old man turned and made his way into the back of the eatery, leaving Rom'n to find his way on his own.

ROM'N KNOCKED the old-fashioned way. He balled his hand into a fist and rapped on the door three times. He waited a few moments, and when there was no answer, he stepped back to see that the house number matched what the man had given him. As he raised his hand to rap again, the door opened the barest crack. The depths were dark against the brightness of the day outside.

"Kreeian?"

"Yes?" The door remained where it was, only slightly ajar.

"It's Rom'n." He heard snuffles. "I'm sorry about last night at the waterfront. Today at the eatery, I was told I would find you here." He watched her open the door until he could just see her reddened eyes, and he stepped forward. He liked this girl, and he was no dunce. She was pulling away from him, curse his sudden memories of Ma'jene. This had to be worked out, and now.

The creaking of an ancient transport arriving on the street intruded on the moment. A horn blew, making him jump.

"Kreeian," he started again, "I'm really sorry for last night—"

"Rom'n!" Kratt's familiar voice yelled at him. "Pay attention." The transport's horn made a second loud blaring sound. "Rom'n!"

He turned to see what was so very important. "I'm busy here, Kratt." He nodded at the open door. "Can I have a moment?"

"No, you cannot. Get in the transport. The river! It's moving. The rains have come to the mountains." Kratt was out of the vehicle, moving at a run up the walk.

Turning to look at the girl facing him in the doorway, he cleared his throat. "Kreeian, I'm sorry. I'll send him away."

"Your friend is correct." She smiled tentatively at him. "It's time. Each year. My telling of it from last night? You do recall it, I hope."

"Bozo!" Another voice, Synrnn's, also from the transport. "Boss, get them out here. We want to see the falls. Hurry!"

"Go," Kreeian motioned, turning to push the door closed. "Your people need you. The river won't wait."

Rom'n turned to glare at his friend. "Kratt, this is very bad timing. Can't you see that?"

Bursting into laughter and reaching around him to push the door open, Kratt returned, "It's perfect timing. Come, Kreeian. Your uncle said you were to see the falls with us. He told us how you love the river, especially when it floods. The shopkeepers near the river in town are already clearing the lower floors. Carry her if you have to, boy. Let's go!" He motioned toward the transport with a jerk of his head.

"My uncle told you this?" A sound of hope found its way into her words.

153

Relieved at her brightening disposition, Rom'n gave Kratt a look of *dare me*. With a laugh, he stepped to Kreeian, slipped his arms under her back and legs, and carried her down the walk.

"Close the door," he called over his shoulder. With Kreeian laughing, he twirled her around, the moment turning the day into a renewed connection with the pleasure of each other's company.

"Take the back of the transport," Synrnn called from the driver's seat, the old vehicle containing room for four.

Climbing over the sides, only a canvas cloth covering the top for shade, Kratt turned to Kreeian. "You're our guide, young lady. Point the way. Wake me when we get there," and he twisted to the front, slouching down in his seat, as he snugged his headgear over his face, his duty for the moment done.

Rom'n laughed at the look Synrnn gave him, and he reached forward and thumped the brim of Kratt's headwear, the man underneath snorting as he did so.

Kreeian laughed at the antics, quite obviously pleased to become a part of this group of friends.

THE AIR WHIPPED briskly past Rom'n's face, his goggles pushed to the top of his head. The sun's glare was broken by the covering of plants over the roadway.

"Rom'n." Kreeian looked at him as she sat under his arm, the ever-present goggles stowed in a rack at her side. "I'm so excited to get to see the falls today. This is a rare event to be able to actually view the water as it breaks over the lip of the basin. The sudden warnings are normally used to give time to prepare the city. It's seldom we can escape just to view the falls. You'll love the excitement of seeing how impressive they are."

He ran his fingertips along the skin on her arm. Forgotten was the flash of intensity from last night's long-ago memories. Now was just Kreeian. Now was the heat of the day and his friends on a grand adventure. He looked around, the world so green and lush. To live here, and to love someone who loved him back. He looked at the picture of perfection in his arms, her beauty wrenching longings from his heart. This could be his world. Kratt had told him so. He could grow to love all this. So different. So vibrant. So intense. He looked to the passing scenery and smiled.

"I already love it," he replied.

"THIS IS GREAT," Kratt yelled with enthusiasm. He stared out at the water, the tumbling and the roiling maelstrom damming up in the basin. The slender channel that normally contained the rushing flow of water was full to overflowing. He turned, his excitement all over him. "I look forward to this each time I visit this world. My timing isn't always so good, though." He looked around. "Where are those two kids, Synrnn?"

"Jealous?" She laughed, knowing him all too well.

"Just keeping track." He looked back to the water. "I don't want them to miss the start of the water breaking over the rim."

"And if they do?" She glanced around at the scattered groups of people gathering to witness the event. "Do you think they'll feel their time together was worth the trade?" She paused. "I suspect from their point of view, the trade would be a very good one."

"Yeah." He took a deep breath. Then he grinned. "But I want them to see this." He looked at her. "I'm headed to round them up."

"ROM'N, YOU KNOW the water'll be up to here before it tumbles over the final height of rocks. We really should go higher." Kreeian stepped around a dry stone. The turbulence of the incoming floodwaters whipped the surface, already wetting her feet.

He took her hand to steady her. "This is better than up there." He found a seat on a tall stone, with Kreeian just below, and he nodded at Kratt and Synrnn much higher up. "They're watching us all the time, hoping we'll decide we're right for each other. They're my best friends, you know."

"You think I couldn't tell?" A fist of water slapped against her leg, and she let out a small cry of dismay, the sound quickly turning into a laugh of pleasure. "It's cold! I forget how much until the floods come again. We really must move higher, even still."

She clambered to her feet, and Rom'n watched her, her arms reaching out to touch the stones, a reaffirmed balance taken from their sturdiness. He joined her as she began to climb upward.

"The air is so cool here. Even the brightness of the sun is less. This place seems like a welcome relief from the city's heat. People must come here often just for the cooling."

She laughed. "It's only like this just before the rains flood the river. Other times, the dampness makes it a muggy nightmare. Will you leave with them?" She stopped and looked at him.

"I don't know." The shift in the conversation was abrupt. Unprepared, he looked down, the water swirling at the bottom of his stone. Then, in a burst, he turned to her, talking rapidly. "We're here for several of your weeks, you know. Kratt's waiting for a job. It's expected, and he's just biding his time." He paused, and then went on at a slower pace. "I know I have to decide what to do. However, I've never lived on a world before. At least not since I was thirteen."

"Thirteen? You've couldn't have been with Kratt on his ship that long. He's not an old man, yet. Not that old, anyway." She laughed, reaching out to place a hand on Rom'n's shoulder as she stepped over a rising whirlpool.

"No, I went to the academy. My first berth was on a military training ship, and I've only spent a few days downside in all the time since."

"Downside? Oh, you must mean on a planet. Which world? I don't recall any with training academies flitting from sun to sun, teaching their children to be big bad galactic soldiers." She giggled.

"What do you mean, which world?" Smiling, he took her hand, and together, the two of them stepped back from the continually rising vortex at their feet.

"You know, what world's military arm?"

"Oh," he laughed. "No world at all." He pulled her to

157

the highest rocks overlooking the submerging basin. The water already roiled wildly just below them. "MegaCorp. I was with their military arm. My brother was with them in the military, and I worshipped him. When the chance came, I went in, too."

"Silly! That's too much, you making that up! MegaCorp doesn't have a military. They just sell stuff. I see how it is to be now, a time of teasing and pranks." She bounced away from him, stopping after a moment and looking back with a smile.

He smirked at her, raising his eyebrows. "Lady," he started in mock earnestness, "I was there. You dare to question my integrity?"

"No, it's just too silly to be true."

He laughed, suddenly understanding. "At least I know why you're confused." He hesitated, putting an answer together, an answer he wasn't sure she'd want to hear. "They used to."

"What? MegaCorp?"

"Yeah. Years ago. I was there."

"How long ago? I don't remember that, ever."

He paused, then shared, "It was a very long time ago. I'm unsure how to tell you, to make you believe my story's true. You might not like it when you hear it. I'm a very old man."

She laughed at that. "Come on. Just tell me."

"Do you know what a cryo pod is?"

"Sure. New colonists come in them."

"Well, I was in one, once." He turned, looking at Kratt and Synrnn. He returned a wave at seeing their hands in the air. "They rescued me. I was almost dead."

"How long?" She pulled herself up beside him. "How long were you in there?"

"A long time." He pulled at his face, stretching the skin tight around his eyes. "How many standard years do you see here?"

"That's funny. Twenty-five? Thirty? Less, I think, although older than twenty, I can be sure." She touched his temples, running her hand over his flesh, the skin smooth under her fingers. "Not old. You're not old at all."

"Not really, but I am, too." He put his hands in his pockets. "I went to the clinic today. They gave me a certificate of verification. Did you know MegaCorp military pay never stops accumulating, not until DNA evidence proves someone's dead?"

"You're certainly not dead."

"That's what I mean. That's why they paid."

"You?" Sudden dawning came over her face. "The eatery. This morning. Some people were in a discussion. They were talking about this, the funds that were paid. It was so much!" She looked at him with her eyes wide. "You're him, the person they were speaking of." Laughing, disbelief coloring her words, she continued, "You really lived back then." She turned away, her hands nervously massaging the fabric of her clothing. "Your name, so old-fashioned. I should have realized." After a few moments, she looked at him. "I didn't think . . . don't know what to think about this."

"My ship was destroyed. All my friends died back then. Not many people escaped."

159

"All those years ago. At least you're still alive."

"Hey!" They heard Kratt's voice yelling. "It's starting. Quit staring at each other!"

Ignoring him, Rom'n slipped his arm around Kreeian's waist, her touch stirring a feeling of longing in him. He whispered to her, "I'm glad I am, so I can be here with you."

She rested her head against him as she whispered, "Let's join the others and watch the falls. I haven't seen this in years."

He brushed the hair from her face to see tears rolling down her cheeks. "Those are tears of happiness, I hope."

She just smiled at his remark, unwilling to share the real reason for her emotions. Satisfied, he turned his eyes back to the water's display in front of them.

They watched as the billowing turmoil roiled to the lip of the basin, churning in its fight to escape. Then, in a flash, it flew into space, dropping the great distance to the base of the falls, spray flinging out, covering those who had gathered to watch. The sound crashed against the on-lookers' ears. Jumping into the air, the mist flung a great rainbow across the sky.

"I had no idea, Kreeian. I'm glad I didn't miss this. It's beautiful."

"Wait until you see the city after the floods spread across everything. It's like a fairy tale. You can stand in a gondola, look down, and there's the bottom, as clear as a bell. You'll be able to see where we sat to have our late supper last night. It'll be beautiful."

"First back to the transport gets to drive," tore by them

as they turned to see Kratt and Synrnn running past. "We want to see the water enter the city. We have to move like the wind."

Tumbling into the transport, Synrnn flying down the roadway before seats could even be attained, Kreeian laughingly fell into Rom'n's arms. Helping her to sit, his hand got caught in her hair. Instead of pulling it out, he ran his fingers through it, letting it brush against his skin; and he brought it to his face, holding it against his cheek, drawing in the breath of it.

"Gods, Kreeian. Only my second day here, and I'm getting attached to this place and you. Are you for real?"

With an intruding cry of triumph, they were forced apart as Kratt jumped from the front seat, landing between them.

"Kratt," Rom'n cried, pushing away his friend's arm. "What's this about?"

"Look at you two." He laughed, grabbing the faces on either side of him, one in each hand. "What do they say? Love is in the air?" He leaned forward to Synrnn. "Was I right? Synrnn, did I tell you? Barely more than one full day. One full day, Synrnn. Our boy, the one we raised from an egg, or from that pod he popped out of like it was an egg, well, our boy has a girl! Who-at!" He reached to grab the front seat and leaped to fling himself back that direction. "Synrnn, I'm so proud of him." He turned to look at Rom'n and beamed. Reaching to pat Kreeian on the knee, he winked. "He's a good one, girl. You can't do better."

"Hold on, guys," yelled Synrnn, as the transport took a

161

corner too fast, the dust flying. "We'll get there in time, if I have anything to do with it, even if a few of us get left along the side of the road." She turned to Kratt and laughed as she wrestled the transport too quickly down the roadway. "How can I top that, Boss? Some fancy driving, huh?" She twisted her head to glance at the back seat. "Kids, you doing okay?"

Rom'n turned to the beautiful girl next to him. "See why I enjoy them so much?" He laughed. "Live with these guys awhile, and no one could ever be the same."

As Synrnn slowed the transport for an upcoming turn-off, Kreeian grabbed the back of Synrnn's seat, pointing. "There! The second road. Turn left there."

"Left? We came in at the road we're passing now, the first one."

"With the river, it'll all be underwater soon. The road will be blocked off. Left will take us just to the edge of the high city, and we'll be able to see it all. Hurry. I do so want to see the water roll in. It's so grand to see the surface roiling and churning!" She turned to Rom'n. "I'm so glad you're here to see this."

"Here, Kreeian? Do I turn again?" The dust from her previous turn still hovering in the air behind them, Synrnn yelled to the back seat. A possible vantage point seemed to be just ahead. "The road, Kreeian. Pay attention!"

"Yes! This is it. Pull up and stop."

The three passengers jumped from the transport even as the vehicle slid to a halt. Rom'n stumbled as he tried to plant his feet, then he clambered up, laughing, and he threw his arm around Kreeian's waist.

162

"This is our best vantage spot, Kreeian?"

"Yes! Right by the steps where they drop to the low city. The water'll come right up to them. In a day or two we'll be able to walk down to the edge and see the steps going on down to the bottom."

"Kreeian—" Kratt leaned out, searching the paved walks and meandering paths bordering the shops fronting on the river. "Where is it? I see nothing. Are you sure it will come through here?"

"Wait. Just wait. Hear it? Hush. Quiet, all." She held up her hands for silence. "There, the rumble in the distance."

Rom'n leaned his head against hers, tightening his arm around her waist. As the water tore through the city below, the noise overtook the waiting group of four, the city below echoing with the onslaught.

"The air," Synrnn cried. "The heat's gone."

"Yes! The coolness of the mountain waters gives us a welcome break. I told Rom'n how much I love this time. For days, the city will be at its most beautiful. You couldn't have come to visit at a better time." Kreeian clapped her hands in exultation. "Wait here for a bit. When the sun sets over the city, you'll see the brilliance of a thousand stars on the churning waters."

She leaned against Rom'n, his arm her guardrail, his closeness her comfort. Gone was the sudden end to the previous evening. Even the tears of that morning were now only a forgotten crease in the unfolding fabric of the day.

"TELL ME, Kreeian." Kratt leaned over the table, his elbows supporting his arms comfortably on the smooth surface. "What do you know of this person the medic told of today?"

"Medic?" She looked at the three faces at the table with her.

"Ah, so." He slapped Rom'n on the back of his shoulder with one hand. "This indolent son of ours didn't tell you the whole story."

"Hey," Rom'n returned. "If you'd give us a hand's count of breaths together, we might be able to share a thought or two."

Synrnn laughed and began the tale. "There's a medic just down from a money house we visited. He said something about a relative doing a DNA scan on someone a number of standards ago. I didn't catch everything, having been banished to the street outside, but I gather it was generations in the past." She looked at the two men for confirmation.

"She was not banished." Rom'n laughed. "I'm hoping to track what might have happened to some of my shipmates who were able to escape with me."

"Escape? I do remember your ship being destroyed. However, other than that, I'm lost."

"Blazing suns, Kreeian. I'm so engrossed in this, I keep forgetting others don't know. I was on a battleship that was attacked while on the other side of the galactic arm. The attack was sudden and decimating." He sat back in his chair. "I only escaped due to the uninvited help of a friend."

"Uninvited? You didn't wish to escape?"

"He pushed me into an escape pod that I was attempting to convince him to use." He shook his head and smiled. "Redzik. He was a good guy. The best. Anyway, I tracked the pods that managed to escape, but only a few came this direction."

"None of them would have reached so close to here, would they? They'd have been rescued far closer to where your ship was destroyed, wouldn't they?"

"Very good, girl," Kratt pointed out. "However, these pods employed a rudimentary tracking and guidance system. They used a form of solar magnetic acceleration and braking that kicked in when they came within the vicinity of a solar body."

Rom'n interjected, "My pod just never intercepted any. Eventually, the internal braking automatically slowed it from what we think was about an initial twenty gees of acceleration to a much slower velocity. I suspect the other pods could have covered twice the distance in half the time. However, if my pod hadn't slowed itself, Kratt's ship would have never been able to intercept and retrieve me, so I guess I should be grateful."

Kreeian thought for a moment. "I do know the medic you speak of, and his family has been in this group of star systems for several generations. I can try to find out something for you. What should I ask about?"

"Rom'n's military organization was MegaCorp, and he was assigned to a starstrike class battle cruiser. The person the medic mentioned was a very old woman several generations back. She apparently received an enormous payout.

The medic didn't say who the payout was from, but he mentioned MegaCorp, so it makes sense to me it was from them." Kratt paused at Synrnn's snicker.

"Enormous is certainly relative in this case, huh, Boss?" She twirled her coaster beneath her finger. "After all, a potato chip is enormous to an ant."

"And a tree is huge to a termite."

Rom'n got in on the wordplay. "A city is big to a group having supper."

Synrnn laughed. "A solar system is big to a moon."

"How about this one?" Kratt hit the table. "A battle cruiser is big to a two-man." He turned to Kreeian. "Your turn, pretty lady. Give us an analogy to follow our pattern."

"Well, I've never been offworld. I don't even recognize some of the terms you've used."

"That's okay," Synrnn encouraged. "Do something you know."

"Go ahead." Rom'n smiled.

"I think love is big to a lonely heart."

Kratt stood and twirled around, his hand on his forehead. "Who-at, boy and girls. We've got a thinker here." He leaned in to give Kreeian a hug. "You topped us all, little miss. You are a gem, that's for sure." He reached to Rom'n, tapping his hand. "I still say she's a keeper."

"Kratt," and he grinned back at him, "that shows you know a thing or two, yourself."

A REPEATED TAPPING, as of a pecking bird, broke the morning. Rom'n stretched, unwilling to wake. The noise

166

came again, refusing to let him sleep. It took a moment for him to decide it wasn't birds as he had first thought, but the door, instead.

"Yes?"

"Rom'n?"

He called, "Come on in; it's not locked," as his head once again found the pillow's softness. He heard the door click as it opened and closed.

"You just let anyone in?" Kreeian stood just inside the door, and she crossed her arms and smiled.

"Sorry," he apologized, his face warming, as he sat up and ran his hand through his tousled hair. "I didn't think. I assumed it was Synrnn or Kratt." Pushing the covers aside, he kept a large section of fabric wrapped around the revealing sleeping attire Kratt had provided as he slipped sheepishly into the adjoining space. He self-consciously pulled a fresh pair of pants from an open box along the way.

"Obviously," and she laughed out loud. "I seem to get to know you better every single day."

"Yeah," he called out. "Not intentionally, this time." He poked his head through the doorway. "Not working today?"

"You asked about that medic and the woman from off-system. I brought the news."

He reappeared, more presentably clothed, although without a shirt. "Let's step onto the balcony."

"Nice," she remarked as she moved outside. She reached to run a finger along the greenery shading the waiting chairs. "It's still so cool here, even though the sun has already grown bright. I think that except for the area by the river, it will be very hot."

"Sit, if you wish. I have some drinks in a cooling box in the room. Let me get you one."

As she dropped onto a low stool, the sounds of a drinking container being opened filtered through the door. Rom'n emerged, the pale coloring of his bare torso crisp against the dappled sun of the balcony. He placed two containers on a low table, and he pointed. "All this will be filled with foot traffic later today. Not even the heat is a deterrent to the people of your world."

"We get used to it. If you should choose to stay, so will you. Rom'n, I've never lived elsewhere, but I know Snowbush is a good world. The river, the sun, the warm nights . . ." She smiled hopefully.

He ran his hands over his shoulders, his thumbs absently tracing his collarbone as he watched the street. "It seems so. However, I need to know about this other, this thing with my old ship. The pleasantness of this world isn't enough just yet. My past isn't three hundred or four hundred years ago to me."

She looked at him, not yet understanding. "Three or four hundred years? You mean your time on the ship with Kratt and Synrnn? That's been only a few years, surely."

"More than that. My life on the military ship. I lived that time nearly four hundred years ago. I also lived that time less than three of my shipboard sevendays ago, three of your weeks past. Things I knew as cutting edge innovations are now antiquated curiosities. My world isn't dead, not in my mind. To turn loose of it so quickly is to lose myself. I cannot lose myself."

"Does that leave me anywhere?"

"In just a few days, you've already grown a place in my heart. You are with me, and I think of you when I'm not with you. My past is also with me." He continued to look out over the street.

"I'm trying to understand how you must feel. This sounds very hard for you."

"You must realize that my friend, Redzik, died less than three of the time periods you call weeks ago. Less than three of your weeks, Kreeian. He died saving me. I fell in that pod, and I could see his face watching me. I could see his lips form his final words." Tears had started to build in his eyes. "I can *still* see it."

She stood to place her hand on his arm. "May I ask what they were? You don't have to tell me if you don't want."

He looked to her. "My friend. That's what he said to me. I had just told him he was the best friend I could ever have, and he saved me, calling me his friend. How could he do that?" He looked away.

"I didn't know. Really, Rom'n. It's so hard to imagine something so long ago still being fresh in your memory, but I can see that it is."

"I have to find out. I know he died hundreds of years ago to everyone else. He was alive to me just the other day." He paused, his eyes following the welcome distraction of events starting up past the edges of the balcony. "Redzik couldn't escape."

She put her other hand on his. "You didn't cause his

death."

"I need to find closure. I need to know the end for those that did manage to get away in one of the pods." He stepped to the edge of the balcony, pulling his hand away from hers and wrapping both his tightly around the metal railing, his head and shoulders shadowed still, the bright skin of his chest and stomach catching the sun, his clothing gently shifting in the breeze. He turned, crossing his arms and leaning back against the railing. "This is beautiful." He motioned to the outside world with one arm. "Everything out there that I've seen is more beautiful than any world has any right to be. You," and he leaned towards her, "are the most beautiful of all." He reached one hand and picked up a lock of her hair. "Your smell has already mesmerized me. Just to smell your hair, Kreeian, is a joy to me."

"But, Rom'n. There is a but, right?" Tears brimmed in her eyes.

He touched her arm, the skin soft and browned with the sun of her world. "Maybe in three of your weeks, Kreeian, perhaps I'll know what I'm to do. I won't hurt you. I wouldn't hurt you. You are already precious to me. To stay? I can't make such a decision just yet. There are too many loose ends in my world. Can you give me that? Can you give me three of your weeks?" He wrapped both her slender, browned hands in his strong, pale ones, pausing to look in her eyes. One tear broke free to run down her face. "Three weeks?"

She tore her hands free, throwing her arms around his neck, her embrace tight. As she hugged him, his emotions were caught off guard, his memories of a lost brother, a friend gone, a lifetime of anguish pouring through him. He burst into wracking sobs, that unexpected set of memories, older than even his MegaCorp days, unexpectedly flooding his awareness. In those days, he had been far too young to understand how to grieve and let go.

Jo'n, his thoughts reached out, as sobs wracked his body. I still miss you, brother.

It wasn't Jo'n he held, though, and after a time, his memories of a long-lost brother were pushed aside. Others of a girl he'd come to know, one filled with kindness and compassion, flooded his awareness. She wasn't lost to him, either. She was right there in his arms, and her touch was something he needed as well.

ROM'N STOOD on the steps reaching into the low city. With his hand in Kreeian's, he led her down to the edge of the water. They stood, the clearness of the liquid like molten glass over the buried steps below. She laced her fingers through his, standing and enjoying the coolness at the water's edge.

"The water's surface, it's become so smooth. How long will it last?"

"The stillness? Until the waters go down." She slipped one foot from her shoe, reaching out to disturb the water with a bare toe.

"The water itself? How long will it cover the lower city?" He moved back up a step, the water splashing onto the ledge from a distant gondola visible down the street's narrow vista.

"Sometimes a week or more depending on how dry it's been. On very dry years, only a few days. Once, when I was small, we had multiple rains in the mountains." She laughed. "That year we used the gondolas for the entire season. Not everyone was as pleased as I was." She turned away from the water's edge, the remains of her laugh hovering on her face.

"Kreeian, tell me more of the woman, the one on the distant world the medic mentioned." He touched her arm. "I have to know about this. I cannot be me without learning how to let go of my past."

"I understand, or at least I'll try to."

He turned at the top of the steps, the leafy ways inviting, and the goggles not needed in this part of the city. As they came to a bench, he slipped his from his face. "Sit with me?"

Kreeian smiled, her goggles already hanging around her neck. "Is this your cue to hear about the medic's story?"

He laughed at her remark. "Please. If you will." He sat, his arm resting on the back of the bench, one hand tracing the contours of her shoulder as she began.

"He says it was a very long time ago, just a story told to him by his great-grandfather when he was at the end of his life. The old man no longer practiced meds, and was so ancient he would sit in a chair in front of the window all day. He called him by the name Great-Gran.

"Great-Gran was an early medic when this series of systems was just getting established. Colonists were scarce, and medics were even scarcer. The medic's great-

172

grandfather only came this direction because our world subsidized his education with the promise of free travel and housing. In his contract, provisions were in place requiring him to travel to nearby systems when the need arose."

"I'd think each system would need its own medic." Rom'n chuckled. "It would certainly be cheaper than paying for the travel of one medic to many worlds."

"I only know how it was done. When the medic's great-grandfather first came to these worlds, he was very young. He had only been here a few years when he got his first offworld call. He wasn't happy about it. He was newly bonded, and his woman was expecting within the year. However, the patient couldn't travel to him, and apparently it was a very important patient, one that people in power were willing to pull very long strings to help. So they threatened to revoke his contract, and he went.

"His great-grandfather never told him the name of the system, or so the medic told me. Only that it was not far enough away to need the use of slow-sleep bunks. The medic remembers that, because as a boy, he was fascinated with the idea of slow-sleep and cryo pods, and he was very disappointed his great-grandfather hadn't used them."

Rom'n interrupted, "Did the medic ever try to find out which system it was?"

"I did ask him that, and he reminded me this was just a bedtime story told by a very old man to a little boy. As a boy, it seemed no more than pretend. Only as he got older and started into the med field did the medic learn that there might have been something to it.

"Anyway, the great-grandfather got to this world and was taken far into the outback. This planet was so rough and haphazardly colonized, it didn't have a central communications system. He said he was very unhappy he had to travel all that terrain just to find out anything about the case.

"When he got there, he found a very old woman, so old she could barely sit and certainly couldn't stand. Apparently, she'd been badly injured when she was much younger. He thinks it might have been in a military conflict. Her face was disfigured, and one of her legs was crippled.

"He treated her for a kidney disease, or perhaps it could have been her liver. The medic was just a boy, remember, and the fact was not one he particularly paid attention to. Whichever it was, she knew her organs were failing and didn't want him there; but her granddaughter was determined, calling the very highest powers to get her grandmother the help the grandmother wouldn't ask for. The granddaughter must have been very beautiful, the medic imagines, with long dark hair and beautiful eyes. He remembers this from how his great-grandfather got tears in his eyes every time he described her, as he told the part of the story where he had to break the news that he couldn't help her grandmother.

"The medic told me his great-grandfather would always tell how one very unusual request was made of him on that trip. He was to make a DNA verification scan of the old woman. No one would tell him when he asked why, and he had no access to databanks to run the verification. All he could do was gather the DNA. He simply sent it back to Earth in care of MegaCorp. It wasn't until years later that the medic's great-grandfather heard stories about the old woman getting a huge sum of funds from the corporation. By the time the great-grandfather heard of it, of course, the old woman was dead, the credits only having come to her just before the end of her life."

"How exciting! That could have been one of the people from my ship." Rom'n vibrated with anticipation. "He never got a name or anything?"

"No. The great-grandfather just knew someone pulled many strings to get him to jump through very elaborate hoops. The old woman and her granddaughter didn't seem to have any credits, so the connections to high places must have been either political or military, the medic figures."

"Can we walk now, Kreeian? I need to think. This story of this woman." He helped her to her feet. "It doesn't really give me much to go on. The time frame could be a hundred-fifty to two-hundred-fifty years or more ago. Life spans are so varied on different worlds with medical care and cryo pod immersion, and then there's travel via slow-sleep bunks. Who knows how many standard years each of these people lived? How would someone even research that out?" He looked up at the trees and laughed, frustration bleeding in his action. "Hey, glass, I'd like you to find me some woman treated by some medic who never even knew her name. Oh, yeah, glass, she lived on some world in some system within a distance to this one that doesn't require slow-sleep during travel. And, glass, two other things. She had a beautiful granddaughter, and the old woman may have died of kidney failure. Glass, did I mention she may have gotten some credits from the largest commercial enterprise in the galaxy?"

"If this is so hard, why chase it? Let it go, and make a new life."

"I need to let this news settle in. It's part of me. For now, let's enjoy our time together. Who knows what the next couple of weeks will hold? Who'd have known a few of those weeks ago that I'd be living nearly four hundred years in the future? You say your family has one of those gondolas?"

She brightened at the thought. "Yes. In the city boat-house."

"How about you and me? I saw one out earlier. Surely we can go out safely."

"I would like that. Come with me, and I'll ask my uncle. I'm sure he'll say yes."

KREEIAN LAUGHED as she pulled the old gondola from the city boathouse. The back was much like a shed with doors, and the front was low and sleek. It was exactly as she remembered it from all the years of her youth, ones filled with hot, lazy days, and the shops all moved to the upper floors, with purchases wrapped in special water-proof wrappings just in case a careless shopper overturned an overloaded gondola.

"For this I can forgive you needing to remind me you may love me and leave me." She ran back inside to dig through a pile of paddles, pulling out two matching ones. "I remember one time," she confided, "when I was a girl, we forgot to return the gondola to the boathouse before the waters went down."

"Not you!" Rom'n smiled. "Not beautiful Kreeian."

She pushed at his shoulder in response. However, the memory was one that was wonderful especially in the retelling, and her eyes sparkled with the wickedness of the story. "It was so very heavy to us as children, and my cousins and I couldn't carry it back. We waited until after dark, telling my uncle it was our neighbor's gondola, and that the neighbor's adult sons had left theirs out. We even moved their gondola to our shed. Knowing the sons often drank heavily and might forget a gondola for weeks, my uncle called our neighbor who insisted her sons come and return the gondola to her shed." As she wiped the dust from the seats, she laughed aloud. "The next day, my cousins and I came and switched the gondolas back to their rightful sheds. No one ever found out."

Rom'n laughed with her. "I certainly hope no one asks me to carry one of these halfway across the city. Could you not have floated it up the river?"

"The current is much too strong when the river is in its rightful channel. Only in this time when all the waters are dissipated over such a wide area is it safe to be out in the gondolas." Together they moved the small boat across the yard to the launching station. "Let me get in first. I can steady it while you step aboard. Have you ever been in a boat?"

"I've rarely been on a planet. Teach me how to do it in small increments. I don't want to fall in. The water must be very cold."

"For the first few days of the flood, it is, indeed, very cold. Then, as the water sits in the sun, it begins to warm. It's already warmer than just yesterday. However," she laughed, "you don't want to go in just yet. You'd have a very chilly ride back."

Slipping one end of the gondola into the water, he held on as she let the other drop until it bobbed gently, the bottom of the boat seeming to float just the smallest of distances above the bottom, although the space was the height of one of the shop's ceilings.

"Do I hold this end of the boat while you step in?"

"Yes." She laughed. "However, you'll show people you know nothing of boats if you continue to say this end or that end. The names for the parts of a gondola are the same as for one of your war boats." Pointing, she said, "Bow and stern. Port and starboard. However," she confided, "most people just say left and right."

"Ah. I can now ride your boat, er, ship, like a capt-gen'l. Call me CaptGen'l Rom'n Rezalton. Man your stations, maties!" He laughed. "Now that I command the ship, tell me, please, how to step aboard."

"Just put one foot in and then the other. Watch." She stepped lightly in, the gondola bobbing in the clear water. "See?"

"Sure. See the captgen'l fall in. Well, here goes." He reached one foot in, only to be off center, causing the small craft to rock precipitously. "Hey," he cried, freezing his body in position, holding onto the launching pole. He waited until the water quit rolling the craft.

"Easy. Step in the middle to keep the boat in balance."

"Just like my war boats. Well, Kreeian, the fact is we never had to keep to the middle on our war boat. No matter where we stepped, the boat always stayed true and level."

"It's not exactly the same, I know. You'll get it, though. Jump in."

With a mind for balance, he did, letting go of the launching pole. Surprisingly, the boat only rocked a bit before settling down once again.

"Oh, Rom'n! You forgot the paddles." She laughed. "Grab them, quickly, before we get too far out!"

He made a grab for them, the boat having moved only a small distance from the shore, and in his haste, he leaned out, one hand bracing on the side of the craft, the rail dipping below the edge of the water. He pulled back to offset the craft's lean, saving the boat, only to unbalance himself. With a look of surprise on his face, into the water he went off the back side, his feet sinking last of all.

"Oh, Rom'n," Kreeian called as his head bobbed back up. "There you are," and she laughed. "This isn't funny, but there you are, and you do look so amusing."

"It's very cold. You certainly weren't kidding. Can I just pull myself aboard?"

"You had better go up on the launching station and try once again." She smiled as she watched him pull himself from the chilly water. "The sun will warm you soon enough. Pull your shirt off and let it dry. Your pants will be dry in a few moments. Remember the paddles this time. Last man in always brings them. I should have let you know."

He pulled his shirt off, letting the water run down his skin, his hair plastered around his face. He grabbed the paddles, and before attempting to board once again, grasped the raised stern of the boat, shaking it violently, just to see Kreeian howl in mock despair.

A lesson learned, he successfully balanced himself into the small craft. His shirt was hung to dry, and his wet pants clung like a second skin, sending shivers running up and down his torso. For the first time since landing at the port, the sunniest spots were where he headed first, the heat finally a desired commodity on this too-warm world.

—Chapter 10—

"You have to turn loose of love, or it will die. Set it free. If it is love, it will return to you. If it doesn't return, it was never truly meant to be."

—Wise advice from an old grandmother to her granddaughter

"SYNRNN?" Kratt sat at the console, the bridge of the ship stretching around him, the bridge of his ship fitting his sturdy form.

"Yes, Boss?" She pressed her lips together, clearly frustrated by something. Her eyes were immersed in the visor, seeing something he couldn't.

"Shall we tell him?"

Without answering, she raised the visor and reached to the panel above her head, the flickering lights indicating green status across the board. All except *that* one. She triggered the query routine and spoke slowly into the visor. "All green except onboard docking bay life support. Please run diagnostics and display report. Notify when compliance has been achieved. Out." Pulling the visor off, she tossed it on the console and stood, looking at Kratt with his feet propped up in front of her.

"Well?"

"Why, Boss? What's the point in telling him?" She turned back to the panel, popping it off, and reaching her hand inside. "We've had trouble with this light off and on since three systems ago. Now's a good enough time to get it taken care of." She fiddled with small items inside, realigning and adjusting. Finally, her busyness apparent as simply that, she closed the panel, looking up at the ceiling.

"Synrnn, hey. Look at me," Kratt gently suggested. "Please." His chair creaked as he sat up.

"I don't have to look at you. I bet your elbows are on the console, and you're watching me fall apart. I'm trying to hide it as best I can." Her voice quavered, but she eventually turned his way.

"Girl, those are tears in those beautiful eyes! Hey, is this more serious than I know?"

"No, Boss. It's not love or anything like that." She sniffled, wiping her eyes on her sleeves. "I don't know. It's," and she sat on the low bench opposite the console, "like, you know, he's special. Do you know what I mean?" She stood, turning around, one hand on her hip, the other at her forehead. "You get it, too. I know you do." She turned back to him to see his eyes still on her face.

"Go on, Synrnn. I'm listening."

"I love you, Boss, you know that. I love this ship with

all its old-ship peccadilloes." She waved her hand around her at the bridge. "I wouldn't space on any other one. But I know you, Boss. You're all about you. That's okay with me. If you weren't that way, you wouldn't be you, and I wouldn't still be here on this ship."

She walked to the door and stood leaning against the metal frame, her arms crossed on her chest. She turned her head to look at him. "A thirtyday ago. That boy woke up one thirtyday ago, and he's changed the way I see things." She turned and spoke into the corridor, her voice one Kratt was forced to lean forward to hear. "Four hundred years ago. A few sevendays. He's been born both, Boss. He was born centuries ago and reborn when we pulled him from that pod. He knows the horror of waking up and understanding nothing can ever be the same again. Not the people he knew, the places he loved, or even the job he worked. He's found something here, Boss. He might have a life here, on the first world we landed on, with that girl."

"It would be a good life, but I think you know that. I gather you have something else that's bothering you."

"Boss, do you know I've never seen him think of himself? Not once. From the moment he opened those eyes, he has never demanded anything from anyone. How can I not love that, not want to take that with us?"

"What do you want to do?" His eyes were locked on her face, but his hands twisted the air within his fingertips.

She turned back to him. "I guess I'm trying to be like him, to learn from him." Tears suddenly ran from her eyes. "I'm just not doing a very good job at it, Boss. I don't want to give him up. Call me selfish, because I am. I just like having that good person on this ship with us. With him around, suddenly I believe in the goodness of the human race. That's what he does for me, Boss."

"You are not sel—" He jumped in, but she leaped back even faster.

"Yes, Boss, selfish, and I don't care. I guess I am in love with him." Finally, her thoughts out on the table, a smile broke through on her face. "Rom'n has stolen my heart, and if we leave him here, part of my heart stays with him." Her eyes teared up again. "I don't think I could take it, Boss, to go back to what I had, the way I viewed my life and the people around me."

He smiled. "At least I know where I stand. In this metaphorical ménage à trois, I'm at the bottom of the totem pole."

"I don't mean that, Boss. You know how much I care about you and being on this ship."

"I'm teasing, Synrnn. I do know what you mean, though." He leaned back in his chair. "Kreeian is a chance for his happiness. Gods!" He leaned his head back and laughed aloud, pulling a smile from her. "All those funds, and he hasn't spent a credit of it. Oh, maybe a few, but it's like it's not important to him."

"It's not, Boss. That's part of it."

"Yeah, I guess you're right about that."

"Boss, do you know we don't have any idea of what he's really about? Sure, what's come out about the cryo pod and a little about being in the military, but he's complained about *nothing*. I watch him, Boss. There are times I see him stop, like he goes into pause mode, and I know

184

there are terrible things he's dealing with inside. Then he brightens, and he's moving forward again, his problems pushed aside. I don't do that, Boss. I can't. I have to vent and wail. Gods," she laughed, "I'm doing it right now."

"That's what I love about you, girl. You wear yourself on your sleeve. No one has to guess who you are. All this brings us back to our original question. Do we tell him?"

"Screw the monkey, Boss, how can we not tell him?" She flicked her eyes at him, hearing a sudden, riotous outburst of laughter.

"That's one I've never heard of, and it's great! Whatever a monkey is, I love it. Screw the monkey! How you come up with these is beyond me!"

She smirked and explained, "At the kibbutz, we had this imported pet, a nuisance, really—"

"No, no. Stop there, Synrnn. I'll enjoy it more if I don't know." He stood, walking to the door, the laughter still shadowed on his face. He stopped and returned to her earlier thought. "He deserves to be the one to make the decision. You're right about that. We can't make his decision for him. Somehow, though, I think Kreeian will wish we had. She'll wish we had just gone, with Rom'n left here in our wake, hers to console. At least I think she would want that. Maybe not. Maybe she would want his happiness first. I hope so. Whatever happens, Synrnn, I can tell you this. If he stays, I'll miss that boy just as much as you. Yep, just as much as you."

As he walked away, she smiled. Reaching and picking up the visor, she whispered, "I knew that. I knew it all along."

185

"KRATT, I HAD another sevenday to decide." Rom'n walked to the balcony door, open to let the coolness from the night soften the heat of the ended day. "Oh, this does cause me to have to make a very hard choice."

"It's your decision. We can't resolve this for you."

He turned to face his two friends. "I think I could love her." He pulled up a chair, swinging a leg over, the seat-back under his folded arms. "I need you guys. The ship, that's my life. How can I turn loose of the only life I've ever known?" He paused, resting his chin on his arms, his eyes thoughtful.

"If you love her, Rom'n—" Synrnn began.

Kratt stood, interrupting, "Rom'n, only you know what you need for your life to hold. Synrnn and I will go on with our lives. If you're not with us, we'll go on. Don't base your decision on that. As far as Kreeian, if your decision is made only because you're afraid of hurting her, she'll find someone else and have a good life here, even if you choose to go. Don't you worry. This is a good world, better than most."

"I know, but I promised I wouldn't hurt her." His eyes roved from Kratt to Synrnn, searching for answers.

Kratt turned to catch Synrnn's eye for a moment, then looked back at Rom'n. "Think of yourself, my boy. You are the only one who has to live with you in that head of yours, and you *have* to be able to live with yourself. For some people, that means choosing comfort and safety. For others, it's adventure and change. Some people must chase purpose and find answers in order to be satisfied." He put a hand on the younger man's neck, looking down at him, only to catch him looking back. He knelt, and their eyes locked. "If you love her and she loves you, she'll still be here if you decide to return."

"You make it sound so simple. If I were the only one living in this head, it would be easier." He stood and reached up, running his hand through his hair. "I have to go with you. I'm lost without the answers I seek. Not even Kreeian can fill that spot in me. Maybe someday, just not yet." His decision made, he turned to Kratt. "Just one thing."

Synrnn glanced at Kratt's face to find him rubbing his eyes with one hand, apparently speechless. She turned her eyes back to Rom'n, answering for her boss. "What, Rom'n?"

"I don't mind my corridor where I have my space, you know, where I sleep on the ship. But, can I at least have a real bed?"

She let out a true laugh of relief as she whacked Kratt on the back, forcing a grunt from him. Leaning in just so he could hear, she whispered. "We get to keep him!" To Rom'n, she hooted, "Whoa, boy, I'm glad to have you back on board!"

Putting her arms around him, her hug was as good a welcome back as Rom'n could have asked for.

KREEIAN TRAILED her hand in the water. "This is the last day the water will be high enough for the gondolas." She leaned her head back on Rom'n's knees. "I knew you'd never stay. When your ship leaves, you won't be able to watch it go without you. Your life is too big; you've got too many unsettled stories woven around you."

She twisted around, her face looking up at him, her arms on his legs. "My life is so simple here. Nothing exciting will ever happen on my world. You're bigger than that. I think I might have even begun to love you, but I need to know you love me above all else. Your complicated life hasn't let go of you." She ran her hand along the fabric of his trousers, tracing the pattern of its weaving with her fingertips. "Still, I've enjoyed our time together." She looked into his eyes. "Come back to me, Rom'n, if you will, if your life ever lets you go. I could love you and would like the chance to try, someday."

She faced the front, dropping her hand back in the water, the ripples spreading out from the boat, filling the water around them. What he didn't see were the tears starting to trail down her cheeks, the wind drying them as they fell.

"CHOOSE QUICKLY, Rom'n. Your credit crystal will get you anything you want. Buy the whole shop, if you wish. You can certainly afford it. Just do it quickly. Our exit window for departure is arriving soon. With the altered departure date for this new shipment, we have little time for preparations." Synrnn stepped to the door of the shop. "I wish we had the extra week we'd expected, but you must make sure they can deliver by our updated departure time, else you'll be back on the bench."

He gave her a thumbs-up sign, the hand signal learned from Kratt, and he turned his attention back to the shopkeeper. "I need one I can assemble. Here are the measurements. It must fit in this space."

He ran his hands down a carved bed frame, one that reminded him of one he remembered from his childhood home, the one his mother had brought from her own childhood home. He had forgotten it until now, the memory just one more cord pulling him back to the ship with Kratt and Synrnn. Things done. People taken. Loves lost. Answers unknown. Could he ever find what he needed?

"Ser?"

He jerked, his past slipping into the recesses of his awareness where it belonged. He knew that for this day, his attention was needed here. "Yes?"

"Will this one do?"

He looked in the clerk's hand at the illustration, the bed one with shelves on three sides and drawers underneath. "How are the measurements?" He traced his fingers along the shelves in the illustration. "This is nice, but it looks very large. I cannot alter the space. The bed must fit."

"I've double-checked each measurement, ser. The size is perfect." The shopkeeper bowed. "May I prepare it for you?"

He paused, thinking, the decision finally made in his mind. "Can you have it to the port by early afternoon?"

"It will be there. I can transfer the funds now, if you wish." He waited patiently to hear Rom'n's answer. When he saw the proffered credit crystal, he carried it away to finish the deal. As the shopkeeper stood at the back of the shop, Rom'n heard him say, "Oh, my. My, my. There will

be no problem at all with getting this to the port on time."
Louder, he heard him call, "Are you sure I can't get you
anything else, ser?"

Just then remembering the enormous funds transferred
by the money house, only a portion of it on the credit
crystal, Rom'n smiled. Maybe he could get to like having
all the credits after all.

ROM'N STOOD, his goggles across his face, the sun on
his shoulders hot. His planetside clothes were his no
longer, the memory of the cool river water flooding the
city only that, and he looked forward to his return to the
ship. Watching the cargo loading from a distance, the
ground crew efficiently moving in and out, he searched for
familiar faces. Seeing Kratt peering from the open bay
doors, his hand wildly gesticulating, he raised one arm in
greeting. When Kratt continued waving, he gave an exag-
gerated shrug of his shoulders, his perplexity clear, he
hoped. Suddenly, Kratt just stopped and pointed, and
Rom'n turned around.

"I wondered how long it would take you to look at
me," a familiar voice whispered.

"Kreeian! I so hoped you'd be here. Our departure being so sudden, I had no time to travel to your home to see
you." He swept her up in his arms, slipping his goggles off
his eyes, burying his face in her hair. "This I will remember. When I think of you, the smell of your hair will be
mine."

"You'd better remember more than my hair! Finally,
you fool, you show yourself for what you really are!" She

laughed in his arms. "Put me down. Your shipmates will think you've changed your mind and leave without you." She pushed at him. "I just wanted to say good-bye."

"I'm so glad you came. Those guys," he motioned to the ship, "can just wait." He wrapped his arms around her again, whispering, "What difference can it make if I take a few more beats of a human heart? The systems in the heavens turn on a galactic scale, and they move very slowly. My heart beats a thousand times, and those systems never even know. A few moments won't change the course of the planets in their race around the sun. The worlds out there will still be hanging in the sky when we leave." His hand tangled in her hair, as he traced the outlines of her face with his lips. "I want to memorize all this, to take you with me to hold forever."

"I only wish—" she began, and then stopped, looking down.

"Wish what, beautiful Kreeian?" He nuzzled her, his lips on the edges of her ears. She put her hands on his chest, making space between them, and then looked up. Finally seeing the tears running down her cheeks, he put his hands to either side of her face. "Oh, my dear Kreeian. I never promised to stay, and you know I would never hurt you, not intentionally."

"Oh, Rom'n. My heart isn't broken. You must be convinced of that." She smiled at him through her tears. "I couldn't have asked for more from you in these two weeks. I just didn't expect it to end so soon."

"Neither did I, dear Kreeian. Neither did I. When the urgent call came through, the window for our departure was exceptionally narrow, and it had to be taken. More time, and possibly I could have found this to be my home. Just not yet, my sweet."

"Without your drive to find your answers, you wouldn't be the Rom'n I'm learning to love. Go! Come back to me, if you can!" Turning, she ran, her hair trailing in the wind as he stood and watched.

Finally, Kreeian gone from view, he turned to the ship, the door waiting, and he walked ahead. The world waited. His world waited. His world, the ship, the only world he had ever really known, welcomed him back.

—Chapter 11—

"If all else fails, please open and follow these directions."

*—On the outside of a sealed
envelope*

"SYNRNN, WHAT can I do about this?"

Rom'n waited patiently for her response, the visor taking her attention at the moment. There was a note of barely concealed desperation in his voice, though.

"Can it keep a moment?" She whispered into the visor, her instructions bringing up information only she could see. "I'm pulling up course corrections as we exit the planetary system. The magnetics and solar flux wreak havoc with the ion drive when we're so close in. I'll be just a moment."

"I'll wait." His voice quavered.

She spoke into the visor a little more loudly, "Systems hold." She flipped the visor off her head, turning toward him, then starting at what she saw. "Leaping jeepers! What'd you do to cause that?" His arm was wrapped with a blood-soaked cloth.

"Umm, that new bed. It doesn't quite fit. I was—"

"Never mind. Thank goodness you had the foresight to at least wrap a cloth around it." She leaped up to give him a hand as he sagged against the wall. "It sure beats all traveling with a couple of jerks who don't pay attention to basic safety."

"I'm sorry. The bed. I think it'll fit once I get it assembled, but I didn't have space to work the parts together. I stepped on it to force it in place, and my arm got caught underneath a rail at the same time I was pushing. I slipped. I wanted to get Kratt to have a look at why the rails wouldn't fit, but with both of you so busy . . ." His eyes started to close as his voice faded away.

"IRaC, we've got a problem. Can Kratt come stat?"

"Thank you for asking, Synrnn. I will check with him and see." The ship's personality paused and then continued, "Yes, he is on his way. I can see there has been an injury. Keep the cloth tightly wrapped, Synrnn. Rom'n will need liquids, and soon, too."

Synrnn helped him to the floor, holding his injured arm above his head. "Gods," she whispered. "If we've pulled this boy from that world just to lose him here." Her words brought tears to her eyes. She looked up as Kratt came running down the corridor. Seeing the tears in her eyes made him ask the first question that came to his mind.

"Is he still alive?"

IRaC broke in, "I am sorry to interrupt, sers. He is not dead, Kratt. He will need liquids soon. Synrnn is performing the proper procedure with his arm. Please continue to hold it high, Synrnn. It will slow the bleeding. Please get him to the medbay. Proper care can be administered there."

Kratt put his hands under Rom'n's shoulders, and Synrnn carried his legs. Together, they made sure he got a quick transport directly to the medbay, and they didn't even demand their two hundred credits.

KRATT LAID the ripper down, the metal shavings scattered around the corridor. "Just a touch or two with this Patch-o-Torch, and I think we'll be good to go." With a couple of jolts of the high-energy beam, the metal was fused into its correct position.

Synrnn appeared at the corridor junction, a look of satisfaction on her face. "Thank you, Boss. The kid's just not good with tools, I guess."

"You know, I don't even think he knew to ask. He was on a military transport. Scabbing wounds, it wasn't even a transport! It was the biggest freakin' battleship ever constructed. What would he know about patching up things with these little-bitty tools?" He reached over to pull out a vacuhose from the wall. The metal shavings soon removed, he and Synrnn inserted the drawers and a sleeping pad. "I think the kid'll be happy with this bed, don't you think? How's his arm?"

"Light use and lots of liquids for several cycles. He's spunky, and tougher than he looks, it seems." She sat on the new bunk. "Boss, for an ol' toughie, you're a softie. At least you are where it counts."

"I'm all about fun and doing what I want," he growled, although there was a twinkle in his eye. "Right now, helping the kid's what I want." He laughed, then a wink flashed across the small space. "Maybe I'll go play racquets in zero gee next."

"Want some company?"

"If you hadn't asked, I might've had to order you to be there." He chuckled. "I wasn't worried, though. You sure the kid'll sleep? I wouldn't want him to accidentally wake up while we're out in the cargo bay having fun together. With that arm, he'd probably be disoriented and might panic."

"Out like a light. IRaC promised another four hours. I'll get the racquets. As far as Rom'n panicking? There's not much chance of that." She smiled. "That's just your soft side coming through."

Before he could come back at her with an answer, she was off, already floating, her last zero gee exercise a very long time ago.

ROM'N SAT, morose, the third wheel at a very small galley table. His eyes were on his bandaged arm.

"Look at this." He held up the arm, the bandage tightly wrapped and making it difficult to bend his fingers. He raised his eyebrows. "Here I am, the useless baggage on your ship once again, Kratt. I had nothing to do before, and now I can do nothing. I wouldn't be surprised to have you take me right back and drop me off with Kreeian. Not that I would mind, but then I'd have to find another way to roam these systems looking for answers I'll probably never find." He pressed pale fingers into tired eyes.

"Minor, minor problems. Time between systems is pretty much playtime for us. Sometimes we complete repairs to the ship, but mostly we babysit whatever we're transporting. Don't you worry about doing anything except healing." Kratt rapped the table, and he nodded once before leaning back and putting his hands behind his head.

"Yeah, Rom'n. That's the point in these slow-boat runs. Lots of time to play. For those of us who really like the spacing life, this is great, the only way to live."

"I've had fun so far." He toyed with his bandage, pulling a loose spot tighter on one side. "If I don't mess it up too badly."

"I admit, it's not for everyone." Kratt patted him on the shoulder. "On most of the big military barges, the people get to live in the same way they do when they're planetside, regular schedules, planned free time, and all. Not here. We work hard a few cycles and then take a couple sevendays off. Then a cycle of hard work, and a couple sevendays planetside rec time. I think you'll fit in just fine."

"I hope so." He looked up, hope returning to his face. "Down sides to being a slow-boat spacer?"

"None," Kratt threw out fast.

"Well—" Synrnn looked at them both. "Small spaces, way lots of downtime—which can a problem if someone gets bored easily—and learning to live with cranky people." She slapped Kratt on the side of his head, prompting him to duck and cry ouch. "Also, no fancy parties." She laughed. "I don't miss the fancy parties

197

much, though."

Kratt crossed his arms on the table and looked at Rom'n. "What have you really thought about our tiny world so far? No hedging, now."

"I really do like it. I've got a place to sleep at night, one that's even comfortable now, I've got good friends, and I'm traveling across the darkest reaches of space." He reached his arm behind his head to scratch his back, before resettling into his seat. "This is what I'm used to."

"Darkest reaches of space," Synrnn mused. "If you really want the darkest reaches of space, it's not here."

"What do you mean?"

"Check the sensors." She reached over and touched a control panel. A frame unfolded from a ceiling track, its display flickering in place. She adjusted the contents being displayed and turned to Rom'n. "Look at that." She raised a hand to indicate points of light covering the display. "Stars, every one. Just think of it like this." She adjusted the display once again. "See how the stars seem farther apart? Our view is closer now. These are just the stars within easy range for cruisers with live-transit capabilities only. That means maximum transit distance of six months' ship time. Any farther than that and regs require either light cryo or full cryo."

"Light cryo? I guess I've never heard of that. All this other is familiar to me, or at least the parts from four centuries ago." He grinned.

"Yeah, you have. Just not by that name. Slow-sleep."

"Oh, yeah. That was old even in my time. Look, I'm saying it now. *Even in my time.* Maybe I will adjust eventually."

"You'll get there. We know you, and we don't doubt you a bit."

"Thanks, guys, but where's the darkest reaches of space?"

"You know the coordinates where your pod originated?"

"I had the ship run them, so I know that much. More? Not really. It's just very far away."

"Farther than this ship's ever been. Farther than this ship's even designed to go. You'd have to have slow-sleep or a full cryo model to head that direction. Either that or a jumpship."

"Been there and done that with the pods, I guess. I just don't remember. You guys know that better than me. You pulled me out of that pod. I've never been on a jumpship."

"Let me show you just how desolate it is." She scrolled the view to the side until the stars abruptly stopped. Finally, several scrolls further, two suns came into view.

"That's it?" He was incredulous. "So, that's the binary system with the twin suns. How did they ever find it?"

"Boss? Do you remember?"

"Maybe a lost ship or something. A probe, perhaps. I really can't remember, but I do know it's supposed to have one of the most beautiful worlds on the intergalactic register of habitable planets."

"I feel I should know this system, but I spent all my time there aboard the ship." He glanced at the other two spacers with him, then chuckled. "Revenant, maybe? I looked it up at one point, but I've forgotten."

"Rejuvenant," Kratt said, smirking. "See, I remember a few things. IRaC, can you access any more for us?"

"Yes. Since my upgrade, I have the most current downloads available. You are correct, Kratt. On official star maps, the planet is known as Rejuvenant. However, there is also a local name. Do you wish it, also?"

"Spit it out, IRaC."

"Se'Yan't. It seems the local name has a special meaning in the local nomenclature."

"Well?"

"I am sorry, sers. It also seems as if the information on the official record has been partially expunged. Someone at some point must have felt the need to limit access to information about this planet."

Kratt said, "That's odd. It's rare to have any information removed or even restricted, unless, that is, the military is concerned. Since MegaCorp was dismembered, even that doesn't happen very often. That makes it especially odd, I think."

IRaC interjected, "This is a very old record, ser. It may have been restricted or expunged a very long time ago. The file does not indicate a time frame."

"Still," he said. "It does seem odd."

"You guys can sit about and debate odd, but I'm bushed. I'm off." Synrnn stood. "Tomorrow." She threw a wave as her two mates tossed ones in return.

Rom'n wasn't quite finished. "IRaC, what's the most recent reference for this world?"

"There are references to the Rejuvenant name for over nine hundred years. Most are simply asides in various sources. No additional information is directly attributable to reports on the planet itself except one. A study by a Ser Alb't deFralin, SSM.rl, was done approximately three-and-a-half centuries ago. It detailed a number of poems collected from the planet. An accompanying reference to the study suggests that about the same time, the planet was deemed off-limits to travel except by special permit. The reasons are unstated. I wish I could be of further help."

"Thanks, IRaC." He sat, thinking. To Kratt he said, "There might not be anything there that could help me in my search, anyway, not after three hundred seventy years. How could there be?"

"Let's think about it in the morning, huh, kid?" Kratt stood and slapped him good-naturedly on the shoulder. Then he exited the room, and Rom'n's own footsteps soon followed in his wake.

After a few moments of silence, the lights flickered out, the room empty. Only the display screen continued to light the space, the two suns buried in a sea of blackness. In time, it, too, flickered off, the frame returning to its resting place in the ceiling.

—Chapter 12—

1. *pound hamburger*
2. *eggs*
3. *celery*
4. *onion*
5. *milk*
6. *seasonings*

—shopping list recovered from
an old-Earth excavation site

"ROM'N!" Synrnn kicked his sleeping pad. "Sleepyhead!" She yanked his thin blanket back. "There's a job I need to do, and even a one-armed weakling can help with this."

"Ow!" he complained. "Just half a yawn. Let me have at least that."

"Come on." She grabbed a foot, pulling one leg off the bed.

"If it weren't for the lights, I'd not know if it was night or day. Thanks for making sure they're on. You know how to make a guy's morning." He yawned, covering his eyes.

The corridor lights had flooded on at full brightness, and the glare cut into his sleep-polluted brain.

"Baby. All the real spacers are already up and about." She laughed, sitting on the edge of his bed and shaking his ankle.

He leaned the back of his head on the empty shelf above his cushion. "Ah. I might leave this empty." A ghost of a grin hovered at the corners of his mouth.

"It's good storage. I thought that's why you picked this bed."

"It's also good for propping my head up so you'll think I'm still awake after I fall back asleep." He grinned, inviting her to grab his foot, once again yanking him, this time completely to the floor.

"That's for threatening to fall back asleep."

"The floor is cold!" he moaned, perhaps a bit dramatically. Grabbing the edge of his bed for support, he stood. "I guess I deserved that. Let me dress in something besides these sleepers. Where to?"

"I'll hustle and meet you in Corridor D."

With those words, the corridor and the woman at his side melted away, leaving him frozen in place, his eyes seeing a scene that wasn't really there. Lights flashed repeatedly around him, immediately going dark between each glaring surge. A man stood next to him in the blackness. In the explosions of brilliance, Rom'n could see his red hair. Men were running. Many were carrying weapons. Rom'n ran without knowing where. The man in the red hair followed him. In one flash, he looked up at a sign posted on the wall. Half as tall as the ceiling was the giant letter D. Wrapping around the corner was a long stairway leading down. He looked behind him, and the man and the corridor were gone.

"Here, follow me."

He turned. The man calling him was already running down the stairs. He was the one with the red hair. As he looked, the first of the stair's treads started to fade, the blackness punctuated with two bright lights bleeding through the previously solid surface.

The man yelled at him, "Jump!" Rom'n leaped the fading tread, following the man. Suddenly he was at the end of the stair, the man running around the corner. As he turned, a bright flash of light showed the wall of the corridor. Another giant D filled the surface from the ceiling halfway to the floor. The man was already in front of him, disappearing as he rounded the corner.

Running faster, not wanting to lose him, he turned the corner to find a wall with the letter D staring at him. He turned the opposite way to see the man who had been ahead of him. He was crouched, motioning to him, urging him to run faster, telling him to hurry. He sprinted toward the man, only to find him farther ahead, already running.

Panting, exhausted, he ran faster, turning a corner after the man only to find the red-haired man running toward him, grabbing his arm, turning him around, yelling at him, "This way, Rom'n!" and disappearing around the corner. When he rounded the corner, the man was nowhere to be seen.

"Psst. Up here."

He looked up to see the man's head and arm hanging

through an open hatch in the ceiling. The man motioned for him to grab his hand. When he did, the man pulled him effortlessly through to the upper corridor. On the wall above the hatch was the letter D on the wall. He stopped, his hands on his knees, his breath coming in exhausted gasps.

Suddenly the man was behind him, leaning over him, his arm around his shoulders, his face next to his. He whispered, "You can't stop now. This way," and he was off again, pulling on his arm. Soon the man was leading him down a long, straight corridor. Lining the corridor was sign after sign, each with the letter D, each larger than the one before, soon each letter filling the wall from floor to ceiling. The end of the corridor was dark, and with dread filling his chest, he began to pull back against the man's hand. However, the man effortlessly pulled him on, turning, yelling something to him. He could no longer understand his words, and the man kept yelling louder and louder, determined to make him understand.

The blackness ahead grew larger and larger, soon filling his view. When he thought the man must surely stop, the redheaded man looked at him, yelled one last time, and he finally understood his words as he wrapped his arms around him, and they leaped together into the blackness.

"My friend!"

When he looked around, the roiling, ebony smoke of unending space revealed the brittle icepicks of jagged stars, and he was all alone.

"Rom'n, wake up!" Synrnn shook him. "Come on, kiddo."

"My friend. He called me *my friend.*" He jerked, back in the corridor with Synrnn. He blinked his eyes at the sudden, steady brightness overhead, and he sat hard on his bunk, disoriented with the abrupt change of scenery.

"Where did you go? It was like you were here, then you blanked out. Maybe you should rest a little while longer. That arm may not be all there, yet." She looked up, calling, "IRaC? Did you follow all that?"

"Yes, Synrnn. I was watching. The flickering eyes, the flush indicating elevated skin temperature, and the sudden return to reality all indicate Rom'n was reliving a very vivid memory. I believe you would call it a flashback. Chances are this was a repeat of a dream he experienced during his recuperation from the cryo-degeneration. Stand him up, Synrnn. He needs to walk. He will be fine."

"Thank you, IRaC. Walk, huh?"

"That is all he needs. It will allow him to reorient himself to the here and now."

"Got that, Rom'n? Up. I'd carry you if I needed to, but IRaC says to walk."

"I believe I can manage that." He paused to settle his breathing, the exhaustion from his imaginary run following him through the barrier back into the real world. "I just had a memory come back, except it wasn't the real memory. IRaC might call it a flashback, but it was a nightmare, a waking nightmare."

"Yeah, I imagine. You haven't told us everything, but I bet you've been through a few nightmares in your life. You must have lived quite a number of them. I'd have to be blind and stupid not to see that." Louder, she called to

206

IRaC, "And you don't have to repeat that to Kratt, IRaC."

"Which part, Synrnn?"

"Duh! The part about me being blind and stupid."

"Understood, Synrnn. My databanks are sealed."

"Thank you, IRaC," she muttered, hoping they truly were.

"HERE, ROM'N."

He took the frozen package in his glove, the slab of food fresh from a liquid nitrogen bath.

"See the one with the blinking red light, the one on top?" Synrnn pointed, and he stood and opened the panel. "Just slide it in, and close the panel. It self-seals as it feeds the slab to the slicer."

"What was that?" He closed the panel to see the light change to green, and he turned to take another slab from her.

"Meat loaf. We stock that just for Kratt. It's the only thing his mother could fix, and I think it brings back memories. Or, maybe he eats it to remember why he left home and came to space in the first place." She laughed. "This one's hot chocolate."

He scanned the panels looking for the words to tell where to insert the foodstuffs.

"Don't read. Just look for the flashing red lights. They're the only ones we replace."

"Much easier. I found it." He slipped the panel back, feeding in the slab. "This is what the reprocessor uses for our meals?"

"Yep. It slices off a frozen hunk, slides it down to the

tray, and heats it to yummy hot, even if not to yummy good. Like the kids on a hundred worlds say, *Umm, umm, flavor!* That should do us for now. I'll probably have to do this again in a cycle or two. Sometimes it's only once a sevencycle."

"I could take this on. Even with my arm. How do I know when to come back to check?"

She grinned with success. "Oh, you don't have to come back here and check. There are three easy ways to find out when to reload. The first is to wait until you dial up a tray and find the food you requested just doesn't show up. Another way is to check the panel on the front of the reprocessor. The third way is my favorite." She stopped as if finished, resealing the liquid nitrogen food storage bins.

"Okay, Synrnn. What?"

"What do you mean?"

"What's the third way?"

"I thought you'd never ask. IRaC."

"IRaC?"

"Yeah. She loves to be busy, too. I've already set it up with her to let you know when the food slabs need replenished."

"Thanks." He laughed. "I appreciate you finding me a job to do, and I didn't have to ask."

"No problem. You can thank IRaC when you get back into her sensor range."

He smiled. "Will do!"

—Chapter 13—

*"Feed the Children provides over one
hundred thousand meals per day to
children who would otherwise starve.
Won't you consider contributing today?"*

—*Solicitation c. 1951 A.D.*
old-Earth

"SYNRNN, YOU'RE sure we can't get to our targeted destination?" Kratt leaned over the console, taking the visor from her, and he glanced inside. "It's just a few cycles more and we're there."

"Kratt, use the sense of a monkey. We can't afford to let this go this time. With just two of us aboard, we might tweak the stores and limp on in, but not with three of us. The reprocessor's supplies won't hold out that long."

"If I just knew what a monkey was." The visor still covering his face, he whispered several commands, continued to look inside for a moment, and then pulled it away. "It's the stores and not the reprocessor. You're sure?"

"I've tied IRaC into the sensor feed, and she concurs. The docking bay life support isn't holding up, and it feeds the pressure lines for the liquid nitrogen in food stores."

His face finally angry, Kratt slammed his fist on the console. "Curse those refitters on that asteroid colony off Carney's World! I paid them good credits, too. Even a bonus for doing the job fast. I should have taken time to put my baby in a real shop instead of trying to skimp on a few lousy credits. Screw your monkey! I wouldn't sell them our stock of old-MegaCorp cryo gel if they paid double for it!"

"Just like with IRaC." Synrnn grinned under her hand.

He turned. "What was that?"

"He heard you, Synrnn. Please salve his pride by being conciliatory. We will need to get this repaired. Our viable food supplies will run short approximately forty-two hours before our scheduled destination can be reached." IRaC made a noise that sounded entirely too much like tut, tut.

Synrnn reached over the console and patted Kratt's stomach. "Hey, IRaC. Why don't you go ahead and skip the repair? It seems it *can* wait until we reach our original destination. A couple days short a few meals certainly can't hurt *some* of us." She lifted her feet and turned her chair in a full circle, her laughter following her, and she turned to Kratt. "That sound good to you, Boss?"

"You know how to hurt a man, Synrnn." He reached for the visor, putting it to his mouth, and speaking inside. "Schematics on the board, foodstores high-pressure lines, liquid nitrogen, quarter field." He put the visor absently aside as he walked up to the 2-D display board. Tracing the lines with his finger, he spoke aloud to himself as much as to Synrnn. "Right here is the reprocessor, and just behind that is the stores. The lines, hm." He reached a hand behind without turning his head. "Synrnn, the visor, please," and feeling the pressure of it against his skin, spoke into it, "Down one layer." Returning his finger to the board, he continued. "Now, there they are. Let me see, if the nitrogen could be recaptured, I could reroute this to the main life support. Hm, counting disconnect and represssurization time, life support would be off maybe, what, a quarter-turn, tops."

"Boss," Synrnn softly interrupted. "Boss."

"Yes?"

"Our high-pressure recovery equipment is also down. Sorry, Boss."

"Crikes, Synrnn. Where's that monkey you were talking about? I think we need it right about now."

"True, Boss. I think he got out of line and became a weekend barbecue after I left. Can't even help you there."

"IRaC, how will this impact our cargo delivery schedule?"

"Ser, I have already notified our destination port. Also, from the cargo manifest, I pulled the contact information for the mining company and have received confirmation of shipment delay approval. An additional three cycles will be added to our total delivery time."

"How about the cost of the delay approval?"

"Ser, the destination port authorities and the mining company have requested a ten percent premium for rerouting other shipments to accommodate our new arrival time. Shall I notify an acceptance of their conditions?"

"Flaming suns, ten percent? Might as well. And IRaC? What's with this ser business? Did that last stop upgrade you to military mode or something? I kinda liked hearing my name in that pretty voice of yours. Can you do that?"

"I certainly can, ser. I will start immediately. Do you think Synrnn and Rom'n feel the same way?"

"Ask them. They can speak for themselves. And if they can't, that's their problem."

"Very good, ser. I will make a point to do so. Synrnn, how do you feel?"

"I was getting to like your personality from before, too. I'm with Kratt. Can you shift to something a little less formal than what we've seen since the upgrade?"

"I will do my best, Synrnn. Thank you for your input."

"Less formal, IRaC," Kratt barked.

"Sure thing, Boss."

Synrnn grinned at him. "Lucky you, Boss. Now you've got two of us!"

"ROM'N, YOU'VE done us a good thing. You don't need to repay Kratt the penalty. He always charges enough to cover things like this. Why, do you know those pods we're carrying, the ones the colonists traveled in, are still earning us credits? We get paid just for transporting them on board until they are returned to their world of origination, whether they are being used or not."

"But Synrnn, if it wasn't for me aboard, the ship could limp in for repairs without losing any time. Here I am with one arm out of commission, due to my own stupidness, I might add, and I can't even contribute to the extra expenses I incur. The only job you've found for me has been restocking the meal supplies. Now, if we don't stop for repairs, I won't even have that job. It seems as if I'm more trouble than I'm worth to you and Kratt."

"Now, you listen to me. If it weren't for you, we might have made it offplanet again before we realized anything was wrong. Who was in the food stores every day, checking, whether IRaC had notified you or not? Who noticed the food slabs didn't feel quite right? Not me. I'd have just slammed 'em into the slots and been back out the door. Where would we have been then?" She leaned in to him and put her fist on his knee. "I didn't pay attention, and that's the problem. I did ask the visor to run diagnostics. I already knew the life-support system in that bay was iffy, but then I didn't go back and check up on it. I just assumed if it went out, we'd keep that bay sealed off." She sat back, a grin on half her face. "So, I should be the one to pay the fine. But, you know, neither one of us will, no matter what we want. This is Kratt's ship, and he always takes the responsibility for whatever happens with it. When you picked Kratt, you picked the best of the best. The nicest?" She laughed. "Well, that's up for debate. Otherwise, I'll take him any cycle."

"It's just that I haven't done anything right since I've been on this ship. I couldn't even put my bed together without failing at that. Just look at my bandage. Gods, I passed out in your arms, and it wasn't even while we were having a good time."

"Don't be a goof." She slapped him on the arm, making sure it was his good one.

"Also, Synrnn. You got to pick Kratt; I didn't get the chance. Don't forget, I was just floating in that cryo pod. I didn't pick anyone. Kratt picked me."

"I can never forget that. I helped him pull you in out of the cold. Neither one of us has any regrets, either. I can assure you of that." She stood, walking to the door. "Now, let's see what foods we can save."

"PUT IT UP on the board, Boss. I want Rom'n to see." Synrnn took Rom'n's arm, pulling him closer. When the information didn't appear, she pushed on Kratt's shoulder. "Kratt, please!" Turning to Rom'n, she mused, "At last, a world I haven't visited at least once. Trasdrom'man. This will be refreshing."

"Why's that? Does it really get that old revisiting the planets? Or, I'm guessing, now," he teased, smiling, "you just really like being out here. A world of green and sky and water holds no interest to you. You're the wanderlust that fuels the spacer fleet. The galaxy is held together by the glue of likes such as you." He cut his eyes to catch hers and found an incredulous expression staring back. "Pretty close, am I?"

"Jumping planetary volcanoes, how'd you do that?"

He laughed. "Do what?"

"Kratt says I'm an open book, that I carry myself on my sleeve, but in all the time we've been together as crew on this ship, he's never seen the real me like you just described." She shook her head, "What else do you see in me?"

"I see that you enjoy fishing for compliments." He laughed, his response bringing a scowl from his crewmate. "Really, I see that you care about others. You just don't always want them to know it." This time when she turned to face him, he saw the moisture in her eyes telling how close he had come to the truth.

"Thank you, Rom'n." She sniffed back a tear. More quietly to herself, she whispered, "That's the real me. At least I want it to be." Then she took a deep breath and put her smile back on her face. Reaching out, she pulled the visor from Kratt's head. "Share, Boss."

"Okay, don't be pushy." He pulled the visor back and spoke into it. "Display to board."

They watched as it did just that.

"Show Rom'n, Boss. Which one is it where we're headed to make our repairs?"

"I get it. I see you want me to give the full tutorial. How much do you really want to know, kid?"

"All this is really interesting to me. If you have the time, I'd enjoy getting to see it all. Even in all my years in the military, I never got the chance to be involved in this side of running a ship." He narrowed his eyes, trying to find something on the display that wasn't there. "Can I see our ship on that? I have no idea where we are, where we're going, or anything." He reached to run his hands over the locations of several stars. "It would really help if I knew that much."

"Sure. That's easy stuff. I can do easy stuff." Kratt glanced at Synrnn, a tart reply not unexpected. He spoke into the visor, and the image of a ship not really all that much like the one they were in appeared on the board.

"This?" Rom'n grinned. "Your ship looks like this?"

"Not exactly. It just shows where we are. Of course, if that were real and our ship were that big, we'd be a few magnitudes larger than Kreeian's sun," Synrnn pointed out. She reached over to prod Kratt's shoulder. "Boss, where we started, get that up, and our destination, too."

The words spoken into the visor, Kratt laid it aside. "Here, Rom'n. Kreeian's world. Now, here's our destination. You can follow our path here. Of course, we really bounce around some. It's not a straight path at all like it looks on the board. The ion drive derives much of its push from the magnetic resonance core inside."

Synrnn whispered to him, "This is a good refresher course for me. I navigate. I don't build the drives."

Rom'n glanced at her, absorbing her comment, and then pressed Kratt, "Bouncing around? I don't get that."

"Yeah. We actually travel faster when we're in an area dense with stars. Their magnetic forces extend out, often overlapping those of numerous other stars. The ion drive uses the magnetic resonance core to ramp up thrust, but to do so, we actually move from side to side, speeding up as we approach a star, the velocity of our approach suddenly releasing us to be flung toward another magnetic source." He stepped back from the board. "In fact, this is the technology that disproved a long-held theory. The shortest distance in space is not the quickest way to travel. We can cover twice the space in half the time if we have plenty of stars around." He touched the board. "Here's a good

216

estimation of the actual travel path." He drew a wildly zig-zagged path from star to star. "In the most densely packed areas of the galaxy, ships often travel three times the distance, getting there in a third the time." He turned, a satisfied smile on his face, his explanation given with gusto.

"I've never seen anything like this before."

"Oh, yes, you have, in every drinking establishment you've been to, this process holds true."

Synrnn barked a laugh. "Boss, even I don't get that one. That's an awfully long way to pull a leg."

"Just think of it, Synrnn," he began to explain. "A guy walks into an establishment, and there's only one girl on the other side of the room. He has a straight shot. Does he go right over? No. He knows there's no one else in the establishment, and she's his anytime, so he steps in, talks to the bouncer a while, fiddles with the jukebox, and *eventually* gets to the girl. Now, the reason he takes so long is really unimportant. He just takes his time.

"The next night, it's ladies' night, and the establishment is crowded with women. That same guy walks in, and that same girl is at the same spot. But there might be opportunities he would miss if he bypassed all those other girls; and the guy is ever hopeful, so he hits on every girl in the room. Yet, that one girl just might get picked up by some other guy if he doesn't get to her pretty soon. In the crowded room, who knows who else might be there for exactly the same reason he is? This night, he keeps his little flirtations brief. He tells a girl she's pretty or rubs his hand on her shoulder as he leans over to whisper a secret to her. In record time he's reached that girl across the room. He's covered maybe three or four times the distance, but it hasn't taken him nearly as long. Now, she knows all this, so when she really wants to pick up a guy, she goes with a group of her friends. They may all get hit on, but she knows, every time, she will get the guy. Every single time." He stood, nodding his head as if he'd experienced his story once or twice.

"Boss, I've seen you in a few of those establishments. The women there know you a city block away. When you show up, I think a few try to go home without the guy." Synrnn grinned at Rom'n.

"Maybe that was some other Kratt you knew," he smirked. "Some Kratts always get the girl, and sometimes they get more than one."

"No, Boss," Synrnn moaned. "That's plain wrong."

"Yeah," he smiled. "That's what makes it so right." He hit Rom'n's good shoulder. "Don't you agree, friend?"

At that, Rom'n shrugged his shoulders, just a touch of red rising around his collar. "I'm more of a straight line type of guy. Sorry to rain on your party." He stepped over to the board. "This little world we're stopping at, Synrnn says she's never been there." He glanced at her for confirmation. "Why?"

Kratt answered, "Not much cause to. In fact, I've never been there that I remember, either. The population is scarce, and not much happens there. You'll see, I think. Kreeian's world was a gem. Most are more like the one we're approaching. You'll see it's certainly livable, if you want to call it that, but certain of the more gentrified luxuries we seem to consider so necessary are considered sybaritic there. Things like lots of showers and green plants to eat."

"That reminds me, Kratt," Synrnn announced, snapping her fingers. "No more meatloaf. *That* nitrogen tank was the first to go."

"Drats! Sorry, Mom!" He chuckled and whispered aside to Rom'n, "Too bad we can't modify the system to use that cryo gel in the hold as a preservative. Never mind. I don't really like meatloaf, anyway. It just brings back unpleasant memories, and I need that to stay out here, sometimes."

"Boss, you eat it just to stay angry with your mother for raising you in that hellhole you grew up in."

"Yeah, maybe that, too."

Rom'n changed the subject. "That world you were telling me about, Kratt?"

"Oh, yeah. Sorry. Synrnn gets me off track so easily."

She poked him. "You get yourself off track so easily, you goofus."

"Can we get back to that world?" Rom'n pleaded.

"It's very monastic." Kratt busied himself at the controls as he prattled on. "Not uncivilized, just distant, socially. The story I get is they won't warm up to you like on the last world. We'll be lucky to find an eatery with even mild drink."

"If you've never been here, how do you know so much?" Rom'n gave him a doubtful look.

"You doubt my sources?" He threw a look of mock hurt across his face. "IRaC?"

"I have been following the conversation, Kratt. May I join in?"

"Please don't jump too quickly," he threw out.

"Rom'n, I assume calling you by your given name is acceptable? Kratt and Synrnn seem to enjoy given names."

"Absolutely! Go on."

"Our destination world is renowned for the severity of its climate. It revolves around its sun in an elliptical orbit, creating unusually hot summers and very cold winters."

"Can people go outside at all, even survive in those extremes?" He made a face. "We're landing there, and the prospect of such harsh weather doesn't seem very appealing."

"Yes. The old-Earth seasons were as severe, just not all in the same place. If an old-Earth location had harsh winters, they were usually balanced by the mildness of the summers. Not so on our destination world. In addition, the weather changes abruptly from one season to another, the time of pleasant weather limited to only a few local weeks, if that. Some years report the change to be so abrupt as to go directly from one severe season to another. Dwellings are constructed accordingly."

"What about cities?" He had no true reference to many of the descriptions IRaC was giving him. He was relieved when IRaC continued, her helpfulness programmed into her.

"There is one major city, and that is where we will land. However, most of the planet's more prosperous dwellers reside in isolated compounds recessed into mountains that surround an interior, landlocked sea. That seems to be a fairly recent transition for this world. For all intents, the city is generally used for political gatherings and for the purpose of servicing the port."

"I've been in some of those port cities," Synrnn ruefully mused. "I know what kind of people service the port." She turned to her friend. "Rom'n, be careful here. For the locals, it's probably perfectly safe. They'll know the unwritten rules and customs. Many of them may try to take advantage of us when they become aware we don't know these rules and customs."

"Synrnn is certainly correct, Rom'n," IRaC confirmed, as she continued with her flow of information. "While our destination world is not known for its violence, it is always wise to be cautious when entering an unfamiliar situation. While our time here will undoubtedly be brief, it is likely that misinterpreted social signals could create difficulties."

"I've been on worse, if it's no more wicked than IRaC's saying. Avoid the dark alleyways, and make sure your pockets are safely sealed. You and I, and Synrnn, too, if we can goad her into joining us, will find that hidden source of liquid refreshment, and we'll have a good night, even if it's only one." Kratt reached to Rom'n's shirtfront and grabbed it in one hand, pulling him close. "We'll show them a time or two and be out before they can say jackrabbit." Retrieving his hand, he guffawed, turning to leave the room. "We'll be the whirlwind they never knew hit them, not until after it's gone."

"I KNOW." Kratt looked up as Rom'n wandered into the galley, glancing down at the tray he held in front of him.

221

"Mashed tubers and cubed orichoke again. I only thought my mom's meatloaf was nasty. You want this, either of these?"

"No sweet carrots left?" Rom'n walked up to the reprocessor, the lights red up and down the board. "I had sweet carrots just last night." He sat without choosing anything.

"I dumped them," Kratt explained. At Rom'n's incredulous look, the precious carrots gone, he went on, "Brown spots. Even I couldn't eat around them anymore. It seems the stores are dissipating more quickly than even IRaC thought possible."

Interrupting, IRaC corrected him, "This is within my projected timetable for expiration of the carrots. A window is just that, Kratt. I cannot predict a precise rate of deterioration in foodstuffs when the thoroughness of the irradiation is unknown. At the present rate of depletion, it does seem the food stores will be exhausted before we are scheduled to land. My apologies for not having more complete information."

"We understand, IRaC. Not everyone's perfect." Kratt smiled.

"I do try my best," IRaC responded.

He smiled even more broadly. "What can you say to that?" He turned to Rom'n. "If IRaC were only a real girl, then we just might have some fun." He laughed. "Did you hear that, IRaC?"

"I did, Kratt, and thank you. I would enjoy having fun with you."

He leaned over to make a wisecrack to Rom'n when

222

IRaC continued.

"However, I am afraid I think much too quickly for you. It would be an unfair game."

Rom'n laughed. "I guess she told you."

Kratt sat back, his comeback gone from his tongue. "I guess she did at that, Rom'n. I guess she did at that."

—Chapter 14—

London (AP News) – New science of DNA confirms babies accidentally switched at birth by nurse. Mother says she knew something was wrong when she touched her baby's skin. It just didn't feel *right to her.*

"GIVE ME a moment, Kratt." The information the visor was feeding Synrnn scrolled from side to side. "This world's magnetic core isn't in the databank experiences, and I need to tweak the propulsion thrusters. How long has it been since you've done a full ion drive survey?" She whispered into the visor, "Course correction three point two degrees port on my mark. One, two, mark." The ship actually shook underneath them, the air turbulence noticeably buffeting their small craft. She glared at Kratt. "Raunchy tomatoes are better than this. Ouch!" She turned her attention back to the visor. "Airspace trajectory registered. All filed plans go. Set. Mark." She slipped the visor off her face.

"We're in, though, aren't we?" He looked at her hopefully. "And that was a sweet deal you brokered, that ancient cryo gel for our repairs. Who'd have thought to find old food preservation devices here adapted to use the stuff? Good flying back there, by the way."

"Good? It was rough. Usually compensating for the drop in the ion drive's efficiency isn't a problem. On this unfamiliar world, it was bone-jarringly rough." She forced her way past him, the corridor her destination, uninterested in further conversation.

He ran after her, keeping pace with her, even as she refused to slow down. "I'll get it fixed, Synrnn." When she didn't pause, he went even further. "Now. While the life support is being repaired. I'll do it now. I promise."

She slowed, finally turning to look him in the eyes. "Will you, really? Or will I just have to wrestle with the ship again next time? That's frickin' exhausting. You just don't have to be in there, tweaking those drives the whole time. That's why you haven't cared." She stopped, leaning against the wall, sliding to sit with her knees at her chest. "I'm tired. Too tired to party tonight. I forget how nice it is to have landings already in the databanks, the work all done, and nothing to do except monitor."

He squatted beside her, his arms resting on his knees. "That's what I wanted to talk with you about. I don't really want the repair crews on board without someone here to monitor their access to the ship. Now, you're feeling out of it, and Rom'n really wants to be outside when we get downworld." He paused, thinking, and then grabbed her hand, pulling her up. "Come on, girl. I have a feeling you could use some rest."

"Kratt, you're not going anyway, are you? You've promised to take care of those thrusters. Please."

"No, I know what it means when you start calling me by my name. I'll come through for you this time." He put her arm around his shoulders, his strength a relief for her tiredness. "I'll spend the night working on them, if that's what it takes. There's not much to miss here, anyway." Once they reached her cabin, he opened the door and helped her inside. Within sight of rest, she pushed him away and dropped on her bunk.

He glanced around, taking in the sparseness of her quarters. "I know space aboard ship is always at a premium, but you keep nothing. Are you sure you don't want a souvenir from this world? Rom'n can bring you something."

"I just want to rest, Boss. Let Rom'n do what he wants. He's a big boy. You just fix those propulsion thrusters."

She was out before he could close the door.

"IRAC, HOW much do you know about the landing procedures on this rock?"

"I know as much as I can access in the ship's databanks, Kratt. What exactly do you wish to know?"

"Synrnn's out. Does the port here require me to be in full visor contact now that our airspace trajectory is filed? If necessary, I can stick around. However, if this is set up, then I have other things I need to attend to."

"Kratt, I believe Synrnn indicated that landing is now

226

completely under the port's control. No further action is needed on your part. If you wish to busy yourself at other tasks, the landing will proceed without mishap."

"Thanks, IRaC. That frees me up to, as you so aptly put it, busy myself at other tasks." As he walked off down the corridor, he muttered to himself, "All right, Rom'n. Let's get you ready for a night out on the town. I think we might be coming into a winter wonderland down there."

"HEY, GUY!" Kratt sat on Rom'n's bunk, the sleeping form beside him face down. He put his hand on the younger man's back, shaking him gently. "Rom'n!" He grabbed one arm, rolling him to his back.

Rom'n settled deeper into his bunk, not yet willing to force himself into wakefulness. As Kratt reached to the younger man's chest, shaking him again, Rom'n used one hand to grab the offending arm, pulling it to him as he dreamed. In his memories, Ma'jene was attached to the other end. He laughed in anticipation.

"Dance with me one more dance, beautiful lady," he whispered in her ear. He cupped the small of her back with one hand, her closeness to him filling him with her smell. His nose in her hair, he closed his eyes, no longer caring where they danced, or even if they danced alone. All he knew was her closeness, the intimacy of her breasts pressing to his chest. The movement of their bodies together was intoxicating. He shifted against her slowly, the world fading to quiet, the sounds gone, the world consisting of just his body against hers.

Sudden clapping caused his head to jerk and his eyes

227

to look around. He remembered: the dance; the band playing, the song now over; people standing around watching, some of the men whistling. They were alone on the dance floor, he and Ma'jene. He stepped back, the moment of magic now broken. With a sheepish look on his face, he took her arm and steered them from the center of attention.

"Ha!" She turned to him, whispering softly so only he could hear. "You look embarrassed." She faced him, running her hand inside his shirt, then sliding it around his waist and slipping her hand underneath his belt. Leaning in to brush her lips against his chin, she worked her free hand up his side, tracing the outlines of his ribcage with her fingertips. "Don't be embarrassed that you want me. I'm not embarrassed by you." She slid her hand across his chest, gently moving her fingers around his neck, tracing his chin and throat with her palm as she did so. Leaning in to him, she gently brushed her lips against his, and then she pulled her other hand free, pushing him to the refreshment bar.

He reached for her, her touch making his head spin.

"Something wet, please." She pushed him away with her hand. "I need you to come right back, though," and she turned away, his hand lingering on her back until he could no longer touch her.

He stood for a moment, the intoxication overwhelming, the *need* to be next to her, to touch her skin, to have her want him.

Suddenly, someone had his arm, and he turned, reaching again for his beloved Ma'jene, only to be jarred by an unexpected voice.

"Kiddo, don't turn back over, and give me my hand back." Kratt peeled the man's hand loose and pushed him onto his back again. "A cold shower would surely wake you up." Laughing, he grabbed his stubble-covered face in one hand and worked his jaw, shaking him. "Come on, pretty boy. The planet's calling."

"Kratt!" He jerked up, sliding back to lean against the shelf. "Oh, wow! I just had an amazing dream. She was the prettiest girl, and then I opened my eyes to you." He laughed. "Please, please don't ever do that to me again. My heart may beat in the body of a young man, but it's nearly four hundred years old. It'd be good for you to remember that. It might not take the shock next time."

"Ha!" Kratt's expansive bolt of laughter filled the corridor that was Rom'n's quarters. "That's the attitude I love to see!" He stood, pulling Rom'n with him. "Get up, my boy. It's time to prepare. You have a world to explore. Proper preparation is your due, and we have lots of preparation to do. Have you ever been to a frozen hell?" He turned to look in the younger man's face. "Well?" He tugged him forward, leading him, his hand pulling him in tow.

Rom'n glanced back at his bunk, and somehow he was surprised to see his youthful flame wasn't wrapped in his bedding, waiting for him still. He chuckled, letting it go, as he turned to follow the man leading him on.

"No, Kratt," he answered. "No, I never have."

—Chapter 15—

*"My God! You have to see the ice! You
stand on it, and it's blue. God, it's blue!"*

*—Blogged comment from
crew wintering on the ice in
Antarctica, old-Earth*

KRATT REACHED inside the stor'lok, throwing out several pieces of soft fabric. "Strip everything off, Rom'n. You'll want this next to your skin." He turned and held several of the pieces against the younger man, measuring with a practiced eye, tossing several others aside, finally deciding just the ones that would fit.

"Just how cold's it going to get?"

"Colder'n space. These things are just the first layer. You've got to be bundled up. Get to going!"

As Rom'n pulled off his lightweight sleeping clothes, he ran a finger along the softness of the fabric Kratt had measured against him. It was no heavier than the items he had worn to sleep in. How could it be warmer? Realizing he had no choice but to trust Kratt, he pulled the cloth over his legs, sliding it around his waist, the fabric soft against his skin in spite of its snug fit. It wasn't bad. Reaching for the top, he pulled it over his head, slipping long arms through the slim-fitting sleeves. Wrestling it over his torso, he pulled it tight and snugged it underneath the lower piece.

"Kratt, this is just like a second skin. I can't even tell it's there."

Kratt chuckled, calling, "Because I'm good. That's exactly how it should feel. Now, these." He tossed Rom'n another heavier layer.

The new layer soon wrapping his limbs, Rom'n began to warm. He glanced at Kratt to see yet another suit of clothing coming from the bin. "More? Why so many layers? I'll be toast before I get off the ship."

"The bottom layer needs to be snug to wick the moisture from your skin. The next layer warms you up. Now, this is the real stuff." He tossed out a number of items that he suggested Rom'n carry until ready to exit onto the planet. "You'll want these once you're outside. However, you wear them now, and you'll overheat. These are what we call *peel-able*."

"Peel-able?" Rom'n snorted with a grin. "What do you mean?"

"You take off one layer at a time to adjust the temperature. If you get cool, start putting them back on again. Get warm, and take something off."

"Surely they'll have some sort of heating down there. Didn't IRaC say this world has extreme seasons? They'll know what warmth feels like and try to keep their buildings that way."

"This isn't a wealthy world. Maybe a few of the people, but not generally. IRaC tells me their planetary resources mostly go offworld to buy foodstuffs that cannot be produced onplanet. Foreigners rarely make it to the surface, either. The transports are typically automated. We're going in on programmed mode, sort of. More like planetary remote control, but anyway, no one on board is controlling this ship. The port is."

Rom'n looked at him with surprise, his socks thick in his fingers as he crouched to put them on. "You let them do that? Just take over your ship?"

"Regulations, boy. If I fought 'em all, I'd never be able to land anywhere. Besides, we need repairs. Sometimes I just have to go with the flow."

Rom'n paused. "Kratt, you're not getting dressed, and where's Synrnn?" He stood, reaching for a pair of sealable overpants, the seals dividing them into two parts attached only at the crotch. "You *are* both going with me?"

Kratt came up and smoothed the top layers of fabric across Rom'n's shoulders, pulling it tight around his waist. "Tuck this in. You want to seal any leaks against the wind and the cold. You'll want to be warm, even if it is just for one night." He walked around the port-bound adventurer, checking the fit, making sure gaps were closed and pieces were overlapped. "We're not going. You're on your own, my boy."

"I don't want to be alone. You and Synrnn are my friends. What will I do without you?"

"You'll have a good time. Besides, inbound navigation exhausted Synrnn, and she's out. I have drive repairs that I've let go too long. You have youth and the need to see the unfamiliar. Let's go."

They both looked up as a rumbling was felt throughout the ship.

"Kratt?"

"Not to worry." He put a reassuring arm on the young man's shoulder. "IRaC told me there'd be a huge ice gate. I guess that's it. They're taking us in." Together they rounded the corner and triggered the pressure plate into the loading bay. When the air pressure seals flashed a welcoming green, he tapped the pad, triggering the outside doors. He pressed Rom'n's credit crystal into his hand and stepped back into the ship's corridor.

As soon as the door into the exposed loading bay opened, Rom'n understood why. As fast as he could, he put on the rest of Kratt's insisted layers, tucking in and sealing places not even Kratt had suggested. He stepped forward into this, his first new world to explore on his own. As he walked down the loading ramp, he noticed a crew already carrying supplies the opposite direction. The loading bay floor would soon be dismembered, starkly revealing the broken lines that had forced them onto this forbidding world. Their faces covered, much like his own, he nodded at the intrepid repairmen, their greeting barely returned.

Looking up at the sky, he saw it was not sky at all but a covering of ice. Could this world really be so cold they could build huge domes of ice in which to land ships?

The further he walked, the more awed by the ferocity of this planet he felt. His lungs fought the inrush of air as the cold crept in and burned his throat. He couldn't do this, live on a world such as this. He immediately understood that. A night would be enough for him.

As the cold continued to seep through even the multiple layers of Kratt's firm preparation, Rom'n strode purposefully forward, the need to find warmth quickly driving him to be anywhere but there.

"DOWN? The city is down?" Rom'n was dubious. At least there was a warmly dressed girl stationed at the port to help out, who he'd learned had been hastily summoned for their arrival. Her obviously temporary enclosure seemed to provide her protection from the worst of the cold, and she didn't lack for company. There were several other girls visiting with her. All seemed very young.

"Well, mas, up you can head if you want. But to be found there, only Summer City be. Lives there now, no one. If to find people you want, to Winter City you need to head. Will lodging for the night you require? Direct you, I can, if you would like."

"The local time?"

"Thirteen-oh-eight."

He pressed, "Is that early or late in the day?"

The girl laughed. "Funny that be, mas. Ahead, the whole day we've got."

"No lodgings, thank you. I'll be fine on my own."

As he headed down the steps, he overheard the girl talking to one of her friends. "So stupid all off-worlders be. Imagine, can you, someone asking if thirteen-oh-eight be early or late?" Then the pack of teenagers began to giggle, the sound fading as he headed into a new world.

Looking up, unsure what the city might be built of, the port having been roofed with ice, he was relieved to see solid stone climbing the walls, the arched stone passageways clearly very stable. Passing a number of landings, he found the air seemed to warm somewhat as he delved deeper into the ground, the bite beginning to be taken out of the air. Although obviously no longer on the surface, the great room the passage had become was gently but well lighted with what appeared to be natural light. Far above, huge panels glowed with softly fractured illumination. He began to see hardy plants in large pots, at first scattered around, and then finding places where they were so dense as to make the buildings almost disappear.

With low walls and thickset windows, very few of the structures glowed with light. Surprised at the emptiness of the passageways, he took time to "peel" a few layers of his clothing, the warmth beginning to be too much. He noticed a person ahead plodding determinedly along, also dressed warmly, but in far fewer layers than his own.

"Hey," he called. The figure turned and motioned to him. He ran to catch up, his "layers" on one arm. "Where is everyone?"

"Not heard, have you?" The figure trudged forward without giving Rom'n more than a quick glance or two. "A gathering there be today. Surprises me, it does, that you do not know."

"What's the gathering for?"

This time the figure did turn to peer at him, his gaze resting on his face for several moments before glancing away again. It was an obviously very old man, perhaps at the end of a harsh life, with wisps of thin white hair protruding from the hood of his garment.

"Why, the Winter Renewing, of course. Scheduled and started already it did, at twelve-oh-eight. From all the compounds, representatives there be; miss this gathering, none dare." The old man smiled, his teeth straight and clean, belying the age on his skin. "Beauties they be, those from Elussie'san 'de Gaso-Fratenni laHolc'm. Beauties they be." The old man tapped Rom'n's chest with the back of one gloved hand, the digits inside visibly gnarled. "Luckiest only be the lads who catch the likes of laHolc'm girls. So lucky should you be, my boy."

Abruptly, the old man stopped walking and faced Rom'n. Reaching a hand to him, he grabbed the younger man's clothing at the chest and pulled him down. One parchment-shrouded eye was nearly closed in a forced squint, as the other studied Rom'n's face. It seemed as if he searched for something familiar in the young man's features. Just as suddenly, pushing him away, the old man continued walking.

"Just a boy you be. A just-grown boy without the etchings of life yet upon your face. Lucky may you yet be, my boy." The man's head swiveled to him. "Bonded yet, you be?" His eyes continued to watch him even as his feet carried him forward, a frank response clearly expected. "Bonded, boy?"

At a loss for words, and not really understanding the

pressing reason for the man's question, Rom'n laughed aloud. "I suppose not."

"Excellent that be, my boy!" The man continued emphatically, "Excellent!" Reaching to place a hand on Rom'n's shoulder, the old man pulled him down again, whispering conspiratorially, although he could see no one else to overhear. "The one you need, I be." As a great double door came into view, the old man stopped and waited. "Well, boy, open it, you must!"

As he rushed to do so, the old man straightened, sliding the cloth off his head and brushing his wisps of hair flat against a smooth scalp. Inside, Rom'n found the great space of a vast amphitheater, all the seating of the bowl of its floor filled with people.

Once the old man removed his gnarled hands from inside the warmth of his gloves, he placed his hand on Rom'n's shoulder for support, leaning to speak to him alone. "Be you here, for that my thanks goes out. Old for this I be." The old man then pulled him inside to a rising crowd of cheers and clapping.

Rom'n walked at the man's side, providing a supporting role in something he didn't understand, wasn't sure he wanted to participate in, and certainly would have avoided if he could.

SURPRISED AT THE warmth in the huge room, Rom'n carried the layers he had removed, until a youngster, a shadowy growth on his upper lip telling of his dance with puberty, breathlessly ran up to him, taking the layers in his hands. With a quick, "To you, thanks, mas. At the desk

237

they be when we retreat," and a smile, he was gone. Rom'n followed the old man, knowing no one or even what this was all about, only that it was a gathering, and that the old man seemed to be of some importance. His host stopping, a greeting given, others received, and the occasional hug gracing the old man's shoulders, they traversed the crowd. Finally seated, the old man before a low table, the other people in the room seated lower still, an unasked-for chair appeared for Rom'n.

As groups, ordered in some way Rom'n didn't understand, stood one at a time to speak, sharing news that seemed important somehow to those gathered with them, the old man leaned to place a hand on Rom'n's knee, a confidence shared and a point of interest noted. "An importer of cloth he be, the biggest in all the compounds. A home in the city he keeps." Another time, with a laugh just for Rom'n's ears, "Six unbondeds she has. Worth the time to pursue, none be."

Finally, as a tall and straight woman of later age stood, one still beautiful in her weathering body, the old man came erect. "Of whom to you I spoke, this be the one. An eye on her to keep, important it be." The old man smiled knowingly. He leaned closely to whisper to Rom'n, "An unbonded she has, my boy. You, I told, I did. For this, your thanks I'll see."

Rom'n placed his hand on the old man's shoulder in response, having no way to know how to reply.

The stories told, the gathering attended and finally ended, the people in the hall moved to congregate in their small groups, sharing confidences important only to them.

The old man motioned Rom'n to stand, and with his youthful arm for support, stood with him. A hand gesture from the old man, and the groups parted for them, the conversations resuming as the pair passed.

"This be she," the old man motioned. Rom'n glanced the direction he indicated to see the elegance of the earlier speaker standing before him. "To her, speak, man. Quickly, lest dim you be in her mind." The old man pushed at him with a shove of his hand, hissing emphatically, "The unbonded one. Under this one's care she be. Speak!"

He raised his eyebrows, knowing only that he was expected to say something. "Um, good morning." He froze when the woman turned and looked at him, her eyes locking on his. He remained still, unsure, as she soaked him up. It felt as if she was seeing something within his face she had not observed in a very long time.

After a time, her eyes shifted unwillingly, finally landing on the old man. Brightening, she spoke. "My precious Cerennt'te Nijenhaus. How sweet it be to see you." She stepped out, reaching to place her hand on his face. "I miss you so through the seasons, Cerennt'te. Your memory be what keeps me going when the winter's cold or the summer's heat refuses to let me enjoy this world we have called our home for so many of its years." Moving her hand to his shoulder, her eyes shifted to Rom'n, again drawn by something she seemed unsure of, then back to the old man. "You have not come to visit me this cold season, Cerennt'te. Surely all the turns of this world have not worn away the spirit I have always found in you."

At that she laughed, and Rom'n was transfixed. He knew that laugh, had heard that sound before, but he could be certain he had never met this woman.

"My dearest and most charming Dóme Elussie'san 'de Gaso-Fratenni laHolc'm. Greeted you be. For the things you say, grateful I be. Fled be our youth, and missed much it be. Years on me weigh, correct you be, and hard it be to travel, taking such as this world's winter and making it to nothing. No longer enduring the cold can my old bones be. Yet, missed you, I have, my Dóme." The old man had a sheen of perspiration moistening his pate, and he reached to his shoulder and placed his hand on hers, his fingers caressing her parchment skin as if that of a familiar friend.

Rom'n watched them together and, with an inner smile, knew. These had been lovers in the past. There was more to this than the surface was telling.

"Cerennt'te," Dóme laHolc'm finally ventured, her eyes now properly on the old man's face. "Your young man. He be unknown to me." Her eyes turned to Rom'n, resting, finally unable to tear themselves away. "I would know this one."

The old man, obviously very pleased with what he was doing, bobbed with excitement, his knees bent and once again straightened in a surprisingly nimble fashion. "Dóme, mine this day this unbonded attendee be. Unknown, his name be. To introduce himself, he will speak." With that, the old man turned to Rom'n, expectation on his face. "Speak words you can, boy. Hold not back. To impress, now be the time."

Rom'n chuckled to himself, his eyes dropping to the

floor, totally out of his element. When he glanced up, the woman was there still, her eyes on his face. A suggestion of a smile, one showing both amusement and yet somehow unnerving, ghosted the lines of her mouth. The expression seemed strangely familiar, reminding him of the laughter he hadn't been able to place. At the twinkle he could see jumping from eye to eye, he smiled.

"I'm sorry, Dóme laHolc'm. I'm at a loss. I *can* introduce myself, however. Rom'n Rezalton. My ship . . . not even mine, really, but one belonging to a friend of mine, undergoes repairs. I'm here alone; and with no one in the city, just the girl on the upper level for directions, I was lost, really. When I saw your friend, here, he encouraged me to join him. As I was saying, I'm at a loss as to what to say." He smiled as he made a little bow and took a small step backward.

"Nonsense. You be quite verbose. Already you interest me much with what you say. Rom'n, you say your name be? How fascinating! We must take you away with us. Cerennt'te seems quite enamored of you, and I must say, that takes some doing. Cerennt'te, can I convince you to join us as we return to our quarters?" Elegant and straight, her presence as commanding in conversation as it had been in her earlier presentation, the Dóme turned, her head inclined in the outstretched invitation. "Yes?"

The old man looked at Rom'n, hope in his eyes, the hope seeming to be that of his new acquaintance earning what he had once held in his hands.

Rom'n questioned, "What of my friends?" Kratt had planned only one night on this cold world, even as he knew this woman called to his heart in some indiscernible way. She tweaked his memories, as well. Just what it was that called him, he couldn't tell. Her laugh? Her commanding mannerisms? He wasn't sure, but he wanted to know more.

"We will send them word. It be settled." She turned to a small boy and pointed her finger. "Go, the foreigners' ship, the one in the Winter Hangar. Take them word their friend be with us." That matter dismissed, the Dóme walked toward the door, a lackey draping fur-lined robes over her shoulders. She called back, her head barely turning, "Cerennt'te, this will be a night to remember, such as you and I have not seen in a very long time."

"Looking forward to it I be, my Dóme. To you, thanks I give." Cerennt'te fell into her wake, content to be one of the faithful entourage following the priestess to her temple.

THE DOOR LARGE, this wall not squat and filled with sunken-in windows as at the edge of the city, the group stopped. Lavishly decorated, the panes jeweled in finery and warmly lighted, it was easy to sense the affluence that lived behind these walls. A great foyer opened past the door, the ceiling decorated, and the air warm. Pulling layer after layer off their bodies, clothing was quickly gathered by younger children and taken to storerooms to be hung and freshened. Feeling cloth placed in his hand, Rom'n looked to see the others, men on one side and women on the other, removing outer clothes to a thin underlayer, donning the brightly colored robes. Following suit, he did the same. One by one, those completing the task wandered inside.

Entering, the main building was stunning, and nothing like what he had expected. The room was elegantly lighted and gracious. Cloth hangings covered the surface of the exposed stone, and low chairs, soft and welcoming, were scattered around. He hung back as servants began offering trays of foodstuffs to tempt the gathering attendees.

From behind him, one of the wall hangings rustled. Out stepped Dóme laHolc'm, and she walked directly to him. "Come converse with me, guest Rom'n. There be fascination in what I find in you. I must hear your story. Where be you from?" She stepped to an open area of the room, a chair appearing beside her as she started to sit. Motioning to Rom'n, a chair was suddenly at his side where none had been before.

He pulled at the unfamiliar silken robes, adjusting them self-consciously as he placed himself on the chair. "From offworld," he began in answer to her question, and was quickly silenced.

"Not enough, young Rom'n. You be the freshest of faces. Your hair be the white of the winter snow. Your skin, so pale. Surely you come from a world of others such as yourself." The Dóme tapped one long, weathered finger, the nail trimmed and shined, against her open palm. "I be not asking just to ask, young Rom'n. Many centuries have my family owned and lived in our distant compound by the landlocked waters we call the Sea of Revenge." She laughed at the expression on his face, her manner relaxing as she warmed to her tale, only a permanent furrow in her

243

brow reminding him of her earlier terseness. "The how is unimportant, but many years ago, the Original Grand-mother was given the great sum of which our fortune has been derived."

"You don't live here?" He motioned around the lux-urious room with one hand.

"Nay, young man. This be but our lodgings when in the city. The Original Grandmother blessed us with finer quarters far away." She leaned in to Rom'n, her face light-ing up with the sharpness of a personal observation she obviously liked to share. One parchment-skinned hand pointed at him in emphasis as she smirked. "That was not the grandmother one would have wanted to know."

She paused as if waiting, looking across the room at the old man who'd exerted himself to befriend the young Rom'n, the expectancy of the glance spurring Rom'n to speak.

"What's the reason, Dóme?"

She laughed, turning back to him. "You wish to know? Everyone wishes to know. That grandmother never learned to disguise her cruelty with oil and honey. Some say it was the leg that was bent, never to be walked upon. Others," and here a wink escaped the old woman's eye, "say it was the disfigurement on her face."

The Dóme suddenly standing, Rom'n rose and fol-lowed as she traversed the room, stopping from time to time to speak to someone before moving on, filling in her revelation in starts and stops as she marked off the empty floor with her footsteps.

"Me? I say it was more, so much more. I've known

244

those with bodies crushed and torn. They be happy if their spirits be happy." Turning and looking directly into his eyes, with a twinkle of amusement in hers, she went on with mock seriousness, as if making fun of those she described. "I've known those with faces like the lowliest of living things. An interest found or a love secured, and the face be transformed. Come, let us rest for a moment." She motioned, a chair appearing as she did so. "The heart. That be the difference."

"How does the heart make a difference, good lady?" Rom'n heard the flippancy in her words, how she spoke with a smirk, belying the philosophical bent of her story. Was she good? He was beginning to think not, but he refused to make that call.

She laughed, and the sound was harsh. "What be it that makes one's anger flash the lightning bolt of hate? It be the emptiness of love. That be something which no man or woman can live without. Give the man or the woman the beauty of the face, yet take the love from the heart, and the beauty be gone. Do you find truth in my words?"

He pursed his lips in surprise, the question unexpected, and then chuckled, taking a chance. "I suppose I must."

Her demeanor shifting, she laughed with more than just a hint of contempt. "So my precious Cerennt'te would tell us. My softhearted words be his. I cannot claim such sentiments." She paused, seeming to gather her carefully mannered graciousness about her once again. With a noticeable release of breath, she turned to Rom'n. "Later this night, I would share with you, newly found friend Rom'n. May I?"

"Dóme, I've nothing to share in return, for I'm a visitor to your world for this one day only." He chuckled wryly. "Besides, I'm no one, and I certainly don't belong with the well-mannered and glittering social elite in which I've been swept up." Surely she could see that. This was not his world, and he had nothing valuable to offer, not even a past. His personal history was nearly four centuries out of date and very dead.

"Nay, my boy." She laughed the laugh of one used to being catered to, seeming to find the sincerity of his consternation fresh to her. "I shall bear the duty of the sharing, and I will pull from you what I will. May I have your permission to call you a friend? I be afraid I did so earlier without asking of you beforehand. I do feel as if I've known you all my life. You be so familiar to me."

"As you have seemed to me, Dóme laHolc'm. That laugh back at the gathering was one that shook my memories, although obviously I've never met you before. It seems I should know you, although I don't pretend to be able to explain why."

"Later, friend Rom'n. I must remember my guests as well as these hangers-on who have come anyway, whether with an invitation or without. Remember," she reminded him as she stood, "I have still to hear of your past. You will hear more of mine."

He let his eyes trail her as she moved from him. He could not shake the feeling he knew her, or at least must have known one very much like her. She was very old, though, her life lived on an isolated world she seemed to have never left, what with her archaic mannerisms and speech patterns. Although, and he smiled inwardly, it seemed a better education must have lessened some of that, for those faults were much less pronounced in her mannerisms than those he had heard in most of the people he had met this day.

He wandered the gathering, aware of evaluating looks from those around him as well as the smells of unusual foods. He also enjoyed the warmth, remembering the cold he had traversed above. From time to time, he stopped to overhear a story or sometimes a joke told, although several times he knew it was a joke only by the laughter at the end.

Several times he approached the Dóme to continue their earlier conversation, but each time she was deeply engrossed in conversation. Finally, he took a seat to pass the time patiently. He didn't know what she wished to tell him, and he wasn't sure what she could want from him, but he did know his ship was scheduled to depart in the morning. When a lengthy amount of time had passed, he searched the room for the old man. His eyes alighting on him in the distance, he walked to stand behind those seated within the group, enjoying his final moments in the city as he watched the elderly ser regale his small throng with a series of hilarious tales.

Catching the old man's eye, a tale just ended, Rom'n dipped his head. "I must leave, my friend. My ship will depart at daybreak. I cannot be late. Forgive me as I abandon you. My outer clothes, I pick them up in the first space we came into, yes?" He raised his eyebrows in question as he waited, pausing for permission to exit. It seemed the courteous thing to do so.

The old man pursed his lips, looking down at the one seated just in front of him, her back turned Rom'n's way. The head turned to face him, and Dóme laHolc'm's response was warm but pointed.

"You must stay, friend Rom'n. We have agreed, have we not? You and I have secrets to share."

"My friends, Dóme. They wait on me. I've enjoyed your company and would choose to enjoy it more, if time were mine to command. However, the choice is not mine alone."

He watched her purse her lips as she considered her response, and then relaxed as he heard her say, "Very well, then," returning to Cerennt'te, motioning for a new tale to begin.

Mystified at the meaning of the strong currents running beneath the surface cordiality of the party, Rom'n dismissed the matter as one not of his concern. Finding a child holding his clothing as he reached the foyer, he began to pull each layer on. Soon he was making his way through the underground labyrinth, eagerly anticipating the excitement of the one who had so looked forward to the newness of this unvisited world. He had a tale to share, one of his own. He felt he was becoming a true spacer. Reaching the end of the warm, underground spaces, he paused, the banks of potted plants long behind him, and faced the expansive rise of stairs. Glancing far overhead, he caught the darkening panels of light. Ice sky windows? he wondered. Not for him to know, now. He tucked the last of his loose clothing, pulled his head covering tightly around his face, and slipped the warmth of his gloves over hands already deeply chilled.

He walked resolutely upward, the stairs the harbingers of winter, each one taking him closer to a frozen land. As the snow started gathering at the edges of the steps, he began to shiver, even wrapped in Kratt's best. He was certain it felt colder than before. Then he realized it was the coming darkness. He looked up, noticing the daylight was gone, and it was, indeed, much chillier. He began to lope the distance to the ship, relieved to find the loading bay complete, the contracted work finalized and the floor plates reassembled and ready to go.

After having braced himself and then endured another trek through the bitterness of this upper world, he was glad to hit a palm to the door lock panel, sealing the cold into the loading bay. Finding Synrnn in the bridge under the visor and Kratt snoring on his bunk, he peeled his layers of warmth, folding them carefully for Kratt to return to storage. Stepping to the ship's facilities, the warmth of the corridor's air against his bare back erasing the goose bumps gifted by the cold outside, he enjoyed the sting of the shower's warm water, his skin red from the heat when he stepped outside. Rewrapping an arm still healing from his earlier self-inflicted injury, he reached his "room." His bunk waited, and with the exhausting day, he was soon out, knowing he would be back in the familiar blackness of space when he next opened his eyes.

—Chapter 16—

"Welcome into my lair,
My sweetest little fly,"
Said the black widow,
With a glint in her eye.

—*Preamble to* Fly's Funeral

"FREAKIN' ostrich eggs! Our schedule! How can a storm keep us from leaving? I bet it's like this all winter here. Now they're telling me the comm sats are unreliable in storms like this, and I can't confirm or deny my delivery delay. For all I know, I'll lose this mining equipment delivery run to another ship. Freakin' jeepers!" Kratt threw himself around the cargo bay, the gravity unusual in this normally zero gee space. "Commerce is my paycheck! No wonder no one ever comes to this hellhole of a rock. They can't get off again."

Synrnn tuned out the distant sounds of Kratt's histrionics and focused on Rom'n lying in his bunk. This was her moment to enjoy, and she didn't intend to share it with anyone but the tale-bearer. Kratt and the rest of the day would just have to wait for the man at her feet to divulge his story of the night before.

"Yes, I hear him, Rom'n," she soothed. "There's nothing he can do. Just like the landing, the takeoff from this port is completely by remote. The only thing I get to play with is the part of the takeoff that occurs above the planet's viable ceiling. Now, tell me about that party." She sat on the shelf at the end of his bunk, her feet resting on either side of his legs. She worked them up under his blanket, remarking, "Much warmer."

"What parts?" He grinned, teasing her.

"The part that's *different*, that's the part I enjoy the most. Tell me that." She leaned over, resting her hands on her knees, her toes working the undersides of his legs.

"The houses were all rock, and they opened underground."

"Underground? Like a cave?"

"Yes and no. More like a roofed city. One with huge windows of ice in the ceiling."

"Windows of ice! I can barely imagine that. Windows of ice in the ceiling of the world. Go on." Her eyes twinkled with eagerness.

"Everyone talked in strange verb tenses, and they spoke even more strangely when it came to syntax. Then there was this old man. At first I thought him just a poor lost person. Soon I found he was an important man in the city. He introduced me to the most elegant old grandmother who must have been his lover many years in the past."

"Wonderful, Rom'n." When he didn't go on, she stretched out both feet, tickling him in the ribs with her toes until his self-control fled, and his eyes bled tears. Soon, he was curled into a laughing ball, pleading with her to let him continue.

"They wanted me to stay longer, but with the ship ready, I could hardly afford to do so." He shook his head. "Now I see I could have taken them up on their offer. But, to look at hindsight is to never look forward. I'm here now, and this is my home."

"Let's go rescue Kratt." She hopped off the bunk. "Spin the bottle might just do the trick. It's his favorite game."

"Sure," and Rom'n joined in, standing in one quick motion. He stretched and started forward, following her down the corridor.

THE FAMILIAR ding announced a message from IRaC, the information something she needed to convey.

"Synrnn, I am sorry to interrupt. A message has been received for Rom'n."

"Hey, IRaC," she shouted, glancing at Kratt sulking in the corner, the ploy of spin the bottle not his desired diversion after all. "Let's have it." She stepped back, panting, the racquetball narrowly returned.

"I am sorry, Synrnn. I must deliver the message to Rom'n, only. No one else can authorize its playback."

She stopped and looked at him. "Hm, Rom'n. Who knows you're on board?"

"Well," he pondered. "You and Kratt, and I did mention this ship to the old woman, but never which ship. I just let them know I had to be back to depart today."

"How many ships do you think are here?"

"Oops. Sorry."

"No harm done, kiddo. Let's see what they want."

He called out, "Message authorized, IRaC."

"Thank you, Rom'n. The message is as follows: *Ready to share? Reply requested.*"

"Is that all? IRaC, check for more."

"I am sorry, Rom'n. There is no more except for a return channel should you wish to reply."

He dropped onto the bay floor, running a hand through his hair, an expression of dismay on his face. "I wasn't exaggerating, I didn't think, when I said the old man was the most powerful person in the city. I guess the old grandmother must have her share of power, also." He looked at Synrnn, seeing Kratt on the far wall still sulking. "I did promise to share. However, I explained why I couldn't. There wasn't time, and everyone was busy with other things."

She came to sit beside him. "Well, we have to tell the boss. What to do? What to do? I think it isn't a pleasant option, no matter what path we take. The results will be the same. Hm." She leaned the back of her head against the wall, her eyes tracing the ceiling in thought. "You know, I've walked that ceiling more times than I've sat on this floor." She put one hand on his knee to help herself up. "It does no good to wait to throw out spoiled milk." She turned and called, "Hey, Boss, ready for some more good news?"

"IRAC, YOU ARE certain this transport will arrive for us as the message says?"

"Kratt, I am hooked in through the comm. I have an additional message that was received just a few moments ago. Your means of passage has arrived. You need to step outside now."

Synrnn reached to the door lock panel and placed her palm against it. With a twist, it began to cycle open, and she began yanking on her glove as it did. Stepping into the ship's exposed hangar bay, the exterior wall already open to the elements, she called to those still inside the ship, "Crikes, it's cold! I had no idea."

Rom'n grinned inside his headgear. "I tried to tell you. It's worse when the sun starts to go down."

Just ahead through the ice canopy's open doors, they could see outside, the swirling snow swept aside to reveal the lights of a transport settling onto the exterior, exposed landing area.

"Let's haul," Kratt yelled. With drifted snow kicking up from their running feet, the three made record time, the doors to the transport and the massive ice door to the enclosed landing area sealing at the same time.

As the craft's warmth washed his exposed skin, Kratt reached up and pulled his head coverings off. He looked around, obviously impressed. "This is like no ground transport I've ever been in."

Synrnn ran her hand over the unmanned consoles. They were filled with flashing indicators, power supply monitors, and cutting edge comm devices. Sitting in the unoccupied operator's chair, she looked out through the forward viewing window. "Hey, Kratt? Do you think this might be glassine?" She stood, reached forward, and tapped it. "By my word, I think it is." Running her hand over the surface of the seat, she looked at her two companions. "Animal hide? If it is, this is luxury beyond belief. This lady must be loaded."

"I tried to tell both of you. Let's find a seat. If this world is like IRaC described, we're headed way out. This ride may take a while, and I want to be rested. Who knows what it'll be like out there? One thing I know," Rom'n remarked, "this is their game, whatever it is. We might as well throw ourselves in the ring and have a good time."

The transport sped over the ground, the inside warm and comfortable, with all three finally peeled from their layers. As the ride progressed, unseen mechanisms made food and drink available, and the pleasantness of the journey was unequaled. Much of the trip's discussions centered around just what the old grandmother's personal world would be like. One thing the three of them knew was that they soon would find out whether they wanted to be there or not.

THE TRANSPORT SPED straight toward the side of the mountain. Below them was the flat, snow-littered surface of the unending wasteland known as the inland sea. Broad expanses of ice glittered among the windblown drifts.

It seemed a dream world.

The Sea of Revenge, Rom'n thought, remembering the old woman's words. Revenge against what? Or whom? He stood, alert for what was to come, trying to connect dots that his time in the city had littered throughout his thoughts. Only, they seemed too disparate to make any sense when he tried to string them together.

Synrnn whispered to herself, "If this baby doesn't slow down, we had better hope this is glassine. That's the only thing that'll hold if we hit the side of that mountain." She pointed directly ahead.

Kratt snored, the sensuousness of the seating surfaces irresistible to his needs. He had been a spacer all his life. When in transit, he'd said more than once, take the time you're given to use as your own, because you can't do anything about what you can't control, anyway.

"Yes!" Synrnn cried aloud, balling her hand in a victory fist. She pointed to a portion of the mountainside as it separated, the lighted interior of a cavernous hangar bay soon revealed. Much smaller lights up and down the mountain's snowy face indicated interior lighted spaces. "There's where we're going. Kratt's missing everything, just like always."

"Not this time, Synrnn." He kicked an unlaced boot at her, missing by half the transport. "I'm just resting my eyes."

"Good," she replied. "Now it's time to rest your snoring."

Rom'n laughed at them. "At least everything's back to normal. You two sound like old bonded people, and that's just what I love about all of this."

"You love all this, being trapped here on this transport?"

"Being a part of your ship, Kratt, and being involved in adventures with the two of you. I missed this before, and I never knew what I was missing. For a long time, all I knew was a woman."

Kratt and Synrnn both turned to look at him. Together they called out, "*Knew* a woman?" When Rom'n didn't seem to catch on, Synrnn explained it was an archaic religious term for copulation.

Rom'n's face warming, he worked his jaw and grinned. "From you two guys, I guess I have to expect that. How about this? I dreamed about a woman."

Synrnn laughed. "Now we're learning the real kiddo who lives in that skin."

"Hey, drop it. Deal?" He turned away, not quite ready to delve too deeply into that part of his past.

"For now, friend." Kratt stepped up and put a hand on his shoulder. "We'll pin you down after we return to the ship."

Rom'n hunched his shoulders. "That's what I'm afraid of."

"Men, I think we're going in. Look at that, will you? These walls are almost as thick as this transport is long. And look," Synrnn said, as the transport slowly spun, the nose now facing toward the closing door. "Wow! The power actuator arms closing the doors are enormous. Someone really wants this place to last."

All three friends turned as the door to the transport opened. A lightly jacketed figure was standing just outside.

"Rikard at your service. Just leave your weather gear,"

he told them. "It will be yours again when you return." He spun and began to walk. "Follow me, please."

Exiting the ship, a blast of warm air swept through the cavernous space. Synrnn pointed to a small stubby-winged craft designed to fly adequately in an atmosphere, yet gracefully in the emptiness of space. "Look at that, Kratt. That two-man you've been wanting? That has full deep-space capabilities. It's red, too. Don't drool, now." She laughed, the familiar joke soothing this unfamiliar situation.

Kratt slowly spun in a full circle as he walked, the ceiling and far walls catching his attention. "Look up there, Synrnn. What is that? Is that . . . nah, not a Cat-Trac? Gods, they've got a full-scale assembly and repair setup here. What else could anyone want? They could fit my ship in here, disassemble it, and never even take up any of the parking space."

Reaching the end of the trek, a door was held open for them, and they stepped inside.

—Chapter 17—

Tip #4 – In case of suspected frostbite, immerse affected appendage in warm water until circulation returns.

—Mountain Climbing for
Beginners, *p. 62*

THE SERVING MAN, Rikard, led the trio through a maze of corridors. All were massive, some crowded with furnishings and tapestries, and others barely more than simple hewn rock.

Rom'n leaned over to Kratt and Synrnn. "I'm lost. If they wanted to torture me, all they'd have to do is tell me to find my way back out again."

They grinned. "It is quite a place."

"I'd be dead before I found the food preparation area." When his two friends laughed, he continued, "I'm serious."

Turning into a wide hallway lined with elegant consoles, recesses, and niches, their guide stopped before a series of doorways. "You may rest in these rooms. They will be yours for the duration of your stay." The man promptly turned and strode down the hall.

"Wow," said Synrnn, walking up to one of the doors. "That sounds like we may be here awhile." She pushed the door open, touched a panel to trigger interior lighting, and paused, her surprise shown in her frozen gaze. "Open a door, guys. You'll be impressed." Leaving them to their own explorations, she left the door wide, stepping inside. "Wow, just wow. This is amazing."

Reaching out to run one hand along the polished rock wall, her fingers traced the myriad fossils of animals that must have lived at some time in this world's long history in the frozen sea they had crossed. The furniture was enormous, sized to a room that would engulf the entire living spaces of Kratt's ship. She walked to the far end and stood in front of a curtained wall. Grabbing the heavily embroidered fabric, she forced it aside, opening it up to a window that cut through the mountain wall. Stepping inside, she stood before a wall of military grade glassine, the surface turning clear when she reached out and tapped it. The near darkness outside glittered with the lights of other compounds far across the frozen water, the reflections on the icy surface leering a drunken grin at her.

She yelled, "I could like this life!" Running back to the hallway, she looked, finding two other doors standing open. She yelled for the two men. "Kratt! Rom'n!"

With a shout, both of them reached arms out of one of the doors, motioning for her to join them. Inside, she didn't immediately see her crewmates, but she saw personal facilities they could all three use and never get in each other's way. Turning to look for them, she stepped through yet another door. Inside, they were stroking their hands down lengthy rows of clothing, tailored either in a variety of sizes, or in styles that required no size. Seeing Rom'n disappear around a bend in the unbelievably long rack of garments, she ran her hand down the line of clothing. She stopped at one, imagining the fabric already against her skin.

"You know I'm not a fancy party girl, but I can see where this might be nice for a night or two. A chance to play before we go back out. Just to see how the other side lives, mind you."

"Don't get used to it, Synrnn."

"I know me, Kratt. The first time I *have* to do this, I'm out of here. It's only fun if I do it for fun. So, don't worry about me."

"That's the pilot that crews on my ship. I'm like you. Love it while we're here, and don't try to keep it when we're gone. Otherwise, it starts to keep you. Then, you're a groundie for sure."

A voice growled at them from inside the main room, its age apparent in its cracks and crevasses. "A groundie? Where did you get that term?"

Synrnn called out apologetically, "We didn't mean to offend. It's an old term where we come from. It means someone who lives on a planet and never gets into space."

"I know what it means." The voice walked in on them, driven forward by an old, very elegant-looking man, one obviously used to commanding others, and also, perhaps, used to being commanded. His eyes fell on Kratt and Synrnn. "It be one of our terms here. No one else on this world uses it. How be it you know it?"

"Spacers, ser," Synrnn coughed out.

"Private transport for hire," Kratt answered in turn.

"Rikard tells me there be a third in your party. Where be he?" He called loudly, "Young man, snap to! I wish to know of you. Your position?"

Stepping smartly from behind the rack of clothing, Rom'n drew himself to attention, the command in the voice recognizable from his military days; and he called out, "Military, ser. MegaCorp Military Arm."

The man whipped around to face him. He paused for a time, his eyes searching out the younger man's features. "Not possible," he whispered to himself. "It be as the old man said." He walked up and circled him, the young man's slender limbs still held at attention. "No," he repeated. "Your name?"

"Rezalton, ser. Rom'n. Underpriv't."

Then, with a sudden change of demeanor, the man put his hand to his chin and smiled. "I'll be spaced, and the cargo be ruined. Ha! Your companions, have they names, also?"

When he laughed, it broke Rom'n's posture, and he relaxed with a smile. "Yes, ser. Synrnn and Kratt."

The man offered a hand to him and shook heartily. "I like you, boy. I like the sound of you and the looks of you. Welcome aboard." Then he turned to the other two. "If you be the friends of this one here, you be the friends of me and my household for this night. Welcome." The man gave Kratt and Synrnn a bear hug, pulling them together in one swift motion. "Kornth be my name. Make yourselves at home. Mealtime be your own this night. Feel free to change. Wear whatever you like. These apartments be your home for as long as you stay. On the morrow we shall gather." Then, his demeanor darkening, the man muttered under his breath, "The sister returns, and we shall gather." With that, he turned and disappeared from the room as quickly as he had come.

"Rom'n, that was odd the way that man treated you when you said you were MegaCorp military," Kratt mused. He walked around the younger man. "What did he see in you that I don't? Hm. Pale skin and washed-out hair. Not that. Features too good looking to be on any real face. No, it can't be that. Well, that trim waistline. That surely impressed him. No, that means you're a picky eater. Synrnn, see anything that might have impressed that man? 'Cause I sure don't." Kratt turned to her with a grin on his face, then slapped Rom'n on the back. "I don't care what he saw, because you're ours, and we're not trading or selling. That's that. Let's go find me a room. Let's do that, shall we?" He stepped forward, trusting the others to follow.

Synrnn leaned forward to whisper to Rom'n, "He's even afraid of the dark. I think the lights might be off in his room, and he just wants company until he can find the switch."

Rom'n smiled as they stepped after Kratt, pulled forward in his wake.

263

"SYNRNN?" Rom'n stood outside the open door listening to the sounds of water inside.

"You found me. Is Kratt with you?"

"Just me."

"Well, get in here."

He walked in to see her floating in a sea of bubbles.

"You know the last time I did this?" She dropped under the surface of the water, coming up, her hair trailing over her face. Reaching her hands to sweep it back over her head, she blew out a blast of air. "Never! This is wonderful. I never thought I'd say it, but hot water, lots of suds, and room to go all the way under. This is the bath for me." Pushing bubbles aside and leaning to the edge of the enormous tub, she crossed her arms on the side, resting her head on her hands. "Come over here."

He walked over, kneeling in front of her, seeing the water drops clinging to her naturally brown skin, so unlike his own. Placing his white arms on the tub next to hers, he was pleased to see her gently run her fingers along the bandaging still covering his injury.

"How many days has it been?"

"Not all that many, but I don't even notice it anymore. It no longer slows me down at all."

"Good. We'll have the old Rom'n back once again." Her hand grasped his wrist as the water around her rippled at the motion. "You can count on it."

Where the suds moved with the ripples, he could just see a glimpse of her shoulder, a hint of bare flesh at her side, and deeper still, a leg, its length curled under her. At the remembrance of an old flame, that one-time lover of his, he paused, and he felt his pulse race with the intimacy of the moment. This woman had never betrayed him. Here she was: the water caressing the smooth brownness of her skin; her face and the caring visible there; her hand on his arm. He felt the man in him respond to her, and in that moment he was overwhelmed with desire. Just a signal from her, and he would gladly rip his clothes from his body and take her. As she looked up at him, tears formed in her eyes, and he was certain it was tenderness, or dare he speak it, love? Yet, when she spoke, he knew where he stood with her, where he had always stood.

"Rom'n, you know we love you. Kratt and I are both so proud of you. No matter what happens or what you decide, ever. We'd keep you with us always. I want you to know that. You've shown me how to believe in people again. You've shown me that maybe I can even believe in me again. We do love you. I love you. You will always be special to me." With that, she kissed the bandage on his arm, her lips' wet imprint still there as she dropped back into the water. She emerged on the other side, bubbles covering her head, blowing water to clear her mouth. "Go, Rom'n. Your room awaits. Mealtime awaits. Be ready or be hungry. And thanks! I'm so grateful you let me take this room with this enormous bathing tub. This is so much better than just having that massive window." With that, she dropped below the water again.

He pulled himself erect, ashamed, glad she wouldn't see how strongly he had been attracted to her, how he had wanted her, and would have taken her if she'd allowed him. He turned, walking out the door and to his room, directly to the massive curtained window overlooking the lake, and pushed his way through. Disgusted with himself, he began pulling his clothing off, one piece at a time, flinging each into a pile at his side. His reflection in the glassine mocked him as he did so, the beautiful backdrop of the sparkling lights across the frozen wasteland the perfect dichotomy for his rising repugnance with himself. Finally, totally exposed, the clothing Kratt and Synrnn had given him cast aside, he stood in the only thing he owned, his skin, hating himself for what he'd wanted to do, for what he still wanted to do. He stood in the darkened window, the sparkling lights all he could see, his reflection repulsive in his eyes, until the tears began to freeze on his face.

THE CURTAIN was drawn slowly back, and then it was jerked wide. Synrnn called into the room, "Kratt, he's here, and it's freezing in this window."

"In the window?" His voice echoed in the vastness of the space.

"Rom'n?" That was when she saw he was wearing nothing at all, his clothes piled on the floor. With alarm in her voice, she called, "Kratt, he's naked and freezing."

At her words, he began to shiver violently, then uncontrollably. "S-S-Synrnn," his voice chattered between clenched teeth. "F-f-freezing." He could get nothing else out.

"Help me get him to the bath," she called to Kratt. "He needs to be warmed, and now. Gods, I'm glad I didn't drain the water." As they began to move, she wrapped her arms around him and rubbed his back rapidly to increase his circulation.

"Let's pick him up." Kratt reached for his legs, and they wrapped arms around him, stumbling into the adjoining room.

"C-c-cold. I'm s-s-so cold." Rom'n's voice chattered.

"Hush. Let's get you taken care of. Then we'll talk."

Slipping him into the warmth of the tub, they held him up until he could sit on his own. Reaching into the water, they massaged his arms and legs, his skin regaining color slowly, eventually turning pink with the heat. Life finally returning to his face, they relaxed and pulled their hands from the water, drying them on towels from around the tub. Synrnn placed her towel across the lip of the tub, sitting on the edge, her eyes on Rom'n as he gently moved with the settling motion of the water.

"Rom'n." She reached out and touched him.

"Please don't." Tears started down his face.

She withdrew her hand, turning to look at Kratt. He shrugged. "What is it? You have to tell us. We can help you, if you'll let us. We've been here for you, and we'll always be here for you. You know that. You're part of us, and nothing can break us apart."

"I'm so ashamed. I don't deserve to be with you, either of you." His eyes closed as sobs began to wrack his body.

"It can't be that bad. We love you. You can trust us."

"All of us," Kratt started, "are a team. We're you, and you're us. One, Rom'n. That's us. A team."

"Gods!" He sank under the water, bubbles rising from his mouth.

"Synrnn, pull him up." He came up sputtering, with Kratt barking, "Spit it out, boy."

"I wanted you, Synrnn. Just then when you were here in your tub. I sat there and wanted you." His sobs starting back up, he sank under the water again.

Synrnn and Kratt looked at each other and smiled.

Pulling him up again, Synrnn held Rom'n's face in both her hands. "Look at me. You didn't try to take me, did you?" She watched him shake his head no. "That's what's important. If you were a terrible person, you wouldn't have walked away. Crikes!" She dropped on her knees and pulled him to her, getting wet no longer a concern, and gripped him in a bear hug, as he slowly wrapped his arms around her and began to hug her back. She whispered so only he could hear, "Oh, I love you so much. You didn't even *do* anything. You just thought it, and yet you felt so bad you've beat yourself up over it. Gods, you are a good person. When you were born, no one else wanted any, so they stuffed all the goodness into you."

With that, he really hugged her back. "Thank you. I'm lucky to have friends like you and Kratt."

She smiled as she looked at Kratt. She knew the truth. They were the lucky ones.

—Chapter 18—

*The police officer knelt by the small boy
and smiled. "Strangers can be your friends,
but only if your parents introduce them to
you first."*

*The boy looked up at his mother and father
with a question in his eyes. When they
smiled and nodded, he turned to the officer,
"Will you be my friend?"*

*The policeman laughed and patted him on
the head. "Of course I'll be your friend."*

*—Public service broadcast
c. 1967 A.D. old-Earth*

"HEY, THERE he is." Synrnn called to Rom'n as she
walked up to him. Dressed in the sharp lines of clothing
bearing a military cut, his paleness drew a sharp contrast
to the black of the cloth, truly bringing out the man he

was. "Nice." She brushed the fabric just to see how it felt against his body.

He dropped his eyes, still tinged with embarrassment about his earlier admission. "I'm so sorry, Synrnn."

"It's okay. I found it sweet and touching. Don't feel bad."

"Um, Kratt's here." He glanced over her shoulder.

She turned around. "Ah, Boss, look at you." Dressed in the soft drapes of an old-Earth formal suit, he could pass for a prosperous businessman.

"What do you think, Synrnn, Rom'n? Do you think this is me?" He laughed. "Even though I could never be a businessman if I tried."

"It does suit you, Boss. You have the build for it." Synrnn smirked, teasing. "Middle years, thickening a bit around the waist . . ."

"Hey, not so far. Some of that may be true . . . well, maybe more than some, but don't rub it in." He laughed again. "Rom'n, my boy, what do you think?"

"Nice, Kratt. You made a good choice." He walked up and pulled on the bottom of the overjacket where it wrapped around the older man's waist. "I think this goes underneath, though."

Kratt looked down, his eyes widening in surprise. "Why, I think it does. I do believe it does." He reached down, pulling the fastening strap from the waistband of the baggy trousers and swapping the layers. "Why, thank you. That does fix the look completely."

"Boss, our boy here just demonstrated some previously unknown sartorial skills. He keeps coming up with this magic that springs from gods know where. Should we keep him?" Synrnn grinned.

"I guess we'll have to," Kratt teased. "After all, there's no girlfriend around here to dump him on."

Rom'n shook his head at the teasing. "Which way, guys? I've got hunger pangs kicking in, and I suspect the torture phase is about to set in." He stepped forward to peer through the most accessible doors and around the first corner, and then he shrugged. "Nothing here to eat that I can see."

Synrnn pursed her lips. "I had hoped there would be someone here to guide us. Perhaps the man who met us in the landing area, Rikard, or even the old man we met in our rooms. Kornth, I believe he called himself." She sat on a bench perfectly sized to a recess in the wall. "Perhaps we should just wait?"

"You know, they can find us if they need us, wherever we are, and I've sat around too long. I'd like to explore. I say we wander the halls of this retreat, compound, or whatever they call it, and let the mealtime find us." Kratt turned to his two companions. "Are you two game, or do we just sit here and slowly starve, turning into mummies buried in the cold mountains of a distant, rarely visited world?"

Synrnn laughed. "There's your flair for the dramatic. How it suits your fancy clothes! I think you could become the businessman, Kratt. You become a good fit for whatever situation you're in. You may be the ultimate chameleon. How nice to know I've been crewing under such an adaptable man!"

271

"Chameleon? I've never heard that word. Old-Earth?" Rom'n raised his eyebrows.

"Ha! Not even close. It's a military term."

"You were in the military?" Kratt stopped. "Talk about not knowing things about someone."

"I guess I should explain that one. No, I wasn't in the military. However," and she winked at Rom'n, "there was this guy, and he was some guy." She cut Kratt a look. "This was before I signed with you, Boss. This man was Special Forces over on Tiaget's Reserve. Aiehhh! He was a man. No slight intended, Rom'n. You're my favorite little brother. He was a man. Arms like tree trunks. Hands like slabs of the finest animal flesh." Synrnn closed her eyes. "Ah, just to remember. And best of all . . ."

"Um," Kratt cleared his throat, "your baby brother's standing right here."

Rom'n smiled, enjoying her reverie.

She shook her head, opening her eyes. "Oh, sorry. It was just a very good memory." She paused, a smile growing on her face.

Kratt prompted, "Chameleon?"

"Right, right. They have this vehicle, all-purpose. I do mean all-purpose. It's only about the size of a two-man, but it does everything. You'd expect it to navigate in both atmosphere and space, and it does. But it converts to a medcenter with supplies to perform field surgery, interactive, personality-assisted field surgery that even a non-com can administer. It carries food supplies for four for two sevendays. Somehow they've also managed to get multiple rounds of high-speed impact weapons squirreled away in that tiny space. It can even dump everything in an emergency, becoming an eight-man transport. That ship's where the word comes from. That military vehicle was called a Chameleon."

"We never had anything like that," Rom'n remarked.

"That you knew of," Kratt laughed.

"Probably you're right. There were bound to be a lot of things I never learned of, need-to-know and all those other chain-of-command concepts we lived under. Sometimes that was nice, though. We only worried about what was right under our noses. The rest was someone else's concern."

"And that's why you were floating in that cryo pod for nearly four centuries. Do you really have no idea what happened to your ship?" Synrnn frowned. "I've been puzzled over that since we picked you up."

"None. But it was big, whatever it was. The whole ship was under attack. All at once, it seemed. I mean, we were moving out the next day, the operation complete." He shrugged his shoulders.

"Well, that's why I like Kratt's ship so much." She gave him a nod. "If I'm going to blow up in space, I at least want to know just why."

"Hey," Kratt interjected. "Blow up? In my ship?"

"I'm just teasing, Boss. It's all in fun."

"I've got a good ship. The both of you know that—"

"A good ship, Kratt," Rom'n interrupted. "However, I'm not getting any less hungry. Let's go." He started off. "Of course, I'm the guy in the story that dies looking for the food preparation area, my torture complete." He grinned. "You people really want to follow me?"

"If one of us starves, we all starve together."

They all three chuckled at the image of three starving people found in one of these sumptuous rooms. Turning a corner at the end of their hallway, they were surprised to find one of the niches contained a lift with a palm pressure plate beside it.

"Do you think," Synrnn questioned, "it might let us on?"

"Can't hurt to try," Kratt offered. He watched as Rom'n strode up, turned to face them with a grin, and slapped his palm to the pressure plate. He turned to the controls just as the pressure plate lighted up a pale orange.

A voice softly chimed, "Please continue to hold your hand firmly against the sensor. Accessing data banks for approval now." He held still as the panel changed to green. "Match found. Welcome, Rom'n Rezalton, Underpriv't, MegaCorp Military Arm. You may remove your hand. Full access to 'de Gaso-Fratenni laHolc'm Compound is now granted. Please enjoy your stay."

He turned to face Synrnn and Kratt. He threw his palms in the air and laughed. "Guys, I guess we're in. Let's see where this takes us." As the others joined him at the lift, he spoke aloud. "Voice command availability?"

"Please place your hand on the sensor to activate voice command." He did so, the voice prompting him further, "Please state your name."

"Rom'n Rezalton."

"Identity not confirmed."

He looked at his friends, puzzled. "Um, not confirmed?" he called to the walls.

"Please try again. State your name."

"Let me see." Then he smiled, copying the way the voice had identified him earlier. "Rom'n Rezalton, Underpriv't, MegaCorp Military Arm."

"Voice command confirmed. Please enjoy your stay."

He chuckled. "At least there's something I'm good for." The lift opening at his command, the three stepped aboard, Rom'n grinning broadly, the other two with puzzled looks on their faces.

Kratt and Synrnn glanced at each other. Leaning in, Kratt whispered, "Rom'n in the data banks of this compound as a MegaCorp underpriv't?"

Hunger, however, won out, diverting their attention as Rom'n tried again.

"Take us to a food preparation area or dining hall."

"Will the galley be satisfactory?" The unseen voice offered them a close option.

"Absolutely! We are starving!"

By the time the doors to the lift closed, all three people inside were smiling broadly, food on their minds.

THE THREE SAT at a counter made of the same material as the walls of their apartments. They laughed, shared foodstuffs from the many open containers scattered among them, and they felt truly well fed for the first time in many cycles.

"Can you imagine this, Kratt?" Synrnn threw her arm in an arc around the massive space. "When that lift asked if the galley would be acceptable, I was expecting, you

275

know, a real galley, not a criking food preparation center for feeding a thousand. I could see maybe what, fifty of whatever those men are called, cooks, no, chefs. That's it. Chefs. I could see fifty of them in here at one time, right now, and we still wouldn't need to move to give them room."

"True, this is a trifle larger than our reprocessor galley. Just a bit."

"Guys," Rom'n mused, "the whole time I've been here, I've been wondering." He took a bite of something from a container on the counter. "Back in the city, it was cold. The only really warm place I visited was the Dóme's residence. Could the city itself have been heated by the people's body warmth?"

"Just with body heat? Nothing else?"

"Yeah. Body heat." He thought for a moment, puzzled. "Maybe the residences I passed possibly had some form of heat, but not the public spaces. In that meeting hall where I met the Dóme, there were lots of people, probably the whole city, I think, plus lots of people from places like this. All those people must have brought the temperature up some."

Kratt nodded. "People do produce quite a bit of body heat. You could be right. Your point?"

"Well, this place. We're not seeing many people, yet it's warm as a summer day in here. I'm sure being in the mountain helps, the rock providing insulation, but when I was on the other side of those drapes back in that apartment, even with the glassine, it got cold really fast. They have to have some form of auxiliary heat here."

"I see your point." Synrnn leaned in, one finger tapping the surface in front of her for emphasis. "When we came in, the side of the mountain opened up. The cold had to have come in with us. Yet, no more than a few moments after we saw the doors close, it was warm in there. I remember our guide telling us to leave our warm outer gear, and there was this wave of warmth that rolled across us as we stepped from the transport."

"See?" Rom'n's face showed the excitement of a shared realization. "The heating plant for this place must be enormous. The cost would be enough to run a small city. Yet, the city itself is left unheated. Maybe it's the wealthy versus the poor, but I'm thinking not. There's some reason these people live out here far away from everything."

Kratt laughed. "It's sure not for the scenery. It doesn't seem to me you'd be on this *planet* if you cared about the scenery." He laughed again. "What are you thinking, Rom'n?"

"Geothermals. There have to be ground-based heat sources for this place to maintain these temperatures in this environment."

"So, I don't have to worry about the power I use with all the hot baths I intend to take?" Synrnn laughed.

"Probably not." After a pause, Kratt chuckled. "I'd be curious to find out, especially since the sea out there is frozen. You'd think geothermals would keep it liquid, unless they had to drill down far into the planet's crust, and that'd take the credits. Plenty of them. It seems we only thought they were rich before."

"Maybe they did all this a little bit at a time. Everything seems polished and well maintained," and she glared at Kratt, clearing her throat insinuatingly, "even though this place looks centuries old. Clearly these people are loaded, but maybe not as much as we think."

"Enough to have a two-man. Besides, who said my ship isn't well maintained?" He frowned as he pushed the last of the food containers away.

"No one." She laughed. "I just hinted."

Rom'n stood, gathering containers. He began looking around, holding them in his hand. "I don't see a recycle slot anywhere."

Synrnn laughed. "Hey, even I know this one. That compound I grew up in was like this." She took a quick glance at the immensity of the "galley" and went on. "Well, not exactly like this, but we didn't have recycle slots, either. We recycled in a very different way. Let me show you." She got up and pointed him towards a depression in the counter. Rooting around, she found pressure points causing water to shoot from an opening in the wall. One she pushed dispensed a cleaning solution. As the suds began to fill the depression, she indicated that Rom'n's load should be placed in the sudsy water. "Now comes the recycle part. You move the dishes around in the water, removing the food residue with your hands. Set them aside to dry when you're finished. Then they can be used over again."

"You're sure about this?" He looked at her hard. After a pause, he laughed self-consciously. "I'm trying to decide if this is a joke."

"Absolutely not. I did this for the first two decades of my life. This time it's your turn, because two decades were enough for anyone." She reached over and pushed up his sleeves, gently patting the arm wrapped in its cushioning bandage as she whispered, "Take care with this," and then grinned as he sank his hands into the suds. When she went and sat beside Kratt again, she whispered to where only he could hear, "Better him than us."

Kratt laughed. "You're right about that, Synrnn. That you certainly are."

—Chapter 19—

Trim woman showing off her massive
diamond ring: 'It's beautiful, but the man it
goes with is like a boomerang. No matter
how far away I send him, he always comes
right back.'

—*Quip from* Marry for
Money – It Lasts Longer

"OH, THIS IS COLD. Rom'n, tell me again. Why do we have to wait here?" Synrnn tugged the fur-lined wrap closer to her face. "With these doors open, the ouside just jumps in and bites us." Her red-tinged face peered from its furry cave.

"Be tough, Synrnn. Look at Kratt over there, his hands glued to that two-man. If he could just get inside, he'd already be gone. That isn't one of those Chameleons, is it?" He glanced at her, her head shaking no. Then, he hunched his shoulders inside his jacket, its lining obviously not designed for such punishing conditions. "I could certainly stand for them to arrive. An extra day in the city for them, and we were sent here immediately. What was the rush for us?"

"A couple of nice warm baths. Some good food with you guys was a pleasant treat, and then there was watching you 'recycle' those food containers." She grinned beneath her layer of furs. "I love you too, Synrnn. Say it, Rom'n. Come on, it's only five words." When he looked at her, his pale skin nearly blue, she laughed.

"Too c-c-cold, S-S-Synrnn." His teeth had begun to chatter, and he stood as close to her as he could get. "N-n-nicer." He looked at her and smiled.

She pointed. "There, I see something. Is that them?"

"Y-y-yes. G-g-get K-K-Kratt."

As the massive transport swung into the open hangar, the doors began to cycle shut, the immediate rush of warm air settling back over the freezing trio. Kratt, finally noticing, waved, pointed to the smaller ship, and grinned, as he began to run back to join the other two.

"I want one of those, just like that," he yelled. "Just like that, color and all." He glanced at Rom'n hopefully, jumping when he reached Synrnn and she hit him.

"Don't you even, Kratt. Don't you even," she hissed.

With a sheepish look, he whispered to her, "You can't kill hope. He can always say no."

"But he won't. You know that, so don't take advantage."

Standing together, they watched the man who'd met them the night before exit the domicile and stride toward them. His arm carrying a cloth and a tray of glasses, he stopped just before the transport.

"He was right," Rom'n said. "Look at him. He has this down to an art. He's not even cold." He chuckled. "I'll listen to him next time."

"If there is a next time," Synrnn added.

As the door to the transport slid aside, it was clear the sumptuousness of this one far outstripped the one they'd traveled in. Inside, the travelers were making merry, unconcerned with the waiting lackey poised patiently outside their craft.

"Rom'n, step forward and see if you find anyone you know." Synrnn poked the man at her side.

"The old man, Cerennt'te. I already see him. I don't see the old grandmother. Perhaps we should wait here until they exit."

Just then the lackey, Rikard, motioned Rom'n forward. He handed him the tray of glasses, pulling a bottle out of his cloth.

"The Dóme and her guests will require additional refreshment before exiting. Please enter. She will want to see you again. The brother has said so. I will carry the bottle to fill the glasses."

Entering the sumptuous surroundings, finding the travelers engaged in reverie, Rom'n and the lackey wandered unnoticed, proffered drinks taken without a look, the thanks murmured without thought. As the Dóme reached for a glass, Rom'n caught her eye.

"You scoundrel." She paused and smiled, her long fingers finally taking the glass, anyway. "You have played the trick on us. You be not my man, Rikard, the one I expected to see. Come, sit. Put those aside. We rest before making our way to more comfortable environs."

"My friends, Dóme. They wait outside." He felt awkward and out of his depth in this gathering, remembering his first stumbled words with the elderly woman, and he phrased his comments neutrally. "We hoped to greet you as you arrived. We waited in the cold, not knowing how to follow the rules of this place."

The Dóme turned to her man. "Rikard, you let them wait outside while the ship entered?"

"They insisted, mos. I did try to dissuade them."

She looked at Rom'n for confirmation. Her face relaxed when he corroborated the man's story.

"We wanted to make a good impression. I see now we made a foolish one." He dipped his head to her. "My friends, Dóme? May I rejoin them until you and your friends are ready to exit the transport?"

At that she stood, finally giving in to what he wanted. "My boy, of course you may. Better yet, they may join us at any time. They should not be left out. Others, listen to me. We have new visitors. Please welcome them." She handed her glass to another and clapped her hands, then casually gathered her drink and smoothly reseated herself.

Rom'n motioned to Kratt and Synrnn. As they entered, the lackey, Rikard, stepped to the door to take the fur coat from Synrnn.

"Dóme, my friends." Rom'n motioned with one arm, instinctively giving a small bow.

"Come in. You be welcome to my home. I understand you met my brother last eve. A most unfortunate event, I be sure!"

A titter of laughter ran through the occupants seated in the transport.

"He seemed most welcoming."

"Welcoming, you say?" Laughing, the old grandmother, Dóme laHolc'm, appearing both somewhat inebriated as well as instantly deferred to, spoke to the crowd. "These be the ones who so recently tried to take my new friend from me." She turned back to them, brushing one finger along Rom'n's jaw. "Ah, it be good you would stay and keep him company. He should not be left alone. One of our world's beautiful girls will perhaps take his heart, and he will be gone, fleet as the wind." She held her glass out for a toast, her laughter echoed by the others around her.

Kratt, grinning, looked at Synrnn. "Did she mention beautiful girls? I could get to like this woman."

"Not too quickly, Kratt," Synrnn whispered, with a smile of her own. "There may be unseen sharp edges. Also, soon she may be in her grave."

He leaned closely to her, his wink to her alone. "Perhaps. Just perhaps. Maybe so much the better."

She laughed as they took a proffered seat. "You would, wouldn't you?"

"Synrnn, Kratt?" They turned their heads to see Rom'n standing beside a stooped old man, his white hair a thin cloud of fog on his head. "This is my friend, Cerennt'te Nijenhaus."

"Loud, please, in conversing with me you must speak. All this noise they do." The old man's eyes crinkled in amusement. He turned to Rom'n. "Needing your company, the Dóme be." He motioned with his gnarled hand. "Go now. Your company she desires." He shook his head knowingly. "Keep these in line I will. Go."

He turned to those in front of him, motioning for room, and it suddenly appeared, the old man stepping in as if the immediate and unquestioned accommodation was no more than he deserved.

Rom'n turned to his hostess. "Dóme laHolc'm." He held her proffered hand, her skin thin in his. Her extreme age struck him anew, more in the touch than in her manner.

"My young man." She nodded her head at him in response.

"You went to great lengths to keep me here. Why? You and I have never met before, and under the course of normal events, never would. May I know the reason?"

"Your answer will come. You will see and know." She riveted him with that striking gaze that had so drawn the attention of the crowd while in the city. "You be meant to share this moment. That be enough for now." She stood. "Friends and others, come. We must find the meal that awaits. I will lead."

And that she did.

"RIKARD WAS right to suggest we dress in the best." Kratt looked around at the grandness of the stylized and very formal meal room, the two large tables that filled it crowded with guests. "We didn't find this place last night, that's for sure."

"I suspect," Rom'n suggested, "the lift would only take us where we were supposed to go." He turned to the old man. "Cerennt'te, is that so?"

The old man turned one eye to him, carefully draping an elbow across the back of his chair. "Surprised, I should be, for you the permissions from the house to get. Somehow, yet I be not. The same as he from long ago, you be."

"What do you mean, my friend? The same as who?"

"Many times I came, and never with the house did I get to speak. Always her. Never to me did the walls listen." He turned his head back and forth as if searching through his past for a long forgotten confidence. "It be true, this name you be called?"

"Yes." He grinned. "It that so strange?"

Cerennt'te replied as if the answer made a real difference in things. "No, not at all, and yes, very much."

Rom'n laughed. "Cerennt'te, I cannot understand what you're about, but I do know you're someone I enjoy having around. Thank you." He leaned to the old man, whispering, "Just a bit ago, I caught a glimpse of a girl coming in to sit at the other table. I didn't see her in the city or earlier on the transport, and I would have remembered. She somehow looks very familiar. You might know her."

Cerennt'te smiled and whispered, "I be the one. I still be him." His eyes danced as he turned his voice to Rom'n. "In the hair, dark she be, and in the face, fair?"

"You know her?"

"Only such as you be whom she needs."

"I would know more of her, whatever you say. Will I get to see her again, perhaps even meet her?"

286

"It must be, my boy. It must be." The old man reached out and pulled Rom'n's hand to him. He stroked the palm, studying the fingertips as he did so. Then he looked up at his face. The old man's eyes glistened with moisture. "Can real, you be?" A tear rolled down his face. "Found you, I did. Come, you have. Never were you real, did I think."

"I'm here. And I certainly think I'm real." He smiled at the old fellow he had come to enjoy.

Cerennt'te looked around the room, the eating finished, and people slowly moving to entertainments unseen. Seeing the Dóme engrossed in a conversation of her own, he stood. "With me, come. You must. Quickly."

With surprising haste for such an old man, they fled the room, a disguised door silently letting them through, with only the eyes of Kratt and Synrnn following their exit.

"WHERE ARE you taking me?" Rom'n was surprised at the vast spaces they traversed, although he knew he shouldn't be. The rooms back in the domicile were enormous.

"Beauties be the laHolc'm clan. Desired by many. Choosing for life, seldom." The old man pulled him down passageways and corridors. Reaching an end, the wall presented a pressure panel to which the old man pressed Rom'n's palm. When the light flashed green, a sharp intake of breath shook the old man. "True, it be," he whispered.

The wall slipping aside, they entered a place more familiar to Rom'n. The metal of the corridors taking them deep into the mountain reminded him of his familiar home aboard his old ship. Soon he saw a great cavern, holding what must be the substantial power plant driving this place.

"Cerennt'te, I saw evidence of other compounds across the frozen lake. Do they have their own power plants? This one seems massive enough to power them all."

"Here in this place, all the power be." The old man pulled at Rom'n's arm, attempting to hurry him along.

"Wait, please." Rom'n, beginning to feel played, and not at all happy with the sensation, refused to go farther without an explanation, and he demanded, "Is all this the Dóme's?"

The old man nodded. "Wealth's source, it be, to be traded for credits. Much power it gives the Dóme. Uses it harshly, she does." He grabbed Rom'n's arm again. "Come. Missed soon we will be."

"I thought there must be something like this." Rom'n smiled in satisfaction. At Cerennt'te's insistent tug, he pushed him for additional answers. "Where are we going?"

"See, you must. Follow," and the old man was away, no longer waiting for Rom'n. "Come," he called, motioning with his hand.

Going under stone archways and down great stairs past massive installations of industrial machinery, Rom'n could see they must be snaking the back way to some place the old man had been before. His hurry was great, his reason unclear, and Rom'n followed, even in his youth finding it tiring to keep up.

"IF IT BE you, then this you must do," the old man whispered, his eyes staring at the pressure plate lock beside the massive door. "Now." He reached to take Rom'n's hand to place it there himself.

"No." He backed away. It had become clear to him that they really shouldn't be down here, and he didn't want to be forced into creating a situation that might get Kratt and Synrnn in hot water. He liked his companion, but his behavior had become disconcerting. "Tell me, first. What is this about?" He saw the pleading in the old man's eyes.

"Please." Cerennt'te's eyes bled tears that seemed as the dreams of lost youth and lost love. "For me, for you. Understand, you will. Answers be inside. Answers you need."

Hesitating only for a moment longer, Rom'n relinquished his reservations and held out his hand. The old man pressed his palm to the plate, the panel glowed green, and the giant door swung aside. Stepping into the room, clearly a vault, the old man paused. "Only one time in here I be. Remember one thing, I do."

As they traversed the space, Rom'n saw Cerennt'te as a young man. His visage graced a painting stored along the wall, and at his side, his companion was a young Dóme Elussie'san. Her unlined face tugged at his memory, the connection one that he hesitated to make. It was an impossible one, and for that reason, he dismissed it. One thing came through clearly in the painting. He had been correct in his earlier determination. They had been lovers when this was done. As they moved forward, he saw a series of

289

older Dóme Elussie'sans, each with a different man next to her. A series of lovers. Poor Cerennt'te. He must have been but the first in a long line.

Suddenly excited, the old man pulled Rom'n hard. "This," he hissed to him. "Was not wrong, this memory of mine. Here." As he pulled him to view his find, he turned to him. "Hear the story, you must. Tell it to you, she will not." His eyes glanced to the ceiling and the rock-carved compound above it. "Told it to me when threatened to leave, I did."

Rom'n saw pride on the man's face when he said that, as if that had been a victory against something very strong, indeed. The old man pointed at a blackened and cracked stack of ID cards and chips resting in a clear case. Rom'n reached in to take them out as the old man started his story.

"The First Grandmother's, they were. Had them with her, she did, when she came . . ."

THE BEAUTIFUL WOMAN in the undergen'l's uniform stood rigid, her fury barely contained. She held the Neuro-Shok in her hand, the power on, as she watched through the glassine. How dare CaptGen'l Willane Bofsky take over *her* job! She excelled at this. How dare he! She had found no answers, because there were none. Even this last man had none to give.

She slammed the NeuroShok back into the weapons cabinet, uncaring if it were thumbed off or not, her anger driving her hard. Forcing others out of her way, she drove herself at a faster and faster pace through the huge ship.

Boarding a lift, she stood alone, others unwilling to enter with her, the solitude her preferred choice. Crossing her arms across her chest, her hand jarred a pocket, driving the contents deep into the side of her breast.

"Ah, at least I have these," she crowed with satisfaction. Slipping the items from their place of safety, she flipped through them with increasing pleasure, their very presence in her hands easing the sting of the captain's betrayal. Finally, reaching one, she spat, "Rezalton!" As she clenched her teeth, she growled out a dire warning, "You and all the others I've come to despise, I'll ruin you. I will *ruin* you. These copies of your service records will soon be altered, and the new ones entered in the data-banks. You'll be court-martialed and sent to Rant, if you're lucky. By the gods, I hope you're not." Throwing her head back against the lift wall, her eyes moist with the emotions broiling inside of her, she abruptly slipped the items back into the pocket.

Exiting the lift, the ship unexpectedly and violently shifted under her feet, the overhead lights flickering off and back on. Klaxons precipitously assaulted her ears, and a voice brayed impossible instructions to the occupants of the great vessel.

"Evacuate ship. This is not a drill. Emergency escape pods now cycling online."

Jerked from the lift's angry reverie into her soldier's well-trained efficiency, her petty revenges pressed aside, she immediately realized the ship must be under attack. From what, she had no idea. Even so, the obvious must be admitted, and she looked for anything she might use as a weapon.

Loping down the corridors, the panels on either side of her sliding into the ceiling, exposing the emergency escape pods, the ship gave another jolt, and the lighting went dead, the escape pods on this level only partially exposed and useless.

Her eyes adjusting to the dimness of the emergency lighting glowing around her, she darted around a corner to continue to the nearest weapons bay. The thudding pops of distant explosions began to resound around her when the floor suddenly ripped itself apart and opened up a chasm directly under her feet. Flame billowed out. Amid a searing blast of heat, she was cruelly flung to the level below, landing hard, one leg bent and twisted grotesquely. Pain shot through her face. Groaning in agony, she reached a hand to her cheek, only to have the skin come away in her fingers.

Looking around her, she recognized dead and motionless troops blasted by the explosion. Her eyes danced along the wall. Every emergency pod on this level had cycled on, the access panels fully retracted. Too bad no one had survived to use them. She smirked in gloating superiority at the irony when unimaginable waves of agony coursed through her body, the damage from the fall finally surging over her in a massive breaker of blinding pain. Dragging herself to the nearest pod, its surface her support, she forced herself to her feet, balancing on her one good leg. She groaned in the blue light from the open pod and quickly glanced away, cursing the fools who were weak and had let such a cowardly device be installed on her magnificent cruiser. To use an escape pod was to run. Only fools ran from battle, and she was no fool.

However, the decision was made for her. With a mighty thump, the floor of the corridor rocked upwards, knocking her off balance and tumbling her into the pod, the contents of her pocket still intact. Sensing an occupant, the pod sealed itself, and within two seconds was a projectile moving with twenty gees of velocity away from the ship.

ROM'N'S HEART beating fast, he held the items. He looked at the lined and tear-streaked face of the old man. "Dóme laHolc'm told you this story?"

"Years ago, many. Lovers, we were. Wanted to tell me, she did not." His eyes drifted to the floor. "Love her still, I do."

"I remember the Dóme mentioning something about the First Grandmother back in the city, but it was just in passing. At the time, it seemed more of a jest than a real story. From what you say, she was indeed this person." He felt as if a hand crushed his chest, gripping him tightly, and the words fell from him in a rush. It was the story of one of his crewmates. It could have been his, except for Redzik. "What happened to her?"

"Meanness. Crippled in leg and scarred in face. The First Grandmother hated everyone, she did. Had only these. Not a man wanted her, until one day the raiders came. Cruel they be. Women and sometimes men, even in the streets they took. Especially the children, if they be big enough. Summer then it be. About the disfigurement, they cared not. That winter a girlchild be born. Carrying the laHolc'm line girlchilds now be, and a strong line it be. Lucky the man a laHolc'm girl gets." Cerennt'te paused, his voice taking on a darker timbre. "Lucky for a time." He glanced up with tears in his eyes. "For some, lucky a lifetime."

"What about a name? Did you get the First Grandmother's name from the Dóme? Do you know who she was?" He squeezed the items in his fist, wondering if this really could have been a crewmember from his long-ago ship. The events of the story, and to have arrived on this world in a cryo pod. Could this person be that connection to his past?

And yet, with a sense of fate kicking him to the ground once again, Rom'n accepted that this First Grandmother had died long ago. Even if she had survived the attack that destroyed his ship, there could be no real connection. The years in between were too great. He reached to place the ID cards and chips back in the container.

Cerennt'te wailed, "See, did you?"

"What, Cerennt'te?" Rom'n let his eyes rove the myriad things gathered together in great excess in the room, not understanding.

"Look, boy. Be you dim? Look!"

Indeed, there on one of the cards was his own picture, and underneath it the words, *Rom'n Rezalton, Under-Priv't, MegaCorp Military Arm.*

He looked up at the old man, his own eyes already burning with the strength of memories old and worn to others, yet only a handful of shipboard cycles gone to him.

294

Holding the cards, finally understanding what they meant, his reality dissolved from under his feet, and to his heart, it was centuries earlier. Only one person would have carried these cards. Ma'jene had made it to this world, just as he had.

Then reality gripped his heart once again, roaring through his mind with untenable ferocity. She might have made it off the ship, but she was dead long ago on this lonely world. In just one day, he had seen her legacy savagely exposed. It was in everything Cerennt'te did and said.

Rom'n whispered sadly, "Your anger was with you to the end, Ma'jene. The cruelty you washed across my life was one you must have burned with to your death." His fingers shifted the cards, his name and those of others he readily recognized held in his hand. "I could have loved you, and I did love you all those years. Somehow I looked past the cruelty, never realizing that the cruelty was you. You never loved me back. Now I accept that you couldn't love me back." He closed his eyes and let the burning flood his face.

He also saw the disaster that Ma'jene's cruelty had foisted upon an entire world, what her bequest to these people had become, and he was mortified to imagine he had worshipped her once. His love had been no more than a dark stain of desire for a woman who knew only how to hate, and it had chased him across the centuries. It was a desire that had brought shame on his head, and it was only now exposed to the scrutiny of reality. In that brilliant instant of clarity, the centuries-old cancer that had eaten at his heart seared itself from his life. The tears that burned his face destroyed forever that black desire as a focused laser vaporizes the accumulated residue of years of abuse. With a new and uncompromising level of sureness that only one reborn can know, he cast her memory from him, seeing her with the glasses of long-ago desire ripped from his eyes.

Cerennt'te, oblivious to the new sense of purpose flooding the man at his side, grabbed Rom'n's arm, pulling his thoughts back to the room.

"See, you do. This be you. Knew it, I did, seeing you there." He pulled Rom'n's free hand to him, running his old, gnarled finger across the younger man's open palm and fingers. "This hand be one she held long ago. Only at the end, the first granddaughter's hand, it be said, did she hold." With his other hand, the old man covered the items Rom'n still held. "Placed these items inside, she did. To the first granddaughter, breathed her last words, it be said. 'Loved me he would, if only I'd let him.' Said by many, it be, loved the First Grandmother much the first granddaughter did, knowing the cruelty to be the pain inside. Only after a great time, when built this place they had, did they understand the Grandmother's final words. But come." Cerennt'te released Rom'n and turned, his old eyes scanning the vault. "Else someone comes, go, we must. Angry, the Dóme would be."

With that, he pushed Rom'n's hand to return the items and hurried him from the memories that had once claimed Rom'n's heart. Pressing a palm to the door, the cruelty of a lifetime was sealed inside, and for the first time in nearly four hundred years, a boy's tender heart, cherished long ago by a beloved brother, and then torn apart by a fierce desire for a cruel and spiteful woman, was freed to find the love that had been stolen from it time and time again.

HAVING RETURNED with great speed along the circuitous paths they had taken earlier, Rom'n looked across the vast room. There was the Dóme, surrounded by those under her command, her laughter directing theirs. His eyes traveled, and he found his friends, Kratt and Synrnn, their attention taken by the man they had met in their rooms, the Dóme's brother. Rom'n watched as Cerennt'te skirted the pockets of people, arriving at the Dóme's side, his bright surprise at finding her seeming real and vastly pleasing to her. Only then did Rom'n feel free to enter the room, the old man's instructions to him clear.

"Enter not, boy, until her attention I have, else guess, she may."

His walk bold, Rom'n caught Kratt's eye as he approached. Kratt motioned to Synrnn, and she turned.

"Rom'n!" Pleasure showed on her face. "And where were you two off?" She grabbed his arm, turning him to the Dóme's brother. She whispered to him in an aside, "I'll want to know it all later. First things first, though." More loudly, "Here's our friend from last evening." She leaned in and whispered softly to him, "You'll want to hear this."

Kratt placed his hand on Rom'n's shoulder. "Rom'n, you remember Kornth, Dóme Elussie'san's younger brother." Laughing, he added, "But according to Kornth, not much younger."

Rom'n saw Kornth smile, his back stiff and still.

"He says he's been keeping an eye on us the past day, and we must meet him to talk. It's very urgent, and most importantly, the Dóme mustn't know."

Rom'n raised his eyebrows. "What are you saying?" He looked to Synrnn, seeing her shrug her lack of information. Then, knowing he trusted *her,* he acquiesced. "Sure," he smiled. Reaching out a hand, he took Kornth's in his. "I would enjoy meeting with you. I've been with Cerennt'te—"

"I am aware," Kornth interrupted. "Forgive me, I know now what I suspected when I first saw you. Possessions be what she wants. You. My sister be a very powerful one. I fear for the granddaughter, her in this place. Later. Please, I must go."

The old brother stepped away, the sudden voice of pleasantries he modulated to the other guests as he walked away melting with him into the room.

GATHERED in Rom'n's room, seated on comfortable couches, with the evening festivities long over, the old brother spoke. "Many old stories be told, the First Grandmother no longer in her mind at the time.

"The First Grandmother shared tales of a world of blue seas and green foliage, the people basking under two suns, swimming in their seas only to come alive again. The stories tell of the old grandmother saying she could be young and whole again if only she could swim under the twin suns." He paused, looking at the floor. "Those gath-

298

ered with her didn't understand the rantings of the old woman, the stories considered only those of an old broken mind."

The others waited patiently on the old man. They had seen his sincerity. It was clearly real.

Then he looked up and continued. "No one lived here," and he motioned to the frozen and unending lake beyond the window, "before our family built the machines and sold the power. Now, everyone wants to be here. The sea had no name then. The First Grandmother had to swim, so the story goes. When youth didn't come to her as she claimed it would, she cursed the sea, calling it life's revenge for the way she'd lived her days. It be the reason for our sea's name. It be known still by that name."

He looked toward Rom'n hopefully, his eyes pleading for confirmation of the original grandmother's rantings.

Rom'n turned from the old brother to his friends, nodding his head in agreement. "I do remember some talk of this aboard the ship, but rumors only. During one cycle, I was present during an interrogation. The proceedings weren't pleasant, and I spent much of the time attempting to blank it out. Some of these things, maybe, were talked about, but I regret that I don't remember much."

The old brother's eyes glistened. "You. You be here, the one of the First Grandmother's anger broken upon her deathbed. How that can be, I don't know, but it surely proves the stories' truth. You must take the beloved Relei'sene away from this place."

"Relei'sene?" That caught Rom'n's attention. His eyes turned to Kratt and Synrnn to find them just as mystified as he was. "Who is Relei'sene?"

"The grandmother will have no competition. None may draw attention from her. Relei'sene has the goodness of heart that skips the Grandmothers. In some generations, goodness and pureness of heart are born into the Grand-mother's line. Not every generation bears one with the drive, the cruelty, one that is strong enough to claim the position of Grandmother. However, that same goodness also allows the Grandmothers to shunt them aside. This must not happen to Relei'sene." His eyes glistened with desperation. "Take her away from here. I've spoken with Relei'sene. She will go."

Kornth stood and began pacing about the room as he continued. "When Cerennt'te spoke with me, I doubted. When I saw you," and he pointed his gaze at Rom'n, "I had my first hope. The old stories, not believed by any, were clutched in desperation by those of us who care, as Relei'sene's only salvation. When I learned the databanks knew you, I began to trust in the stories, and I spoke with her." He returned to sit before them. "Please." His eyes brimmed with moisture.

"You're the reason we arrived a day early, to meet you." Rom'n laughed. "Of course."

Kornth nodded in agreement. "I had to be for certain."

"We have no way to leave, good ser." Kratt massaged a fist. "Even back at the city, our way was blocked by your sister."

"I have connections she be unaware of. Your ship can be released if you can get back to the city."

Rom'n stepped forward and questioned, "What of me?

Can I not talk with the Dóme? She seems somehow attracted to me, as if she finds me fascinating."

"My sister collects only, and then when tired, she throws away. She can charm, but don't trust her. She has the Original Grandmother in her. She will rule until the deathbed takes her, and she won't leave another who might take her place. You must get Relei'sene away."

"Couldn't this girl simply move to another city, just leave this compound?" Kratt frowned at the obvious solution no one was considering.

"If she stays on this world, she will die. This year or in five years, once she bears children, there will be an accident, and her life will be gone. My sister fears for her position, and she will see to it. Trust me in this. It has happened many times before."

"Boss," Synrnn exclaimed, appalled at Kornth's vision of Relei'sene's bleak future. "That two-man. Could four fit inside?"

Kornth looked at her with fresh hope in his eyes. "This, you could fly?"

"Not me!" She laughed in surprise, pointing to Kratt. "He is the best, though."

The old man thought. "Four, I think, yes. Four. It will be tight, but four, yes, for the distance to the city." He smiled. "Give me one day. Friends must be contacted and permissions gained. One day and we will do this. Not a word must be said."

Turning, he walked from the room without a backward glance.

301

—Chapter 20—

The coach pulled her team in, her voice urgent as she spoke her words of encouragement. "They are beginning to tire. Your opportunity will come, but it will be unexpected. Don't hesitate. Grab the brass ring, and victory will be yours."

—Said before taking the Ganymede Gaming Trophy

KRATT AND ROM'N were gathered, surrounded by the most formal of wear strewn about the vast suite, the grandest of events planned for the evening.

"Rom'n, we don't even know this girl." Kratt paced the room, his sartorial accoutrements mostly complete.

"You didn't know me, either." Rom'n grinned. "You took me in. We get along well." He stood, his shirt in his hand, and walked to the window, the draperies open, the first rays of sunshine to be seen since arriving on the planet streaming through. "The sun feels good. Not warm as on Kreeian's world, but good, anyway." He turned back to his friend, raising his eyebrows as he stressed his point. "Just look at us now."

"I'm looking. What am I supposed to see?" Kratt paused, consternation cutting across his face. "To take this girl sight unseen on my ship . . . it's madness."

"You're in the finest home, probably, that you've ever stepped foot in, you've been given the choicest of clothes to wear, and tomorrow you may have your new two-man after all." Rom'n slipped his arms into the shirt, pulling it over his head. "Have I brought you luck, or what?" Turning to look out over the lake, he commented, "This place has a rugged beauty in winter. It must be very beautiful in summer." He shivered in the warm room, the idea of the heat he had been told of appealing, but accepting from his knowledge of the history of this place, that the fact might well be otherwise.

"All this finery, and all the old man wants is to help his grandniece to escape from it, no matter how or where," Kratt mused, beginning to sway. "I can understand escape. I'm a spacer. I'd drown in the luxury of this place if I thought I could never be free. Already we feel it. You, me, and even Synrnn. Where have our jokes and word-plays gone? Our teasing? That's how we know the others care." He stood and walked to the door. "We'll make our try possibly during the evening meal? Is that what we're told?"

"That's the message he sent. I must admit, Kratt, the old woman's laugh had me hooked. I knew I should know it. It was the laugh of an old love, the many times granddaughter of a woman I once knew. Now I'm finally able to release what I once craved. In fact," and he turned and smiled, "I feel it's already gone. I don't know how, but there's something in me that feels free to love again. You may complain, but coming here is my life given back to me. I want to know this young woman the old brother describes. She might be someone I'll be able to love. I'll never know if we don't do as the old man says, will I?"

At his words, Kratt laughed, his sense of adventure stoked once again. "I see you've learned from me well, my boy. Very well, then. Let's have an adventure. Surely Synrnn will want to join."

"As if she has a choice." Rom'n laughed.

"As if she ever has a choice." Kratt joined in, his laughter filling the room.

"YOUR THINGS, you have them ready," Kornth stated, only confirming earlier instructions to the trio. "I will have a pretense to pull each of you away, and the game must be set into motion without delay. If she finds us out, we all may pay."

Rom'n turned conspiratorially to Kratt and Synrnn, "If the Dóme truly has the spirit of the Original Grandmother in her, I don't want to be found out." He grinned. "Remember, I knew the original, and I was at the receiving end of her spirit a few times."

"I, too, have been on the receiving end a time or two." Kornth's face cracked into a rare and broad smile. "Your sense of play will serve you well, young Rom'n. It be something to see one so like my Relei'sene. I do wish it could have been Relei'sene you had known all those many years ago instead of the Original Grandmother." Pausing, he looked at each of the three visitors in turn. "I only wish we had more time to spend together." The old brother stepped back, turning to leave. "Rikard will have your things by the ship. It will be crowded. Carry nothing else." Then, he was gone.

"Boss, it feels good to get to go home again." Synrnn put an arm around his waist. "You do realize," and she started to laugh, "the females on your ship will now have the deciding vote, since we'll be in the majority."

Kratt turned his head and looked at her, putting his hand on his hip. "The majority? Count like I do, Synrnn. Man, man, woman, woman. Seems pretty equal, doesn't it? Rom'n?" He looked at him for support.

Rom'n just grinned, waiting for the wordplay to sort itself out, enjoying the much-missed interaction between the two.

"No, Boss. Try again. Count it this way: captain, pilot, crew, passenger, and IRaC." Synrnn grinned with triumph.

"Gods, no!" Kratt threw his hand to his head, dropping onto a chair. "She's right. Once again, she's right! Rom'n, gods help me, she's right!"

Rom'n and Synrnn laughed as their captain cried with frustration, his tears staining the front of his shirt.

"AH, MY MUCH vaunted new friends. Welcome to our humble meal. We wish to dine this night in your honor." The old Dóme stood, gracing the huge table surrounded with guests standing behind their seats, the second table still empty. Her hair piled high, she sparkled in her fine

305

fabrics, with just a hint of glittering adornment showcasing the quality of her choices.

New in his assurances, finally set free, and knowing now the broken attraction, from his end of the table, Rom'n matched her words.

"Most gracious Dóme Elussie'san 'de Gaso-Fratenni laHolc'm. From early 'til late, your hospitality abounds. My friends and I are honored to be in your home, the recipients of your largesse. We are excited to have this opportunity to form new acquaintances, and we hope we will find those that will be long and honorable."

As the Dóme seated herself, the rest of the guests quietly following suit, Synrnn leaned in to Rom'n. "I had no idea you had that in you."

He laughed. "I did spend seven standards at the military academy, even if the Original Grandmother stole them all from me. We spent a year learning formal etiquette. It was something all officers were required to know."

Kratt grinned in anticipation. "Just like we plan to steal something from her."

"Shush!" Synrnn motioned with her hand. "Do you want to be overheard? Just act normally. Gods, what am I saying? Act properly, you two, not normally. The both of you. Now!" She turned back to the table, and then motioned for them to sit up. "The food's here. Behave!"

Dodging the many dishes handed over their shoulders and placed before them, Synrnn soon motioned to Rom'n with her hand. Catching her attention were the guests arriving at the second table. Among them was the one Kornth had told them to expect.

Relei'sene 'de Gaso-Fratenni, beautiful in unimaginable finery, her hair done in jewels and fine metals, and wearing clothing cut for her alone, entered the room. Rom'n was transfixed as the girl ran her eyes along their table, finally resting on him.

He had received only a glimpse of her the evening before, but to look her directly in the face was uncanny. Cerennt'te and Kornth had both said Ma'jene died so many years ago. The stories were so old as to be just that, stories. Still, he knew as he looked, if the truth were not already known, he would recognize this girl as Ma'jene. Not the Ma'jene that had become hard in her cruelty and anger, but a Ma'jene in the sweeter moments of her youth, the Ma'jene he could have loved, the person his Ma'jene never was. Only by having broken the bonds of the old Ma'jene was he able to see this new face in her own right as the beauty she was.

Kratt punched him. "That's really her? Then I'm sold. Where do I sign on the dotted line?" He laughed as Rom'n stuttered out a reply, dropped his eyes, and his cheeks started to warm with embarrassment.

"You think you'll be glad I turned you down, Rom'n? Or do I get a second chance?" Synrnn gibed.

"Shush!" Rom'n pinched his eyes shut, and then opened them wide to clear the sudden fog in his head. "Creepin' flamerunners, guys," he started, then paused, overwhelmed with the thought of this girl being on the ship with him, with *him*.

"Planetside Comm Station calling Rom'n. Planetside Comm Station calling Rom'n. You are now passing the outermost planetary orbits. Contact will soon be lost. Come in, Rom'n. Come in, Rom'n," Kratt teased, the opportunity too much to pass up.

Synrnn kicked Kratt, eliciting a low yelp. "Stop it, Boss. She *is* beautiful, and he did just find out she's the great-something-granddaughter of his lost love."

Kratt put his hand out to quiet the voices as Kornth stood to speak, and the conversations settled down along both tables.

"My most gracious sister, Dóme Elussie'san 'de Gaso-Fratenni laHolc'm of the 'de Gaso-Fratenni laHolc'm Compound, I would like to present our guests tonight with a special treat." He turned to the adjoining table. "My grandniece, Relei'sene 'de Gaso-Fratenni, will be presenting a special dish, prepared by her own hand." With that, everyone up and down the tables clapped. "Furthermore, since our honored guests from offworld be the reason for our celebrations, I would like to excuse them to watch Relei'sene put the finishing touches on her masterpiece. My sister, if you please?"

The grandmother's brother waited, his sister's acceptance of his ploy crucial to his plan. At the Dóme's nod, he breathed a sigh of relief and motioned for his grandniece to stand and exit to the food preparation room. Once she was gone, he turned again and made a motion. The three offworlders stood to follow.

"Brother!" All eyes turned to the Dóme. "What be this special dish our own granddaughter has so studiously prepared? I be unaware of her skills in this area."

"Sister, be not fearful that your guests will suffer the

indigestion of an amateurishly prepared dish. I have been overseeing the preparations this very day. And sister, a surprise must be just that. If I tell you," and he looked around the room as if inviting the other guests to join in a jest, "where be the surprise?"

A tittering of laughter was heard, most guests afraid to risk offending the Dóme. Finally, the old grandmother nodded her head, allowing Synrnn, Kratt, and Rom'n to join their fellow escapee in the other room.

THE THREE OFFWORLDERS entered the room to find no food preparation being done. Instead, Relei'sene was standing, her clothing stripped and piled by her side. She was leaning over, running her fingers through her hair, the jewels and metal falling into the fabric of her recently worn finery.

"Smart," whispered Synrnn. "A second layer of clothes under the clothes. I should have thought of that."

Rikard stepped up to them. "We must hurry, mas, mos. Please. Touch nothing. Walk quickly." Stepping through a hidden door, Relei'sene leading, the three followed at a fast pace, Rikard bringing up the rear. He called forward, "Exiting the compound will be easy enough. Exiting the city will require exquisite timing. Hurry!"

Reaching a service door to the landing platform, Relei'sene stopped and turned, speaking in a quiet, assured voice. "The outer doors are open. It will be very cold. Take your things and prepare to enter quickly. It will be even colder at Winter City. I'm sorry about your winter things. They will be lost. Rikard, their bundles?" Once

Rikard had given the bundles to their respective owners, Relei'sene reached to him, grabbing his shoulders and pulling him close. "You have been a good friend, Rikard. Thank you for all you've done. Please give Great-Uncle my love." With that, she opened the door, and they ran, the cold urging them on.

At the two-man, Relei'sene slapped the access pad, the side swinging open. Urging the others inside, Kratt and Synrnn clambered through first, crowding the pilot's seat.

"Close," Synrnn breathed to Kratt.

"Too close. Can I even fly it crowded in here like this?"

"I'm giving it a shot if you can't," she breathed back.

Rom'n leaped into the remaining seat, his bundle thrown at his feet, and suddenly Relei'sene was there with him, sliding down into the recess of his arm, her face beside his, her hair smelling so very good, the sides of the craft closing the cold out. As Kratt hit the ignition pad and the small ship surged forward, Rom'n knew that for this trip, a two-man was the perfect size. Any larger would be too spacious, indeed.

"Which way, Relei'sene?" Kratt cried. "I knew I shouldn't have slept on the way out here."

"I cannot navigate, but I've made this trip many times. Go across the lake. On the far side is a large rock outcropping. From there, go left. After some time, we'll come to a large drop off. Stay on the top, and follow it. It will take us directly to the city. I'll close my eyes for a time. Please wake me if you have need of my assistance."

By the time her head was against Rom'n's shoulder,

her eyes were closed, and she was breathing evenly. With the warmth of the woman in his arms and the steady pulse of her breath next to his face, soon Rom'n's eyes began to sag, and then they were open no longer.

"Synrnn," Kratt whispered. "I think you just lost your chance."

"No, Boss," she whispered back. "Rom'n just found his."

—Chapter 21—

spit·tle *(spĭt′l) n. saliva, especially when outside of the mouth*

—*NewWebster's Thirty-Seventh Secondary Dictionary*

"I'M SORRY, Synrnn. It just jumps. It's the air turbulence." Inside the cramped two-seater's cockpit, there was little room to fight the craft's errant motions. "Oomph!"

"Boss, they are, oomph, sorry, sleeping like babies."

"More like lovers," he whispered.

"You devil." She grabbed his skin and twisted until he cried out. "Shush," she hissed at him when he did.

"That hurt! How can you expect me to be quiet?"

"You know, Boss, your heart's gold, but your sense of shame is nonexistent."

He beamed. "That's the type of compliment I like to hear. Thanks, girl."

"It wasn't supposed to be a compliment."

"I'll take 'em any way I can get 'em."

"Just fly, Boss. That old woman probably has your ship under lock and key already. I sure hope Kornth has gotten whatever connection he needed taken care of."

"Like the 'let the ship go' part?"

"Yeah, that'd be good. Then we could actually get off this planet."

"Hey, Synrnn. Look right over there, right at the horizon. Do you think those might be the city lights?"

"Rom'n said the upper city was completely closed down, so I don't know. Sorry." She looked over, the drop off just where Relei'sene said. "I trust her. The lights, could they be beacons, possibly to pull ships in? They seemed aimed very much at . . . no . . . surely not." It was hard to tell, but after a few moments, she confirmed, "Yes, Boss, they seem to be searching. I think those lights are for us."

"That can't be good."

"Let's hope it's Kornth's doing and not his sister's." She reached over and touched Relei'sene just where a hand rested on Rom'n's shoulder. With no other sign than her eyes instantly being open, she was alert. Her eyes moved, glancing through the glassine, taking in everything.

"The lights are just as Great-Uncle promised. Stay very low. There's a weakness in the city's perimeter sensors. Great-Uncle has arranged to take advantage of it. There will be an opening, just the size of this vessel. It's designed for ground transport, but it will allow us to arrive undetected. The opening will allow us direct access to the ice hangar."

"The lights. How do they fit in?"

"They are what they appear, lights for navigation when the remote systems are nonfunctional. My great-uncle has arranged for those systems to be off-line for diagnostic subroutine maintenance."

Kratt grinned. "So, they cannot be brought back on line, and the light lets everyone know to fly in under manual control."

"Yes. Great-Uncle arranged to have the subroutines cycle on a day early."

"Aim for the source of the lights?" Kratt glanced at the girl who had not moved more than her eyes and mouth, and he was very impressed. This was no empty-headed teenager, brought up in a rarified world of generous funds and household politics.

"Yes. They will lead you in. The weakness is in between, at the junction of the two. Your ship, you can access it from the outside?"

Synrnn spoke softly, "The bay doors were left open. Access to the rest of the ship is by palm lock. Boss, you'll be able to fly directly inside, won't you?"

"Synrnn," he glanced at the girl in Rom'n's arms, "if I can take this little beauty with me, I'll fly her through the gates of any hell in any religion that has ever been thought up."

Relei'sene murmured softly to herself, "We are not away, yet. Be careful of what you speak." Louder, to Kratt, she instructed, "If possible, you *will* need to land inside your ship. There will be no way to leave this small vessel behind. Once your ship begins to power up, my

314

grandmother's notice will be quick."

"What can we expect?"

"Her power to stop you will not extend further than the city walls. Our planet has no attack capabilities. Also, if she understands I am being taken off this world, she will soon accept the facts. This is where her life is; this is the limit of her concern with her power. She doesn't relinquish control easily, but she's a pragmatic woman. She won't pursue me offworld, so my great-uncle believes."

"Will your great-uncle be safe?"

"Great-Uncle has resources. It's Rikard I worry most about."

"Your great-uncle can help him, no?"

"Rikard knew the dangers. He was willing to accept the consequences to help me. He has truly been my dearest friend." Tears rolled unimpeded down her face. "Now we must make his sacrifice one worth the price he will surely pay. The opening is just ahead. The gates have been released. Now is the time to show just how well this ship can be flown."

Kratt shifted in his seat, Synrnn shrinking back into the crevasses where she could. With internal dampers offsetting the worst of the tearing inertia, Kratt deftly manipulated the craft's controls, proving Synrnn's statement to Kornth to be much more than boasting. With a hand's breadth to spare, the small two-man, overloaded with four, danced through the city's wall directly under the lights and toward the ice hangar their own ship had entered just days before.

With the ice ceiling domed high overhead, and the

barely visible status lights on their own waiting ship flashing the siren call of space, Kratt swirled the wind-blown snow left from the storm that had ensconced them days earlier. He circled and aimed for the opening yawning in his ship's side.

"Kratt!" Synrnn's cry slipped out, her spoken caution an involuntary one in response to the sight of the opening rushing at them.

"Shush," he returned.

Synrnn flicked her eyes to Relei'sene, still unmoving, the dried streaks of her tears all that told of her world being torn apart inside of her. The surroundings suddenly darkening, she looked out to see the familiar walls of the ship that had been her home and would carry her away again. She let out a breath of tightly-held air as she felt the small shiver that told of landing gear settling on a firm surface.

With his arm, Kratt hit the release pad, and the side of the small craft disgorged them. Synrnn and Kratt scrambled out over each other. Relei'sene moved more gently, her shifting body bringing Rom'n to wakefulness.

"Ah, so my dream hasn't faded upon awakening."

Relei'sene glanced at his face, a flicker of a smile hidden from the man against whom she had been resting, and she withdrew from the cockpit. "Come. We are aboard your ship. We must prepare to exit the city quickly."

He jerked his eyes from side to side, the visible interior of the loading bay jarring him to full wakefulness. Seeing Relei'sene's offered hand, he reached out, allowing her to assist him from his cramped position.

316

Kratt, waiting at the door, his palm on the interior pressure plate, called, "Now!" As they entered, he rotated his hand once, then twice, and both doors, the outer bay doors and the inner corridor door, began to close. "IRaC?"

"Welcome back, Kratt." The familiar warmth of that melodious voice softly washed the corridor. "I see we have a new passenger aboard. Synrnn is at the bridge, and the ion thrusters are coming online. It also appears the city's remote routines that guided us in are off-line, and the ice doors are retracted. Synrnn has indicated she will be piloting us out. How may I help you?"

"Can you calibrate which bay flooring plates that two-man is resting on?"

"Yes, I can, Kratt. My new Vid monitors have excellent visual capabilities. Plates 16D, 20D, 16H, and 20H. I do believe there is some overlap on two of the plates impacting 21D and 21H."

"Thanks, IRaC." He slid open an access panel and punched in a code bringing up a display of the bay floor. Tapping six sections, each lit up red, and through the wall, the shifting of the two-man could be heard as the flooring's magnetic grapplers stabilized the small ship. Slamming the panel shut, he leaped into motion, sliding into the bridge to stand behind Synrnn. Tapping a little-used wall comm, he whispered, "IRaC, can you give me a split visual off the visor without impacting Synrnn's feed?" Immediately, the 2-D version of what was in Synrnn's visor was on the board.

Barely heard, just loud enough for Kratt's ears, IRaC whispered, "You have it now, Kratt."

317

An absent, "Thank you," was returned. However, Kratt's attention was already on the images overhead, the numbers scrolling past, and numerous smaller views of the interior of the ice hanger. He watched the readouts that showed the withdrawing of all landing gear and the ship moving effortlessly through the great ice passageway, out of the ice dome, and into the world's open skies.

"Crikes!" Synrnn cried out. "Override attempt."

With only that for a warning, the entire overhead display board flashed red. Synrnn's hands moved in the air as she manipulated the environment in the visor. Kratt remained frozen and let her do her job. With relief, he watched the red bleed from the display, pooling at the bottom, and finally fading away. From overhead came the sound of IRaC's voice.

"Override attempt aborted."

Synrnn paused, her hands still manipulating something unseen. Then, speaking aloud, she questioned the shipboard personality, "IRaC, why did you announce that externally?"

"You have an audience, Synrnn. By the way, very nice work."

She turned, pulling the visor from her head and laying it aside. "Boss! Nothing else to do, huh? Came to see the best out-navigate the rest? Ha! I almost doubted Relei'sene there for a moment, thinking Kornth might not have been able to get it all done, but here we are." She laughed. "Suck it up, Boss! I'm good, and wow, those ion thrusters are working fine! I do love you." She stood, placing her palm on his chest. Patting it one time, she walked out the door. "I think it can fly itself on out of here."

After she was gone, Kratt ventured, "IRaC, can it do what Synrnn said?"

After a pause, IRaC answered, "Sorry for the wait, Boss. Synrnn says she knew you would ask me, and yes, the ship is fine. Synrnn also says you prefer to go by 'Boss,' and I should use it all the time. Is there anything else, Boss?"

Kratt sank into the seat, putting his arms around his head as his forehead hit the console. "No, IRaC. Thank you," came the muffled reply. More softly, to himself, he said, "Women, women, women. Why do I keep bringing 'em aboard?"

"RELEI'SENE, I'm wondering one thing." The galley was very crowded with three seated and Rom'n standing, his shoulder pressed against the wall. Synrnn continued, "Your speech is perfect galactic standard. Why is that?"

"The Original Grandmother came to our isolated world with the strange speech of an offworlder. Only the Original Grandmother spoke after her fashion. Even before she was gone, the native speech patterns had begun to infiltrate the compound. When Great-Uncle and Rikard started their plan for my escape, they knew I would be marked on the outside as backward. My training started years ago."

"What about your grandmother? Did she not guess that something was up?"

"I always spoke in the way of the compound when in public. Only with Great-Uncle and Rikard did I practice

319

my learned speech patterns."

Kratt jumped in, taking the conversation a new direction. "We're glad to have you along no matter what speech patterns you choose to use. However, we will need to work out accommodations for your stay." He glanced to Synrnn and Rom'n before going on. "Quarters will be tight, but then, we'll just get to know each other pretty well. Had you or your great-uncle made any plans past just getting offworld?"

At his question, tears filled Relei'sene's eyes. "We knew of little offworld. None of us had traveled, and there was little information flow. We only knew to make what plans we could in the hopes an opportunity would arise. Thank the powers that be for your opportune timing."

At her tears, Rom'n placed his hands on her shoulders. He prompted her, "Surely you would have been safe even if we hadn't come."

"My mother was not of the Grandmother. My parents were sent far away, and I was retrieved as a child to be brought up at the Compound. I was found unsatisfactory, and come the summer, my sending away, also, was to be complete."

"But where? To whom?" Rom'n questioned.

"My grandmother would choose for her own ends, but be sure of this, it would not be a life of luxury and ease. Those women in my family who are not of the Grandmother live not long. Once they bear children, circumstances work to take them quickly, whether by accident or design."

"You must be grateful you had your great-uncle and

Rikard to look after you."

"We used to have such times together. Great-Uncle is old now, but we were often teasing with each other." At the memory, a smile of mischievousness crawled across her mouth. "We used to play great pranks on each other." Her eyes teared up again. "Now that is gone."

Seeing the smile fade, Kratt leaned in, "Trust me, girl, if it's pranks you want, this is the place." He turned and laughed. "As we say, when the going gets tough, we laugh until it's over."

Synrnn frowned. "Boss, I've never heard you say that."

He leaned to her. "You have now, and now's all that counts. The past is something to let go. You can't call it back again, so enjoy what you have."

"Um, Boss." Synrnn nodded her head toward Rom'n, who was still standing with his hands on Relei'sene's shoulders. "I need to readjust your thinking on that. *We* didn't let the past go. Remember? We opened it up, thawed it out, and it's been riding along with us." Kratt gave Synrnn a puzzled look. "Rom'n, comet-brain. He *is* the past."

"Oh!" Kratt pursed his lips. "Yeah, doggie! I keep forgetting."

"Rom'n doesn't, I'll bet you that. Does he have to wear a sign that says: I'm four hundred in thirteen more shipboard cycles?"

Relei'sene looked blankly from one speaker to another. "Does this have anything to do with the stories they used to tell about the First Grandmother? The stories said the people from her faraway world didn't die, or at least they came back alive after a time." She looked at the man standing beside her. "Rom'n? They're talking about you, right?"

"Well, that's sort of like me. I did kind of come back alive after three hundred seventy years."

Synrnn laughed. "Kind of!" She turned to Kratt. "We've even got the egg in the cargo hold."

"What? I'm even more confused, now. Great-Uncle told me what he could, but I didn't understand about Rom'n being able to access the house security. It seems the house recognized him, or so I've been assured. Even though I didn't see how that was possible, Great-Uncle did insist, so I knew it must be true."

Synrnn stood, pushing Rom'n into her seat. "Tell her. She has to know."

He glanced at Kratt for confirmation and then turned to Relei'sene. "The Original Grandmother and I went to the military academy together—"

"We have never had a military academy," Relei'sene scoffed, laughing.

"Have you ever heard of MegaCorp?"

"Certainly. Who hasn't? Some of our food shipments come from them. They contract with an independent shipper for delivery, usually using automatic drones the city can take over remotely once they drop into our airspace."

"MegaCorp used to also have a military operations arm years ago."

"I've never heard of it."

"Well, it did." He glanced from Synrnn to Kratt and

then back to Relei'sene. "It seems no one now knows what was real to me just a few sevendays ago. I know there isn't a military arm under MegaCorp's umbrella anymore, but hundreds of years ago there was, because the First Grandmother was an UnderGen'l in it. UnderGen'l Ma'jene Holcum."

Relei'sene glanced around the small space, her eyes catching each person around her as her mind made the connection. "As in laHolc'm Compound?"

"The very same. That grandmother and I were at MegaCorp's training academy together."

"How . . . never mind." She held up one hand. "I'll suspend disbelief. You tell the story, and I'll laugh at the end. I've not forgotten what you said about pranks, Kratt."

"This is no prank." Rom'n watched her smile at his denial. "The First Grandmother and I were even lovers." This time he laughed as she made a horrible face. "She wasn't a grandmother at the time. She was very young and beautiful. In fact, you could pass for her in front of anyone who knew the First Grandmother. I know. I was at the First Grandmother's side just a few sevendays ago."

This time she laughed in spite of her earlier promise. "This *is* a prank after all. I see the matter of it."

He smiled at her response. "That does sound odd, but it's true. It wasn't really just those sevendays ago, but in my mind, it was. See, the First Grandmother and I were serving on the same ship together. When it was destroyed, we both managed to get away. The First Grandmother must have made landfall here not too long after the explosion that destroyed our ship. I was rescued only recently by Kratt and Synrnn. Does that make more sense?"

"Some, except how could you have still been alive that long?"

Kratt jumped in. "He almost wasn't. Do you know what a cryo pod is?"

She nodded. "I've never seen one, but I do know people travel in them, usually people with little funds who are forced to go long distances. We have several in the city from when our world was colonized, non-working, of course. Your ship's accident must have been three or four hundred years ago, though. The pods don't sustain life that long."

"Old-MegaCorp military equipment was the best ever made. Full cryo pods were rated for over three hundred standard years full cryo-suspension before decay would begin to set in. Rom'n was inside his for three hundred seventy. We've still got the pod aboard. When he was picked up, the pod was entering failure mode, and cryo-decay had already set in. He spent multiple sevendays in a full medbath, and then several more on a med table before he could be resuscitated."

Synrnn crouched, leaning over Relei'sene's shoulder, and she smirked at Kratt. "Kratt was afraid he'd have to do 'potty duty' if Rom'n's cognitive ability was compromised."

Rom'n looked aghast at Synrnn, then turned to Kratt.

"Just let it go, boy. Let the woman talk. There's three of them, now." Kratt shook his head.

"Why did you come to us? Did you have suspicions?"

Relei'sene rubbed the tip of a finger on one hand against the back side of one on the opposite hand. "Our world rarely had manned vessels land. You must have provided a very good reason, or you would have been denied access."

"Emergency shipboard repairs. Your world was the closest. It helped we carried high-grade cryo gel, and your world was in desperately short supply." Kratt grinned.

Synrnn stood and explained more of what Relei'sene seemed not to know. "The first grandmother, Ma'jene Holcum, had military record information with her when she entered the pod. One of them was Rom'n's. Do you know Cerennt'te?"

"One of my grandmother's earliest consorts. The first, I believe."

Synrnn continued, "That first day when Rom'n was in the city, Cerennt'te recognized Rom'n from something he had seen at your grandmother's. However, no one knew for sure he was the same person until Rom'n was able to work the house controls. It sure surprised us when the house knew him by name."

Relei'sene remained seated, looking at one of her new companions and then another. "I must admit, I cannot honestly laugh, not at this. Although Great-Uncle didn't tell me all this, it matches what he did, and it also matches some other things I already knew or suspected. Where do the old stories come in, the ones of the world where the people never die?"

Rom'n shrugged his shoulders. "That part's a bit of a mystery to us, too. I do know my ship was around a world in a binary star system, probably the First Grandmother's twin suns. I wasn't high up on the ship's ladder of important people," and he gave Relei'sene a knowing look with a nod of his head, "thanks to the help of the First Grandmother, but I was aware we were looking for something, something worth decimating the planetary population to get our hands on. It could have been this live-forever-rebirth thing that your stories about the First Grandmother reference. I can only surmise about it, though."

"Does anyone know where the First Grandmother's storied world is? The one she told about under the twin suns?" Relei'sene looked from Kratt to Synrnn to Rom'n, seeing nothing but the resignation of the unpleasant fact known by the others. That world was far away, and it could never be reached by Kratt's ship. When they didn't answer, she prompted them, "What?"

Synrnn touched Relei'sene on the shoulder. "It took Rom'n's escape pod three hundred seventy years to get to us. It's a long way back there, and this is a very small ship. Besides, we've got a cargo to deliver."

"Not actually," Rom'n drawled. Contrition painted his face. "There was a message earlier. IRaC routed it through the visor when I was checking to be sure of our clean getaway. They've cancelled our contract. It seems they wanted this shipment stat, and we didn't quite make it. Kratt will have to find another buyer for our cargo."

"Pigs are what they are. Old-Earth pigs," Synrnn groused.

"I didn't think," Relei'sene apologized. "You have a business to run. My rescue interrupted that. I am so sorry." She reached into a pocket, pulling out a credit crystal, holding it out with tears pooling once again in her eyes. "Great-Uncle sent this with me. It was all he could get together, but I'm sure it will be adequate compensation for your troubles. Please, take it."

The three rescuers glanced at it, remembering Rom'n's long-ago offer. Rejected in principle then, it would be rejected now.

"Keep it. You may be in far greater need of it at a later time."

"Thank you, friend Kratt. Your generosity is magnanimous."

"Speaking of small ships," Kratt, now embarrassed, interrupted, "and I hate to change the subject, what with traveling to the far side of the arm sounding so interesting, but we've got to get our new passenger a bunk. Any ideas?" He peered at his two crew.

Relei'sene offered, "Anywhere will be enough. I'm just grateful to be here."

Kratt chuckled and reached to touch her on the arm. "Anywhere is about all we have to offer."

"This is a two-cabin ship." Synrnn pressed her lips together in a matter-of-fact manner, and she glanced at Rom'n, waiting to see what he could come up with.

"Hey," he interjected, identifying with Relei'sene's discomfiture, and refusing to allow her to be put on the spot. "I slept on a bench before, and I can do it again. We have a bunk for you, Relei'sene. We'll get it made up, and you'll even have a bit of privacy. Not really much, I admit, but a bit."

Kratt and Synrnn looked at each other with a puzzled

expression.

"Bunk, Rom'n?" Kratt glanced into the corridor, turning his head both ways. "Did I miss something here?"

"Bunk, Kratt," Rom'n hissed. "In the corridor. Remember?" He turned to Relei'sene. "How does that sound? Workable?"

Relei'sene smiled. "I would appreciate that. Any place at all."

Kratt turned to Rom'n and grinned. He nudged Synrnn and hissed, "If the boy wants to give up his bunk, that's his business. Where he'll sleep is also his business. He can work that out between you two."

"Boss! Shush!" Synrnn put her finger to her lips.

"You two go and freshen things up," Kratt suggested, motioning to the door with his hand, "and I'll keep poor Relei'sene company. The conversation will the best I've enjoyed in some time." When he saw them hesitate, he continued, "Go! The girl's exhausted. Now, go!"

As they stepped out the door, Rom'n turned to Synrnn. "I guess this means I'll need a place to bunk, now that I've given away mine. I didn't think of that, just that I knew how she felt, the feeling of being here, intruding unexpectedly into someone else's world. I couldn't bear to think of her feeling like that."

She laughed at his new predicament. "Well, it does, indeed, seem that you've put yourself in a spot. Ever wanted to try sleeping in zero gee?"

"Zero gee? Are you teasing? Is that even possible?"

"Certainly, it is. We actually have zero gee sleepbags aboard. They are required on all cargo ships when the bay comes equipped without full grav capabilities. That's us."

"They don't float all over?"

"That's what makes them zero gee bags. They have straps to keep you in and hooks to attach them to the wall. There's only one problem with sleeping in a zero gee environment."

"What's that?"

"Zero gee." She chuckled maliciously. "Spittle from your mouth tends to drift out during the night, and when it floats around and slaps you in the face, well, it isn't my favorite alarm clock."

"Gods, Synrnn, you sure know how to make this sound appealing."

She laughed out loud in anticipation. "The really fun part, Rom'n, is getting up to go to the facilities at night. Try swimming for the door lock with the pressure in your bladder doing everything it can to make its escape. That'll be a fun night for you."

"That's the best you can do? You're sure?"

"Well, my cabin's taken, and Kratt barely fits in his with all his stuff. That leaves the zero gee bay or your old bunk with Relei'sene." She watched his eyes brighten for a moment, and then she laughed when his face collapsed with the realization that this was a girl he didn't even know.

"Okay, Synrnn. When we're through getting my old bunk made up for Relei'sene, I'll get you to show me how to work the zero gee sleepbag. Thank you, anyway." He trudged after her, his enthusiasm not quite as clear as it had been a few moments before.

—Chapter 22—

Notice: Management is not responsible for
loss of income due to bodily injury or
damage to personal items.

—*Faded sign on old bus*
station wall

ROM'N OPENED his eyes to darkness, something wet clinging to his hair. *Oh, great blazing suns! I've been impacted by spittle again.* He considered reaching a hand to wipe it away, but he knew the consequences of any movement.

Inertia was the force that controlled his existence during the nights, now. He decided to just leave it alone this time. Moving one leg to shift his position, he felt the bag begin to swing, and as it had last time, no matter how still he held once the motion started, he finally impacted the wall.

Ow! That's the sore spot, again. He knew he could make it through the night, though. He only had to do this one sleeptime at a time. Just tonight was all he had to worry about.

If I just hold still and don't move, he told himself. He was motionless for a time and then felt that familiar itch start on his leg, the kind that wouldn't let go, wouldn't let his eyes sleep or his brain rest until it had received the attention it demanded. *Don't move,* he told himself. The muscles in his hand unable to resist, he shifted a finger to scratch his leg, and once again, he felt the bag start to move.

Oh, crikes! Here it comes again. His movement smaller, the impact would take longer. He had found that out already. But how long? It was anyone's guess. He just waited . . . and waited . . .

ROM'N SAT on the corridor floor, the metal cold through the thin fabric of his sleeping shorts. He leaned his head against the wall, the sound of the running water on the other side of the door making him intensely uncomfortable. Kratt's personal facilities were occupied. Synrnn's personal facilities were occupied. His facilities, rather, this one he shared, were occupied. He needed to be occupied. *Oh, boy,* he thought, as he squirmed. *One, two, three, four. Think of anything except the cold of the floor. Five, six, seven, eight. Oh, no!* He moaned as the pressure mounted.

Finally, he heard the door latch. It opened a crack, and he heard a familiar voice.

"Oh, Rom'n. I'm so sorry. I must be in your way. These are your facilities. I should have thought of that. I'll be out in a moment. I need a few more moments on my hair." With those words, the door clicked shut.

Oh! He thought. *Nine, ten, eleven, twelve.*

"IRAC, PLEASE display star map, full version. Highlight current position and binary destination star."

"It is done, Boss." The map appeared as the onboard personality spoke.

"Thank you, IRaC."

"Anytime, Boss."

"Synrnn," Kratt chided. "Any way we can undo that little personality modification?"

"I like it, *Boss*." She winked. "You did say you wanted her to be more casual."

"This about takes the cake, though, don't you think?"

"Just about, Boss. Just about. We'll wait and see if anything else comes along."

"A dozen Rom'ns! Gods! Just give me a dozen like him!"

"But you've already got us, Boss. Isn't that right, IRaC?"

"That is right, Boss. Take or leave us. But I am telling you, taking us is better than leaving us. We make your world go round."

He gave in with a sigh. "I know, IRaC. I know. I'll keep you. Now, about this star chart. It's a long way from here to that binary system. What are our options?" With distaste, he ventured, "Those cryo pods? Is that even a possibility?"

"No, Kratt," IRaC replied. "We do not have the proper preparation systems available. However, this is a heavily traveled section of the arm. I could try to hail a ship to initiate transport."

"Boss, that was amazing." Synrnn turned to him and put an arm around him to hug him. "You hate those cryo pods, and just for you to offer." She planted a kiss on his cheek. "Thanks, Boss."

"Stop that." He pushed her face away, a red flush crawling up his neck.

Turning to the board, she called out, "IRaC, post all known ships with adequate space to transport this vessel intact."

Kratt grabbed her arm. "Synrnn, do you know how much that would cost?"

She laughed. "Not as much as Rom'n's got, and he's already volunteered to pay for the transit fees."

"You told me I couldn't take his credits."

"I didn't say he couldn't offer. Pick one, Boss. Pick two, or pick 'em all." She pointed to the board where several lights were now seen very close to their own. "I'll sort out the final cull," and she walked out the door.

"BOSS, I'VE GOT replies with two offers. Pick the one you want." Synrnn spoke into the visor. "Ships' offers on board, full stats." A bevy of information flashed across the board above her. Flipping the visor off, she leaned back into her chair. "Your choice, my man."

"Well," he began, looking over the display. "Both are within easy pickup and require us to live aboard during the transit. So, the real choice concerns payment and transit time."

"There is one other difference. The slower, more expensive ship is fully documented and legal. Quite a bit more expensive. Fees, contingencies, and the like. The second is quicker on the transit time. I suspect their official navigation charts reflect an honest path of transit, but the real charts cut the corners to increase the time advantage. Our addition to their load will be strictly off the book, so it saves us both tons of fees."

"Make it easy for me next time, Synrnn. Give me a third choice that lets us hobnob with the crew of the main ship. Then I won't have to decide. The choice'll be obvious."

"I had a few of those offers, Boss, but the transit time jumped up considerably. Didn't think you wanted them. I can call 'em back." She picked up the visor as if she really intended to do so.

"How much cheaper is that one on the board?" He scratched his forehead as he pointed to the second one, weighing the options.

"Like half, Boss."

At that, his eyes opened wide. "Have you tried to access anything about their TDH ratings?"

Synrnn smirked. "Only one bad mark, but it was a doozy. Several standards ago, probably close to ten subjective, they were boarded. Dumped their cargo. Someone happened to be in the cargo bay for an inspection for some reason. He got spaced and died."

"That's it? Nothing else?"

"They did pay restitution to the man's company."

"It's a high speed jumper with full bay transport?"

"You're thinking about it, Boss. I can see your brain working."

"You're right. I'm thinking that's a pretty good record." He walked behind the counter and touched the board. "Pick us up here, jump to there and there, and we're delivered and done. At fifty percent. Even though it is Rom'n's account, I'd still like to spend it wisely."

"I understand, Boss, just for the fun of shaking the system for the best deal. Right? You want I should contact them?"

"I should want, pilot. Get us passage."

She slipped the visor back on, and whispering, soon had a digital contract up and ready for their junket to the world of the twin suns. Kratt stood looking at her as she slipped the visor off her head. She turned to see him still there and just grinned.

"How'd you get that taken care of so quickly?" He reached out a hand and tapped her on her nose. "Magic?"

"Yeah, Boss. Magic. All I had to do was finalize the deal. Just a call, because I know you. You like the edge. Safe is boring. Boring is dead. I want you alive, so I picked interesting. All right?"

"When you signed on my ship, Synrnn, you were my best contract ever. However, you know something? I don't need an illegal ship to keep me on the edge. You do that just fine. Every day." His face somber, he stood staring at her.

Her grin fell away. "Boss? You mean that?"

"I sure do." He turned and walked from the bridge. She jumped up and stuck her head out the door, looking into the corridor after him.

"Kratt, you really mean that?" After a moment he turned around and looked at her.

"Hook, line, and sinker, Synrnn. You took it hook, line, and sinker. Ha!" He turned and laughed all the way down the corridor.

She leaned against the door, her legs and arms crossed as she shook her head. As she turned back into the bridge, she muttered with a grin, "I sure did, Boss. I took it, whatever a hook, line, and sinker are." Sitting down, she laughed out loud. "I sure did."

"LET HER SEE, Synrnn. Give her the visor. We're already on remote. You just don't want to share." Rom'n started to tug it off her face.

"Rom'n! Synrnn doesn't have to do that just for me." Relei'sene laughed with embarrassment, pulling his hand away.

"No, no, Relei'sene. You have to understand. That's what Synrnn's like. She's got it, so you've got to take it. Otherwise, you never get access to it." He smirked and turned back to Synrnn, demanding, "The visor."

"Bully. Here." She handed it to him. "You two play. But, this is huge. I'm telling you, this dwarfs anything I've ever been on. Whew!"

As Rom'n explained to Relei'sene what would happen when she put the visor on, Synrnn stepped away, already forgotten, his words focused on their passenger as the pilot moved out of range.

"Here, Relei'sene. On your head like this. What you

336

look at will be identified by the visor. However, if you want, you can speak to it and tell it whatever you want to see."

"Help me put it on. Oh!" Her hands began to move in front of her as she caught sight of whatever Synrnn had been looking at.

"Here." He gently took the visor off her head. "Let me look for a moment." Slipping it on, he responded, "Whoa!" When the image inside stopped moving, he understood instantly. "Real time forward," and he added, "Dual display to board."

The visor back on the console, he pulled Relei'sene with him to the board. The approaching transport was more comparable in size to his long-ago military craft, the starstrike battleship. A commercial vessel, this one was enormous. It was capacious enough to carry small vessels like the one they were on without even impacting its available hold space. He pointed out the open hangar door they were approaching and would soon enter.

"There! We'll be inside, soon. Just watch."

His arm around her waist, he was more focused on the view from his fingers than the view from his eyes. In fact, he didn't realize he'd stopped talking until Relei'sene pushed her hand against his chest, repeating herself several times.

"We're in, Rom'n. What next?"

A sudden stumbling jerk interrupted his answers as the great ship's magnetic grapplers stopped the smaller ship, knocking the two of them to the floor, the suddenness too much for their own ship's inertial dampers to completely compensate for.

He stood, helping Relei'sene to her feet. "I guess we make ourselves at home for a few days. At least I'll have gravity in the cargo hold. That'll be a welcome change for a while."

Relei'sene laughed, even if she couldn't be sure just what he meant.

"NONE OF US thought about this." Kratt flipped an old-fashioned card Synrnn's direction. "At least I have these."

Rom'n picked up his card, turning it over to see both sides, and laughed. "Where did you ever find these? Real paper?"

Kratt laughed. "Some worlds still use this a lot. By the way, Rom'n, no one else is supposed to see the side of the card with the numbers." He flipped one to Relei'sene. "Have you ever played this?"

"Similar games as a child," she said. "I'm sure I'll pick this up quickly. At least I don't show all my cards to everyone." With a smile she reached to Rom'n's cards and turned one so the numbers could be seen by only him.

"It's just that I thought I'd still have the visor to play with. Not in transit. Oh, my! It might mess up the main drive engines. Ha! They just want us to pay more for access to their 3-D comps. Crikey, that just makes me angry."

Rom'n turned to her. "We can afford it, you know."

"It's principle, now. I wouldn't use their system unless they gave it to me for free, and then I'd have to think about it. It just makes me angry, and truth be told, it was right there in the contract. I didn't catch it, and IRaC didn't think it was important."

"I am sorry, Synrnn," IRaC's voice softly intoned. "I have registered this concern as a top priority for the future."

"Thank you, IRaC. I know you couldn't have known. Next time we'll just negotiate this out of the small print."

"I appreciate your understanding, Synrnn," and IRaC grew quiet.

Synrnn muttered, "As if I ever want to travel this way again."

"At least we're down to one full cycle to departure." Kratt played out his final cards, the game easily won in the others' confusion over the unfamiliar rules. "Anybody want me to leave these?" He stood to exit the small room.

"I'd like to play with them a bit." Rom'n held the deck of cards in one hand. "Can I get these to you next cycle?"

"Leave them on the table, kid. Just stack 'em and leave 'em out of the way. I'll pack 'em before we get underway." Kratt left, a wave of his hand his nightly farewell.

"He'll pack them." Synrnn grinned. "As in pack *rat*." Her eyes quickly cutting to the other two, then back to the card she'd pulled from the stack in Rom'n's hand, she laughed at her own joke.

"Rat? What is pack *rat*?" Relei'sene took the deck from Rom'n and began to shuffle them in an organized manner, instead of the clumsy way she'd watched Kratt do it. "A rat. This is a creature of some kind?"

Synrnn shuddered. "Awful! Ech!" Smiling, she handed her cards to Relei'sene to shuffle into the pack. "Gods, I can't imagine an *animal* in there. No, it's the noise. Pack in too much stuff, and it's the vibrations that do it."

"What vibrations?" Relei'sene raised her eyebrows, looking around.

"Ship's engines. When they're running, things packed too tightly sometimes rattle. Get it? Rat? Rattle? It's kinda ship slang." Synrnn motioned with her hand to indicate everything around them. "Now we're running life support only, what we call screensaver mode, except, I suppose, for the magnetic grapplers powered up on the two-man. IRaC? Can you check and tell me if the magnetic grapplers in the bay are on?"

"My internal ship's logistics tell me that life support is running in full function mode, as you indicated. However, the magnetic grapplers for the transport in the docking bay are now off-line. Our current low-power mode requires minimal accessory usage. Even internal gravity is presently powered down. Kratt has set the magnetic grapplers to reactivate upon release from our transport ship. Internal gravity will self-activate when external gravity is no longer detected."

"Thanks, IRaC." Turning to the others, "Well, I'm off. Tomorrow I start to earn my paycheck again." She turned to Relei'sene. "Teach him a trick or two, okay? He could use a heads-up." She slapped Rom'n on the shoulder as she left, her voice drifting in from the corridor, "And I was talking about the cards, Rom'n. The cards!"

He laughed self-consciously, clearly less interested in the cards than he was in Relei'sene, and he was embarrassed it was so easy for Synrnn to see. He turned, carefully watching the cards in Relei'sene's hands as she shuffled them, painfully aware of the urge to look that kept pulling his eyes her direction.

"Rom'n!" Relei'sene rapped the table in front of him. "Do you want me to teach you this game or not?" She held out several of the cards, laughing. "Here, you need all these. Lay a row out like this, then you flip through the ones in your hand and try to match them up."

Clearing his throat, he tested his voice. "Name? Does this game have a name?"

She laughed, the sound of her grandmother's laugh and the Original Grandmother's before that. "No, silly! How could it have a name?" She flipped through the cards, counting out three and turning that one up. "See, it matches here." She placed the card on one stack and flipped through the remaining cards in the deck. "I was bored one day. Rikard was out managing what he had to manage, and Great-Uncle was working on business affairs. No one was there to play, and I had just been shown these cards. So, I invented this game." She looked up with pleasure in her eyes and a smile on her lips.

"Name it, then." He laughed. "It's yours. You must give it a name."

"Name it?" She tapped the stack with her finger as she looked over the cards on the table. "Like, Relei'sene's Game or something?"

"That's it. Your game now has a name. Relei'sene's Game. We'll have to teach it to the others."

"Tomorrow we'll all be too busy to play a little girl's game. But it's fun to think you helped me give it a name.

Now, it will always be mine. And yours."

Without raising her eyes, her fingers reached across the table and found his. The flush around her collar finally matched the red already underneath his.

—Chapter 23—

Fine for Littering $200

*—Sign posted along old-Earth
roadway c. 2009 A.D. old-Earth*

"ROM'N?"

Freshly showered, his hair damp, and only his sleeping shorts on, he stood in the corridor, his old bunk to his right, and the navigation cockpit to his left. In the relative darkness of the ship's low-power mode, he was unsure if he truly heard anyone call.

"Rom'n, are you there?"

Relei'sene. His heart suddenly driving his breathing faster and deeper, he turned to where he had slept only a handful of cycles before. He could picture her, hear her laugh, and feel her touch. He reached his hand out and powered down the remaining lighting throughout the corridor. The sound of his driving heart loud in his ears, he softly stepped her direction, desire in his every movement.

"Relei'sene?"

"Come this way. I would enjoy speaking with you. Come and sit."

Not trusting himself to respond aloud, he trailed his hand along the wall, just the glow of various indicator panels along the corridor to show his way. Turning the corner, just a darker shape in the darkness, lay Relei'sene. He bent to touch the edge of the bunk and sat down, his side touching her leg, the covering of her blanket sliding gently between their skins. Taking a deep breath, he blinked his eyes, squeezing them tightly to focus his attention, the very touch of her leg threatening to overwhelm his senses.

He cleared his throat and croaked, "Yes?"

"Give me your hand."

His hand taking hers, she rested it at her side, his wrist now pressed against the curve of her hip. His world spun in his head.

"Tell me of the First Grandmother. All I have are the old stories. You actually knew her. She was alive for you."

Relei'sene shifted, the touch of her skin beneath her blanket sliding against his like a spark of super-charged electricity through poorly insulated wires. He felt his breath tear through his chest each time he drew in a fresh gulp of air.

"Tell me of when you were young together. What was she like then? You've said I could pass for her, even to people who knew her well, and that you remember her from just handfuls of weeks ago. Am I much like her in other ways? Rom'n? Will you tell me?"

Her voice pleaded with him, and he couldn't say no.

He fought to modulate his voice as he tried to focus his words. "The first time I met her, I was in love with her." He paused, the painful memories no longer holding him, seeing only the sweet. "She was a year late to the academy, and the only empty bunk was under mine. We were fourteen then, and I didn't want that bunk to go to anyone. I didn't know it was the First Grandmother that was taking it. I just knew a new recruit was on the way. I was furious. Then, I looked over the edge of my bunk at that new recruit sitting below, and my world changed. She was beautiful and strong and witty, everything I wasn't. To me, she was a goddess."

"What happened? How did she become all the things that are in the stories I know? How did she become so hard and cruel?"

"Sometimes we bring baggage with us." Images of his brother, Jo'n, more of his first friend at the academy, killed, and even those of the cruel things he had helped Ma'jene do flashed through his mind. "Sometimes we can't work through that baggage without tearing up the lives of others as we do so." He took a breath, the touch of Relei'sene at his side giving him the reassurance that his memories were no longer his life. "I see now that the Original Grandmother was acting in the only way she knew. Her life had taken her down a path that was her own, and she walked that path because she couldn't deal with something that had happened to her many years before I met her, something that haunted her. It haunted her to her death. I only feel sorrow for her to have lived out a life in the anger that I now know was the core of her cruelty. How miserable she must have been!"

"You are so kind. Who else could forgive such a person?" Relei'sene pulled herself up, reaching out to him. She touched his face with a hand.

He pulled her to him, burying his face against hers, the smell of her hair so much like that of so long ago, yet new and fresh, the smell of the new love he wanted so badly. In that moment of sweet acquiescence, Rom'n giving in to something he could no longer resist, the ship lurched around them, and flashing red lights filled the air. IRaC's voice intruded into the corridor.

"Supplemental gravity off-line. Ship's engines reengaging. Prepare for immediate transit. Emergency override of all systems in progress."

Rom'n grabbed for a shelf as he felt himself start to float from the bunk. Relei'sene grasped at the bedding, and then harder, she grasped at him. For a moment, they hung suspended in the air. Just as suddenly, they both fell jarringly to the bunk, crashing against each other, still in one another's arms.

A resounding jolt vibrated throughout the ship.

Overhead, IRaC's voice rang out, "Artificial gravity restored. Magnetic grapplers reactivated. Propulsion at thirty percent. Awaiting further orders."

The lights throughout the corridor flickered on.

"No crickeys, the artificial gravity's been restored. I wouldn't have noticed," Rom'n muttered. Relei'sene turned her head to face him, their eyes a hand's breadth apart.

"What was that big noise?" she whispered.

346

He looked around. "Probably the two-man reseating itself with the floor grapplers." He pushed himself up. "At least I hope so. I need to go find out what this is all about. Will you be fine here?"

"Go. I cannot help, no matter what. I'll be strong." She pulled her blanket around her. "Go."

Rom'n stood and looked at Relei'sene. He'd found in himself a deep attraction to this woman, and he so hoped she wasn't just feeling sorry for him. He smiled at her and turned to run down the corridor.

RELEI'SENE SAT, and the fear she should be feeling just wasn't there. Instead, she knew the confidence that no matter what happened, she was in it with a man she felt she could possibly learn to love. She ran her fingers down the soft swell of her breast, the memory of his arm touching her there still like burning embers. There was no problem with the ship as long as Rom'n was with her.

She closed her eyes and continued to relive the previous few moments in her mind, as the events around her played themselves out.

ROM'N BURST through the bridge door to find Synrnn already under the visor, giving directions to the flight module as she triangulated their location.

"Seen Kratt?"

Her hand waved him away, and he dashed to the galley to see if he'd holed up there. Not finding him, even Kratt's quarters empty, he stopped to think. The two-man! Rom'n found himself at the door to the landing bay. Slapping the lock and cycling through, he floated over, better now at kicking his way across the zero gee space.

No one was visible.

"Kratt?"

"Yes?" A head popped up on the far side of the two-man.

"Is she all right, Kratt?"

"They dumped us. With apologies afterwards, but they dumped us." He continued to inspect the two-man.

"You knew they had a track record. They've dumped before. At least with us, no one died."

"Ever the see-the-silver-lining kid, always ready to forgive. Well, me, I'm just angry."

"Your ship is in one piece, right?" Rom'n watched him nod his head. "The two-man doesn't seem any worse for the event, I don't think."

Kratt pursed his lips as he listened, anger still flashing in his eyes.

Rom'n continued, "How close are we to where we were headed, that binary star? Do you know that?"

Kratt began to take on a sheepish look. "That's why we were out of jump mode."

"So, I guess we're just about there."

"Pretty much."

"How did you bargain the price? All up front, or some behind?"

Kratt dropped his head. "Sixty up front, with forty behind."

"So," Rom'n chided, "you chose an illegal transport so you could cut the cost by half. We're here, and you get dumped, saving you nearly half again. Then, you get irritated. It seems to me, you should be thanking the guys who did you a favor."

"Was Relei'sene okay during that zero gee thing?"

"Everyone's fine. Let's get busy on what we need to do next. I think we should get back into the ship." Rom'n kicked off in the zero gee, his movements much improved over just those few sevendays ago.

"Um, kid."

He twisted to face Kratt, gently floating backwards toward the door.

"When we get inside, do you think some clothes might be in order?"

He looked at himself. He gave a sheepish grin, moving to grab his pants from beside his sleepbag, before cycling through the door. Pausing to slip them on, an unexpected movement in the corridor made him look up.

"Rom'n?"

"Relei'sene, you're safe?"

"This ship is fine?" The question was in her eyes, but her hand reached and found his arm.

He coughed and looked away, quickly slipping his pants on. "All is fine. We're in the vicinity of our destination."

"Kratt and Synrnn?"

He reassured her, "The urgency is over, IRaC has the situation under control, and we can sleep once again."

The spell with Relei'sene was now broken, but his body's longing for her wasn't. He didn't dare return to her bunk with her. He wished her a night of sleeping well, and as she stepped away, he quickly palmed the corridor lights off.

He moved to step back into the bay. His enthusiasm for sleeping in zero gee already worn off, he stripped back down to his shorts, tied his clothing to the bag, and slipped inside, dousing the lights as he did so. Holding his lips shut, he didn't want any spittle floating around tonight. Now, if only he could keep from moving. Shaking his head, he felt the bag start to move.

Oh, crikes! Here we go again.

Just then, a voice rang out in the darkness. "Hey, who turned out the lights? Rom'n? Are you in here? Rom'n?"

—Chapter 24—

To get the most in donations, when you see the following people, beg as indicated:

1. Businessman – funds are needed for the new library

2. Housewife – funds are needed for runaway children

3. Family – funds are needed for hungry children

4. Student – funds are needed to improve our technology infrastructure

Please return all collected monies to John in the park. Look for the red vest.

—Card passed out to fundraising volunteers

"THERE REALLY are no visible stars this far out, are there?"

"Just that binary system, Relei'sene. That's why this world was isolated for so long. No one knew it was here. Once it was discovered, however, we did what humans always seem to do. We stepped in and wrecked it." Rom'n called to IRaC, "Surely you can surmise something, IRaC. All records about this world disappeared from public data sources nearly four hundred years ago. You now know my version as well as I remember it. You've listened to what Relei'sene heard about her first grandmother. Put it all together. What do you come up with?"

"Rom'n, I have assembled a theory, but it is just that. I cannot validate it without additional information."

"Just give it to me, as best you can." He drummed his fingers on the tabletop impatiently.

"The theory I have assembled suggests MegaCorp unsuccessfully attempted to wrest information about a 'fountain of youth' found on the planet Rejuvenant from the native population, decimating them in the process. MegaCorp was blasted with punitive blows that crippled the corporation and eventually caused the dismantling of its military arm. Afterward, the planet was declared off-limits, possibly to enable either restoration or recovery efforts. I have also factored in the publication by deFralin and what little I can surmise he discovered after the MegaCorp incident. The population does seem to have renewed itself via a sudden influx of young children, hence the collection of poems deFralin published. Please understand that I am acting on out-and-out supposition from here on. With no additional information from the planet for nearly four centuries, it would seem highly probable someone with a special interest in the world, its people, or perhaps the planet itself, is still suppressing knowledge from getting out. My best guess, and it is only a guess, would be illicit financial gain. Find what this planet has that could be highly profitable, and you have your nose aimed in the right direction."

Synrnn hung her head in the door. "I didn't think she had a nose, Rom'n. How would she know about aiming it?"

"Maybe using those Vid cameras we had installed?"

She glanced at the ceiling. "I guess she gets it all from us, nosy girl."

Rom'n grinned as he glanced from Synrnn back to Relei'sene. "I just hope she doesn't watch *everything* we do."

ROM'N AND Relei'sene watched Synrnn tap her finger on the table over and over. Finally, Rom'n stopped her.

"What is it, Synrnn?"

"I've just been thinking. What would provide a lucrative enough credit supply from Rejuvenant that would warrant someone suppressing outside contact with the planet for this long? There are only three things we know for certain about this rock we're headed to. The populace was decimated long ago. I can't see any financial windfall there. Not at this distance in time." She looked at the other two sitting with her. "We also have proof the book of poems was collected and printed, and by a very well-known man, also. If there are any funds there, he's already collected them." She started tapping again. "It's the third thing I can't figure out."

"What's that?" Relei'sene tried to pull it from her.

"It just sounds stupid. It's the only other thing we

know, though."

Rom'n prompted, "And it is?"

Synrnn clicked her tongue. "It's just once it's said, it won't go away, and I don't want to be called a fool."

"Kratt's not here. You're safe." Rom'n winked at Relei'sene.

"The children." Synrnn shook her head, rubbing a hand over her eyes. "See? I told you it was silly."

"How would they be a big cash source?" Relei'sene gave a quick frown, puzzled. "They are just children."

"Think about it. According to deFralin, these kids appeared with no knowledge of who they were or who their parents were. All were eight years old. They were perfect."

"What do you mean, perfect? Perfect in what way? Perfect for what?" Rom'n looked between the two women, also puzzled.

"Illegal adoptions. Take the kid, and no one questions where the kid comes from. There's not even a birth parent out there to come back and haunt the new adoptive parents. Plus, it's all clear profit. Just pick up the kid on the surface and deliver them anywhere. Pretty ideal, huh?"

Rom'n sat looking at the two women for a moment before he began to smile. "Well, I like the one about sucking up all the water on the planet, packaging it, and selling it for drinking water. It could even be enclosed in individual clear containers so people could see the pureness inside." He winked with the outrageousness of that idea.

"No, I think Synrnn might have something here. May I try your ship's voice?" Relei'sene looked hopeful.

354

"Ship's voice?" Rom'n and Synrnn looked at each other quizzically, and with a grin shared, they replied, "Sure. IRaC, answer Relei'sene's question, please."

"Hello, Relei'sene. Please state your question, and I will do my best to answer it."

"Thank you, IRaC. Please check on adoptions over the last four centuries."

"I will be glad to, Relei'sene, but that is rather broad. May I narrow it down? A few moments ago, Synrnn mentioned eight-year-olds. Would you like me to check on adoptions of eight-year-olds?"

Relei'sene laughed. "That makes much more sense."

"I have them, Relei'sene. What would you like to know?"

She looked at the other two with pleading in her expression. "This is new to me. Help me, please."

Synrnn rapped the tabletop, excitement starting to show in her voice. "Numbers. Changes. Abrupt shifts in information. Anything that breaks a pattern. Thanks, Relei'sene. If there's something to this, we might know why that world's been out of touch for so long."

"SYNRNN," Kratt called from under the visor. "We've got a visitor shooting some questions at us."

"Like what, Boss?"

"About our reasons for being here, for being anywhere close to this binary star."

"Ask him for his credentials. See who he is."

"I have. He just talks past my request as if I haven't asked it. He's trying to bully me, but I don't know what he

355

has to back it up."

"Can you put him off for a while? I have some information you might be interested in. It might affect what this visitor's all about."

"Sure." He spoke into the visor. "Pssst, squaak! I'm sorry. I'm breaking up. I'll see what's wrong and get back, pssst, squaak, to you." He yanked the visor off and turned to Synrnn. "Okay, what's it all about?"

She grabbed the visor and spoke into it. On the board flashed the scrolling information of hundreds, then thousands of children all adopted out at eight years old. The list went back hundreds of years. Over three hundred, not to put too fine a point on it.

"What do you see, Boss?"

"Um, nothing?"

"Look harder, Boss. Look at the sport each, *each* one excelled in. Now pick a few and see what their annual physicals revealed. *Every one,* Boss. Every one without exception. You know, only one known race in the galaxy produces this combination of characteristics. One. And we're above their world. Right *here*, Boss. Look, webbing between the toes. The fingers, the *fingers! Webbed!*" She pointed excitedly to several individual sets of information. "Here are where records show that a number of them had surgery to close what appeared to be *gills* along their lower shoulder blades. *Gills,* Boss. That's why this planet is incommunicado. Somebody is stealing and selling the children."

"Come on. Don't you think people'd notice? Twenty Thousand Children Stolen from Planet near Binary Star.

Some headline that'd make! Synrnn!" He snorted and reached for the visor.

She grabbed it from his hand, forcing him to listen. "Who's to hear? This world was declared off-limits centuries ago. It's out in the middle of nowhere, literally. Nobody knows. Well, some people do, obviously. Some of the parents probably suspect or maybe even realize. If you were one of the parents of one of these kids, would you tell and invite someone to take your son or daughter away? Or would you try to convince the school medic it's a recessive family trait?" She paused and flicked her eyes to the visor. "Boss, you've been talking to the people who are doing this. Please be careful."

He turned back to the visor, his eyes playing with it. "What sport have they all been so good at?"

"For the sake of all the gods, those in the water. Swimming, Boss. They can all stay underwater long enough to set every record in every book on every world where one of these kids has ever been adopted out, and I don't think they've missed even one of the major worlds. Flaming stars, Boss, we've got to get down there on that planet and find out what's happening."

"You know it's not our problem."

"Boss, it's Rom'n's problem and Relei'sene's problem, and I want it to be my problem, because I care so much about those two. How about it, Boss? Can you make it your problem, too?"

He turned to slow her down, her rising irritation more and more apparent. "I never said I wouldn't get involved. Rom'n's my problem, and Relei'sene's my problem. I haven't regretted getting involved with either one of them." He traced a circle on the top of the console with one finger. "We just can't have any regrets on the other side of our decision if we jump in."

She grinned. "No regrets, Boss."

His head jerked up to look at her. "Since when does your voice operate in stereo?" Two other faces looked at him through the doorway, grinning widely.

"When we're on her side, Boss," both Rom'n and Relei'sene chimed, once again in full, surround sound stereo.

SYNRNN SAT at the console, the visor covering her face. Her hands manipulated the space around her, their contact with the substance of her perceived reality inside the virtual world of the visor apparent only to her. Speaking softly into the visor from time to time, giving the guidance inputs the course corrections and atmospheric permutation overrides, she forced Kratt's ship to slide through the unfamiliar air of an unknown planet.

"Kratt, what did you tell those bozos?"

He murmured, "Bozos?" He studied the 2-D representation of her virtual world, the board overhead lit with the scrolling numbers and shifting pictures she was seeing,

"Boss, those clowns on the visor, the bullies trying to scare you off."

He continued to look at the scrolling numbers. "I'm not as adept as you at understanding all this," he remarked. "It's good I'm content to let you handle the technical aspects of a planet's first landing."

"The ship will learn the quirks of landing on this unfamiliar world, but yeah, Boss, only a human interfacing during the actual passage can pull us through a successful first landing. Thanks. It's what you pay me for. Those clowns? You said?"

Almost absently, he replied, "Oh, nothing."

"Nothing, Boss? What did they say?"

He stepped over and leaned in close to her ear. "I never contacted them back. I put up a distress signal that's going out now. That's why I asked you to go in fast and hard." He stood, and after a pause, finished, "They'll probably come looking for us, but maybe not. Not if they think we crashed and burned. Can we do that?"

"Crash and burn? I don't think that would help us out much."

"No, just get them to think we crashed and burned. Can we do that?"

"And you want me to do this, keeping us in one piece? Um doggies, Boss."

"Um doggies?"

"Hold that thought for a bit," she barked, and began to speak rapidly into the visor. Something jarred the ship, and Synrnn's hands danced in the air. The ship vibrated as if buffeted by unusually violent air currents. Then, as quickly, it settled into its customary smoothness once again.

"Whew! That was a rough moment." She pulled the visor from her face. "These ships aren't really meant for atmospheric flight, not smooth atmospheric flight, any-way. At least I've got an easy spot coming up that the ship can handle for a moment. Let me see what the big guns say. IRaC? Crash-and-burn protocol?"

"Hello, Synrnn, Boss. Synrnn, there is no viable crash-and-burn protocol."

"I know that, IRaC. How about a way to make our craft appear as if we had crashed and burned?"

"We would have to eject something from the ship to simulate an actual crash, Synrnn. I have come up with several possibilities."

"Like?" Synrnn prompted.

"We do have the eight cryo pods stored in the cargo bay. Ejecting them would not affect the integrity of the ship or the safety of those aboard," suggested IRaC.

"Um," Kratt interjected, turning to Synrnn. "At what cost? That's a pretty chunk of credits if we don't get those back sometime. I don't think that would divert their attention, anyway."

IRaC interrupted, "Kratt, in the mining shipment, there are some interesting possibilities. The cargo manifest indicates several compounds designed for explosive use."

"What? I shipped explosives for them, and they're still on board?"

"Kratt," IRaC soothed. "The compounds are extremely stable unless combined and set off with an ignition device. This could be done by loading the compounds into the cryo pods and igniting them after ejection from the cargo bay."

He retorted, multiple reservations written across his face, "This sounds dangerous. Is there a chance my ship might blow up with all this combining going on?"

"There is an element of danger, Kratt. However, it is the ignition device that causes the mixture to explode, not the chemicals themselves. We must hurry, though. Synrnn will be able to delay landing for a time, but we must appear to be in distress for a short period only."

"Got it, IRaC." Now that he had a mission, his decision made to do this, Kratt leaped into action. "Get Rom'n and Relei'sene to Cargo 4 to prep our explosive cryo pods." He was grinning as he ran out the door. As he did so, Synrnn turned back to the visor.

"IRaC, what's the deal with this visor today? The color is off. Everything around us is this goofy yellow."

IRaC suggested, "Look again, Synrnn. It is only the atmosphere of the planet we are approaching that shows as yellow. That is the normal color this sky refracts from the light of its twin suns."

"Oh," Synrnn said sheepishly. "I should have known that."

KRATT SLAPPED the palmcrypter on another crate. Opening the door, he tore through the contents, pulling out boxes of chemicals, sliding them across the bay to land close to the stored cryo pods.

"IRaC says to just dump one of each box in each cryo pod. Just dump everything, the box and all. I'll get the ignition devices."

The pull of gravity from the planet below was making it much easier to work in the cargo area than it would have been in zero gee. As he moved the palmcrypter to yet another crate, he turned to see Relei'sene and Rom'n placing the boxes in the open cryo pods. Centering his hand on the palmcrypter yet again, he rotated it, and the crate popped open. He tossed out packages and machinery until he located the boxes of igniters. Opening one, he looked at it.

"IRaC, what do I need to do to set it off remotely?"

"Kratt, I have checked my databanks on this type of ignition source, and there should be a timer on the side. Each press on the pad should increase the time increment before ignition. Hold the pad, and the timer will start to count down."

"Got it, IRaC. People," he called to Relei'sene and Rom'n, "one per pod." He stopped and figured out the time needed for opening the bay doors and dropping the pods out. He instructed them, "Press the pad on each one three times and hold it to start the timer."

"What if we can't get the pods out fast enough?" Relei'sene wondered aloud.

He grinned. "Then we don't have to worry about whether we make it down safely or not. So, let's just make sure the pods all get off my ship before they blow."

Relei'sene looked at Rom'n with concern. "Is he always this cavalier?"

He laughed. "No, sometimes he's worse." Turning to Kratt, he yelled, "Ready, Boss. We're prepared to seal the pods and for you to open the doors."

Rom'n showed Relei'sene how to seal the pods, and they ran down the row, triggering each to close. As the cargo doors opened, the noise of the lower atmosphere's dense air swirled in the bay, assaulting the trio's ears.

Pushing each pod to the edge, the brilliant yellow of this world's foreign sky reminded them they were far from home. They began tipping the pods over the side, watching as each fell, each successive pod exploding closer and closer to the ship. Realizing the timers were all set to go off closely together, the only difference being the time it had taken to place one down and pick another up as they were setting them, the three shipmates began to push each pod out as quickly as their awkwardly coordinated movements would allow. As the last one dropped off the side, a wave of heat and noise blew the demolition team from their feet.

Kratt looked at Rom'n and Relei'sene. "IRaC," he yelled. "That was kinda close, don't you think?"

IRaC answered, "I would have recommended four taps to the pads, Boss. No one asked me."

Rom'n and Relei'sene laughed, relieved to have completed the job and survived.

—Chapter 25—

*" . . . and God cast the serpent from the
garden and crushed his head beneath
his heel . . ."*

—*Excerpt from the* Latter
Works Holy Word of God

WITH A SOFT jolt, Synrnn settled the ship to the ground. Emerging from the bridge, she joined with her companions as Kratt cycled the doors open.

"Gods, who would have thought?" She blinked. "It's so beautiful." She stepped into the open, gazing at the two suns casting opposing shadows, one from high in the sky and the other from its position low on the horizon. Motioning for the others to follow, she looked out to the sea in front of them. "Have you ever seen anything so stunning? Why would anyone want to destroy this?"

Rom'n joined her. "Nearly four hundred years ago I was here, and I never saw this place from the surface. I only saw it through the viewwalls of my ship." He waved for the others to join them. "I understand your question. What could have been our motivation?"

Kratt touched her on the shoulder. "Did you see any signs of cities or anything on the visor that would indicate people living here?"

"Nothing, Boss. No energy sources, nothing. Yet, there must be." She turned toward the sea lapping the shore in the distance. "I want to walk to the water. Relei'sene? Come with me, if you would." Together the two women stepped that direction, the rich blue color of the water a siren's song.

"Rom'n," Kratt wondered aloud. "Is there anything you remember that might help us know what's going on?" He moved away from the ship, the lushness of the greenery pulling him forward.

"I was only in interrogations a few times and tried to block out what was happening then. I remember, though, repeated references to the sea. Not much else. I'm sorry I'm not more help. Just looking around might be of benefit."

Kratt laughed. "Well, with what we know, that's about all we can do. We didn't exactly come equipped for a survey mission. All we have is a lot of mining equipment, minus a lot of the explosives." He pushed aside the concealing greenery as he stepped into the undergrowth. "I certainly don't see how that can help, though."

Rom'n knelt, making himself small, his attention suddenly alert, as he hissed, "Kratt, shush. That noise, did you hear it?"

"What noise?"

"Shush! Listen," he whispered. Sure enough, the rustle of plants could just be heard above the faint sounds of Synrnn's and Relei'sene's conversation drifting up from the water's edge. A sharp series of three high-pitched whistles pierced the air, then a stick cracked as if stepped on. "It's moving away from us. This way." He bolted through the underbrush.

Chasing whatever had gotten his attention, he dodged massive fern-like trees and copious roots crisscrossing the ground, drawing closer and closer to the movement of the leaves and fronds, sprinting until they were just ahead of him. No longer trying to remain hidden, something was running at full speed. Finally overtaking it, he leaped, tackling his prey.

When he landed, he found himself holding a boy who was panting from his run for his life, one who was golden-skinned, blond-haired, and no more than twelve years old. In addition, to Rom'n's surprise, there wasn't a stitch of clothing on him anywhere.

WARY, THE BOY looked back and forth from Rom'n to Kratt as they led him back to their ship. Rom'n, firmly holding the boy's arm, was unsure what to say after the boy's initial refusal to speak. He walked with him in silence. Kratt kept looking at the boy, miming friendly gestures. Hoping the women would have better luck, he called to them.

"Synrnn, Relei'sene," Kratt yelled. "You've got to see this." He laughed when he saw the two women get their first sight of the boy and break into a full run to get to him.

When they arrived, he teased, "Now I know what it takes to get you women to come at my beck and call. A younger man. Sorry, Rom'n." He looked at him with an amused expression. "It seems you're no longer young enough to do the trick."

"Where—" Synrnn began, with a look of undisguised astonishment. "I can't believe this, Kratt. Maybe our suspicions weren't correct, and there's not anyone stealing the children."

For the first time, the boy stood tall, as if preparing to speak. His eyes glanced back and forth at the adults around him. He seemed to clear his throat as if dropping his voice into an unfamiliar register. Then words came forth, hesitant at first, then faster. "You are not here to take me away?"

Relei'sene, so close to having just escaped from a horrible situation herself, stepped to him, putting her hands on his shoulders. "Is that what you think, that we are here to take you away? No." She looked directly into his eyes. "We were worried that others have been, though."

The boy watched her intently for some moments, then turned to look thoughtfully at the rest. Shifting his eyes to stare at their ship, he studied it, his eyes resting on the open hatch for a short time, and faced back to Relei'sene. "True. Your ship is not as the others' ships are. They come and grab and go. I think you can be trusted. The Mother should know. Follow me." With those words, the boy turned and walked swiftly into the woods. His invited visitors quickly moved after him, struggling to keep up.

After a distance, slipping along trails snaking through

challenging understory and past burbling streams, they approached a verdant, greenery-faced escarpment thrusting broad shoulders into the yellow sky above. The boy walked up and whistled a series of high-pitched notes, almost out of the hearing range of the adults behind him. Soon, a rope ladder trailed from a dark recess in the greenery. Down climbed a middle-aged woman with gold-flecked eyes who looked at the boy first. Her mouth opening and moving as if speaking, only a beautiful, high-pitched melody of sounds tickled the ears of Kratt's crew. As the boy ran off, the woman turned to the four standing before her. Clearing her throat, the sounds from her mouth were now in the human range of hearing.

"Hali'ka tells me you can be trusted. However, I am not sure. Please tell me why I should believe Hali'ka." With no further information, the woman stood and watched them, waiting for answers.

Knowing this was a test of sorts, and being given no clue what the passing standard was, or even the penalty if they failed, they hesitated. With trepidation, Relei'sene stepped forward.

"Mother, I am Relei'sene." She paused, during which the woman matched Relei'sene's information.

"I am Var'elen. I still do not know why I should trust you."

"Mother Var'elen, thank you. I am traveling with my companions to seek out the answers to a very old story. My Original Grandmother from many years ago told stories of this place, unbelievable stories. My friend, Rom'n," at which she motioned him forward, "was here many years ago, although he never landed on your planet. The other two, Synrnn and Kratt, are our traveling companions, providing us transportation." Relei'sene dropped to one knee, the formality of her family making her no stranger to the importance of rank. "On our way here, we uncovered terrible information suggesting your world's children were being stolen and given to others for their own. We have seen Hali'ka, and we know we've been mistaken. Our apologies, Mother Var'elen." She rose, stepping back to the others, pulling Rom'n with her.

A sad smile crept across Var'elen's face. "You have not been mistaken, child. Hali'ka is one we have managed to save. I can see why he trusted you. Please come with me." She turned and began to climb the ladder.

Looking at each other, Kratt motioned for the others to go ahead. Rom'n took Relei'sene's elbow to start her forward, and Synrnn followed in her footsteps. Kratt fell into place last.

Stepping up to the rope, in a whisper, Synrnn leaned close to Relei'sene's ear. "Nice going. Thanks." She handed the rope to her and prompted, "You, first."

Following one at a time, soon they were standing on the top of the ledge, and they turned, overlooking the path they had recently come down, the beautiful blue of the ever-present sea beyond fading into the distance.

"Please, inside," Var'elen directed. "We do not dare remain on the ledge long. We might be seen." She took arms, pulling each one in with her.

INSIDE, THE FOUR visitors were amazed. The room, or

rather, cavern, was large, well-lighted, and comfortable. Simple furniture abounded, and soft rugs were spread across the rough stone floor. Most amazing were the children everywhere.

Synrnn burst out, "I would have never known. The number of children. You've saved all these? How, if all is so bad, Var'elen, have you done this?"

Var'elen laughed what seemed to be an old, well-used laugh. "You are the one called Synrnn. Welcome. When necessity is your mother, you do what must be done."

Kratt fingered a wall hanging done in vivid colors. It was a mixture of threads, some closely cropped, and others long and lush. It was also well worn. After a moment of studying it in silence, he looked up. "It's true, Var'elen? The children, they are being taken from you? To suspect such a thing is bad enough. To be in the midst of the reality is unfathomable." He dropped the corner of the fabric, and he put his hands behind his back, waiting.

"Yes, one called Kratt. Our children are born from the sea. Eight years we must wait for them to return from Se'Yan't's waters, and for more years than you know, the stealers have patrolled our shores, taking the unwary as they emerge from the depths. We have learned to watch without seeming to watch, so that we may rescue those we can. My Hali'ka was doing just that as we speak. A family of re'anlts is expected to emerge any day. We must have watchers. Alas," and Var'elen looked around the cavern, her eyes sad, "our space is full. None have been stolen for many of our years, but others around our world are also finding their hiding spaces are able to take no more." At

370

this, she turned to the wall, her voice cracking in anguish. "How can we not rescue those who need us most?"

Rom'n reached out and touched her on the shoulder. "Var'elen?" When the older woman turned, the streaks of her tears still on her face, he continued, "We want to help. What would you have us do? We have a ship for transport. We have credits, if you need." He looked up and caught Synrnn's eye, her nod of approval at his words confirming his determination to give of what he had. "Please let us assist you."

Her eyes still red and wet with tears, Var'elen cried in her native, high-pitched tongue, the beautiful notes ringing throughout the stone room, "Can you bring us more caverns? Can you dig through the rock with your bare hands? The stealers will go, someday, when they tire of having none to steal, but for now, we must protect our own."

Kratt's crew didn't understand the oddly-spoken words, but they found the grief clear, and they looked at each other helplessly. One of the children walked up to them.

"Mother says you cannot help. We must learn to dig through the very rock of the walls with our hands to make room for new children. Even your offworld hands cannot do that." The child nodded respectfully and backed away.

Kratt turned to look at his three traveling companions, a look of excitement on his face. As the others returned puzzled looks, he jerked his thumb to the cave entrance. "The ship. The cargo. Remember? Mining equipment. We can give them all the room they need."

Turning to the tear-stained face of Mother Var'elen, Kratt said, "Var'elen, we *can* dig through the very rock of your cavern walls."

As the four began explaining what they had brought with them on their ship, her face began to change from disbelief to joy. Her people would be saved. As the word began to spread among those in the cavern, a great cheer of joy could be heard echoing throughout the redoubt hidden underneath Se'Yan't's yellow skies.

"ONE CALLED Kratt, how long until you choose to leave us?"

He jumped, not used to how quietly these people moved, and he handed Synrnn the tool he was using. "You surprised me, Mother Var'elen. My heart won't take many more surprises like that." He took a cloth from a pocket and wiped the sweat from his face.

"My race seems to surprise many people. In addition, I would not worry about your heart, one called Kratt."

He leaned against the side of his ship, giving her a bemused look. He knew better than to doubt any claims to knowledge she might make. However, he would like this one explained. "Why do you say that? What do you know about my heart that I don't?"

She smiled at him. "I think you know what I am about to say. You have a roughness about you, one called Kratt. Yet, that roughness is not you. Inside I see a very strong heart, a heart that is full of goodness and caring for other people."

He glanced over to see Synrnn loosening the mining

bits and grinning. "How can you see that in my heart, Mother Var'elen? For over half of one of your years, I have assembled and disassembled the mining equipment that I've transported all over this planet, hidden my ship under plant fronds and woven mats, and ferried you along to help us reassure the other groups we've helped. I've groused about it as often as anyone else and more than most. It's those two that your children adore."

Var'elen turned to watch Rom'n and Relei'sene engaged in rambunctious play with a large group of Se'Yan't's children. As one of the children fell, crying, Relei'sene ran to her and knelt, concerned, and as quickly, the child jumped back up, laughing, her trick having fooled the visitor. Rom'n ran to Relei'sene, laughing at the trick, and bent to put his arms around her waist. Leaning his face close to hers, he whispered something to her, her face lighting up in a smile. Standing, his arm around her waist, he leaned to her and touched her lips with his, then they were off after the errant child who had so unwisely played the trick on poor Relei'sene.

"Ah, those two. Of what have they given more? The young man's credits have done much, and the young woman has a teacher's touch. Yet, those gifts, as appreciated as they have been, have not been their greatest. Those two find a pleasure in each other. That is what the children love. Those two may decide to stay with us, or their journeys may travel other paths. Only time will tell. They will find their happiness either way. For now, with each other, they find the joy of the morning and the sweetness of the evening." Var'elen paused in her sharing.

373

Then she looked at Kratt. "That is the particular blessing of the first-alives. As they mature, their needs may continue to be met in one another. Who can tell? The future will reveal the answer to that."

She turned wholly to Kratt, her focus now on him alone. "You, though, one called Kratt, have had no impetus to stay here. You brought us a great gift in the equipment we have used to enlarge our places of refuge from those who would steal our first-alive children. We could not have asked for more, nor would we. You would not have been faulted by anyone if you had given your gift and gone from this world."

She motioned for him to walk with her. Coming to the edge of an escarpment, she looked out over a beautiful landscape of verdant green understory, vivid blue waters, and a lemon yellow sky. "This is what your heart has given my people, one called Kratt. You have given us the chance to reclaim our world from those who would steal it from us. It was nearly stolen once before, many years ago, and that attempt has been made again. Without the help you have taken the time to provide, who knows but that they might have been successful this time.

"Yet, I know your heart is not here, one called Kratt." When he started to protest, she quieted him. "No, not here. Your heart is there." She pointed a long finger to the emptiness in the sky between the two suns low on opposing horizons. Turning her face to him, she spoke the softness of truth. "That is how I know your heart. To give up your heart's desire so others can live a better life, what is that if not goodness and caring?"

Kratt turned to follow as she moved back in the direction of the children.

Her words continued, speaking as if making a prediction that must surely come true. "You will follow your heart. You will not stay with us. No one could expect that of you. We have had you long enough, and when it is time for you to go, I wish to be there to say good-bye."

Synrnn stepped up as Var'elen walked away. "So, Boss. What was all the private stuff about?"

He grinned. "She told me she's fallen deeply in love with me and wishes to be my navigator when I ship out. I told her I already have a navigator. Um, Synrnn, do you know what it means to have a duel? Is that dangerous?" He winked and walked away.

She called after him, "I would have faulted you, Boss. If you hadn't stayed, I would have faulted you." Quietly, to herself, as she turned back to her machine, she murmured, "But you wouldn't have gone. You wouldn't have been able to live with yourself."

ROM'N PULLED off his shoes and then reached to tug his shirt over his head. He stood and looked at himself in the reflection in the water below. He was four hundred years old, and he wore the body of a young man. His waist was tight, his hair was full, and his flesh was unlined. He guessed Relei'sene might not do too badly with a man the age of her great-times-ten-grandmother. He dropped his pants and dived head first into the waters of the sea.

As he swam up behind Relei'sene, he wrapped his arms around her waist. She jerked in surprise, forcing his hold loose, and as his arms tightened to keep her in his grasp, he felt her softness yield to his arms.

Not so much like Ma'jene after all, he thought. This is better. Much better.

As they swam in the water, he soon found other parts of her that were much better, also.

"SYNRNN, YOU'VE got to come see this!" Kratt was gone before she could reply.

Pulling her head out of the access panel, she knew if this generator wasn't fixed, they wouldn't get any credits for the slightly used mining equipment in the cargo bay, once they got to that mining world Kratt had contacted. She also knew she could do this tomorrow. She slapped the panel shut and ran for the corridor, Kratt's voice egging her on.

"Quick, Synrnn!"

Entering the bridge door, she saw Kratt with the visor already over his face.

"I found this one, Synrnn. I was sitting right here when IRaC picked it up. It's a pod just like the one Rom'n was in, MegaCorp signals and all." He yanked the visor off and turned to her. "There's no telling just what we might find in this one."

She looked toward the ceiling. "IRaC?"

"Yes, Synrnn." If possible, the voice sounded nervous.

"I thought we talked about this."

"Yes, Synrnn, but Boss Man used the override code to pick up the pod's signal before I could delete it from the input feed."

"Boss Man?" She looked at Kratt as he grinned at her.

"So, Synrnn. Want to go and catch me a new toy? I just learned of this old-Earth game called baseball. The object was to catch a ball flying through the air. If one team could catch it enough times, the other team would lose the game."

She looked back up to the ceiling as she vented her frustration. Her one word said it all.

"IRaC!"

Glossary

3-D comps . . . . three dimensional computers; often used for gaming

3Vid . . . . high definition Vid using 3-D technology

academy . . . . MegaCorp's military training division; later a generic term

Aregas 4 . . . . originally started as a trading outpost; by 3170 A.D. (old-Earth timeline), it is a center of commerce

auto program . . . . tabulates and lists items shipped in a cargo hold

automated rescue ship has full personality interface for assistance in operations

bay doors . . . . allows for egress from the ship's cargo bays

bay flooring plates . . . sections of a bay floor that can be calibrated individually for specific tasks

bedframe . . . . support system for a sleeping pad

bridge . . . . command center of the ship

bunk . . . . shipboard sleeping location

Cargo 4 . . . . the largest cargo bay on Kratt's ship

Carney's World . . . . . has nearby asteroid colonies that refit ships for profit

Cerennt'te Nijenhaus . Elussie'san's first consort

chameleon	a specialized troop transport that can be converted to a medcenter or a weapons transport
civvies	civilians
clinic	term for a small, planetside medcenter
coldpaks	self-cooling refrigeration packs
comm	slang for communication device
comm sats	communication satellites
computer	term still used in 2800 but archaic by 3170 A.D. (old-Earth timeline)
Correigo Prime	heavily populated; encourages emigration
corridor	shipboard passageway
crate	used to ship items in the hold of a ship
credit crystal	storage device for storing money or credits
creepin' flamerunners	invective
crikes	invective; also crikey
cryo pods	cryogenic life support pod; uses cryogenics to suspend life for later reanimation
cryo-decay	occurs from the breakdown of a cryogenic life support pod
cryo-rejuv	the process of reanimating an occupant of a cryo pod
D Corridor	Rom'n's location when Redzik pushed him into the cryo pod

databanks	information storage
DeathMaker	colloquial name given to the battle cruiser Rom'n served on
decoder	overrides encryptions
dermal readers	info-readers implanted directly under the skin
DNA verification	proof of identity
DNA verification scan	medical procedure for determining identity
downplanet	also downship; used when aboard a ship
eatery	restaurant
electro-biometric patterns	the specific electrical pattern of individual people that can be read by sensor pads
Elussie'san 'de Gaso-Fratenni laHolc'm . . .	the current grandmother in 3170 A.D. (old-Earth timeline)
ESS	emergency survival suit
exosuit	latest in self-powered working spacesuits
feed	information channel
foodstores	food carried in nitrogen storage
foodstuffs	edible items
forty-two occupied systems	total count as of 3170 A.D. (old-Earth timeline); does not include research stations, moons, or occupied asteroids

381

full grav capabilities .	the entire ship is under artificial gravity, even the cargo bays
Ganymede Gaming Trophy	highly sought after Zero Gee Butt Ball trophy; winners receive full scholarships to any higher learning institution in the Sol System
gel	cryo gel – carries the photonic cryo compounds necessary for cryo sleep; civilian gel is green; yellow is the highest quality military gel; must be energized to work
geothermals	power source for the compounds around Trasdrom'man's great inland sea
glass	computer interface; outdated by 3170 A.D. (old-Earth timeline); many were wireless or personal glass units
glassine	super strong polymer that has strength excelling that of steel
goggles	worn for eye protection on worlds where the intensity of the sun's rays exceeds human tolerance levels
Goltine's Treasure . . .	one of the more pleasant worlds; trees, grass, and pleasant temperatures abound

gondola	decorative boat
gravity well	any area of the ship with artificial gravity capabilities; can apply to the gravitational pull of any number of celestial bodies
green code	permits opening of a cryo pod
ground transport	transport with wheels instead of rotors or magnetic pulse drive
groundie	anyone who lives on a planet
gyros	stabilizers
Hali'ka	Rejuvie boy who leads the visitors to the redoubt
hallway	planetside passageway
high-pressure recovery equipment	used to recover and repressurize fluid lines
info-comm	ship's internal communication device
Interlink	Internet
intersolar law	laws applicable to all occupied worlds
ion drive	main propulsion system
ion thrusters	main drive engines
ionic-pulse key	low level energy pulse designed to trigger a hidden lock; military
IRaC	Information Retrieval and Communication module; also known as a ship's personality or artificial personality
klaxons	alarms

Kornth ('de Gaso-Fratenni laHolc'm) . . — the Grandmother's brother

Kratt Balanchine . . . . — captain of a transport-for-hire ship

Kreeian Potgieter . . . . — girl attracted to Rom'n onworld

Lacy's Veil Prime . . . — Synrnn's homeworld; originally settled by Separatist Jewish Fundamentalists

leaping jeepers . . . . . . — invective

life-force regeneration — one part of the process of reanimation from cryo sleep

liquid nitrogen . . . . . . — used to store foods in transit aboardship

live-transit capabilities — traveling without cryo capabilities; six standard months' travel time is the maximum allowed before cryo must be made available

loc-seals . . . . — environment seals between a ship's various sections

Ma'jene Holcum . . . . — betrayed Rom'n Rezalton; Original Grandmother (a.k.a. First Grandmother)

magnetic grappling arm . . . . — used to draw in metallic objects encountered in space; also useful for docking

magnetics . . . . — supplemental drive system; often used in conjunction with the ion drive

manifest	list of goods
mas	Trasdrom'man term of politeness for a male
mech preassembly programs	diagnostic algorithms used to verify functionality
mechanical grapplers .	used to draw in non-metallic objects or for pulling items directly into the cargo bay
med bed	medical bed
medbath	one time use self-sealing emergency medical bag; self-liquefies after use to prevent transmission of infectious organisms
medcenter	medical center; also sick bay or medbay
medchamber	sealed medical chamber
medic	medical doctor
medkit	medical kit
medscan	medical scan
MegaCorp	galactic corporation
MegaCorp Military Arm	originally part of the MegaCorp corporation
memory crystal	information storage device
message-ding	attention signal
military emergency escape pod	highly developed; can "gel" an occupant from eighty-five

	injectors and reach twenty gees in under two seconds; had rudimentary guidance and propulsion systems using solar magnetic acceleration and braking; capable of sustaining life for over three hundred years
military overlay	extra information encoded over civilian transmissions
mos	Trasdrom'man term of politeness for a female
nodes	interchangeable hardware
nutrient pack	concentrated form of revitalizing paste especially formulated for revival from cryo sleep
offsystem	originating outside a world's solar system
offworlders	anyone from offworld
old-Earth	anything from before the Collapse; also, anything from Earth
optical sensors	camera-like information feeds
orange code	prevents a cryo pod from opening
orichoke	a type of foodstalk
overjacket	worn for public display
overpants	insulated covering
pain blockers	medication
palmcrypter	overrides encryption codes
personal facilities	toilet

photonic compounds .	medical compounds that distribute and enhance projected energies
planetside	having to do with anything on a planet's surface
powerpack	carries the charge for an exosuit
prisonplanet	used for the most incorrigible convicts; secretly MegaCorp's depository for political or military embarrassments; most notorious is Rant
priv'tshorts	boxer-like underwear; worn by males and females
propulsion thrusters . .	drives, as in ion drives
pudz	stupid person; often used affectionately
pudzo	variation of pudz
Rant	MegaCorp's prisonplanet
realcloth	woven cloth, unlike the disposable shipboard variety
recycle slot	used for disposal or reprocessing items in order to retrieve the raw materials
Redzik Ajadijon	Rom'n's friend aboard the battle cruiser
Regglet Colony	fueling station; few families live there, mostly young adults with a high turnover rate
regs	slang for regulations
Rejuvenant	locally known as Se'Yan't

release pad	sensor pad for opening protected doors; can be set to ignore specific hand electro-biometric patterns
Relei'sene 'de Gaso-Fratenni	girl rescued from Trasdrom'man
reprocessor	food reprocessing unit aboard Kratt's ship
res	short for resolution
Rikard	the top Man in the laHolc'm compound
ripper	powerful tool for cutting metal
Rom'n Rezalton	rescued from a cryo pod
Rutger's World	pleasure world run by organized crime
scab blisters	invective
screensaver mode	low power mode
Sea of Revenge	Trasdrom'man's inland sea
ser	term of respect; formally as Ser, plural as sers
Ser Alb't deFralin, SSM.rl	collected poems from Rejuvenant
sevenday	old-Earth week
shipboard cycles	compatible with a planetary day; used with varying degrees of uniformity depending upon a person's affinity with shipboard life
shipmates	crew; slang as shippies

slowboat	sublight
slow-sleep	partial "cryo" used for shorter trips; the bodily processes are only slowed down; capable of sustaining life up to 100 years
Snowbush World	Kreeian's homeworld
starstrike class battle cruiser	the most powerful of MegaCorp's military armaments; the final few built were highly classified and contained cutting edge weaponry; no more were built after the Rejuvenant incident in 2801 A.D. (old-Earth timeline) when MegaCorp's military arm was broken up and sold off
stor'lok	specialized shipboard storage; storage locker for personal goods aboardship
Synrnn Har-Zahav . . .	Kratt's pilot and navigator
T404Pocket Trainer . .	training vessel without a personality interface; also called a T404Trainer Pocket Ship
THD ratings	rating system for cargo vessels; determined by reliability and performance
tight-beam focus	narrowing the magnetic grappling arm for selective pickup of an object

Timons	cadet killed by Holcum while attending the academy
transport	any vehicle used to convey people or goods
Trasdrom'man	where Rom'n meets Holcum's descendants
two-man	small, personal transport
unbonded	Trasdrom'man term for unmarried persons
underjacket	worn for less formal situations; slang: unders
underpriv't	lowest military rank in the MegaCorp Military Arm
undershorts	outerwear for less formal situations; slang as unders
vacuhose	vacuum hose
Var'elen	Rejuvie adult over the redoubt
velocity regulators . . .	power feed; referred to when under manual control
Vidpics	images displayed on a Vid, or video unit
virtual displays	displays overlaid on an exosuit's faceplate
visor	virtual interface; sometimes called an info-reader
watersynther	unit used to synthesize water from basic available elements
Winter Hangar	Trasdrom'man's seasonal port hangar made of ice
world's magnetic core	used by a ship's magnetic drive

zero gee . . . . no gravity
zero gee sleepbags . . . contains straps to prevent the occupant from floating out

Read all the books in this vibrant new series!

The Se'Yan't Chronicles

Get Yours At:

www.ThreeSkilletPublishing.com

THREE SKILLET

www.ingramcontent.com/pod-product-compliance
Lightning Source LLC
Chambersburg PA
CBHW071156250626
47159CB00001B/115